ALL THE KING'S MEN

REBEL OBSESSION

Rebel Obsession

Published by Phoenix Press

Copyright © 2013 Donya Lynne

ISBN: 978-1-938991-24-0

Cover art by Reese Dante.

ACKNOWLEDGEMENTS

First, a special acknowledgement goes to Zach Tesar, my cover model, and Joem Bayawa Photography in Chicago. Joem took the fabulous shot of Zach that appears on the cover of Rebel Obsession. Both Zach and Joem are talented, wonderful people I've gotten to know through the course of writing Rebel, and I am so thankful they granted me permission to use Zach's picture. He made the perfect Io, and the photo represented Io's personality impeccably. I hope we get to work together again on another project. Many blessings to both of you.

Thank you to all who have joined me on this journey. Each book brings new readers, and I'm grateful for each and every one. I want to issue a special shout-out to my fans in Italy who continue to push for an Italian publisher to print these books in Italian. I hope you'll be pleased to learn that I'm trying to learn Italian so I can better speak to all of you.

To my beta readers goes my gratitude in helping me to make these books better than even I thought they could be. The feedback you gave me for Rebel helped me to find Miriam's voice and guided me to make the story and characters stronger. I love the discussions I have with each of you. You truly are what make these stories as good as they are.

And finally, thank you to Laura, my editor, for keeping me on course and finding new ways to reach new readers.

BOOKS BY DONYA LYNNE

All the King's Men Series

Rise of the Fallen
Heart of the Warrior
Micah's Calling
Rebel Obsession
Return of the Assassin
All the King's Men - The Beginning

Strong Karma Trilogy

Good Karma
Coming Back to You
Full Circle

Hope Falls Series

Finding Lacey Moon

Stand-Alone M/M Titles

Winter's Fire

Collections and Anthologies

All the King's Men Vol. 1 (books 1-3)
All the King's Men Vol. 2 (books 4-6)
Strong Karma Trilogy Boxed Set
Whispered Beginnings - A Romance Sampler

ALL THE KING'S MEN

REBEL OBSESSION

DONYA LYNNE

DEDICATION

To you. You're a tough one. I didn't think we could make readers like you, but you proved me wrong.

CHAPTER 1

"Hi, my name is Io, and I'm a cobalt addict. Welcome to our first meeting."

Six new faces sat around Io in a circle. One particularly scrawny male squinted and blinked as if his eyes hurt.

"Is everyone comfortable?" Io gestured toward the light dimmer. Cobalt detox was hell on the eyes. "Should I turn down the lights?" He nodded for effect, receiving a couple of polite nods in return.

He had a shy bunch this time around.

The meeting room inside the AKM facility was small, and in a jiffy Io had dimmed the lights and was back with the group. Each of them wore a similar visage, all in various states of shame. Io had seen faces like theirs over and over in these meetings. Hell, he had *been* one of those faces.

A year ago, he had dragged himself into his commander's office, head bowed, disgusted with himself. *Tristan, I need help.* Four simple words, but Io had never found it more difficult to speak than he had in Tristan's office that day.

When had he ever needed help? When had he ever fallen so low he couldn't pull his own ass back up? Talk about a disgrace.

Had it really been only a year ago that he had confessed he was an addict and admitted himself into the drug treatment program? Now he served as one of AKM's drug counselors, leading a group twice a week to help other recovering addicts as they fought through withdrawal worse than anything humans could imagine.

Tonight was the first meeting for this group. These six

vampires were fresh out of a month-long detox, but they still had a long journey before they could consider themselves recovered and in remission, because cobalt wasn't just an addiction. It was an affliction.

"I'm an enforcer here at AKM, but obviously, not even enforcers are immune to cobalt." He held out his arms, presenting himself.

For recovering addicts, hearing his tale gave them hope and made them feel less ashamed. If an enforcer, whose job it was to battle the drecks who manufactured and sold cobalt—or *blue* as some called it—could become addicted to the drug, then maybe they weren't the total losers they thought they were. The sentiment was painted all over their faces, just as it was over every face that passed through the door to participate in one of these sessions. Each one of them carried an incredible amount of humiliation and guilt for being an addict, and it was Io's job to show them they didn't have to shoulder that burden. Not anymore. As a member of AKM's rehab team, he was committed to making sure as few people as possible went through what he had. If only he could get someone higher up to listen to his ideas to proactively seek out the true origins of the drug.

AKM stood for All the King's Men, an agency set up to police the drecks and maintain the tenuous truce established between the two races centuries ago. Drecks historically resented the strength and stronger genes of the vampires, which had led to several wars as they tried to rise up and overtake the vampires. This was why Io didn't trust for one second that the drecks were blithely sitting by, not trying to find a way to rise up against them again. Cobalt gave them the perfect means to do so.

Io couldn't deny the irony. This was the king's agency, set up after the last truce had been agreed upon so that the king could keep an eye on the drecks. Rightfully so, he didn't trust them and feared they would attempt another uprising, despite the peace agreement. And yet, King Bain refused to see the threat cobalt presented, even when the danger and evidence were right under his nose, hitting him at home.

Io's mind flashed to Princess Miriam. Two weeks ago, she had been brought into AKM suffering from an overdose. Her first, or so the report had said, but who really knew? He hadn't known she was the king's daughter. Not at first. Not until later, after she had already burned a place in his heart, had he found out that the most beautiful female he'd ever seen was the one female he could never have. Never touch. Never see again. The short time they'd spent together was all they would ever get unless he found a way to steal time with her again. Fat chance of that happening with all the rules the king had instituted to keep Miriam sheltered.

What was she doing now? Was she keeping clean? Most likely she was still using, so it was only a matter of time before they brought her back into AKM from another overdose. Io frowned and pressed his teeth together, because the thought of Miriam coming back under such circumstances shouldn't have given him hope the way it did.

But Miriam overdosing again *was* Io's only hope of seeing her again, especially since her father had refused to admit her for treatment, which Io didn't understand. King Bain's daughter was on a fast track to death by cobalt. Why wouldn't he admit her to the treatment program?

It wasn't like her overdose and drug use were big secrets anymore. Rumors of Princess Miriam's overdose and subsequent drug-induced forays into the public eye had been splashed all over the Internet in the past two weeks.

But his hands were tied. He had been commanded never to attempt contact with her again. Even when he had approached Tristan with his concerns, Tristan had told him that Miriam wasn't his problem and that her condition was to remain a private affair of the royal family. Io had left Tristan's office feeling helpless, relegated to see her picture only on the gossip sites littering the Internet. And he was sure that pleased the king to no end, being that he had worked so hard to keep Miriam's identity and reputation protected since she had been born.

He smiled weakly at the six sets of eyes staring at him. He hadn't said anything for nearly a minute. Nothing like making them feel more uncomfortable than they already did. Bonehead. He needed to get his mind back in the room and out of the Miriam-induced clouds.

"Sorry, I lost my train of thought for a second there." He paced to the side and cleared his throat, pushing Miriam to the back of his mind as best as he could before continuing. "For me, using cobalt was about taking a risk." He steepled his fingers in front of his torso. "It was about rebelling against society, as well as myself." He walked slowly around the circle, touching the shoulders of each vampire as he passed, connecting with the members of his group. "See, I'm a gambler. I like to give life a run for its money. To me, life isn't worth living if you don't take chances once in a while. And if you never experience the bad, how can you appreciate the good?" He stopped and shrugged. "Think of me as the human who rides a motorcycle without a helmet and his mouth wide open. You know, so I can swallow as many bugs as possible."

As he had hoped, that got a few yucks and a couple of quiet chuckles, which was good. Io needed them to open up. He needed them to feel safe here, and smiles and feedback were signs they were beginning to feel that way. Trying to be funny always seemed to help make that transition happen.

"I know, I know. Pretty stupid, huh?" Io continued his slow trip around the circle, chuckling to himself. "But I thought I could beat it. I thought I could be that one person who wouldn't get addicted."

A few nods answered him, the six vampires watching him with more interest now. They could relate.

Io smiled to himself. Each opening speech was the same, and each group reacted the same, too. In a few weeks, they would think of each other as family.

"How many of you felt the same way? That you could do the blue demon once or twice and never need another hit?" He raised his hand, glancing around the circle.

One by one, the hands of the six members crept upward.

Had Miriam thought that way after taking her first hit of cobalt? If she were in the room, would her hand be in the air with all the others? And what were her reasons for turning to cobalt?

Io dropped his hand, acknowledging them with a compassionate nod. "Sucks, doesn't it? Feeling so helpless, wondering how you got to this point so quickly, trying to hide your drug use from those around you while falling deeper into its grasp."

Io's arms began to itch. He noticed a couple of others scratching their arms, as well. Would the itching ever stop?

"Some days I fear I'll never lose the physical symptoms of what getting off cobalt felt like. What it did to me..." Io clenched his fists in front of him as if wringing a wet towel. "Cobalt is the one thing I regret. It's the one thing I'll never do again, because I know now that it's stronger than I am. For us"—Io waved his tattooed arm in an arc to encompass the members of the group—"Not much can kill us. As vampires, we heal quickly and don't die easily. But cobalt?" He spun around in the middle of the circle, eyeing each person, pointing his finger for emphasis. "Cobalt can kill us. It's one of only a few things that can."

And the drecks knew it, didn't they? How could they not? Cobalt was the ultimate weapon to weaken the vampires. A way to even the playing field. And the drecks were winning. For every vampire who got cleaned up, two more began using. And half of all overdoses ended in death. At least that's what the numbers indicated from arrests, street talk, and medical records.

How was the drecks' agenda so obvious to Io, but not to everyone else? Especially the king?

His fingers curled into fists, and he clenched his teeth. Knowing in his heart that cobalt was a weapon more than it was a drug infuriated him, but losing his cool in front of the group wouldn't be a good idea. But it didn't stop him from eyeing his empty chair like it was a football and he was being called on to kick a game-winning field goal from the fifty-yard line.

Io had no doubt the drecks who were making cobalt knew what they were doing. What better way to get rid of your enemy than to create a drug that was not only highly addictive and could affect vampires in a way no human drug could, but also kill them? He wouldn't be surprised to find out their scheme went all the way to the top, to Premier Royce himself. They didn't fool him, even if they did have King Bain snowed.

How could the king not see what was happening? His own daughter was an addict, for God's sake. Drecks had invaded the royal home, even if only by way of infecting her with their fucking toxic blue shit, made of their venom, made of their blood. How could King Bain not see this as an attack? He had to be blind.

Io returned his attention to the group. "Each of you should be proud. You've defeated the demon. You've survived." He clapped, encouraging the others to do the same.

Once the applause quieted, Io sat back down in his chair before he could follow through on making like a placekicker. "Let's go around the room and everybody tell us your name and how you got here."

He motioned to the first person to his left, sat back, and listened as each told his or her story. Io was always amazed to hear the painful tales of how people became addicts and how they had finally conquered their addiction. Recovering addicts were some of the strongest people he had ever seen. To fall into such hell and still be able to find a way to fight out of it was nothing short of remarkable.

By the end of the hour, many tears had been shed and hugs given as new friendships were forged in the support system Io was so committed to.

The drug rehabilitation program had been a part of AKM for a while, but Io had made it his passion in the past year. He could practically oversee the entire program if the enforcers weren't so short-staffed. That was his dream, to quit enforcing and run the program full time. Just the way Arion had quit to follow his dream of—

Io sighed, cutting off the thought. He had been doing so well, not thinking about Arion all day. And now, wham! He'd gone and re-opened that wound. Just pulled the scab clean off.

Arion hadn't spoken to him since the night Io had met Miriam. The same night he'd found out Arion was gay. *Gay.* How had that happened? He'd never seen that coming, but sure as shit filled the crevices in the sole of a tennis shoe after being stepped on, Ari was as gay as the ocean is deep. And he had mated Severin, the newest member of the team.

And now Io missed his best friend—or maybe ex-best friend by now—like crazy. Io had been a homophobic gay basher since forever, never missing an opportunity to bash the gay lifestyle. Hell, he had even bashed Severin...to Ari, of all people. After they had already *done stuff* with each other. Io's lip curled, his stomach knotting. *Stuff.* Would he ever be able to get used to the idea of Ari and Sev together? Like *that*? Could he get past his prejudice to mend the friendship he'd once had with Ari? Why did he even give a flying rat's ass what a guy did with his own dick, anyway?

He couldn't think about that right now, though. People were waiting on him to wrap things up.

After giving the final group member a hug, Io straightened the room and pulled out his smartphone to check his schedule. With Arion leaving AKM, scheduling patrols and shifts had become a day-to-day routine, and no one knew until right before a shift where they would be stationed.

When he saw who he was scheduled with, a pit opened at the bottom of his stomach, making his balls try to creep up and fill the void.

"Oh, come on! You've got to be kidding me," he muttered under his breath. He would patrol with Micah and risk having that bastard dip into his private thoughts all night, but this? Anything but this.

He groaned and closed his eyes then opened them again to make sure he had seen right. Yep, he was scheduled to patrol with Severin tonight.

Sev.

Ari's mate.

Shit just got better and better.

Tonight was going to be about as much fun as chewing glass.

CHAPTER 2

Bishop strolled across the darkened den of his Arizona ranch house, his long smoking jacket hugging him like expensive wrapping paper tied with a gold bow at the waist. A plume of smoke blew from his nostrils and swirled around his head as he inspected the cigarette tucked between his index and middle fingers. His other hand was stuffed inside his pocket where his fingers smoothed over his gold, engraved lighter, rotating it slowly.

When the gold tip of the cigarette touched his lips again, and he inhaled the glorious smoke, all felt right in the world. For that brief moment, he didn't have a completely inept brother who had fucked things up so badly in Chicago that he had been forced to rethink his entire operation. In this smoke-induced perfect world, his other brother still lived, and the only use he had for his pet scorpions was to admire them.

He eyed the cigarette between his index and middle fingers. The Sobranie Black Russian. The most exquisite cigarette ever made. One of life's simple pleasures. One that took away all the shit for that single, indulgent moment when the smoke filled his lungs.

Bishop kissed the tip of the cigarette again, drawing in long and deep to hold the flavor against his tongue and feel the exquisite expansion as his lungs filled with smoke. After a moment's hesitation, he breathed out the succulent richness and walked toward a line of aquariums along the far wall.

Time to return to reality and the pile of shit his last remaining brother had created.

Inside each dark, black-lit glass tank, a glowing arthropod

skittered almost eagerly toward him as he approached. Scorpion exoskeletons contained a chemical that glowed under black lights, and the effect on those he tortured with his pets was always quite striking.

Only one thing mattered more to Bishop than his Sobranies: his scorpions.

"I knew I shouldn't have sent Deacon to Chicago." He sighed with irritation, snuffing the glowing end of his cigarette into a crystal ashtray sitting on a round, wooden table.

A form shifted in a darkened corner of the room as if he had awakened it. Or maybe even scared it. The disgusting human form was cast in shadows, and Bishop squinted in that direction. Contempt oozed from every pore. His brother's failure was a personal affront that Bishop had made him pay for since he'd shown up here two months ago.

Sucking his teeth, tsk'ing with a shake of his head, he reached into one of the aquariums. A small, black scorpion, which appeared blue under the black lights, flared its pincers, curling its stinger-tipped tail as if preparing to strike.

"Do you think your brother's life meant nothing to me, Apostle? It's your fault he's dead, you know. I should kill you for that simple fact alone." He refused to look back at the shifting form in the corner, even when a groan broke from his brother's throat. *Weakling. Deacon wouldn't have groaned like a sniveling human. Deacon was stronger than that.* "I sent him to help you because you asked it of me, and look how you thanked me. You let him die. How are we to correct this travesty, brother?"

Bishop wiggled his fingers at the scorpion, encouraging the arachnid until it scampered onto his palm so he could lift it out of the aquarium. Slowly rotating his hand as the creature crawled around to the back, he walked to the corner and knelt down, not taking his eyes off the tiny but deadly scorpion.

"Do you know that in some countries, they use scorpion venom as an anti-inflammatory? In others, they make the venom into wine and drink it as an analgesic." His voice crooned softly as he admired his poisonous pet.

His brother disgusted him. It mattered not that he was Bishop's own blood. Deacon had been the real treasure of the siblings—the one who had held the most promise to oversee Bishop's growing operation. But now Deacon was gone. Dead at the hands of the vampire enforcers who dwelled in the cesspool known as Chicago. And that left this poor excuse for a dreck, shivering naked in his human form, to be Bishop's second in command.

"You will require a new human form, my brother, as the fool vampires believe they killed you when they killed Deacon in your place."

"Why?" The broken voice that came back at him sounded weak and shaky.

His brother was struggling to accept the amount of venom the scorpions had injected into him in the two months since Deacon's death. But in time he would see how beneficial the venom was from these special, altered scorpions. Altered by Deacon. The scorpions had been Deacon's idea. Who would develop such pleasant, torturous methods and experiments now? Torturous yet progressive. Methods of strengthening their race while diminishing the strength of the vampires. Oh yes, his sniveling brother would thank him someday for his gift. With time, his body would assimilate the poison, and then he would become stronger and deadlier than he could imagine. Unfortunately, the scorpion venom wouldn't make him smarter. Oh well, two out of three wasn't bad.

Bishop lifted the scorpion to his lips and kissed it. "Isn't it a beautiful creature?" He seemed not to realize his brother had asked him a question.

"Why do I...n...need...a new...human f...form?" His brother shook so violently, he could hardly speak.

"Kiss my darling pet, dear brother." Bishop extended his hand toward Apostle even as he shuddered and shoved back against the wall. The chain restraining his ankle jangled and slid across the floor, going taut, pulled to its limit.

Bishop tenderly lowered his hand until the scorpion scurried off and onto his brother's stomach. The blood-curdling scream that followed the scorpion's sting was sweet music. Bishop closed his eyes and grinned as if listening to his favorite opera. He stood and swayed, dancing, his head tilted back, his blue lips curling in pleasure as his brother continued to sing for him, the scorpion performing like a maestro, stinging repeatedly, just as it was trained to do.

Scorpio venom and dreck venom were similar concoctions. And even if they weren't, a scorpion's sting couldn't kill drecks. That whole immortality thing made sure of that. But these were special scorpions, their DNA spliced with that of vampires. Their sting was more painful because their venom was more potent. As a result, a dreck subjected to repeated doses from these creatures developed deadlier venom—strong enough to kill even a vampire, according to the experiments Bishop had conducted—and became physically stronger, as well as highly resistant to pain. But the treatment was uncomfortable, even excruciating at times, to the point that some of his subjects died. Still, Bishop enjoyed using it as a torture method for those needing a reminder of who held the power around here.

The fact that Apostle had survived this long was surprising, and it was the only reason Bishop considered him strong enough to be trained in Deacon's place. Lesser drecks would have died weeks ago from what Apostle had endured for almost two months.

Even so, how dare Apostle let Deacon die! He had earned this castigation. Still, it was time to put the past behind them and plan their retribution against those who had taken Bishop's favorite sibling. Deacon's death was hard to accept, but it was time to move on. There was work to do and vampires to kill, and he needed Apostle for the tasks ahead.

After enjoying Apostle's cries of pain a moment longer, Bishop opened his eyes and knelt back down to retrieve his pet and return it to its aquarium with a fond stroke over its curled tail.

Harsh, ragged breaths burst in a panicked, terrified rhythm from the corner.

"Why do I require you to take a new human form?" Bishop

finally addressed Apostle's question. "If you are to return to Chicago, you will need a new face, my brother."

A tortured groan shuddered from Apostle's throat. "Not... going...back. No reason...to."

Oh, he wasn't going back, was he? When had this cretin begun thinking he made the decisions around here? If Apostle wanted to live, he needed to know who was in charge.

Bishop snarled and leaped forward, landing in a crouch over his brother's naked body. His eyes glowed red briefly as he growled, his hair hanging down like long, black fringe. "You will do as I command, Apostle. Or I will put an end to you. Is that understood?"

Apostle shot back toward the wall, pulling against the short length of chain restricting his movements. His body was covered with swollen, red bumps where the scorpions had stung him.

Bishop tracked Apostle's movement, glaring at him through the long hair that hung over his eyes. He snarled again. Apostle's obstinacy would not be tolerated, and he would learn never to tell Bishop no. If Apostle thought to bring his idea of pithy leadership to Bishop's dominion, he was delusional.

Pushing up from the floor, Bishop's boots struck down with two heavy thumps and planted on either side of Apostle's torso. He bent forward with a backhand that nearly shot Apostle's head off his shoulders. "Do you understand me, brother?" His eyes glowed red again, his upper lip curled back. "This is *my* house. You came to *me*, remember? What *I* say goes." He leered ever closer, practically kneeling over Apostle, who cringed back and tried to look away. "If you don't like my laws, I'll throw you back to those jackals in Chicago myself so they can finish what they were too *inept* to do the first time."

Apostle trembled uncontrollably. From fear or the venom? Maybe both. Probably both.

Bishop stood back up, stepped away from Apostle, and sat down in a nearby chair. He plucked another Sobranie from the case on a small, round, cherry wood table and lit it, inhaling its glorious taste as he glared at Apostle cowering in the corner. He'd seen jellyfish with more spine.

"Do we have an understanding then?" He spoke as if there was only one acceptable answer, and he would continue to ask the question until he got the one he wanted.

It didn't take long. Apostle nodded shakily, fearfully. "Y... yes."

Finally! Why did Apostle always have to be so argumentative? Couldn't he be more agreeable? He would have to groom this disagreeable nature out of Apostle. Make it perfectly clear that he expected only compliance.

Bishop took a victorious, satisfying draw on the cigarette then pulled a key on a round ring from his pocket and tossed it so that it landed on the floor and slid toward Apostle.

"Good. Now release yourself and get cleaned up." Bishop rose dismissively, slipping the cigarette between his lips.

A plume of grey smoke followed him and dispersed into the air as he left the room.

He didn't want to be near his disgusting brother for one more second.

CHAPTER 3

Io SAT IN THE PASSENGER SEAT of the Suburban next to Severin, and wasn't that about as comfortable as being rubbed with barbed wire? Sev had effectively stolen Io's best friend, Arion, away from him when the two ended up coming out about their homosexuality on St. Patrick's Day, which was also when Io learned they had mated each other.

Io still hadn't wrapped his mind around how his best friend could have turned out gay after all the chicks they had bagged together, but there was no mistake. Ari and Sev were mated to one another, and the bond that connected them was one of the strongest Io had ever seen between mates.

Just the thought of what the pair had spent the past two weeks doing to each other through their calling phases was enough to make Io squeamish. He just couldn't picture Ari fucking a guy, for Christ's sake, and if he tried to, his stomach lurched.

To say Io was homophobic was an understatement. But now he was all confused, because he had never imagined his closest compadre would turn out to be batting for the other team.

Sev turned down the heat in the cab and pulled into a parking garage where drecks liked to deal cobalt.

"How you feeling, man?" Io quickly dashed an awkward glance toward Sev before looking away uncomfortably. He knew that Sev knew how he felt about gays. Or at least how he *used* to feel about them. Now Io wasn't sure *how* he felt.

"Good." Sev inclined his head warily, almost as if he suspected his question had come with ulterior motives.

"Your chest okay?" Io fiddled with the zipper tab on one of the pockets of his military cargo pants.

Sev's chest had been blown open by that assassin, Gina or whatever her name was, the night Ari and Sev had come out. Sev had been lucky to survive, flatlining once during surgery before pulling through.

"Yeah, it's fine." Sev threw Io an inquisitive look.

Io bobbed his head in acknowledgment. "Good. Good. Glad to hear it." He averted his gaze and looked out the window, feeling like ants were crawling up and down the back of his neck. Being around Sev was fucking awkward.

"I'm glad you're glad." Sev spoke in a measured cadence, as if he sensed the tension in the cab of the Suburban and was beginning to get pissed off about it, or maybe he was just irritated.

They circled up to the top level of the parking garage.

Io cleared his throat. "So, uh…how's Ari?"

Despite his purveying homophobia, he missed his best friend. As in, really missed him. A lot. Like he didn't know what to do with himself anymore, because he missed him that much. Io and Ari had been inseparable forever. Io's gaze drifted to his right arm, which was covered with an impressive tattoo sleeve under the jacket he was wearing. Ari had gone with him that day and had tattooed his left arm. The two had been closer than brothers then. And now Ari was…*gay*?

Sev shot him a quick glance then turned his gaze back to the road. "Maybe you should ask him yourself, Io." Sev's tone wasn't angry or judgmental, but he did sound suspicious about why Io was asking about Ari. But then, mated males were pretty protective of their mates, and Io hadn't exactly given Sev—or Ari, for that matter—any reason to think he wasn't a threat. On the contrary. After bashing homosexuals for the better part of his adult life, Sev and Ari had reason to be wary of him.

Io shook his head. "No. Um, no way. He's got to be pissed at me." It was a cop-out. Ari being pissed off to the point that he wouldn't even speak to him was about as likely as Kim

Kardashian's ass deflating.

"Actually, no. I think he'd like hearing from you." Sev kept his eyes forward, his hands square at ten and two on the wheel. "I mean, he hasn't got the warm and fuzzies going on for you right now, but I wouldn't say he's pissed. Hurt maybe, but not pissed."

Io got the impression Sev was just as uncomfortable with this convo as he was. Io fumbled with his gun, releasing the clip to check the bullets then slapping it back into place. Twice.

The two rode back down to street level. Patrol was damn slow tonight. Too slow. It made Io fidgety, because all this inactivity made the polka-dotted elephant in the Suburban that much more apparent. At least if they came across a dreck skirmish or maybe a cobalt deal, he could push that damn pachyderm into the back of his mind for a while as he dealt with business.

Not that Io normally patrolled. He was more of the team's intel guy. Io was a hacker more than a patrol grunt, but he could multitask and do both, and now with Arion gone, it left a hole in the team that needed filling.

When had Io gone this long without seeing Ari? Had it really been since before they had even met over a hundred years ago, because from day one, the two had been like Siamese twins, pretty much doing everything together.

"I don't know what to say to him anyway," Io blurted.

"Huh?" Sev glanced over, frowning. "Oh, you mean Ari."

"Yeah. I don't know what to say to him." He was repeating himself like Rain Man. *I don't know what to say, don't know what say to him. Yeah.*

"Well, Io, it's not rocket science," Sev said. "What did you guys talk about before?"

Good question. What hadn't they talked about? But that had been when Arion was heterosexual, or rather, when Io hadn't known Ari was gay. Shit! They had fucked women together, for Christ's sake. It made Io mad that Ari had gone along with him and fucked females sometimes three at a time, but the whole time, Ari had been gay. So, a lot of their conversations had been centered on females, and now Io didn't know how to deal with that. He didn't understand.

"He's gay, Sev."

Sev shot the Suburban to the shoulder of the road, slammed the brakes, threw it into park, and spun in the driver's seat to look at Io. "Excuse me?"

"No offense." Io held up his hands. "I'm just saying—"

"You're a dick."

Io ricocheted backward, body bristling. What the fuck? "That was uncalled for."

"Fuck you. Your idiotic attitude is uncalled for, too, but I don't see that stopping you."

"Just wait a second—"

Sev threw his hand up, stopping him. "No. You wait a second. You're saying now that you know Ari's gay, you don't know how to talk to him. Just because he's gay? Seriously?"

Io was starting to see Sev's point. "Um...yeah. I guess so." He didn't even sound convincing to himself.

"You really are a bonehead."

Io frowned. "Fine. Okay? Just..." He huffed and looked away. If only he had kept his big mouth shut. Sev was on a roll.

"You're such a typical homophobe." Sev snorted. "Ari hasn't changed, Io. He's still Ari. He's still your best friend. And he misses you like crazy, asshole. He misses you every day. So, what is it you're really fucked in the head over? Huh? Are you worried his *disease* will rub off on you? Are you worried he'll talk about how much he loves me? Are you worried he'll disclose what goes on in our bedroom? Is that it?"

Io squirmed and pushed away. This conversation had taken a turn for the worse. Couldn't Sev just drop it?

Oh, no. Not Sev. He forged onward like a bull in the streets of Pamplona. "Does it make you uncomfortable to think of your friend making love to another man? Fucking a dude? How about the thought of my dick in his mouth, or his in mine?" Sev's voice took on a dramatic tone, as if he was mocking someone. *Hmm, wonder who?* "Oh yeah, Io, Ari and I have tasted every inch of each other." Sev pushed toward him, barreling down like a steamroller on steroids. "His ass is so fine. Damn. I've never seen a finer cut of meat on a guy." Obviously, Sev was making a point.

"Okay, stop it! Just stop! Fuck!" Io's stomach roiled, bile rising in his throat. He couldn't digest dicks on dicks.

Sev sighed long and deep and eased back against the driver's side door. "You know, what's funny is that you carry on about women like that, Io. You fuck 'em, spill the details, talk about them like they're nothing more than cattle to your prod. It's degrading. It's irritating. Now you know how it feels."

Io hung his head. Was he really so bad? Well, yeah, now that he thought about it, he was.

Sev surged on. "Ari and I don't feel like we have to go around bragging about our sexual life. We don't treat each other like the next big conquest. We love each other." Sev sighed and shook his head. "And you're such a hypocrite. I know for a fact that you get off on the idea of two girls together, and that you've actually lived out that fantasy more than once. But...two guys?" Sev shook his head. "The thought of two men together makes your stomach turn. So, what's the difference? Two girls, two guys?" Sev lifted his hands palms up and moved them up and down like scales. "One's okay, but not the other? As long as they don't have dicks, stack 'em one on top of the other and enjoy the party? Is that it?"

Io didn't know what to say. Sev was right. It was as if the guy had read his mind. Until this moment, Io hadn't made the connection. Two girls, two guys. Really, what *was* the difference? Why did two girls together stoke his sexual fantasies, but two guys made him squeamish?

Great. One more thing to shame him. First, cobalt, and now his own prejudice. Would a time ever come when he wouldn't make himself out to be such an ass?

Sev turned and sat back heavily, looking out the windshield. "Look, Io, you do what you have to do, but Ari misses you like hell. I'm not saying it will be easy, because he's just as hurt as you are, but my mate misses you and would love nothing more than for you to be a part of our lives. But neither of us will tolerate your gay bashing. So, if you can't open your mind and accept us for what and who we are, then it's your loss. It'll kill Ari to lose your friendship, but that would be better than letting you hurt either of us with your ignorant bullshit."

Io looked away, feeling about as tall as an ant. Sev had just royally chewed his ass out, and he really didn't have a counterargument that made sense and wouldn't make him look like an even bigger fuckup than he already was.

Sev put the Suburban in gear, pulled back onto the road, and they drove in silence for a while.

Finally, Io said quietly, "Okay, I hear you."

Sev nodded, his long, blond hair like a golden waterfall over his shoulders. "Well, that's a start." He made a left turn toward a part of the South Side known for its growing cobalt traffic.

Io glanced out the window. "A fresh start." He said it quietly, as if he were trying the words out on his tongue. Io was more than familiar with fresh starts. His meeting earlier tonight was evidence of that. Only, starting over with Ari felt like it would be impossible. How did you start over with someone you had thought of as a brother for nearly a century?

Sev cleared his throat uneasily. "Okay, so Ari and I plan to go to this bar in Lakeview on nights I have off. It's called The Blue Turtle. Arion has talked to the owner, and he's allowing Ari to play a one-hour set twice a week there starting next week. It's a gay bar, but if you want to see him on more neutral ground, that's where he'll be on our next night off, okay?"

Io wasn't sure going to a gay bar was something he was comfortable with. "You guys could come to Four Alarm, too, you know."

Sev nodded once, pursing his lips in consideration. "Yeah, we could. But we're not the ones with a problem over all this. You are."

In other words, Io needed to make the first step, and maybe they would make the next one.

They. He had to start thinking in terms of *they* with Ari, now. Because, whether he liked it or not, Ari was no longer just *he.* He was mated. Part of a pair. Which was another point of contention. Io had thought he and Ari would never take mates, and if by some fluke they did, it would be at the same time, two twins or some shit. He had always seen the two of them doing everything together for the rest of their lives, and now all that was shot to hell.

For the first time, Io was afraid of what the future held.

CHAPTER 4

"I'M NOT A PRISONER!" Miriam threw her napkin down on the dinner table and spun for the door, chin high, lips pinched tightly together. Her gaze darted back and forth between the guards who stepped in front of the exit. She really *was* a prisoner, wasn't she? She couldn't even leave the dining room without permission from her father. How fitting.

"Get back in here!" Her father's booming voice projected with the power of a king. And why shouldn't it? He *was* the king. A fact she was reminded of every day.

Was this the life of a princess? Did she have nothing but this...*servitude* and oppression to look forward to for the rest of her life? Her father wanted more from her than she wanted to give. More docility, more pretty-pretty figurehead, more fake smiles and propriety. *Vomit.*

Freedom and normalcy. That's what Miriam wanted. To choose where she went, when she went there, and who she saw. In short, she wanted to make her own decisions.

Her throat constricted and her jaw clenched as she stopped abruptly and crossed her arms over her chest with a huff. Her eyes narrowed on the two guards. At one time this had been her home, but somewhere along the way, it had become a jail. One day the doors had closed with the clang of barred prison cells, and the mood had only worsened in the days since.

She was constantly thwarted by everyone around her. The guards, her mother, her father, even her brother, who remained servile and meek—they all contributed to her not being able to find herself.

At forty-seven, she was old enough to be grown up, but

not wise enough to be mature. That was Miriam to a tee, and she acted it, sneaking out, running off, partying, rebelling, arguing with her father constantly, and now dipping into drugs. Cobalt was the only thing that relieved her of her anguish. Only cobalt took her to a place that made her feel free and alive, unlike how she felt at home.

But the jig was up. She had experienced her first cobalt overdose two weeks ago. Now everyone knew how she self-medicated, even if they didn't want to accept it. Case in point: her father. After being retrieved from AKM by one of the family servants, her father had greeted her with about as much gentility as a gnat. His temperament hadn't improved since.

Arms still crossed, she spun on the heels of her designer shoes and stared her father down. He stood at the head of the lavish, oversized table in the equally luxurious dining hall. His corded arms were extended straight down to hands twice the size of hers, pressed against the lacquered walnut table. Her mother, the queen, sat straight-backed beside him, her gaze giving nothing away of her thoughts as she watched Miriam.

"Miriam. Sit. Down. I'm not finished," he said, standing tall and pointing to her empty chair.

"With dinner or with me?" Miriam rolled her eyes, her words dripping with sarcasm, and flopped back down in front of a plate of half-eaten cuisine.

Cuisine. Not food. It was not called food in this home, which was as large as three city blocks. King Bain's family ate *cuisine*. She mentally scoffed at the silly way things were done here.

All of it—the opulence, the money, the ass-kissing servants, the even bigger ass-kissing guards...the *cuisine*—just wasn't her. She knew it wasn't, but trying to figure out *who* she was and where she fit in was as difficult as a mouse trying to defeat a cat with all the overbearing control her father tried to weigh her down with. Couldn't she just call it food, for God's sake? Couldn't she just wear jeans or sweats to dinner once in a while?

She looked down at the stylish, expensive pantsuit that had been laid out for her.

Everything was *always* laid out for her. She never got to decide for herself. From her clothes to her bath towel to her food—no, *cuisine*—nothing Miriam did was of her mind unless she forced her will. And when she forced her will, she was branded a trouble maker. She couldn't even speak without permission most of the time.

Her father sat back down, tossing her a cross look. "Both," he said, answering her earlier question. "What's gotten into you?"

She gave a flippant, one-shouldered shrug. Her father refused to admit she had overdosed. He hadn't spoken of it once, and Miriam imagined that he thought if he didn't acknowledge her drug use, in his mind that meant it didn't exist. But that was how he was, always sweeping the family problems under the rug instead of dealing with them. After spending all day handling the issues of the entire race, he must not have any energy left for her or the rest of the royal family. But especially her. She was invisible to her father. He saw her, but he didn't see her. Really *see*.

Case in point, if he had been paying attention, he would have known by now that nothing had gotten into her. She had been behaving this way for a while, but he chose not to see it.

Her father huffed, undeterred. "What were you thinking last night, Miriam? How am I supposed to rule a race when I can't even rule my own daughter?"

Last night, she'd snuck out with Persephone again, hitting a dealer and ending up at a party with less than agreeable humans pawing her as she had only just barely refrained from passing out. She had openly fed from a human's vein, in front of other humans—most of them high, none sober. When the guards had fetched her, they'd had to clean every mind at the party to ensure no one remembered the pretty vampire girl who'd bitten the neck and drank the blood of their friend.

Her brilliant sapphire eyes whipped toward her father.

"Excuse me? Rule me? Is that what you said?"

Her younger brother, Colin, ducked his head across from her just as her father slammed his fist against the table. The loud boom echoed around the room, and her father's anger hung like an ominous storm ready to let loose.

But Miriam wasn't afraid of him. Not like her brother, and not like the spineless, sniveling liaisons who kissed her father's royal ass on a daily basis. Unlike all the rest, Miriam's inner package had come with fortitude and an iron will which rivaled her father's in every way, which was probably the source of her growing antics. Antics that outraged her father. But why should she care what he thought when he didn't care enough to treat her like a living, breathing person who bore half his genes? And with those genes he had given her, she matched him rage-to-rage and fist-to-fist across the spectrum.

"This is my home, Miriam, and you—"

"That's right." Miriam sat back and threw her napkin on her plate of cuisine. "I'm just some stray dog you took in. I should be grateful you even allow me to live here."

"Goddamn it, Miriam!" Her dad glared at her.

For most people, his stern frown was enough to send them yipping in the opposite direction with their tails tucked between their legs and fear in their eyes, but Miriam wasn't like most people. Not anymore, anyway. At one time, she had reacted to her father with fear, too, but those days were over. With narrowed eyes and crossed arms, she glared right back at him.

"What? Not used to someone talking to you like they have a pair of balls? Funny that it takes a female to remind you what courage sounds like, isn't it? You're spending too much time with your—*ahem*—liaisons and counselors, Father. You've forgotten what it sounds like when someone actually has a spine." She pushed away from the table, and this time she wasn't going to let her father pull her back in. Conversation over.

"Miriam. Miriam!"

She waved over her shoulder, her Manolo Blahniks

clacking over the hardwood floors, and stared down the guards who stepped in front of her to block the exit again.

"Get out of my way or lose your jewels." She hit them with a downward glance aimed at their crotches.

As her father continued shouting at her from the table, neither guard budged, their faces still as stone and their eyes full of dark resolve.

"Suit yourself." She feinted as if she was going to roundhouse the guard on the left. When he ducked, she leaped and somersaulted like a graceful cat, punching the other guard in the face as he tried to catch her.

"Bring her back here!" Her father's voice bellowed through the entire house.

As soon as her feet landed on the opposite side of the guards, she kicked off her designer shoes, turned, and sprinted down the hall, leaving those lackeys behind. After all, she *did* have her father's genes. The guards would never catch her.

Leaping and dematerializing, she instantly reappeared on the landing at the end of the main foyer and darted down a long hallway as the guards struggled to keep up. Breezing through her room, she grabbed her coat, another pair of shoes, her keys, and her bag, then burst onto her balcony before jumping four stories to the ground below. Security from all over the house was after her by now, but they would never catch her. They never did. She was too smart, too fast, too strong. Not even her own father could tie her down anymore.

Materializing into the driver's seat of her Jaguar, she cranked the engine and gunned it, top down and radio blaring.

The wind whipped her long hair around her face, and she quickly pulled it back in a ponytail, driving with her knee. Then she floored it. Destination South Side.

Destination Cobalt, more like it. She *needed* the cobalt. Cocaine, heroin, meth. Miriam had tried them all, but that shit didn't work on vampires. At least not in the way she needed it to. Nothing helped ease her except cobalt. Dream-inducing, stress-relieving, take-me-away cobalt. It was the only thing that enabled her to deal with the shitty life Fate had racked up for her.

Damn it, but she just wanted to be herself. She only wanted to live her own life, but her fucking father and everyone else in that prison she called a home refused to let her.

After nabbing her cell from her bag, she punched in Persephone's speed dial and pulled the phone to her ear.

"Hey you!" Persephone said.

Miriam smiled. Seph was her partner in crime and a sweetheart.

"I'm picking you up, Seph. I'll be there in five."

Miriam and Persephone had been friends since they were kids, but Seph's family had only just returned to Chicago a couple of months ago after living in Italy for the past ten years.

"Where are we going?" Seph asked her.

"The usual."

"Thank God. I'm almost out."

Out. Out of cobalt. Just like Miriam. And being out was a bad thing. Very bad.

These little fights she had with her father pushed her to need the blue elixir more and more. Or the blue powder. Either way. That was the nice thing about cobalt. It could be inhaled or injected. She liked options.

Miriam pulled up the long, turnaround driveway at Persephone's house. Within seconds, the door opened and Persephone darted out and hopped in.

"Hurry before Father stops us," Seph said, throwing a hasty look over her shoulder.

Miriam was already hitting the gas and speeding back down the driveway.

After getting back on the road, Miriam glanced over at Seph, who had been through a lot in the last few weeks.

"How are you coping?" Miriam said. Persephone had been engaged to Arion Savakis for about a minute before finding out that Arion had already taken a mate. A male mate he worked with at AKM, from what she had heard. Talk about a blow to a girl's confidence. Seph had taken the broken engagement pretty hard, especially since she had been dumped for another male.

"I'm okay. Easy come, easy go, right?" Seph brushed her lustrous, blond hair off her face, but her easygoing attitude wasn't fooling Miriam. She knew Seph was devastated at losing her chance to be mated, especially to Ari. Seph had really liked him.

"Shit sucks," Miriam said, hitting the highway.

The two hadn't talked much since *that* night. That night being when she had overdosed and Seph had been a happy bride-to-be for all of an hour.

"Yeah, but what are you gonna do, right?" Seph shrugged and offered a weak smile. "What about you? I heard that tone in your voice when you talked about that guy. Eo, Io, or whatever his name is?" She laughed. "Ee-eye-ee-eye-oh!"

Seph seemed too pleased with herself. "Or is that 'heigh-ho, the derry-o'?"

Miriam laughed. "You goof! Stop playing. That's not funny." She smacked Seph's arm. "And it's Io." Her cheeks heated, her breath hitching over his name.

"A-ha! I heard that. You do like him."

"What if I do? He sure beats anything my dad has ever presented me with." Her father had introduced her to a lot of handsome, *worthy* young males over the years. Holiday parties and countless political functions had become a cattle parade of males all vying for her hand. She stiffened and scowled. Her father needed to mind his own business and leave finding a mate in her hands.

He thought that if he introduced her to countless males, the one who would soul-mate her would magically appear, but that wasn't how it worked. Not for her. She was in charge. She would choose. Her father's only saving grace was that he didn't just want to marry her off the way Seph's parents had tried to do with her. Everyone saw how disastrous that had been. Poor Seph.

Besides, Miriam wasn't interested in taking a mate right now. She just wanted to have a little fun. She wanted to experiment, make out, touch and be touched—learn what this thing about the opposite sex was all about without having to worry about anyone getting arrested or killed for touching her. But her father wouldn't even give her that much. At the times when she was able to break away from the ever-present watch of her father's guards, it was never long before they eventually caught up to her, such as they had last night. She had been so close to tasting her first real kiss, but the guards had busted in and broken up the party before she'd had a chance to sample more than just the human's blood.

But the human wasn't who she really wanted. The gentle male from AKM, Io, who had brushed her hair and made her feel things she had never felt—that was who she wanted. She had been thinking about him a lot. What did his lips feel like? How did he taste? Would he be afraid to touch her like all the others, or would he be brave enough to break the rules with her?

Io.

Such a simple name. But she got the impression he wasn't as simple as his name sounded. His hypnotic gaze, his tattoo, and his shrewd manner hinted at a male who wasn't as gentle as he seemed, nor as compliant as her father would have liked. Was it the glint in his eye or the way he seemed to smile out of one side of his mouth as if he had a secret that gave him away? Or was it something else? Whatever it was, Io was the one she really wanted to kiss and get to know better.

"So? You going to see him again?" Persephone said, as if reading her mind.

Miriam snapped out of her fantasy and smiled. She would love to see Io again. He was handsome and tragic in an odd sort of way that made her feel like she had more in common with him than the fact that they were both vampires. Io had demons haunting him just as she did. She could see it in his eyes. And what amazing eyes he had. Green and golden brown mixed, and intense in a way that touched her all the way to her soul. It warmed her to think about him and the short time they had shared while she had been recovering at AKM from her overdose.

And it had been obvious he had been attracted to her, too. However, reality made it clear that she and Io had about as much chance at seeing each other again as a fly had against a fly swatter. As in, zilch. No chance. Nada.

"Yeah, Seph, like that'll happen," she said, rolling her eyes.

"You never know."

"Pah-lease. Do you want to know what would happen to Io if I saw him again? Father would ruin him. Io would lose his job, his credibility, his livelihood, everything. Maybe even his life."

It sucked having the king as a father. He did a decent job ruling the race, but he was a lousy dad. Domineering, controlling, completely out of touch. The simple fact that he had made reference to ruling her earlier was a huge clue that he needed parenting lessons in the most severe way. His idea of parenting was keeping Miriam under lock and key and preventing any male from touching her.

And if she saw Io again, she would most definitely encourage his touching her, which was why Io would never survive if she somehow managed to find her way back to him. Father would destroy him.

Her thoughts went back to that day two weeks ago, when Io had been brushing her hair while she had been in AKM's medical ward. Io's boss had busted in and reprimanded him for being so casual with her. *You're not allowed to touch her,* he had said. The words had echoed like the lyrics of a bad song that had engrained itself in her mind, playing over and over ever since.

No one was allowed to touch her. As if she were some paper-thin, crystal egg shell.

"Still, you like him, Miri. I can see it all over your face." Seph's voice was soft. "I've never seen you so starry-eyed over a guy."

Okay, so Seph was right. She hadn't been able to stop thinking about Io since meeting him. "He brushed my hair," she said, blushing.

Seph's face screwed up in a cheesy half-frown, half-grin. "What? You didn't tell me this before." She sounded accusatory, but in a playful way.

"I know, I know. It sounds lame, but"—she sighed wistfully—"it was the most romantic thing, Seph. He brushed my hair. He got right up on the bed and sat behind me and just...brushed my hair." She could still feel how tenderly Io had smoothed his palm over her hair as he slowly swept the brush through it. His body heat had been intoxicating behind her and she could have sworn at one point he had wanted to reach his arm around her waist and hold her. Damn, her nipples hardened even now at the thought.

"Oh boy, you're completely smitten," Seph said.

"I am not."

"Are to."

Miriam giggled. "Okay, maybe a little."

She had needed this. After the fight with her father, she had needed to get out and find a way to laugh and smile. Funny how thinking about Io over the past couple weeks had been about the only thing that had been able to do that.

CHAPTER 5

AFTER UNLOCKING HIS SHACKLES, it took Apostle over an hour to crawl out of the corner he had been confined to for the past several weeks and reach the bathroom on the opposite side of the room. Who would have thought a commode would feel like a luxury item? But after weeks with only a pot to piss in, properly relieving himself like a civilized gent brought him back to the land of the living.

Bishop had always been ruthless, but he seemed even more so now. Apostle never would have imagined that Bishop would subject him to such abhorrent accommodations, or that he would have allowed those scorpions to sting him. But not only had Bishop allowed it, he had encouraged it, pulling each deadly creature out from its aquarium, one-by-one, and placing it on Apostle's body. The fucking things seemed trained to sting only him, because they never hurt Bishop.

Maybe it would have been better if he had died in Chicago, after all, because at least he wouldn't feel like death without the funeral right now.

Through the poison haze in his mind, Apostle recalled walking into his Chicago home two months ago to find his twin brother's decimated body alongside those of his team. Something very powerful had crushed them from the inside out, leaving them in virtual puddles of flesh. The entire living room had looked like it had been through both a tornado and an earthquake, the floor ruptured and the furniture broken and flung in disarray.

The only answer as to what had caused so much damage was a vampire. Well, more like a mixed-blood vampire. Only a mongrel could possess power like that. Full blood vampires certainly didn't come pre-packaged with an instant natural disaster at their disposal, but mongrels could possess powers strong enough to do that kind of damage.

That fucking Micah obviously had powerful friends. Two-faced, Indian-giving asshole. Micah had come begging Apostle to kill him—a task Apostle had gladly accepted. To kill a vampire as old and strong as Micah would have been a marvelous notch in his belt, and he had wanted the notoriety of taking down the legend himself. Micah was well-known in the dreck community, and he was highly feared for his lethal skills with a knife and his fearless manner of fighting first, asking questions later. No one wanted to cross Micah, and Apostle had been *thisclose* to removing him as a roadblock that stood in the way of dreck progress.

Which bit Apostle's ass no end that his moment of triumph had been thwarted by that human wench, Samantha. The bitch had shown up and shot him in the shoulder before he could finish the job on Micah in that goddamn parking garage. Apostle knew he should have killed her when he had the chance, but she had startled him and his team, and they didn't want to risk exposing themselves further than they already had. Still, not a day went by that he didn't regret not taking her down that night.

Oh, but he had gotten the last laugh. It had taken him some time, but he had tasted revenge when he had tracked her to Micah's apartment to come face-to-face with the bitch again. This time, she had been helpless—no gun and no Micah to protect her—and Apostle had bitten her, giving her a lethal dose of his venom. No doubt, the catastrophe at his Chicago home had been retaliation for her death since Micah had allegedly taken her as a mate.

Touché. Except that they had missed the real target—him— and killed Deacon, instead.

The irony of enduring Bishop's punishment after surviving the attempt on his life had made Apostle delirious with laughter more than once. Micah and his powerful mongrel friend had wished him harm, and in the end they had gotten it, hadn't they? But Apostle wasn't dead, which was the only in-your-face he had against Micah. Still, all the agony he had endured at Bishop's hand over allowing his twin to be killed in his place had been worth it, because at least he had taken something away from Micah and had left him just as empty. Apostle knew how shit worked for mated male vampires, and Micah was as good as dead without Sam.

Which made his desire to go back to Chicago about nil. His job there was done, as far as he was concerned, and he felt no compulsion to return to oversee his drug-dealing operation. No use tempting fate.

But now Bishop had told him he wanted Apostle to return there. Why?

Probably because he was absolutely livid over Deacon's death and wanted a slice of his own payback against the Chicago bloodsuckers. A fact Apostle knew all-too-well, because he had lived through Bishop's immediate fury over Deacon's death. His itching, swollen flesh made him feel like he was on fire and near death himself.

What was with the scorpions? When had Bishop become so enamored of those vile creatures? Apostle swatted his arms like he was having a seizure just from the thought of those tiny stingers piercing him and pumping his body full of poison.

Were the scorpions simply used for torture or were they a part of some larger experiment?

Apostle knew that in addition to producing the mother lode of cobalt for distribution around the globe, Bishop conducted genetic experiments in his underground laboratory here in Arizona, but Apostle had never been involved in that side of the family business. He had been in charge of distribution, based in Chicago, which was an ideal location for shipping within the United States. So when it came to the Dr. Frankenstein shit Bishop had going on, Apostle was relatively clueless.

His twin, Deacon, had been in charge of the lab and the production facility, but when Apostle had to travel outside of Chicago for any length of time, Deacon usually filled in for him to keep up appearances in the Windy City. That was why Deacon had been in Chicago two months ago. He had been there to pose as Apostle while Apostle traveled to New York to deal with mafia entanglements and a rising turf war over cobalt distribution. He had only been gone a day.

In Chicago, Apostle had posed as a police officer. What better role to play to get cozy with the criminal element responsible for pushing product? And being a police officer had lots of helpful perks, such as doing pretty much what he wanted, when he wanted, and to whom.

Yes, the persona known as Officer John Apostle, Apostle's human visage, had been on the take. Big time. None of the humans he had worked with knew he had been anything other than another human named John. They had never seen him in his dreck form: Blue skin, blue blood, blue-black hair, gaunt features, fangs…real horror movie kind of stuff.

As such, he and the other members of his team, drecks who had also posed as cops, had received a hero's funeral. He hadn't seen the TV broadcast of the funeral personally, because he had been chained to the floor, but Bishop had told him about it between litanies of profanities. Bishop's anger over Deacon's death had since cooled, but those first few days back had been brutal, both physically and mentally, as well as audibly.

Which brought his thoughts full circle. Because it hadn't been Apostle the police force of Chicago had mourned. It had been his brother. Deacon had only needed to stand in for Apostle for one shift, but it had proven to be one shift too many.

The door opened and the overhead light flipped on, causing Apostle to cringe and blink rapidly against the sudden pain. You knew you were fucked up when just light hurt you.

"You're still not cleaned up?" Bishop sauntered in, one of those goddamn brown cigarettes between his fingers.

In the weeks Apostle had been here, he had grown to hate the smell of those shit-assed stink sticks.

Bishop approached him. "We have work to do, Apostle, if we're to get you up to speed so you can take Deacon's place."

DONYA LYNNE

Under his breath, he added, "Not that you'll ever be as good as he was." He turned toward the armoire in the corner of the room.

"I can't take his place." Apostle frowned and scratched the swollen bumps on his arms.

Bishop rummaged through the garments in the armoire one-handed, seemingly reluctant to part with his cigarette, and pulled out a shirt and pants. He tossed them haphazardly toward Apostle then walked around behind his desk.

"Of course you can take your twin's place. And you will." Bishop sat down, glaring pointedly at him.

He flipped through a file of what appeared to be photographs, hesitated, then picked one up and flicked it toward him.

"This will be your new human form."

Apostle's lip curled at the thought of doing what Bishop told him, but right now he was in no shape to argue. He picked up the picture. The man looked normal enough. Black hair, blue eyes, strong physique. Apostle imagined this guy had no trouble getting chicks.

"What does he do?" Apostle looked up at Bishop.

"Did," Bishop said, standing up. "What *did* he do." He slipped his cigarette between his lips, took a long draw, and blew out the smoke as he came around the desk and sat down on the front edge. He pointed with the cigarette. "Nothing. He was one of our earlier subjects. A beta tester for some experiment we ran several years ago. Here's what he looked like when we were finished." Bishop reached around, picked up another picture, and tossed it at Apostle.

The picture spun and danced in the air before landing in front of him on the floor. When he picked it up, the resemblance between the two images was nonexistent. The man's skin was mottled with what looked like bruises. He was naked and his hair had fallen out, and his emaciated body hung from the ceiling like a starved side of beef. His wrists were bound above his head with chains and cuffs.

Apostle really didn't care about the human, but he was curious what they'd done to him to make him look like this.

"What did you do to him?"

Bishop gave a flippant shrug as he inhaled on his cigarette. After exhaling a plume of grey fog, he said, "We were trying to alter humans into half-drecks to use them as foot soldiers or slaves."

"Soldiers?" This was news to Apostle.

Showed how out of touch he'd been with his brother's operation.

Bishop nodded. "Yes. Soldiers." A wicked smile curved his blue mouth.

No further elaboration was given other than they had been trying to build soldiers. Did that mean that the dreck council was secretly trying to amass an army for an uprising against the vampires?

"Are you still trying to turn humans?"

Bishop shook his head, his smile widening. "No. We've found a better source than humans for our soldiers." Those azure eyes of Bishop's twinkled.

Apostle bristled. This could get interesting. "What?"

Bishop took one final draw on his cigarette then crushed it out in an ash tray behind him on the desk before turning back around, a satisfied smile on his face. "Mixed-bloods, dear brother. Mongrels. In time, we will use their own kind against the vampires. And we will destroy them for good."

CHAPTER 6

Io was staring out the window of the Suburban when his phone beeped. He looked at the screen. It was a message from AKM Dispatch.

"What is it?" Sev said.

Like Io, Sev was probably hoping it was a call. It was damn slow tonight and the two simply couldn't rock the warm and fuzzies between them.

Io frowned at the message. "Nine-one-one from Dispatch for me to call someone, but I don't recognize the number."

Sev exchanged curious glances with him, then Io punched in the number and waited. Who the heck would call him personally besides his immediate family or someone at AKM, especially while he was working?

"Hello?" A female's panicked voice answered, but she didn't sound familiar.

"This is Io from AKM. You wanted me to call you?"

"Thank God. I need your help. Miriam's in bad shape. I'm not sure, but she might have overdosed again. Her father can't see her like this. Oh my God. Please—"

"Whoa, whoa, whoa! Slow down. Who is this?" He didn't know who the female was, but he did recognize Miriam's name. That had been enough to lock up his balls and knife his gut. And if Miriam had overdosed again, shit could go critical in a heartbeat if it hadn't already.

"My name's Persephone. I'm Miriam's friend."

"Persephone, where are you?" Io sat forward in his seat, fear gripping his gut for the beautiful raven-haired female who had rocked his world two weeks ago. He motioned toward Sev.

"Um, I don't know…um…." Persephone sounded like she was looking around.

"South Side? North Side?" Io said, trying to prompt her.

"South Side. We're on the South Side. Oh God, she's unconscious. Um…"

Fuck! Io needed to get there. He needed to save her. As a former addict, he knew what needed to be done, but he needed to get to her first. *Come on, Persephone, where are you?*

"Are you at an intersection? Are there any landmarks, Persephone? How long has Miriam been unconscious?" Io raked his hand through his thick, brown hair.

Sev suddenly stopped the Suburban and got out. Io wondered what he was doing as he stood and sniffed the air.

Persephone started to cry. "She passed out about five minutes ago. I told her to stop. I told her she was taking too much." She was panicking.

"Persephone, calm down. Calm down. Stay with me. I want to help, but I need you to stay calm."

Sev jumped back in and threw the Suburban in gear and gunned it.

"I'm trying, I'm trying. Oh God. She's going to die." Persephone was in hysterics, obviously cranked on the blue buzz, too. "There's an old warehouse, um, I think, I don't know. I can't see any street signs. Wait. Someone's coming."

Io looked up as Sev barreled around a corner. About a block down, a silver Jaguar was parked on the side of the road and a blonde with long hair was pacing at the side.

"I see you. We're almost there." Io looked over at Sev as he disconnected. "How did you know…?"

"I marked them that night I gave them a warning. This is the same neighborhood they were in before, so I hopped out back there to see if I could catch their scent. Didn't know they'd be so close, though. Talk about right place, right time."

Io's eyebrows popped. "Good thinking."

"Eh, just doing my job."

They pulled up alongside the Jag and Io jumped out and rushed toward Miriam. Just seeing the state she was in brought back memories of his own addiction. He scratched his forearms as they began to itch. It had only been a year since Arion had helped him kick his own cobalt habit, but the damn itching of withdrawal persisted. Would it ever stop? For six months he had been on the using end of that nasty shit, and he feared he would pay for it for the rest of his life. He wondered how long Miriam had been using. It only took a few uses of cobalt to go full-blown addict, and he already knew she had been using for at least a month, from what Sev had said.

Sev rounded up Persephone, and Io lifted Miriam out of the driver's seat. She was in bad shape.

"I'm taking her to my place," Io said.

Sev gave him a look. "No, you aren't."

"Yes, I am. Meet me there."

"Io!"

But Io had already connected with Miriam and pulled her with him into the ether, shooting their molecules to his home on the North Side. Within seconds, he had pulled her through the mist and appeared in the shadows of the backyard, Miriam cradled in his arms. He ran to the back door, yanking his keys out of his pocket as he reached it. Quickly, he unlocked the door, rushed in, gently laid her on the bathroom floor down the hall, then ran for the ingredients he had used to help get himself cleaned up.

When Io had been fucked up beyond all recognition, Ari had stayed with him every day, helping him detox, feeding him the concoction he was about to give Miriam and injecting Io with his own venom to fight the addiction. Ari had sacrificed so much to make sure Io got better and kicked the blue shit. He'd sat with him, held him through the violent chills, cleaned him up after vomiting God only knew how many times. Ari had never given up on him, saving Io from himself.

And now Io had to do the same for Miriam.

He pulled out the tin of ancient, powdered herbs and scooped out a quarter-teaspoon, mixed it with water, and then put it on the stove. He added raw vinegar and a drop of an elixir that had been provided by AKM's medical center.

Phew! The shit stunk. It was enough to bring back bad memories.

While the brew heated up, he hurried into the bathroom. Miriam was slumped on the floor, and her long black hair draped her body like a death shroud.

"Time to get up, baby. Come on." Io lifted her and crushed her body to his as the glands in the roof of his mouth kicked into gear, churning up his venom. *Vampire blood trumps dreck blood. Vampire venom trumps dreck venom.* Being that cobalt was made from dreck blood and venom, vampire venom was a key antidote to detox an overdose.

He bit into her neck. Back at AKM, the medics would have put in an IV and injected it into her system. He didn't have time for that shit. She needed his venom now.

Miriam shuddered and drew in a shaky breath as his venom burst into her veins. First would be euphoria then would come the pain as he pushed more venom into her than he would during a simple feeding. And fuck him if she didn't purr. He had never known a female vampire to purr in the way a male did when aroused, but shit, Miriam was purring deep within her chest. But then, Io had never known a female with such pure bloodlines as Miriam's, either. Perhaps that was what made her different.

Soon enough, the purring stopped, and her body quivered. Then shook. Her teeth chattered and her long fingers dug into his shoulders. The pain was breaking through as his venom sought out the intruder and destroyed it. She whimpered and groaned then finally let loose a scream so full of despair tears welled in Io's eyes.

But at least she was alive.

CHAPTER 7

MIRIAM CAME OUT OF UNCONSCIOUSNESS SCREAMING, her body convulsing with pain. And what the hell? Some crazy-ass fool was biting her. Too bad she couldn't control her limbs enough to punch the guy. And her voice was too busy screaming to be able to form coherent sentences to tell him to fuck off. Not that coherent thoughts were in big supply right now. Her brain was a pile of cobalt-stomped mush.

For several seconds, she jerked and spasmed as her screams echoed and choked her throat, but finally she was able to squeak out, "Stop."

In her head, she had heard that coming out a lot differently. Louder, for starters.

She tried again. "Stop." That was a little better. It sounded more like an actual word and not a mouse trying to speak.

"STOP!" Wow! That time she hadn't even tried.

Her attacker released her neck and jerked back to look at her.

Oh my God. Io. Where had he come from? Was she only hallucinating? She had hallucinated on cobalt before, but not like this. He looked so damn real.

Gorgeous, greenish-brown eyes bore into hers, full of concern, and she reached for him, wanting to brush her fingers over his thick, dark brows. Instead, she punched him. Okay, yeah, so she didn't have complete control over her faculties.

He ricocheted to the side from the impact but seemed unfazed as he swiftly turned back.

"It's okay," he said. "I've got you. Hold on, I'll be right back."

No, no, don't go! But she couldn't get her voice to work again. It was like a bad case of Tourette syndrome. When she tried to speak, she couldn't. But then out of nowhere...

"NOOO!"

How embarrassing he had to see her like this.

"Don't worry, I'm still here," he said from the hall. "See, you can hear my voice. I'm still here. I'm not going anywhere." His voice grew more faint, but he continued calling back to her. She heard the sound of cabinets opening and pans and cups hitting the counter. "This is my house. You're in my home. I'm going to take care of you. See, you're safe. I'm not going anywhere."

He sounded like he was talking to make sure she knew he hadn't forgotten about her and hadn't poofed into ether. That was nice. Very nice. Comforting.

As soon as he reappeared in the doorway, holding a large mug of something that smelled atrocious, her mind relaxed again.

Io!

She reached for him, her arms flailing out of control, heat still rippling through her limbs in waves as the pain and burn continued to subside. Instead of taking her hand, though, he knelt down beside her and lifted the mug to her lips.

"Drink," he said. "You have to drink this."

One whiff and she knew there was no way.

He shook his head and huffed. "You have to. You need it to detox the cobalt out. It will make you feel better."

Her eyes snapped to his doubtfully, but she found trust and honesty in his gaze. She could trust him. He wouldn't hurt her, and somehow he knew what was happening to her. She could tell Io had done this before.

She nodded, or at least tried to, but she probably just looked like a bobblehead for all the control she had over her muscles right now. He grinned compassionately, caressing her face with his free hand, trying to reassure her. He knew. Damn, somehow he just knew how to help her.

"Okay, drink. I'm here to catch you."

She held her breath and let him tip the cup to her lips. Hot liquid touched her tongue and she winced before taking the fluid down her throat in heavy, disgusting gulps.

"Keep it down," he said. "At least for a few minutes."

Keep it down? At least for a few minutes? Oh, God. How bad was this going to be?

He emptied the cup and quickly set it aside before lifting her into his arms and holding her close in a gentle, rocking motion. She gagged at the aftertaste, but he simply kept rocking her, making shushing sounds.

Her stomach was not happy. At all.

"This is a more effective treatment for overdose and addiction than what they gave you at AKM a couple of weeks ago," Io said. "This is much better."

Better? She and Io would have to talk about his definition of the word *better*, because even though she still couldn't talk, she could feel, and right now it felt like World War III was about to go postal in her stomach.

"Keep it down as long as you can, Miriam."

Dear God, she was going to throw up.

Not in front of him. Please, not in front of Io.

How much more was she going to humiliate herself in front of this male who made her heart do flips at just the thought of his hands in her hair? She had nearly upchucked in front of him two weeks ago at AKM, and here she was, in his home, about to do it again. And it felt like this time would put last time to shame. Nothing like being an overachiever.

"Sssshhh," Io said, trying to comfort her.

But she couldn't be comforted. Her stomach was a roiling inferno. She tried to shove away from him. This was it. She couldn't hold it back any more. *Toilet, toilet...*

"TOILET!"

He lifted her away from him and held her body as she lunged and heaved a mess of blue shit into the commode. Great, gasping, body locking spasms that seemed to go on forever and empty her to the point where she didn't think she could empty any more decimated her, and still she continued to retch. Through it all, Io managed somehow to hold her body up with one arm while holding back her mane of hair with the other.

After what felt like ten minutes, she finally stopped and fell back against him in a spent heap as he flushed the toilet.

She was exhausted. The soothing chill of a damp cloth being rubbed over her face and mouth relaxed her. After he had cleaned her up, Io gently lifted her in his arms, cradled her, and carried her out of the bathroom. She closed her eyes against the soothing, rocking motion of his body, and then she felt him lower her to a soft, cushiony surface.

He didn't say a word, but she heard him walk more calmly into what sounded like the kitchen. Yes, it was the kitchen. The refrigerator door opened and then the faucet turned on. The rush of water stopped a few seconds later, and then she heard the sound of a light switch being flipped. Next thing she knew, he was back at her side and his fingertips were brushing her face.

She cracked open her eyes and blinked at him.

"How do you feel?" he said.

"Better. Tired." Her throat was raw, and she coughed.

"Here." He handed her a bottle of water, already opened. "Don't worry. It will stay down," he said when she hesitated.

She had regained the use of her limbs, although they felt weak and heavy, and she took the bottle and lifted it to her mouth. Yes, the cold liquid felt good going down.

Io lifted the damp cloth and wiped her face again, and it felt wonderful. Refreshing.

"You need to rest now, okay?" he said. "A short rest and you'll feel better. I promise."

How could she say no to those eyes? "Okay."

He stayed with her until she finally nodded off.

IO SAT ON THE FLOOR NEXT TO MIRIAM, watching her sleep.

He hadn't thought he would see her again after their encounter at AKM, but here she was. Fate had seen fit to thrust her back into his life. And damn if he was going to waste this chance to be with her. All he had wanted was another opportunity to see her, and his prayers had been answered. Someone up there sure liked him. He glanced to the ceiling, placing his hand on his chest. *Thank you.*

When had he ever been around a more perfect female? Miriam was everything he had ever been attracted to. Other than her cobalt addiction, she was the definition of perfection. He had captured enough of a glimpse of her mental fortitude at AKM to know she was no soft-footed glamour puss, either. Something about Miriam told him she was intelligent and powerful, which begged the question, why was she doing the big blue monster? What drove her to shoot up cobalt?

For Io, he had just been plain stupid for taking on cobalt. He had always been more of the daredevil, trying new things just because he could. He was a risk taker, a rebel. Not a rebel in the way Micah was, but a rebel in that he took dares no one else would take. He liked to gamble and go against the odds. It made him feel alive.

As he'd told the group earlier, cobalt had been one of those gambles. Turned out to be a stupid one, but one he had taken nonetheless.

Maybe Io just liked feeling as if he could beat the odds. Playing it safe was for other people. Boring people. Not him. Io wanted to experience life. All of it. That couldn't truly happen without taking risks and experiencing the bad alongside the good.

But that still didn't explain why someone like Miriam, who had it all, and who obviously had the brains and the brawn to go along with all that beauty, flirted with the blue beast. This intrigued him. What made Miriam tick? What pushed her to drug up?

A vehicle pulled into his driveway.

Sev.

He rushed to the door and quietly opened it as Severin and Persephone came up the walk.

"Just what in the hell are you thinking?" Sev sounded like a snarling pit bull.

"Ssshhh," Io motioned for him to keep his voice down. "She just fell asleep."

"Is she okay?" Persephone raced past him before he could stop her, but at least she ran tippy-toed.

Sev glared at him. "What are you thinking?"

Io ushered him inside and shut the door. "I knew I could take better care of her here than they could at AKM," he said.

"Why's that?" Sev kept his voice down as he entered the living room and saw Miriam passed out on the couch.

"Didn't Ari tell you?"

"Tell me what?"

"I used to be an addict, Sev."

Severin's head shot around, his gaze lighting with surprise. "What?"

"Yeah, about a year ago, I was strung out on that shit. Ari didn't tell you?"

Sev shook his head. "No. He mentioned you two had been through some heavy shit over a year ago but wouldn't elaborate."

"Well, yeah, not many knew about it. Arion. Tristan. Probably Micah, because you know he can't stay out of people's heads. But that's all."

"Shit." Sev turned and looked at Miriam again.

Persephone was kneeling beside her then quietly got up and returned to him and Sev. "So, she's okay?" Her gaze darted uncomfortably from Severin, and emotion flickered in the depths of her eyes before she met Io's gaze.

That's when Io remembered that Arion had briefly been engaged to Persephone before the truth had come out that he had already mated Sev. No doubt she felt awkward in the presence of the male who had ended up stealing her fiancé's heart...and soul.

That makes two of us, sweetheart.

Io nodded. "I was able to treat her and get her settled down."

Sev sighed. "You can't keep her here, Io. She has to go home, or at least to AKM."

"No," Persephone said, looking worried. "No, she can't go home."

"Why not?" Io asked, startled by how upset Persephone was about the idea.

"Her father doesn't understand. He doesn't get Miriam." Persephone looked down, the telltale shame of drug addiction evident on her face. "He doesn't understand that she's an addict."

"What do you mean, he doesn't understand? What is there to *not* understand about what's happening to her?" Io pointed toward Miriam, angry over what he was hearing.

Persephone looked between him and Sev. "Miriam says he pretends he doesn't see it. Her drug use. It's like he thinks it will just go away if he doesn't acknowledge it."

Was the king insane? Ignoring cobalt abuse was the worst thing anyone could do to stop it. This just proved the point that the vampire society needed better education about cobalt. If the king himself didn't understand it, how could he expect to get control over it?

"Home is the last place Miriam needs to be right now." Persephone gave a pleading glance toward Io then Sev. "Please let her stay here."

Severin shook his head at her then turned a warning eye on Io. "She can't stay here, Io. You know she can't."

True, if Tristan found out he had kept Miriam in his home, he would be up shit creek, and not just without a paddle, but without a boat, too. But he couldn't send her home, not after what he had just heard. Besides, he couldn't let the most beautiful female he had ever laid eyes on leave his home before he'd even had a chance to talk to her. Io just wanted her to open her gorgeous blue eyes and look at him. No way was he going to spit on this gift God had given him.

"Sev, come on. You know I can do more for her here. I can help her through this. AKM won't do anything but turn her over to her father, and he won't do anything to get to the bottom of this."

"You don't know that," Sev said.

"Didn't you just hear what Persephone said? Her father refuses to see what's going on here."

"It's true." Persephone's face was a mess of fear as she turned toward Sev, practically begging him. "Please. Her father doesn't try to understand. He's the problem. He's why she uses."

Io and Sev both frowned at her.

"What do you mean, he's why she uses?" Io said.

Her face screwed up like she was afraid of speaking out of turn. "God, please don't tell anyone I said this." Clearly, Persephone knew how much trouble she could get in for speaking ill of the king. After wringing her hands and making a pained face, she said, "He keeps Miriam like she's a prisoner. She feels like she's trapped there. He doesn't let her do anything, and she's always saying how much she hates it at home, how it feels like a prison." Persephone paused and looked at Miriam, who remained asleep on the couch. "She just wants to be free. She uses cobalt because—"she looked down with that familiar shame in her eyes again—"she says she uses because it's the only time she can feel free from her father."

This was bad. Real bad. He could get Miriam off the shit, but if she just went right back into the environment that had caused her to use in the first place, the chances of her staying clean were slim.

"I can help her, Sev," Io said. "She needs me. You know with my past that I'm the best one to help her through this. I practically run the cobalt rehab program at AKM, for God's sake. You know I can take care of her."

Persephone turned to Severin. "Please don't make her go home. Please let Io keep her here."

Severin let out a growl of frustration as he turned his critical gaze on Io. With an aggravated shake of his head, he said, "Okay, fine. One day, Io." He lifted his index finger in the air and shoved it toward Io. "You can keep her here for one day, and that's all. And then she goes home."

Io had been ready to do his own thing, anyway. No way was he going to let Miriam leave under the circumstances. She needed him right now. And he needed her.

"Okay, take Persephone home and I'll see you tomorrow," Io said. Then to Persephone, he said, "I've got your number on my cell if I need you for anything. And you've got mine if you need to contact me, but she'll be in good hands here. I know what I'm doing."

Persephone nodded. "Thank you. You have no idea how much she needs someone to help her." She started to follow Sev out then stopped and turned back. "Don't be too hard on her, okay? She needs someone who understands. Someone who will listen."

Io gave her a reassuring smile. "Don't worry. She'll be fine here. I'm a great listener, and I've been through this once or twice." More like a few hundred times.

Sev grumbled unintelligibly under his breath and scowled back at him. "Don't do anything stupid." He ushered Persephone toward the door.

"Me?"

Sev cocked his head as if to say *really?* "Yeah. You."

"Don't tell Ari, okay?" Why he didn't want Ari to know stemmed from the hope that he and Ari could still find a way to be friends. This would be just one more boneheaded move to push Ari further away. Why he would think Ari would think that, though, didn't make sense. Ari had always had his back. But that had been before...well, that had just been before. Things were different now.

"Are you kidding? I'm not telling anybody about this. I don't want to go down with you when the shit hits the fan. How 'bout you do me a favor, and when you're caught, you say I had no knowledge of this shit you're pulling."

Io nodded. "I can do that."

Just as long as he could keep Miriam with him for one day, he would do anything. Just one day with her. Then he could let her go back home. Right?

Right?

His inner voice refused to answer.

CHAPTER 8

MALEK DROVE AROUND THE BLOCK FROM FOUR ALARM, the club where he and the others usually hung out after their shift ended. But he wasn't looking for a parking place. What he was after was something totally unrelated to Four Alarm. It just so happened that the ladies-for-hire hung around the place like bees on honey, waiting for drunk patrons to come out looking for a date. A date who wanted only one thing.

Except Malek wasn't drunk. He was cold stone sober and riddled with guilt so thick it felt like another person was in the SUV with him, riding his ass over emotions he had no right to be feeling.

His eyes roved, searching. One after another, the females selling themselves stepped away from the shadows, hoping to catch his attention, but he wasn't looking for just any female. He needed one in particular.

Too bad Gina was long gone, fleeing from her own guilt after nearly killing Severin two weeks ago. And thank God she was gone, because as much as Malek's soul wanted her, he refused to disgrace Carmen's memory by taking another. Carmen had been his mate centuries ago. She had been human, but his biological makeup hadn't cared, fusing with hers in the way vampires chose their lifemates.

Malek blinked hard against Carmen's memory. He still refused to accept her death, even after all this time.

Unfortunately, his body had other plans. His mind may not have been ready to move on, but his body was, and for the first time in hundreds of years of abstinence, he needed release by something other than his hand. That need consumed and drove him, and his dark brown eyes searched the faces of the females who lined the sidewalk.

Where was Gina now? Gina. The female his body longed for? Had she stayed in Chicago or gone back to Atlanta after Sev had forced Tristan and the powers that be to pardon and release her? Perhaps she had taken off for someplace new to wallow in her guilt.

His eyes fixed on a petite female with short, black hair. *That one.* Yes, she would do nicely.

Malek pulled over, reached across the seat, and opened the passenger door as his gaze caught the one he had chosen.

"You need a date, baby?" The woman stepped forward and peeked inside. She was human, but that was okay. She looked the part.

"Yeah. Yeah, I do. Get in." Not since the Middle Ages when he and Micah had caroused in the king's city had he bought a woman's services.

She arched an eyebrow as if considering he might be some psycho, so he smiled and said, "I'll give you a thousand to come with me. We can stay here if you want, but I can assure you, my place is way more comfortable."

She bit her lip. A thousand dollars was a lot of money to turn down. "Okay, but no funny business." She got in.

Malek put his SUV in gear and hit the gas harder than intended. He needed to get her home fast. His zipper was ready to bust.

"What's your name?" he said, pulling out onto the main road.

"For a thousand dollars you can call me anything you want, baby."

Without hesitation, Malek said, "Gina. I want to call you Gina." He glanced at the female. She had short, blunt-cut black hair and a petite frame. The eyes were different, and so were the clothes, but she was close enough to the real thing for his fantasies to take him there. Maybe if he pretended with this one, he wouldn't need the real Gina to fulfill what his body was demanding of him.

"Gina it is, baby." She licked her lips and flashed him a come-hither glance.

If he tried hard enough, he could almost see the real thing in her. Almost. "Please. Call me Malek."

CHAPTER 9

MIRIAM WOKE UP TO FIND IO SITTING ON THE FLOOR next to her. His gaze brightened and he smiled.

"How do you feel?" he said. He helped her sit up.

"Like shit." She groaned. "Don't get me wrong, I feel better than I did, but damn, this shit sucks." Who the hell had let in the army of Terminators to play Rock 'Em Sock 'Em inside her body?

Io chuckled at her surprisingly unfeminine manner of speaking and sat down beside her. "I gave you a potent detox with my venom. I needed to get the cobalt out of your system."

"Ah, I see." She leaned her face into her hands. "Great. Just great. I don't know whether to thank you or hit you." How did she always seem to put her worst face forward around this guy? The one male she wanted to impress and all she did was behave like a strung-out junkie around him. The vampire version of Amy Winehouse. How could he not be impressed? Uh-huh, right.

He caressed her back, his palm rubbing up and down slowly. "You'll thank me later." His fingertips traced soothing, slow circles.

"That feels nice," she said, peeking at him. His right arm rested across his lap, and she caught herself before she could reach over and follow the swirling lines of ink down his forearm. "That really is an amazing tattoo." She remembered it from when she saw him at AKM two weeks ago.

He lifted his arm. "Thank you. I've been thinking about getting the left arm done, too, but haven't had the time."

She wondered what kind of tattoo she would get if she

ever got one. A dragon, or possibly a heart broken in two. That would be appropriate for her life. Or maybe she should just get her name tattooed on her forehead. Her father would surely find that suitable. Not.

Io shifted beside her and brushed her hair off her back so he could rub her shoulders with both hands instead of just one. "Is that better?"

"Mm-hm." She took a deep, relaxing breath and felt the tension melt away a little bit more.

She liked it here. Io's home was comfortable. Cozy. The furniture was nice, but not too nice, and the appliances were more functional than artistic. She felt like her home was a museum to be visited and viewed, but Io's home felt like... well, like a home was supposed to feel. The couch was soft and well-used. And there was dust on the end table. Not much, but enough to make it clear this was a living space, not a sterile room where you couldn't touch anything for fear of breaking it or leaving fingerprints.

"I like your home," she said.

"Not what you're used to, though, is it?" Io's hands worked her shoulders gently, and with a hint of something deeper than innocent intentions.

"No, but that's why I like it." She looked over at him. "This is what I envision a home *should* look like." She smiled and glanced down at the coffee table and traced the tip of her finger around a ring where a glass had once sat. "A water ring." She grinned.

"I'm a slob, what can I say?" Io sounded humored.

"No, that's not what I mean." She started to laugh, but the Terminators inside her head hadn't finished decimating her brain yet. She cringed then continued. "I wasn't pointing out that you're a slob. I was saying that it's nice to be in a place that feels lived in."

His sexy, see-everything gaze penetrated hers, and Miriam felt certain that he was burrowing into her deepest secrets and desires, seeing how much he affected her and reveling in the knowledge that her insides had turned to mush at just being this near to him.

Hadn't she and Seph just been talking about Io earlier? At the time she had been certain that she would never see him again, and yet here he was. She was in his home…and he was touching her.

Look at me now, Dad. She blew mental raspberries at her father.

"How did you find me, anyway?" she said. The last thing she remembered before waking up and tossing blue cookies all over his bathroom was dosing on cobalt, the euphoric high, and then blackness.

"Your friend, Persephone. She called me."

Persephone had called him? "She did? Directly?" She wondered what Seph might have said to him. She hoped to God Seph hadn't said anything that would embarrass her. As if she needed help in that department.

"No. Well, not really. She called AKM. But she asked for me directly." His hands stopped briefly. "You know, I didn't even think to ask her how she got my name or why she called me. She was in a bit of hysterics when I talked to her on the phone."

Her face heated. Maybe it had been a good thing that she and Seph had talked about Io tonight. At least it had given Seph someone to call after she had let her I'm-temporarily-stupid gene take her down Overdose Lane again. "She got your name from me," she admitted.

"Oh?" His mouth curled at the corners and he cocked his head curiously, watching her with more interest.

She glanced away, unable to hold eye contact when he was looking at her like that. "Yes. I told her about you."

He shifted closer. "You did, huh? How interesting."

Biting her lip, she ducked her head and huffed out a self-conscious exhale. Could he see what she had told Seph? Was he peeking inside her thoughts to see how she had blushed and carried on like she had a human teenage crush on him? She swiped a curt, sideways glance toward him. "Stop looking at me like that." She averted her gaze again, heat blazing from her face to her neck and chest.

"How am I looking at you?" He bumped his arm against

hers. A playful gesture.

She smiled. Why did she feel guilty? All she had done was tell Seph about him. But then, that did make her guilty, didn't it? "You're embarrassing me."

He sat back, obviously amused. "I'm sorry. I'll stop." The tone of his voice implied that he wasn't really sorry but was simply appeasing her.

"Thank you." She nibbled her lip. His reaction to learning she had been talking about him made it clear he was pleased to learn she had. Which meant...what exactly? That he liked her? That he was attracted to her? Both?

After several seconds, he cleared his throat. "Yeah, well, like I said, Persephone was pretty distraught when I talked to her."

She groaned and shook her head. "She was?"

"Yeah, she was really worried. She thought you were going to die."

Miriam cringed hearing that. "Oh man. Shit. Poor Seph." She dropped her head into her hands, feeling like an idiot. "She's been through enough already." She shook her head, her arms rocking side to side as she did. "I royally fucked up." And in her case, she could really say *royally*. Too bad she was the only one who got the joke. Miriam kept her face hidden against her palms.

For a second, Io quieted as if her use of the f-word had caught him off guard. Most likely it had. The *princess* wasn't supposed to use such language, after all. Well, fuck being a well-mannered princess. She wouldn't be what others expected. She would be herself. If only she could figure out exactly who that was.

"No, you didn't fuck up. You just made a mistake. We all make mistakes." Io leaned toward her, holding her arms in a half-hug. "If you'll let me, I can help you."

Miriam looked over her shoulder. His face was so close to hers that she momentarily caught her breath and lost her train of thought before getting herself back on track. "My father will never let you. You know that. If he saw what you're doing right now, he would cut off your hands. You heard your boss two weeks ago. No one is allowed to touch me, remember?" Resentment clipped her words.

She couldn't let herself get too close to Io, even though she wanted nothing more. But her father would never allow it. He would destroy Io if he knew what had happened tonight, even though Io had only been trying to help her.

"Do I look scared?" Io said, brushing his palms up her arms, over her shoulders, and down either side of her spine.

Well, actually, no he didn't, and she almost smiled at his bravado, impressed that she had found another like her: someone who didn't wilt under the power of her father the way most everybody else did. Still, she couldn't let Io get hurt.

"Look, Io...." She huffed and pursed her lips. "I appreciate what you've done for me tonight, but—"

He pushed forward and kissed her. Not a passionate, open-mouthed, let's-get-naked kind of kiss. It was a simple press of his lips against hers.

Her first real kiss. And it was Io giving it to her. Her heart went from zero to sixty in less than one second.

A squeak broke in the back of her throat and her eyes shot wide as she froze, but no way was she going to pull away. His lips felt too inviting, too warm, too firm. Too perfect. She had dreamed about what her first kiss would feel like and how it would happen, but she had never imagined that such a simple, innocent meeting of lips would set her insides into fits of somersaults on a lava flow.

For several seconds, he held his mouth against hers then drew back, his lips clinging to hers for a second before pulling away, leaving cold emptiness in their wake. The stunned shock written on her face apparently amused him.

"What?" he said, grinning.

Miriam opened her mouth, but no words came out. Only a quiet huff of air. No male had ever had the balls to break her father's rules and kiss her, but Io wasn't following in the footsteps of those others. Maybe that was why she was so drawn to him, because she could sense his fearless drive to do what he wanted when he wanted, despite the rules and acceptable social customs.

Of all the elite males who had wanted her hand over the

years, and who had been flatly denied by her father when not a single spark of the mating call revealed itself in them, here was Io—who was a whole lot of nothing special—and he was the one she wanted. He didn't have super powers as far as she could tell, and he didn't come from any of the aristocratic families in her father's circle, but she was drawn to him as if he were a magnet and she were steel. Io had dared to go where no male had gone before, simply taking her mouth with his without preamble or warning, and that simple, brazen gesture made her want him in a way she had never felt.

"Why did you do that?" She touched her fingertips to her lips, still in shock with her body doing a lot of dipsy-doodle in her tummy that radiated out through her limbs.

"What? Kiss you?"

She nodded.

"Well, because I wanted to." He shrugged one shoulder. "And because I wanted to shut you up. It sounded like you were about to say something I didn't want to hear."

"Such as . . .?" She bit her lip and answered his charming smile with one of her own.

Io chuckled. "It sounded like you were getting ready to say something like, 'I can't stay,' or 'I can't be with you.' And, frankly, that's unacceptable."

Her heart skipped. She had wanted to see Io again but hadn't dared to hope he would feel the same way. And she had been scared to see him for this very reason. Now that he had kissed her, she wanted him to do it again. In fact, her body squirmed for him to do a lot more than just kiss her. In the history of bad ideas, this had to be the worst ever.

A lifetime spent not knowing the feel of a male's kiss or his touch left her yearning for more. Like a fire doused with gasoline, control fell away and only one thought remained. More. More Io. More kisses. More touching. More of all of him.

The only male who had ever touched her more intimately than those in her family had been the family physician, but Miriam didn't count him. The doctor was clinical and unattractive. Io, on the other hand, was very much the opposite. Io was warm, open, and beyond what she heard human girls describe as hot. *He's hawt!* they would say. Io was definitely hawt!

Heat pooled between her legs, and she shifted on the couch to ease the tightness in her belly and thighs, her eyes trained on his mouth.

"Unacceptable how?" she said, her voice breathy.

Io stood up and held out his hand, his gaze locking on hers, his eyelids hooded. "Because I haven't been able to stop thinking about you since I met you."

Miriam's breath caught. She was in so much trouble.

CHAPTER 10

Io wrapped his hand around Miriam's and helped her up. Just like when he had seen her two weeks ago, it didn't matter that her hair and clothes were in disarray. Miriam was the most beautiful female he had ever met. He couldn't take his eyes off her.

"Come on," he said. "Let's get you cleaned up and into bed. You need to rest."

"I'm not going home?"

He shook his head. "No. You're staying with me today. Besides, it's almost dawn."

"What about my car?"

"I'll take you back to it after sundown."

She took a deep breath that sounded like resigned acceptance and followed him into his basement bedroom, where he flipped on the lights. She hesitated when she saw there was only one bed.

"Where will you sleep?" She bit her lip, but Io sensed she was secretly pleased with the accommodations.

Which secretly pleased him. He liked feeling her attraction to him bubbling just beneath her reserved exterior. He couldn't be imagining that. Miriam clearly liked him, and she had liked the kiss he had given her just a few minutes ago, too. The scent of feminine arousal hadn't been in his imagination.

"It's a big bed," he said. "My side, your side." He gestured back and forth.

Miriam nodded once. "Okay." She rubbed her palms nervously over the sleeves of her blouse.

He led her to the bathroom and turned on the light then started the shower. He heard her gasp and turned to see her looking at her reflection in the mirror. Her eyes met his. She looked mortified.

"Why are you always seeing me when I look so awful?" she said, turning away.

He sighed and brushed his hand down her back. "Miriam, you really need to stop with this obsession over how you look. Because I'll let you in on a little secret." He lowered his voice to a reverent whisper. "You're stunning."

Her head whipped around. A suspicious frown furrowed her brow. "You're lying just to make me feel better."

He shook his head. "Like hell I am."

Io had to stop himself from kissing her again to prove his point, brushing his fingers over her cheek and taking a deep, steadying breath instead.

Her bright blue eyes opened wide then flicked down toward his hand as if she wasn't used to someone touching her face like that.

"Does my touching you bother you?" Io pressed his palm against her cheek.

"No. It's okay. I'm just..." She looked down.

"Not used to being touched like this?" Io stroked the pad of his thumb across the apple of her cheek, right under her eye.

With her head still turned downward, she looked up through her lashes at him. "No. I'm not."

"Do you want me to stop?"

The air was thick with sexual tension. He knew what he was doing was wrong and that he was breaking all kinds of the king's laws where Miriam was concerned, but he couldn't stop himself. Miriam did things to his heart no female ever had, and he felt emotions with her he had never felt.

Miriam blinked and gave a single, subtle shake of her head. "No." The single word trailed off as if she wanted to say more.

"But?" Io dipped his head, gazing heavily into her eyes, prompting her to finish her thought.

"But I'm scared."

Scared? He hadn't expected that.

"Of what?"

"What my father could do to you if he finds out."

"Your father isn't here, Miriam. You are. And that's all that matters to me."

She inhaled and her eyes fluttered as she dipped her head into his hand, nearly melting his heart. With such a simple gesture, she made his body sing with desire in a way no female had ever come close to.

"You make me feel things," she said, but stopped short of going into detail.

"You make me feel things, too." Io pressed his nose into her hair and inhaled as his lips pressed against her forehead.

For several long moments, they remained still. Io could hear the heavy beating of her heart and feel the way her chest rose and fell deeply as she leaned ever-so-slightly into him. One graceful hand pressed hesitantly against his chest, her fingers bending as if she was afraid to fully touch him, almost as if she wasn't sure she should. In a way, it felt like Miriam feared letting herself take that final step.

"Touch me, Miriam," he said, whispering against her forehead. "Don't stop halfway. *Touch* me." He didn't know why, but he needed this from her, and he felt like she needed it, too.

For a heartbeat, he thought she would, her hand stilling and her breath catching. Io could feel her press forward, but then she pulled back, shaking her head almost apologetically.

"I really should get cleaned up," she said quietly, looking down and gesturing toward the bathroom as she took a step back.

She left a void where she had just been, and Io felt naked without her beside him.

What kind of life did Miriam have? From the sound of it, her father didn't allow her any latitude. No wonder she felt like a prisoner in her own home. Even now she acted as though she wasn't quite sure how she should behave. She was caught between two worlds: one where she had to follow rules and one where she was free to make her own choices and do as she wished.

Io had a feeling that the rules of protection her father had erected around her went a lot further than just preventing males from touching her, too. Io imagined that no male could even speak to her without the king's permission. And even then, it was likely that her father had to be present. Hell, Io would bet his life Miriam's father wouldn't even allow a male to simply *look* at her without his approval.

And the way she had just reacted to him all but confirmed his suspicions.

It was becoming more and more clear that what Persephone had said was true. Miriam used cobalt to find freedom. Freedom from rules, her father, and the oppressive state she lived in as the princess.

Squeezing his eyebrows together, his muscles tensed and he bowed his head. Surrendering her upset him. What was this pull she had over him? She was a light in the darkness, and he was the moth drawn to her. "Come on, Miriam. I'll grab you a towel and scrounge up a spare toothbrush and some clean clothes for you."

She was almost as tall as he was, even if she was quite a bit more slender. He could probably find her a pair of drawstring sweatpants that she could cinch around her waist. The thought of seeing her wearing one of his T-shirts about made him spring his zipper, though.

Okay, so it was time to leave her alone before he did something he would really regret.

He handed her a towel then closed the bathroom door and rummaged through his closet before pulling out a faded red T-shirt and a grey pair of sweats.

While she showered, he went to his linen closet, where he had a shelf of toiletries. Surely he had an extra toothbrush he could give her. Yep. He had two. Io grabbed the one with purple accents and set it on the neatly folded clothes he had picked out for her. Then he sat down in the chair beside the bed and waited.

Sleeping in the same bed with her could be hazardous to his health, but when had he ever taken the safe route? Even so, he couldn't stand the idea of being more than a few feet away from her. What if she needed him? What if she went into withdrawal? It could happen and probably would after the purge he'd given her earlier. He didn't want to risk being in another room where he couldn't tend to her immediately if she needed something.

Speaking of which, he hopped out of the chair and took the stairs two at a time to retrieve the elixir from the kitchen. If she did go into withdrawal, he would need that.

MIRIAM FELT WEIRD TAKING A SHOWER in Io's home. She had never showered anywhere but her own bathroom, which was three times the size of this one. But this was nice. Cozy. Comfortable. And the idea that this was where Io showered made her feel like she was doing something naughty, being naked where Io had been naked.

And his soap smelled good. Like him. Tangy and a bit citrusy. She inhaled the scent as she rinsed the shampoo from her hair.

That kiss. Her belly went all light and airy again as sensations pulsed through her belly and...lower. For a moment, she hesitated as she worked conditioner through her hair. She just wanted to remember how his strong lips had felt against hers, as well as how he had looked standing so near her, touching her face in a way no one had ever been allowed to touch her.

Io sure did enjoy flirting with disaster. He knew the laws. He knew her father would punish him if he discovered how reckless he had been.

Wait a minute. What was she thinking? What did she care what her father thought? Wasn't she trying to break free from being under his thumb? Io had touched her...had practically begged her to touch him. And she had walked away. Her one chance to be her own person and explore her curiosity about him, and she had wilted like old lettuce under the domineering shadow of her father, which seemed to follow her everywhere.

What a dope she must have seemed like, ruining a perfect moment of intimacy between her and Io, all because she still felt burdened by her father's inane rules.

Even so, Io surely hadn't been impressed by her novice lips. Io was the type of male who had probably kissed hundreds of females, both human and vampire alike. Her inexperienced lips had to be a far cry from what he was used to. Hell, when he kissed her, she had locked up like a dummy. What kind of female froze like that when a guy kissed her?

One who had never been so much as touched, that's who.

With a soft groan, she slapped her hand over her face and grimaced with embarrassment.

For all her verve and rebelliousness, this was the one thing she had never done. She had never had sex. She had never felt the weight of a man above her during carnal relations, never been caressed by his hands, never been groped, felt up, cuddled, or so much as nudged by a male. And she had never felt a male's lips against hers. Until tonight.

The reason for this was clear. No vampire male dared approach her for fear of her father, no matter how much they admired or longed to be with her. The cowards. And while humans were none the wiser and more bold about their intentions, Miriam wasn't that careless. She had no desire to mate with a human. Not that she was racist. Human males just weren't strong enough to handle her physically, and the thought of what her father would do to a human who dared to defile her in that way prevented her from even thinking down that road. Miriam didn't care what happened to her, but she cared immensely about what happened to others, and her conscience wouldn't allow her to be that reckless and irresponsible with a human.

But Io. He was another story. Io was a vampire. He was a warrior—tall, strong, virile, and brave. He had kissed her despite knowing she was the king's daughter. He knew the consequences, but still, he had kissed her anyway.

Her lower belly and between her legs lit again with warmth and butterflies. Io's devil-may-care actions excited her and before she realized it, a gentle purr bloomed in her chest. Wow. Io made her feel things she had never felt. He made her body sing.

And he was sexy as hell. And hawt! His hair was short and thick, a rich, dark brown. She imagined her fingers combing through it. How would it feel against her hand? Was it soft? Coarse? Would he close his eyes and moan with pleasure at her touch? And what of his eyes? Io had the most incredible green eyes with brown highlights, and when he looked at her, she felt like he was seeing right inside her.

A knock came at the door, jolting her out of her Io-induced fantasy.

"You doing okay in there?" Io spoke through the door.

"Um...yeah...yeah. Almost finished." How long had she been in the shower? Apparently too long if Io was checking on her.

"Okay, I've got some clothes for you. I'll slip them in when you're done. Just let me know when you're ready."

She quickly rinsed the conditioner out of her hair then shut off the water, towel dried her hair, and wrapped the towel around her.

"I'm ready," she said.

A moment later, the door cracked open and a toothbrush came through, held in Io's large hand. She took it, smiling at his modesty. Next came a T-shirt and sweats.

"I hope they fit well enough to get you by," he said.

"They'll be fine, I'm sure." She took the clothes.

His clothes. The thought that she would be wearing clothes he had worn gave her a perverse thrill.

She pulled the shirt over her head. It was four sizes too big and hung on her like a blanket, but it worked. The sweatpants weren't too bad. They were only an inch or two too long, but the waist was obviously too big. She pulled the drawstrings as tight as they would go, and even though they were still far too loose for daily life, it would do for tonight.

She quickly brushed her teeth then opened the door and stepped into the bedroom. Io was sitting on the edge of the massive bed and looked up.

Miriam held her arms out to the sides and pulled a three-sixty. "What do you think? Am I ready for the catwalk?"

He smiled and stood up. "Absolutely." One of his eyebrows quirked ever-so-slightly, his gaze growing dark and appreciative. "Oversized is definitely the look this year."

"Then I'll fit right in," she said playfully. "Okay, so...do you have a brush or a comb or something for my hair?" She glanced around.

He went to his dresser and picked up a large-toothed comb and handed it to her before retrieving her clothes from the bathroom. "I'll put your clothes in the wash."

She winced. There was only one reason why he would need to wash her clothes. "Did I throw up on them?" She hadn't even noticed, apparently too concerned with her hair and face to see vomit on her clothes.

"Just a little." He winked reassuringly, his smile warm and inviting. He crossed the room and disappeared through a doorway. The light came on and she heard the sounds of a washer being started. A moment later, he reappeared, turning off the light and shutting the door.

"I'm so embarrassed." She looked down, holding the comb against her stomach.

"Don't be," he said. "I've seen worse done by less beautiful people than you."

"Liar."

He shook his head. "It's the truth."

Normally, she loomed over males. It was nice having to look up for a change, at least to meet someone's eyes other than her father's.

"Thank you for the comb." She lifted it awkwardly as if he wouldn't remember giving it to her. Her mind traveled unbidden to when he had brushed her hair at AKM, and she bit her lip, her gaze darting away from his as heat burned her face.

"What?" His eyes twinkled as his smile widened.

"Nothing."

"Come on. I can tell it's something."

With a sigh, she met his gaze again. "It's just...well, I..." She puffed out her cheeks and blew out an exasperated breath. "I was just wondering...." She nibbled her bottom lip. "If you'd like to finish brushing my hair? Like you did at AKM?" She had fantasized about him brushing her hair for two weeks.

"I didn't think you wanted me touching you." He was teasing her.

"I changed my mind."

Io took a step toward her. "So, you want me to brush your hair?"

She nodded. "Yes. If you don't mind."

The look on Io's face was pure mischief and self-assuredness.

"Don't look so self-satisfied," she said, teasing him back.

He chuckled. "Self-satisfied?"

"Uh-huh." She was shamelessly flirting with him, but she didn't care. She enjoyed it. And he seemed to, as well.

"Well, since I *was* interrupted last time"—he took another step toward her—"I would like to finish what I started." He brushed a wet strand of hair out of her face. "I can even dry your hair for you if you'd like." His eyes smoldered as if he knew how often she had thought about that night at AKM. The night they'd met.

Could he see inside her thoughts? Did he somehow know that she had thought of those few precious minutes with him repeatedly ever since? Him brushing her hair had been the most erotic thing she had ever experienced...until he'd kissed her earlier, of course.

Heat flushed her face. "If you want to...yes, that would be nice."

What game were they playing? It certainly felt like they were playing a game akin to cat-and-mouse, but Miriam didn't know which she was, the cat or the mouse.

"I do want to." His voice was low, his gaze following his hand as it caressed the side of her face and his fingers dipped into her wet hair.

Miriam's pulse raced, her heart thumping so hard she was sure he could hear it. Still, she forced herself to maintain propriety.

"You're flirting with disaster, Io. You do realize that, don't you?"

"You can stop me. Just say the word." His hand pushed further into her hair.

It took all her willpower not to lean her head into his palm.

"Normally, males refrain for fear of my father. I have never had to tell a male to stop, for none have ever touched me as you are now."

"Never?" he said, his eyes narrowing. His hand stilled on the side of her neck.

"Never." She had a feeling he had already expected as much.

He seemed to think about that a moment then grinned. The upward turn of his lips and the way his eyes narrowed and sparkled with what looked to be satisfaction appealed to her, and her heart skipped.

"Well, I'm not like other males," he said.

"I'm beginning to get that impression."

The sound of her mobile phone ringing made her jump away from him. She laughed self-consciously and reached for her purse then pulled out her phone.

It was her father calling.

"Speak of the devil." She dropped the phone back in her purse.

"You're not going to answer it?" Io stepped up beside her, placing his hand on the small of her back.

She held her breath at his touch, and then turned her gaze toward him. "No. He probably just wants to yell at me."

"Maybe he wants to make sure you're safe."

She shook her head. "I doubt it. He hasn't cared about my well-being in years."

Io stared at her lips as she spoke, and her gaze followed suit, dropping to his mouth.

"Well, rest assured that your well-being is in good hands here, Miri." His hand caressed lower to the curve where her back met her bottom.

Oh, Io was definitely tempting Fate.

She inhaled as warmth cascaded through her body. "I'm where I want to be."

The air crackled between them, but she remained still despite an unbelievable desire to kiss him again. Even if she wasn't educated in the art of kissing, it didn't diminish her excitement when she thought about his lips on hers. But she wanted him to come to her. She had liked how it felt for a male to throw caution to the wind as he had earlier.

Io was so close now, his body heat blending with hers to warm her. He leaned down.

"Give me five minutes?" His lips brushed her cheek beside her ear as he spoke.

Was he seducing her? Because if he was, he was damn good at it.

"Five minutes?"

"To shower," he said. "Five minutes and I'm all yours for the rest of the day."

Why did that sound so damned enticing? He would be all hers.

"I'll be right back," he said. "And then I'll comb your hair, and dry it...." His lips brushed gently over her eyebrow. "And I'll take care of you."

Miriam closed her eyes, his deep voice and his words making her feel decadent. But then he drifted away from her, and she opened her eyes to watch him grab a change of clothes from the dresser, step into the bathroom, and shut the door.

And I'll take care of you, he had said. She exhaled, not even aware she had been holding her breath.

Something told Miriam that simple statement meant more than Io was willing to admit.

CHAPTER 11

THE MUSCLES IN MALEK'S BACK CLENCHED and his hips slapped hard into the woman he called Gina. For over an hour, he had fucked her with everything he had, and only now did his cock cooperate and let loose into the condom she had insisted he wear, even though he knew he couldn't give her any diseases.

As a vampire, his blood was pure. Disease couldn't live inside him, so there was no way he could pass any on to her. Still, he could get her pregnant, so the condom had been a good call, because the last thing Malek needed was to sire young. And just his luck, he would be that one vampire in ten thousand who could impregnate a human when he wasn't in his calling.

Growling out a groan of relief and frustration, he thrust again then again, feeling the effects of the first orgasm he had allowed himself to have with another woman since—

His stomach lurched violently.

Like a shot from a gun, he yanked himself away and rushed to the bathroom before disgracing himself in front of her.

"Oh my God! Are you okay?" The woman hurried in after him, still naked, still looking not at all like the one he really needed…or the one he wanted, now that he took a good look.

He needed Gina, but he wanted Carmen. His sweet, perfect Carmen. Guilt ripped through him. What had he done? He had defiled Carmen's memory by fucking this whore while fantasizing that she was Gina. He hated himself right now for his lack of self-control.

"I'm fine." He avoided the woman's eyes, wiped his mouth, and stood up before flushing the toilet. Then he bent down in front of the sink and turned on the faucet.

"Can I get you anything?" The woman was genuinely concerned, even though she didn't have to be. She shouldn't have been, because Malek wasn't worth her worry.

"No. I'm fine." Embarrassed and ashamed was what he was. Add to that a side of self-loathing and disgust, and he had a four-course meal of anguish to digest.

He scooped water to his mouth in the cup of his hand and sipped then swished the water around and spit it out before drinking more.

His long, black hair draped down on either side of his head, getting wet as the ends fell into the rush of water pouring from the faucet.

The woman hovered and Malek could feel her discomfort. He could see inside her thoughts and saw that she found him attractive, despite his gastrointestinal pyrotechnics. She wasn't sure what to do. Should she stay? Go? Rub his back?

Just what he didn't need: an admirer.

Before exiting her mind, Malek caught a further glimpse of her feelings for him. She was grateful for the way he had treated her. Unlike most of the men who bought her services, he had treated her with respect. She thought he had a heart.

If only she knew the truth. He had no heart. He had lost it a long time ago. Then Gina had come along, stirring his soul in a way only Carmen had so long before her. Malek slammed his eyes shut. No. He couldn't acknowledge the way his heart had begun to open again when he met Gina. He refused to recognize how Gina had held him captive the moment he had laid eyes on her two weeks ago, and he certainly didn't want to address the nagging questions about where she was now or whether or not she was okay. She was gone. As soon as Severin had forgiven her for what she had done, Tristan had released her. It was anyone's guess where she was now.

No doubt her guilt over what she had done to Severin was eating her alive, but Malek didn't want to think about that, because then he would go crazy wishing he could be with her to soothe her through the gnawing despair, because he knew the feeling all-too-well. He knew what it was like to feel lost and broken.

He had sensed disgrace in Gina before she left, as if she felt unworthy to continue living. She had thought she was avenging her brother by going after Sev, but once she had learned the truth—that Sev had been framed by a jealous commander—she had been beside herself with grief. Gina prided herself on being the best. In her mind, she felt she had allowed herself to be duped, as if it was somehow her fault and she should have known better. The thought she had almost killed an innocent male had mortified her. She had even tried to get herself killed by faking her own escape attempt—a death wish Malek had barely prevented when Sev's father, Lakota, had almost blown her head off.

God, he hoped Gina hadn't done anything to hurt herself or worse now that she was out in the world alone. If only he knew where she was, he could see her through this.

Once more, Malek smashed his eyelids closed, scrunching up his face. He couldn't think like that. Gina had no place in his life. None. Only Carmen belonged in his heart.

"Hey, are you sure you're okay?" the woman said, breaking him from his thoughts.

"Yes. Yes, I'm fine." He stammered over his words, feeling helpless and breathless as he shut off the faucet, pushed himself up off the edge of the sink, and turned around before peeling off the condom and dropping it in the trash.

Dawn was about to break, and he could sense the woman's fatigue. He had kept her here longer than he should have, but he hadn't thought it would take so long for his body to release itself. Then again, he wasn't used to being with women. Malek's hand had been his only sexual partner for so long it was amazing he even remembered where his pecker went during intercourse.

He combed his wet fingers through his hair and glanced at her. "Look. You can stay here in one of the spare bedrooms if you like, or I can call you a cab. It's up to you. I won't hurt you if you stay."

She licked her lips, obviously interested, but then shook her head. "No, that's okay. I should go home. You look like you need some rest."

Malek nodded and steadied himself as he walked weakly from the bathroom. "Okay, let me get your money."

He opened a drawer and pulled out a leather pouch that looked like a bank deposit bag. After unzipping it, he pulled out ten one-hundred-dollar bills. Then he grabbed a few more for good measure.

"Here." He handed the bills to her.

She frowned, realizing he had paid her more than he said he would. "What's the extra for?"

"Buy yourself something nice," he said. "A pretty dress, a nice dinner." He brushed a hand over her hair. "A day at the spa. Just do something nice for yourself, okay?"

"Okay, sure." She smiled and folded the money into her fist.

"So, what's your real name, anyway?" He didn't want to call her Gina, anymore.

"Jess." She smiled and blushed. "Well, Jessica, but everyone calls me Jess."

"Jess? That's a pretty name, Jess."

"Thank you."

He glanced away then back. "I'll call you a cab. Feel free to grab a quick shower before you dress. I'll make you breakfast while you get ready."

She nodded and smiled again. Malek got the sense none of her other customers treated her so well. From the bits of thoughts he had snagged from her mind earlier, they probably didn't.

A half-hour later, Jess was freshly showered, dressed, and had put away three scrambled eggs, two slices of toast and jam, and four sausage links. A honk out front signaled her cab was there.

Jess started down the front hall to the door while Malek stayed behind in the safety of his kitchen, where the sunlight wouldn't hurt him once she opened the door. Suddenly, she stopped.

"Hey, if you ever need a date again, look me up, okay?"

"Thanks, Jess, but I think this was a one-time thing." Malek met her gaze.

She sighed. "Oh well. You take care."

"You, too."

She hurried to the front door as if she were regretting her decision not to stay and felt that the sooner she got out, the better, so she wouldn't be reminded of how she could have slept in a comfortable bed for at least one day.

The door opened and closed, and a minute later, Malek heard the cab drive away.

Yes, last night had been a one-time thing. He couldn't let himself fall prey to his weakness like that again. From now on, he would go back to using only his hand when he felt the need to get off. No more women for him.

Uh-huh. Yeah, sure.

CHAPTER 12

APOSTLE'S ENTIRE BODY ITCHED AND TINGLED from several weeks' worth of scorpion venom and stings. And clothes weren't doing it for him. They hung off his starved body, and the fabric felt like sandpaper on his raw, sensitive skin. He didn't know how much weight he'd lost, but it was a lot, and he had to keep hiking up his pants, which aggravated the latest scorpion stings to make him itch even more.

He had already adopted the human form Bishop had chosen for him, but not even his changeling powers could overcome being so weak and emaciated. He would have to do some serious eating before he resembled the man in the photograph.

Apostle followed Bishop from the room where he had been kept since arriving, through the main hall toward the back of the sprawling ranch-style home, through an elegantly arched doorway that led into the living room. Large picture windows and a pair of glass double doors overlooked a rocky decline down into a valley. Finally they made their way through the kitchen to a locked, metal door past the laundry room.

"I've made some changes since the last time you were here," Bishop said, unlocking the door and pulling it open.

It had been years since Apostle had seen the laboratory and production facility built beneath Bishop's home.

"Such as...?" Apostle wanted to know what he was in for, especially if he was expected to take Deacon's place at the helm of the operation.

Bishop casually descended the stairs, puffing away on

that goddamn cigarette of his like it was his lover.

"The experiments we're conducting now required the construction of holding cells."

"Holding cells?" Apostle's brow wrinkled into an inquisitive frown.

"Yes." Bishop kept a steady pace, his eyes straight ahead.

"Why do you need holding cells?" But Apostle was beginning to get the gist of what types of experiments Bishop and Deacon had been running here.

Based on the two pictures—a before and after?—of the man whose form Apostle had now adopted, and on what Bishop had said about using the vampires' own kind against them, Apostle suspected his twin and Bishop had been working on some kind of biological experiment.

"Who do you keep in the holding cells?" Apostle stopped behind Bishop on the landing in front of another metal door.

"See for yourself." Bishop pulled the door open and stepped aside.

Apostle walked into a giant beehive of activity. Drecks in both shifted and unshifted form worked at lab tables, wearing white coats, plastic gloves, and goggles. Some even wore masks.

Along both side walls were ten-by-ten rooms with steel-reinforced Plexiglas fronts, and inside each small cell was a vampire. Some paced, some slept, and still others screamed at the top of their lungs over and over again, their faces a display of agony.

"What are you doing to them?" Apostle walked toward the cells on the left.

"Some we are training. Others we are using for analysis and study." Bishop stopped in front of one cell with a particularly large vampire inside. The tag on the door read *Maddox*. Maddox was a big fucker, with long, dark hair and dull, lifeless eyes. "And still others we are using for gene splicing." Bishop's lips quirked into a lusty grin as he stared at Maddox, who sat in the corner of his small cell, staring at nothing and everything, unmoving and unmoved.

"Who is he?" Apostle noticed how Bishop gazed at the

naked male who seemed not to care—or even know—where he was.

"Our future."

Apostle frowned, not understanding. Clearly, Bishop had special plans for this one.

"Where did he come from?"

Bishop took a deep, wistful breath and finally began walking down the row of cells again. "I bought him."

Fucking hell, getting information out of Bishop was like trying to milk a bull. "From whom?"

"A pair of business associates." Bishop hesitated to watch as a one of the lab assistants approached a cell with a syringe of cobalt.

The vampire inside, who had been one of the shriekers, quieted and perked up, shooting forward and staring at the syringe of blue liquid. The vampire licked his lips and pushed his arm through a small opening in the thick Plexiglas after the lab assistant unlocked and opened it.

"We usually pick up those who are buying from our dealers," Bishop said quietly, standing aside so Apostle could watch. "We make junkies out of them. This one..." Bishop gestured toward the vampire inside the cell, "...is a mongrel. He's almost ready for phase two of his...*training.*"

Apostle had no idea what phase two was, or what Bishop meant by training, but he was sure he would find out soon enough. In the meantime, he watched as the mongrel was injected and fell into the characteristic convulsions associated with cobalt use. In a matter of seconds, the vampire had fallen to the floor, twitching uncontrollably, a smile on his face and sweat pouring out his body.

Whatever Bishop had planned for these vampires and mixed-bloods, it was big. That much was obvious.

CHAPTER 13

IO WAS IN AND OUT OF THE BATHROOM in record time. Took him all of five minutes to shower, brush his teeth, and put on flannel pants and a T-shirt.

The idea of being away from Miriam, even if he was only in the next room, urged him to rush.

Had he heard her right a few minutes ago? Had she really said no male had ever touched her the way he had? And if so, what exactly did that mean? Was Miriam a virgin?

On one hand, he couldn't believe a female that exquisite had never taken a lover, but on the other, she had a point about her father. Most people, male and female alike, cowered at mention of King Bain. Her being a virgin made sense considering everything he already knew.

Maybe he was crazy for being so candid with Miriam. Maybe he *would* find himself at the receiving end of a knife to the heart for his cavalier behavior when this was all over. But one day with her was worth it.

Io couldn't explain what drove him. He only knew that he had to know Miriam better. He had to take this one opportunity to simply exist in her presence, if only for a day.

No female had ever drawn his attention like she did. Usually, he took what he wanted from those willing to give it then he never looked back. Oh, sure, he occasionally double-dipped and took the same woman again as his whim dictated, but what he felt for Miriam was different. *She* was different. Miriam was at once strong-willed as well as innocent. Something in her eyes and body language told him that much. This made her infinitely more interesting than some girl he'd picked up at a bar with her legs already halfway open and her hand massaging his crotch.

Io opened the door to the bedroom and shut off the bathroom light, holding his hair dryer in his hand.

Miriam was sitting on the edge of the bed, running the comb through her hair.

"You ready?" he said.

She glanced down at the hair dryer and smiled. "You're seriously going to dry my hair?"

Hadn't he made that point perfectly clear only a few minutes earlier? "That was the plan." He plugged the hair dryer in then stood beside her.

"You really have a death wish, don't you?" She looked up at him through her lashes, her cheeks flushed. "If my father could see me now, he'd blow a circuit."

"And that thrills you, doesn't it?" Io took the comb from her hands and sat down beside her.

"What do you mean?" Miriam's sapphire blue eyes pierced him as she glanced over her shoulder.

He chuckled. "Something tells me you don't like following orders."

"I follow orders just fine." Her chin jutted out with coquettish flair.

"Whose? His or your own?" Io lifted one eyebrow as if challenging her.

Her eyes narrowed, but she didn't reply, her demeanor suddenly growing cold.

Ah, so there it was. Her trigger.

"Is that why you use?" Io said, speaking in measured syllables, his voice quiet as he ran the comb through the ends of her hair to loosen the tangles she had already started working on. "Or does your father typically allow cobalt use in the royal home?" He was wrecking the mood, but he needed to get her talking about her addiction, or at least thinking about it. He didn't have much time with her, and if he was going to help her, he had to dig, and if that meant pissing her off, oh well.

Her scowl deepened and she huffed. "No, he doesn't allow

it." She turned away, a mixture of shame and anger rolling off of her.

"There you have it then. You don't follow orders." He kept himself calm, feeling her emotions rise on a tidal wave.

This was what cobalt did. It burrowed in and fucked with the minds and emotions of those using it. Miriam would be like a roller coaster for the next couple of months as she went through withdrawal, her moods changing in a snap, even if she wasn't showing other symptoms. And if he was allowed to help her through the worst of it, Io would likely trigger her to snap as often as he could just so she could learn how to identify what was happening and cope with it when she did.

She spun around and pointed at him, banging her hand against the comb, causing it to fly across the bed. "Look, no one orders me around." Her eyes blazed with defensive anger even as she glanced sheepishly at the launched comb. "Least of all my father." She jutted out her chin again, bringing her gaze back to his.

Miriam was clearly someone who was fighting to find her own voice. Fighting to be heard within the royal cacophony surrounding her father. Io got that, but he needed her to see that there were better ways to go about making her voice heard than going off in search of her next high. He stood up and calmly walked around to the other side of the bed and retrieved the comb.

"I'm just saying, Miri, if the shoe fits—"

"Excuse me? If the shoe fits?" Now Miriam looked hurt as well as angry. "Didn't you hear me? No one controls me, especially not my father." She crossed her arms. "I can't believe you're saying this to me. I thought you were on my side. I thought you were different."

Io knelt in front of her, his elbows on his knees. "I am on your side, Miri, but you have to take responsibility for your actions and own up to them. You use cobalt. You're an addict. A junkie. And you use because, whether you admit it or not, your father made you. That's your excuse for using. In your head it's his fault even though you're the one who made the decision to shoot up. You let him dictate your life even in this, Miri."

She looked away from him and tried to get up, but Io grabbed her hands and pulled her back down.

"You're wrong," she said, frowning.

"Am I?" His grip tightened on hers as she tried to pull away again.

"I do what I want, when I want. My father has no control over me."

"Really?" Io wasn't buying that line of shit for a second. "Admit it, Miri. You've let your father control you. You've let him direct everything you do. Even your drug use."

She refused to look at him. "Why are you doing this to me?"

"Because you need to see it, Miri."

"There's nothing to see."

"Of course there is. Open your eyes."

"I don't want to open my eyes!" She turned her fury on him, unleashing her voice like it was a whip. "Damn it! There's nothing wrong with me! Just dry my hair, for God's sake. That's all I wanted. Not this"—she inhaled sharply, her eyes darting around since she couldn't free her hands— "inquisition from you!"

Io released her hands, but before she could get away, he grabbed her around the waist and pulled her to the floor, pressing his mouth against her ear as she tried to push him away. "I don't take orders, either, Miri. Not even from you, who I would die for." The words had left him before his brain-to-mouth filter could engage, but in that moment, he knew he had never made a more honest statement. He would do anything for Miriam. Even die for her if he had to. Where was this profound devotion coming from? How had she gripped him so tightly in so short a time?

In an instant, she stopped struggling. "You would die for me?" Her voice sounded small and confused.

"In a heartbeat." He ran his palm down her back, knowing in his heart he had found a female worth going to the ends of the Earth for. "And I am different. I'm different because I won't close my eyes to what you're doing. I'm different because, unlike your father, I want to help you find who you are. I'm different because I'm not afraid to touch you." At this, he paused, his mind going back to earlier, before her shower, when she had been so close to opening her hand against his chest to fully touch him. "And damn it, I want you to touch me, too. Really touch me, Miriam. If you want to, touch me." His voice dropped to a whisper. "Without fear. If this is what you want, then please…" He trailed off, waiting, hoping, needing her to touch him.

"I don't know how," she whispered. Vulnerability didn't seem to be a trait she liked to show, so for her to trust him enough to let him see her weakness meant everything to him.

"Why not?"

The two seemed to be balancing on the edge of a razor, both of them hardly breathing as they settled against one another on their knees, the quiet stretching between them even as they spoke. Io felt like Miriam was on the brink of a breakthrough, as if she was wrestling with admitting the truth to herself, let alone out loud to him.

"Tell me, Miri. Why is it you don't know how to touch me?"

She trembled, her arms barely around him, her hands curled into protective fists. "Because…" She shivered again and Io smelled the telltale scent of tears.

Io's hold strengthened. "Because why, baby? Tell me."

Miriam exhaled and dipped her head until her forehead rested on his shoulder. They sat together like that for a long time, neither speaking, both hardly breathing, until finally she said, "Because my father won't let me."

Ah, surrender.

Finally. She saw. She could admit it. Her father had more control over her than she wanted to acknowledge. And if she admitted his hold on her here, she would eventually see—if she didn't already—that Io had been right about her father's control over her drug use and every other facet of her life.

"I know, baby." Io smoothed his hands up and down her back. "I know, but he's not here now. And if you'll let me, I'll teach you how to touch."

Strange how something so simple could be so monumentally difficult, but after living in fear of touching and being touched all her life, he could understand her hesitance, even if he couldn't relate. What must her life have been like under such strict rules? Io couldn't even fathom what life without touching another person outside his immediate family would be like. And Miriam didn't just live without touch, she lived in fear of it, because anyone who laid hands on her would be punished, perhaps even put to death, depending on the circumstances.

He flattened his palms against her back. "Feel that?" he said. "Feel my hands?"

She nodded. "Yes."

"Put your hands on me this way." He pressed his palms against her back, his fingers splayed.

Miriam trembled as she slid her arms more fully around him, stopping once self-consciously before opening her fists. Her fingertips pressed into his back, and then as if she had taken a deep breath and jumped into the deep end of the pool, she flattened her hands.

"See, that wasn't so hard, was it?" Io said.

She shook her head, and a weak breath of air that sounded like a feeble attempt at laughter escaped her throat.

He began caressing her back with slow, tender circles. "Now, do what I'm doing."

This was a first for Io. He had slept with more women than he could count, but he had never had to teach any of them how to touch him. On the contrary, most had been well-versed in how to touch a man.

Oh, he was sure Miriam knew the mechanics of intimacy, and she had certainly seen others engage in caressing and feeling, but knowing how things worked and actually experiencing it were two totally different things. It was like driving a car. You read your driver's manual, learned all the rules, and had probably watched others driving to the point you knew the mechanics. Even so, that first time behind the wheel was a scary thing, and when all that knowledge was put to a live test, nerves could get in the way.

Miriam was taking her first real drive with a male. She was assimilating everything she had read, seen in movies, or witnessed first-hand, but for the first time she was in the driver's seat. What she had read or seen with others was now happening to her.

And for a first-time driver, she wasn't bad. Not at all. On the contrary. Io only hoped he would have the strength to stop before things got out of hand.

MIRIAM MIMICKED WHAT IO WAS DOING with his hands, letting hers ride up and over the gentle, sloping contours of the muscles in his back and shoulders.

"Close your eyes," he said. "Just feel me."

She did as he said, shutting down her sense of sight and using her hands to see him, much the way a blind person would.

"That's good," he said.

He felt bigger and stronger than he looked. How strange that eyesight could diminish the power she could feel simply by touching him.

She smiled as he leaned back and wiped a lingering tear from below her eye as his free hand ran down her hip and thigh.

Keeping her eyes closed, she bit the inside of her lip as her fingers drew over his shoulders and down his arms. He flexed, making his muscles pop out more sharply under her palms. Passing over the edges of his short sleeves, she found his skin to be warm and soft, smooth, but underneath was like stone. He slowly raised his arms, taking her hands with them.

"What do you feel?" he said, his voice coming from beside her face. So close, in fact, that she felt his breath on her cheek.

"You're like a sculpture. Carved and solid. Hard like stone, but warm." She grinned as his cheek pressed against hers, rubbing her the way cats rub their humans with their heads. "You feel bigger than you look, too."

He let out a quiet laugh, and his cheek rose against hers as he smiled. "I do, huh?"

"Yes." She bowed her head bashfully.

Only minutes ago, she had been angry with him, but now she couldn't imagine why. Touching him was fascinating and provocative, sensual in the purest form. She skimmed her hands back up his arms and inward over his hard, rounded shoulders before dropping them down to his chest.

"Mmm." A quiet purr broke behind his sternum and vibrated against her palms, his solid pecs lifting as he moved against her, sitting taller. His left pec popped once against her hand, and she gasped.

"Do that again," she said on a breath, pressing her hands more firmly against his chest.

"What? This?" His left pec jumped again, followed immediately by the right.

Miriam inhaled sharply. She didn't know why, but him flexing his chest like that turned her on. "Yes."

"Do you like when I do that?" His body crept closer to hers.

With her eyes still closed, every other sense was heightened. The scent of clean skin assaulted her, and the way another quiet purr bubbled in his chest was like a roar.

"Yes," she said.

He moaned as she skimmed her hands down the sides of his torso, feeling each ridge of muscle.

"How am I doing?" She opened her eyes to find that Io's were closed.

"You're a natural," he said.

The chemistry between them was undeniable. She felt it, and it was more than obvious he did, too.

"So I passed?"

He nodded and opened his eyes to look into hers. "With flying colors."

What was happening here? Between them? Whatever it was, she didn't want it to stop.

"I'd better dry your hair before this goes much further." Io cleared his throat and took a deep breath then blew it out as he scooted back.

She stared in wonder as he reached for the hair dryer and stood up. As she drifted up from the floor to the bed, her gaze ranged down his tattooed arm and back up his torso to his chest as he turned and faced her. Using only her hands, she had discovered Io in a way her eyes couldn't capture.

"I liked touching you," she said, blinking her gaze up to his.

Shadows turned his hooded eyes smoky, and he hesitated for a heartbeat, his lips parting on an inhale as if he could taste her on the air. "I liked it, too." He held her gaze through another breath. As he exhaled, he said, "Which is why I had to stop."

With a lick of her lips, she looked down. Miriam understood what he was saying, and she agreed that letting themselves go down a more physical path with one another probably wasn't the best of ideas. Not that she didn't want to, because all that touching had set her imagination—as well as her libido—into motion. Io was the sexiest, most alluring male she had ever met. He was the first male she had ever wanted to do bad things with...or good, depending on whose point of view she was referring to, hers or her father's.

In only a couple of hours, Io had changed her life. He had shown her so much already, awakening her to a way of living she had never thought possible.

She knew that no matter what happened from this point on, her life would never be the same.

CHAPTER 14

IO TOOK A STEP BACK and held the hair dryer down at his side, his groin tightening. He hadn't thought it possible, but Miriam looked even better with wet hair that hung down in tangled tendrils over her face.

He took another deep breath, beginning to doubt he could make it to nightfall without doing something that would be bad for his health, such as grab a fistful of that lustrous hair, yank her head back, and bite her while his other hand shot up her T-shirt to cup her breast.

God, he was in deep here. And the way she was looking up at him through her lashes, her cheeks flushed, wasn't helping.

He reached out and gently pushed the strands from her face, letting his fingers glide through her hair as he swept it over her shoulder. "Turn around for me," he said quietly, lifting the hair dryer.

Throwing him a come-hither look, she did as he asked and shifted around to face away from him. Did she even know what she did to him?

The air in the room was electric, and it felt as though they were both only barely holding back from taking their affection further. The semi in his sweats indicated he was more than ready to take the next step.

"You're a beautiful female," he said, letting his palm smooth down the length of her straight hair.

She bowed her head. "And you're a beautiful male."

Io had never been called beautiful before, but he liked how the compliment sounded coming from her, especially in that quiet, husky voice that set his heart to beating a new rhythm.

"I'm sorry I upset you earlier," he said, standing so close that his torso almost touched the back of her head. "But I want you to see what you're capable of, Miri. I want you to see how special you are and that you don't need cobalt to help you deal with your problems. And the only way to do that is to help you be honest with yourself."

"I know. I think I'm beginning to understand." She kept her head bowed, her voice quiet. "I'm glad it's you helping me."

"Why's that?" He combed his fingers through her hair.

She didn't answer right away, as if she were carefully choosing her words. "Because I like you. And I get the feeling you understand. I feel like you get me better than anyone ever has. And...well...no one ever stands up to me like you just did." After a short laugh, she added, "It was nice...in a way."

Io hadn't been expecting that. "You're not used to someone like me, are you?"

She laughed softly, glancing to the side without turning all the way around. "No, actually. I'm not."

"And you like it."

Her brow arched. "Cocky, aren't you?"

With a chuckle, he leaned forward and draped one arm over her shoulder before kissing the top of her head. "Maybe a little cocky. Is that a problem?"

Fresh laughter, light and airy, burst from her as she reached up and touched his hand. "Not at all, actually. It's kind of refreshing."

Now it was Io's turn to laugh. "Refreshing?"

"Yes. Most of the males I've met are spineless wimps who would let me walk all over them if I gave them half a chance. I like that you aren't like that."

Io didn't like hearing about other males she had met and he stiffened, standing back up. "You don't need to worry about those spineless wimps anymore, Miriam."

"Oh, why is that?" She sounded like she was flirting with him again.

"Because now I'm here. And I don't like to share." With that, he switched on the hair dryer.

As he gently pulled long strands of her hair out and away from her body, he wondered over what he had just said. He had never felt possessive of any of the females and human women he had been with. In fact, he had enjoyed sharing them on occasion, and he had with Arion before the truth had come out about Ari's sexuality. But the idea of letting anyone else touch Miriam caused the hair on the back of his neck to bristle and his muscles to twitch. He didn't like the idea of any other male even looking at her.

He turned his attention back to the way his fingers threaded through all that black silk spilling over her shoulders. He gently pulled her hair away and let it fan out as the hair dryer blew hot air against it. Over and over, he pulled and fanned, pulled and fanned, her hair drying and falling over his hand and forearm in lustrous, shiny waves.

She dropped her head back, eyes closed, relaxing as he brushed drying sections of her hair aside with his fingers to reach for others as yet untouched. Finally, he grabbed the brush and ran it through the nearly dried strands, gently pulling them straight as he aimed the dryer and drew it down the length with the brush.

All too soon, he was finished.

"You're done?" She sounded disappointed as he set the hair dryer on the nightstand.

"Yes."

"Shit."

He grinned. "I guess you liked that."

"It felt nice." She sounded like she was holding back.

"I can keep going if you like." Io would brush her hair all day if she asked him to. Right now, he would do anything to please her. Shit, he would paint her nails for her if he had polish and thought it would make her feel good.

She let out a heavy sigh. "No, that's okay. I'm actually kind of tired."

That wasn't surprising. She'd had a long night.

"Just tired? No withdrawal?" He needed to make sure she stayed comfortable. If withdrawal set in, he needed to be Johnny-on-the-spot with the elixir.

Miriam turned on the bed, looking pensive, as if she was feeling out her body. "Actually, I feel pretty good. No withdrawal." She sounded surprised, as if she hadn't expected that.

"Is that unusual?"

She pulled her hair back with her fingers, stretching. She looked like a feline lengthening her body. "Yeah, it is. I normally start feeling it within a few hours if I haven't taken a hit."

"That's how it was for me, too." Io winked at her. "I'll be right back."

"Where are you going?"

"To put your clothes in the dryer so they'll be dry by nightfall." He grinned then went to the laundry room, took care of her clothes, then returned to the bedroom to find her getting situated on the far side of the bed.

He pulled the covers back and climbed in beside her. Tension bristled the air and Miriam stiffened and stared at him as if he were fire and she didn't want to get burned.

He cautiously slid toward the edge of the bed, keeping his demeanor non-invasive.

"I'll stay on my side, I promise."

The bed was large enough that even if the two tossed and turned with flailing arms they wouldn't touch each other as long as they both stayed on their sides of the bed.

Miriam looked away and blushed. "I'm sorry. I didn't mean..." She shook her head, embarrassed.

"It's okay." Io sat back against the headboard.

"I'm just not used to sleeping with someone."

"Me neither." Io held her gaze for a moment.

He hadn't had a female in his bed for sleep in...well...it had never happened. Usually, if he had a female in his bed, he was fucking her, not sleeping with her. And when the fucking was over, it was clear the female had to go. Some resisted, trying to woo him to let them stay, but he never gave in, which was why he usually preferred to fuck them in their beds, so he could leave when he was finished.

Man, he was an asshole. Why had it taken him so long to

see this about himself? First with Ari, and now with females. He was a lousy friend, a lousy partner, and just plain lousy overall. He needed to reboot his system in the most severe way, but he didn't know how. What he did know was that he had a feeling the stunning female hugging her knees to her chest and eyeing him nervously could help him figure out who he was now that he was becoming Mr. Self-Revelation.

She looked away, and Io felt as if they had silently made a truce about the sleeping arrangement.

"What did you mean a couple of minutes ago? When you said, that's how it was for you, too?" she said.

"You caught that, huh?" He leaned forward and propped his arms on his bent knees. He might as well tell her. "I'm a former addict, Miriam."

She stared at him for a moment, not saying anything. Silence stretched between them until she finally said, "When?"

"Last year."

More silence.

"How did you get clean?" Was that hope in her voice, along with a deeper understanding of why he had gone after her so hard about her father earlier?

Io's mind went to Arion, sitting on the bathroom floor with him night-after-night, nursing him through the shit Miriam had just endured a few hours ago. Io's heart ached for his friend, but he tried to shrug it off. Right now, he didn't want to think about the best friend he wasn't sure he still had.

"A friend helped me," he said. "Like I helped you. I was way fucked up. Worse than you are. I was overdosing every night. Arion—my friend—stayed with me and poured that shit I gave you down my throat and held me as I threw up night-after-night. He never complained, either. Man, he was always there for me. Without question, Ari was always there when I needed him." Io's gaze drifted away into introspection. Ari had sat with him every night, giving him his venom, doing whatever it took to clean him up and keep his addiction a secret, fully committed and faithful that the two of them could get him through.

What a poignant thought. Arion had never walked away from him. Not even when Io had pulled that boneheaded cobalt shit every night. Ari had been there for him one hundred and fifty percent. For nearly six months, Ari had all-but-lived in this very house to see Io through his addiction, his recovery, and the horrid withdrawal that had made him want to die. Ari alone had saved him from himself and from the cobalt. Ari had been the one to pull Io back to sobriety and help him beat the blue devil, even stealing the elixir from AKM's medical supplies and jeopardizing his job so he could keep Io's addiction a secret from the rest of the team.

And what had Io done when Arion had needed him most? He had run. Io had deserted Ari. What a horrible friend he was.

"Your friend sounds like he really cares about you," Miriam said.

Salt, meet wound.

"Yeah. Yeah, he does." Io nodded stiffly. "He sure does."

At least he used to.

CHAPTER 15

KING BAIN PACED IN HIS STUDY. He couldn't sleep. After the argument with Miriam, she had run off and still hadn't returned. She could be anywhere.

He had tried calling her, but she hadn't answered. Was she avoiding him or was she simply unable to call because she had been captured by one of his many enemies. King Bain trembled briefly as he sat down behind his desk. With his elbows propped on his blotter and his fingers joined together as if in prayer, he rested his chin on his hands and took a deep breath.

He didn't understand Miriam's behavior, and she clearly didn't understand why he was so protective of her. Forces in the world would stop at nothing to get their hands on a member of the royal family in an attempt to hurt him. King Bain had enemies all over the world, and not just dreck enemies. Vampires weren't always cozy bedmates with one another. Just as within the human race, vampires had a bad element who served their own purposes, not caring who they hurt.

In fact, King Bain knew of vampires who worked with drecks to follow more criminal pursuits. And if the rumors were true about what was going on in the dreck underground, keeping Miriam under lock and key was even more important than ever.

The king leaned back in his massive chair, making the rich leather crackle under his shifting weight. His fingers remained laced together, and he steepled his index fingers under his chin, lost in thought.

He met with Premier Royce, the dreck leader who served as King Bain's counterpart, once every month, and they spoke by phone even more frequently. All part of interracial relations and truce management. The dialogue between them had to remain open and steady to allay the aggressive intentions that seemed to hover between the two races like a constant scourge.

During their conversations of the past several months, King Bain had brought up the rumors coming back from AKM, VDA, and his undercover spies that dreck cobalt dealers and other dreck affiliates were capturing vampires and hauling them away to an unknown location. In fact, one of his own spies had suddenly disappeared over a month ago.

Premier Royce denied any knowledge of funny business and had sworn to look into it on several occasions, but as yet, Royce's *investigations* had turned nothing up.

It made King Bain suspicious. And nervous for his daughter.

With a swift dive of his hand, the king hit a button on his phone.

Immediately, a crisp male voice answered. "Yes, my lord?"

"Donovan. Can you track my daughter's cell phone?"

"Of course."

"Do it. She left hours ago and hasn't returned. Find her."

"It will be done, my lord."

The king disconnected and pushed forward to rest his elbows on his desk once more, his forehead pressed against his fists. If anything happened to his daughter, he would destroy anyone who'd had a hand in harming her, even if it meant breaking the truce between the two races.

And as far as Premier Royce was concerned, King Bain had a feeling it was time to bring in a few more specialists.

His thoughts went to his old friend, Maddox, who had disappeared centuries ago after he'd married a human witch. Damn, but Bain missed Maddox. If he were here, the king would have nothing to worry about.

But he feared Maddox was long gone, in more ways than one.

His phone beeped.

He smacked the speaker button. "Yes."

"We found her," Donovan said.

"Where?"

"A location in the suburbs. House belongs to Iobates Liatos. We checked him out and confirmed he works at AKM on Tristan's team."

Io? King Bain knew Io's reputation. The hair on the back of his neck prickled just knowing his daughter was in the home of such a philandering womanizer. King Bain's blood surged as he shot from his chair. If Io had defiled Miriam, King Bain wouldn't hesitate to exact the highest penalty within his power to punish him.

"Go. Get. Her." Each word seethed between clenched teeth as the king practically growled them past his voice box.

Donovan paused for only a heartbeat. "And if he has—?"

King Bain didn't let Donovan finish the thought. "If he has, kill him."

Everyone knew the law surrounding his daughter. No one touched Miriam without his permission. Not even a member of Tristan's team. Especially not Io, whose reputation preceded him in the most unflattering and unimpressive way. King Bain would die before letting the likes of Io touch his daughter.

"Yes, my lord." Donovan quickly disconnected.

King Bain burst from behind his desk, consumed in a fit of ferocious pacing. What was that bastard doing to his daughter? This very minute, he could be—King Bain slammed his eyes shut and hissed low and deadly at the image of Io seducing his daughter.

With a rush of energy, he was back behind his desk and punching in the speed dial for Gregos Savakis, his liaison who oversaw several teams at AKM, including Tristan's. Gregos's son, Arion, had been a member of Tristan's team until recently.

Gregos answered, his voice groggy from sleep. "Yes, my lord. What's wrong?"

Clearly, Gregos knew King Bain wouldn't call him in the

middle of the day unless something was wrong.

"We have an incident." There was no might or maybe.

"An incident?"

"Yes, I want you up to handle the fallout if what I suspect has happened."

"What's happened." Gregos suddenly sounded more awake.

"My daughter. She's with Io."

"Oh," Gregos said flatly.

The king imagined that Gregos's face had just gone stark white. Gregos knew exactly what Miriam's proximity to Io meant. King Bain didn't have to spell it out for him.

Gregos cleared his throat. "Okay, so how would you like me to proceed?"

King Bain shook his head, livid, and filled Gregos in. He had a bad feeling about this. A very bad feeling.

CHAPTER 16

THUNDER RIPPED THE AIR OUTSIDE, jolting Miriam awake.

She sat up, gasping. She looked down to see red streaks where her nails had scraped her forearms in her sleep. Her skin itched. And not just on her arms. She itched everywhere. Panic made her heart race and her breathing quicken. What was happening to her? It needed to stop. She needed to keep scratching…to peel off her skin…to scream. A dull throbbing pulsed behind her left eye and she slapped her palm over the left side of her face and winced.

Cobalt. She needed a hit. God, she needed her dealer. Now!

"Are you okay?"

She jumped and swung her gaze around toward the voice. Who was with her? Someone she knew. Someone she trusted. He was someone she liked. She thought for a moment, searching the dark shadows before vaguely remembering where she was.

"I…Io?" Her voice trembled and she frowned. The male's name was Io, right?

He sat up just a few feet away from her and turned on the light. The quiet click sounded like an explosion and she jerked and curled in on herself protectively, shivering, shielding her eyes from the light with her hand.

"Miriam?" Io's voice was filled with worry.

She swallowed impulsively and looked over her shoulder at him just as a hot flash worked through her body and sweat bloomed over her neck and chest.

Well, well, well. He was attractive. The most attractive male she had ever seen. She could swear she knew him from somewhere, but she couldn't think straight.

"I n...need a h...hit. My d...dealer." She struggled to sit up and crawl toward her purse.

"Hold on." The male threw off the covers and rushed across the room and grabbed a dark brown bottle off the dresser. The bottle reminded her of prescription medicine.

"My p...purse." She reached but fell over and rolled to her back on the bed. "Need m...my phone." She tore into her forearms again, scratching and shivering.

"No. You won't be calling anyone, Miriam." The man—Io—appeared beside her, holding a cup in his hand. His voice was quiet, measured, and calm. "No more dealers. No more cobalt. Understand?" He sounded like he knew what was happening to her, but he was wrong.

Miriam stared at him, her eyes wide with anger. No, she didn't understand. She wanted a hit. Now! Who was this male who dared tell her what she couldn't have? She was sick and tired of people telling her what she was allowed to do and what was forbidden. Miriam wanted to live her own life. If only all the assholes would get out of her way.

Arching her back, she slapped her arms out to the side on the bed and shrieked like a banshee, outraged that this male was keeping her from what she needed. He would pay. She wouldn't stop screaming until he gave her—

Vile liquid poured into her mouth, and she sputtered and coughed. She'd tasted something similar before. Recently. It had made her throw up. Miriam gagged and snapped her mouth closed then rolled and pounced to all fours before spitting the putrid liquid at the handsome man beside her.

He sighed and looked away before calmly wiping off his face.

Miriam bared her fangs and hissed, curling her long fingers into the blanket so that it bunched up under her hands.

"You have to drink this, Miriam."

"Fuck you!" She smirked at him, feeling victorious. "You can't make me."

"I don't want to make you. But I will if you force me to."

Why was he so damn calm?

She hissed again, completely lost to her addiction. Nothing else mattered right now except getting more cobalt. Vaguely, she realized she had never felt such a strong pull toward needing the drug before, and she had a feeling that throwing up earlier was tied to her cravings. All she wanted was more cobalt. Everything else was secondary.

The male drank the remaining contents of the cup, his nose curling slightly as if from an unpleasant odor, and then he lunged for Miriam, picking her up and throwing her back on the bed before landing on top of her.

She tried to lash out, but somehow he had gotten hold of her wrists with one of his hands and held them down over her head. The other clamped onto her face, around her mouth, squeezing her cheeks until she couldn't resist any longer.

Growling, her jaw gave and opened as she tried to kick herself free. The male quickly subdued her, thrusting his knees down against her thighs, and lowered his mouth to hers as if to kiss her. His mouth pressed into hers and he spit the vile liquid down her throat before pulling back and flattening his palm over her mouth so she couldn't spit the nasty-tasting water back out.

She struggled and squirmed, growling, moaning, trying to cry out, but he held firm, keeping her pinned and her mouth sealed.

Finally, he took his hand away from her mouth and she spit at him, but it was useless. She had already swallowed what he'd given her.

He wiped off his face, keeping her wrists locked down with his other hand, seeming to take her behavior in stride, as if he expected her reaction and wasn't fazed in the slightest that she was unloading a string of profanities at him that would make a sailor blush.

"Mother fucking cocksucker!" She spat at him again. "Prick! Fuck you! I hate you!"

That seemed to crack his stoic shell, and his brow ticked slightly before smoothing out. "That's fine, Miriam. You can hate me, but it doesn't change how I feel about you. And it won't stop me from taking care of you. I'll get you through this, baby." He caressed her cheek with his free hand.

She snarled and flinched away as if his touch burned her. But that didn't make sense. He had touched her earlier, and she had liked it. She was sure of it.

"This will only last a few days if you stay off the drugs. Your withdrawal is going to be magnified because of the tonic I gave you earlier. It kick-started a detox, but if you'll let me, I'll take care of you. I promise to take care of you."

He sounded so sincere and concerned for her. So handsome. Who was he? It was on the tip of her tongue.

Minutes passed, and the itching subsided. Her headache eased, and recognition returned. *Io*. She looked around. This was his house, his room. His bed. And she had said awful things to him. He had been helping her and she had behaved like a child.

"Oh God." What had she done?

"Sshh." Io gazed down at her, his hands still holding hers against the bed.

Uncontrollable shivers wracked her body, worsening in a matter of seconds. In fact, the more her other symptoms eased, the worse the shaking became. Her teeth chattered and her entire body quaked as if in fever.

"W...What's wrong with m...me? I c...can't stop sh... shaking." She couldn't meet Io's eyes. How could she after the way she had behaved? She had acted horribly in front of him. Again. She had...oh God, she had spit on him. She had told him she hated him, and to fuck off. Her chin quivered and she looked away. If only she were a turtle, she could crawl inside her shell and hide.

"Miri. Ssshh, baby. It's okay. You're going to be okay." He released her wrists and slowly slid his knees off her thighs, situating himself beside her. Propped on one arm, he caressed her face. "It's adrenaline, Miriam. The tonic you drank is forcing you to come down from the withdrawal, but it will take a few minutes to work the adrenaline out of your system."

She turned away, curling in on herself through another

wave of the shakes, hugging her torso as she drew her knees toward her chest. She'd find a way to hide yet.

"I'm s…sorry about wh…what I said to y…you." She buried her face against the mattress. Would she ever be able to be around Io without making herself look like a fool? He was the one male she wanted to impress and all she did was make an ass out of herself around him.

"Miriam, look at me."

She burrowed further into the bedding.

Io's hand smoothed over her shoulder, gently tugging on her as she trembled again. "Miriam, please. Please baby, look at me."

How could she? She was a disgrace to herself and to her family name. Io was a better male than she deserved.

"Miri?"

Fine. She would get this over with. Let him see her, be disgusted by the awful person she had become, because only a wretch would treat someone like Io the way she just had. She lifted her face and looked over her shoulder.

Before she knew what was happening, his mouth was on hers, his arm winding around her waist from behind, pulling her back against him.

Heat blasted through her body as the adrenaline coursing through her found a new—better—outlet.

"Miriam." Her name left his lips on a whisper even as they pressed against hers in another mind-blowing collision of flesh and tongues.

Fire expanded from her belly, right underneath where his palm flattened and seared her, urging her back, pressing their bodies together. She reached around and gripped the back of his head, holding him in place, devouring his lips.

"God, baby." He moaned and shifted, spinning her around until she faced him. "I need you."

"I need *you*." Their mouths danced, a fierce tango, locked one to the other, giving and taking in urgent turns.

A waterfall of warmth spilled through her abdomen as he sucked in her bottom lip, licking it before clutching it in his teeth. His gaze connected with hers, their breathing heavy and quickened, and desire gazed back at her.

She was no longer trembling. Io had seen to that quite nicely, hadn't he?

She searched his face, her lips still captive in his teeth. God, she wanted him. Needed him. Would die to have him. Moaning, she pressed forward, captured his top lip between her teeth, tasted him, then moaned again as he surged against her, arms securing her as he claimed her mouth completely once more.

Another rumble of thunder shook the house, but it was nothing like the storm brewing inside Io's basement bedroom.

His lips were incredible. Strong and firm, yet soft and smooth. And he knew how to work them against her mouth to tease, cajole, and persuade her to open for him so he could find the tip of her tongue with his, hold for a moment, then dive in to taste her over and over.

With the fluidity of melted chocolate, she undulated beneath him as he rolled her to her back. She needed him in the most basic way, her body a gentle wave that reached toward his so her curves kissed his hard edges as their mouths fused more deeply together. Her nipples hardened as her breasts brushed against his chest. Her abdomen quivered as it rolled along his. And when her pelvis raised off the bed, they both moaned as his hard shaft teased her through their clothes.

Io sank lower, his own body responding to the feel of hers riding up and down against him, their mouths locked in a never-ending, deep, breathless embrace.

He sank fully against her, all of him feeling all of her, his hips nestled snugly between her legs.

Miriam had never known such physical pleasure. Even fully clothed, this was more erotic than she could have imagined, and she couldn't stop. Not now. Not when she could feel an orgasm building deep within her belly.

Every part of her body seemed to call to every part of his, reaching for him.

Io's hips pushed forward, and she opened her legs wider.

He moaned approvingly and pushed his pelvis against

her again. One long, persistent, thrusting motion.

This time, she moaned. Everything was a blur, a rush of excitement and lusty arousal, and it had all happened so fast, coming out of nowhere, sweeping her up and away. Had Dorothy felt this way riding inside the tornado that took her to Oz? Grounded one instant, flying to a fantastical land the next?

He smiled against her mouth, and she opened her eyes to look into his. He was devilishly sexy, and he watched her closely, enthralled with her.

"You're going to come, aren't you?" He rolled his hips against her again, more persistently this time, letting his steely shaft tease her in just the right spot.

Choking back another groan, she nodded briskly and licked her lips. "I think so."

His eyes flicked to her mouth and he leaned down and teased her lips with his tongue as he thrust against her again. "You think so?"

God, yes. Yes. She nodded again. "Uh-huh." She could barely breathe, too caught up in what was happening inside her. Muscles bunched, nerve-endings fired, everything seemed to be getting tighter, pulling toward a snapping point.

His movements were measured and paced, persistent. He needed to keep going. *Don't stop. Please, yes, this is good. So good.*

"You're going to come for me?" He pressed his lips to her ear, his devilish smile showing through his voice. "You are, aren't you? Bad, bad girl." He chuckled, a quiet, deep sound that sent a delicious chill down her spine.

"Io!" She gasped and dug her fingers into his ass as he rolled against her again.

"That's it, baby." He pulsed his hips forward and back, forward and back in tiny movements that kept the pressure squarely on her clit.

"Hurry!" She practically breathed the word out, clawing his buttocks through his sweatpants. But hurry to where? It wasn't as though Io had a whole lot of control over how quickly she came.

He tucked his face against the side of her neck, kissing her, licking, sucking.

Miriam wanted him to bite her, but he didn't. She sensed he wanted to, but for some reason he held back. Why wouldn't he bite her? *No, don't think about that now.* She was about to come. Her entire adrenaline-laden body was about to come unglued, and it was all because of...

"IO!"

Her climax roared, making her feel like a one-woman earthquake as she shuddered violently, crying out as wave after wave pummeled her, ripping her apart.

Io rolled violently against her, his back arching as he pressed his groin between her legs. Ragged breaths burst against her neck where his teeth clenched her skin in a show of self-restraint worthy of an Olympic gold. He could easily sink his fangs into her flesh, but he held back, his entire body paying the price for his withholding as he tensed and shuddered.

She held him tightly as the initial swell broke and crashed through her muscles, pounding her, drawing her in as if sucked into a rip current, until finally, the violent sea of bliss released her and she floated to the surface once more. Miriam opened her eyes and brushed her hands up Io's back as his face swayed into her field of vision. She was smiling as if she had been starving and had just been served the most heavenly cuisine—no, not cuisine...food—she had ever eaten. Completely satisfied, Miriam stretched and purred under him, reveling in how exquisite her body felt in its post-orgasmic bliss.

Io shivered, breathless. "I've never heard a female purr before." He pressed his nose against the side of her neck and inhaled, his body sliding against hers in a way that reminded her of a cat. A very large cat. Maybe a panther. Mmm, yes, she liked thinking of Io as a panther.

She blinked and her smile widened as she lazily traced the swirls of ink on his right arm. "Mmm, is that so?"

She felt fine, as if she'd just slipped on her favorite silk robe after a long lavender-scented bubble bath in her Jacuzzi tub.

She felt sinfully decadent in the way the woman in the Dove chocolate commercial appeared to feel after biting into one of those delicious, creamy, bite-sized squares of chocolate. Io was her silk. He was her Dove chocolate. Only he had ever made her feel so luxurious and debauched, but in such a wonderful way.

"You're amazing," Io's gaze raked her face and neck as he pushed himself up.

She was beginning to come back from Cloud Nine. It had been a lovely trip, but as much as she was drawn to Io, she couldn't forget who she was, and especially who her father was. The possibility of her being allowed to stay with Io was about as likely as an asteroid hitting the Earth tomorrow.

What had just happened between them had been incredible. No, it had been more than that. Stellar. Beyond words. The most wonderful thing she had ever experienced. Miriam's body still sang from what Io had coaxed out of her, but this had to remain a one-time thing.

"We can't do that again," she said sadly, knowing full well what would happen if her father found out.

"Why not?" Io bent down and nudged the bottom of her chin with his nose so he could circle his tongue inside the tender hollow of her throat.

He was flirting with disaster.

"My father." She closed her eyes, enjoying too much how well he worked his tongue. "He'll never allow us to see each other."

"I'm seeing you now," Io said against her throat.

Io did have a point, but was he seeing hers?

"You know what I mean." She pushed playfully against him, giggling as he nibbled the tendon that stretched from her collarbone up the side of her neck.

He sat back and rolled to the side, grinning and resting his hand on her stomach. "He doesn't have to know."

She rolled to face him and propped herself up on one elbow, craving to have him back on top of her even though she knew it was better that they remained apart.

"What are you saying? That I purposely defy my father?"

As if she didn't do that every day.

As if reading her mind, he said. "Aren't you defying him already? By using cobalt? By being here now." He brushed his fingers over her cheek. "By letting me touch you even though you know it's against the law?"

Io's brow lifted as if challenging her to deny it.

She sighed. "This is different."

"How?"

Good question. Because really, how was him bringing her to orgasm and touching her sexually any different than all the other acts of rebellion she had exercised against her father's wishes?

"It just is."

"Why? Because you think he'll hurt me?" Io scooted toward her, but she pressed her palm against his chest, pushing him back.

"Yes."

And then she realized how this was different than any of the stunts she'd pulled before. Because before, she was the only one subject to punishment. And her father couldn't contain her. His threats of punishment on her were just that. Threats. He never followed through. But Io would feel the full wrath of her father's idea of justice.

"My father could destroy you, Io." She searched his face.

For several seconds, they only stared at each other, neither knowing what to say next as the full weight of her words sunk in. Then Io sighed and rolled to his back, flopping his arm out to the side.

"You're right." He turned his head back toward her. "But, Miriam, you're the most beautiful creature I've ever seen. I can't accept that this is all we'll ever have."

She knew what he meant. She couldn't imagine not having Io in her life, especially now that he had given her such incredible pleasure and awakened her to a way of living she had always wanted but feared she would never know.

But it was more than just that. Io was strong-willed, carefree, a rebel like she was. He understood her when not many did. Not only did he understand her need for freedom, but he knew how to treat her addiction, which was something her father refused to see. And he saw through her. He saw the lies she tried to tell herself about how she didn't let her father control her—because he did. Even down to her cobalt use, her father had a hand in affecting her decisions. Io could see that, and he had forced her to see it, too, not allowing her to hide behind excuses.

Io filled all the empty spaces she had yearned for her father to fill since she was young. With him, she felt safe in a way she hadn't felt at home in decades. Her father had abandoned her when she had needed him most, treating her more like just another of his subjects instead of his daughter. There had been a time when she had been able to count on him, but as she grew older and came into her womanly body, her father had distanced himself and had continued treating her like a baby. He didn't understand that she needed him to let her grow up.

Io got that. Io treated her like an adult. Io would never baby her.

"I wish there was a way," she said, tucking her hair behind her ear. "I wish things were different. I like how you make me feel." She blushed and looked down at the sheets.

Io shifted toward her, and this time she didn't push him away.

"I like how I make you feel, too."

She could hear the mischievous smile in his voice and looked up to see his eyes twinkling knowingly at her. The look on his face made her laugh.

"Oh, do you now?" She playfully pushed against his shoulder.

"Oh yeah. Feeling you come against me, and knowing I'd given that to you..." He paused and took a deep, satisfied breath. "Well, it gave me pleasure to know I'd made you feel that."

The tips of his fingers skimmed over the side of her breast and down to her hips.

"Stop that." She slapped his hand away and gave him a warning look, but her mental fortitude was waning. If he continued to make such advances, she might reconsider her position on whether or not they should perform an encore.

He chuckled and pulled his hand away. "Fine. I'm stopping. I surrender."

She lay down beside him and listened to him breathe, thinking about all that had happened since she woke up in a fit of itching and violent withdrawal.

"What happened to me, anyway? I've never had withdrawal like that."

Io reached for her hand and she took it, liking how his strong fingers felt tucked between hers.

"The tonic I gave you earlier kick-started a detox. I won't lie. Cobalt detox is a bitch," he said, and then added, "More like a bitch with horns, a pitched fork, and breathes fire. You sort of lose your mind on a cobalt detox." He sounded like he was reliving old ghosts from his own detox.

"Well, thanks for the warning." Miriam let out a heavy breath. "Is this what I get to look forward to after I leave here?" She sensed Io's concern. "Don't answer that," she said before he could say anything. "I think I get the idea of what I'm in for."

"The elixir I gave you helps curb the worst of it."

"Too bad I don't have your nasty-ass elixir at home." She sucked her teeth and rolled her head toward him as he did the same toward her.

"Hey, it's nasty, but it works."

"So it does." She couldn't deny that. Within minutes of swallowing the vile concoction, she had calmed like a baby drinking from the teat.

They stared at each other, her thoughts filled with worry over how she would get through detoxing without his elixir— or him—to take away the violent withdrawal when it rose up as it had a little while ago.

"You could always stay here with me." Io spoke softly, squeezing her hand. "I'll take care of you. I'll see you through."

She rolled her eyes and turned away to stare up at the ceiling. "Yeah, right. As if my father would allow that."

"He might. If we approach it right, your father might allow me to treat you."

She looked back at him. Was he serious? Could they really convince her father to release her into Io's care when he didn't even want to admit she had a drug problem in the first place?

"I don't know, but we could try." She bit her lip, her mind alighting with hope.

CHAPTER 17

THE STORM OUTSIDE RAGED ON, but Io was more concerned with the storm that seemed to be raging behind Miriam's crystal blue eyes. Was she trying to figure out a way to convince her father to let him treat and care for her during her recovery? Even after all her protests about how they couldn't see each other and how her father would destroy him if he knew what they had just done, could she now be searching for a way for them to be together just a little longer?

And a little longer was all Io wanted. Longer to see her, feel her, and imprint her on his soul and in his memories. He knew that after she left here the odds would be against them ever seeing each other again.

The thought angered a primal part of him that thrust itself forward in his mind, snarling at the idea of never seeing Miriam again. She was his, damn it. She belonged to him. He had a right to—

Whoa! Had he mated her? Io physically swayed at the thought. Was that what was going on here? Had his vampire instincts fired up to form a bond with Miriam already?

This was one area where vampires differed from humans. Whereas males of both species played the field in similar ways, a human marriage had nothing on a vampire mating. A marriage could be dissolved by a judge with a little slip of paper. A marriage could be ended in a blink if the humans got tired of each other or fell out of love. With vampires, there was no dissolving a mating. A mated pair didn't grow tired of one another, and they certainly didn't fall out of love. When two vampires mated, a link formed to tether them to one another on a level that transcended the physical plane and fused them into one on a spiritual and emotional level, which was why the loss of a mate left a male in a state of despair if it didn't kill him outright. A mating was for life and plainly demonstrated the vampire race's link to the animal kingdom.

How had he connected with her so quickly? It was too soon. Wasn't it?

When he gazed back into her eyes, he knew he had to have her forever. His heart beat harder at the prospect, and his body warmed at the thought of seeing her belly swell with his child.

Damn, but Io was in it for real with Miriam. This was bad. Real bad. Because if she thought her father would blow a gasket over his giving her an orgasm, he would likely stroke out if he knew Io was forming a mating bond to her.

Armed with the knowledge that she was his mate, Io latched on to what little momentum he had going for him, because he had to find a way for them to stay together.

"It could work, Miriam. I can talk to Tristan and convince him that I can quietly see you through your rehab here." He lowered his voice. "No one would have to know. We could keep it from leaking out into the community. Surely your father would appreciate that."

She eagerly rolled to her side and propped herself up on her arm. Io could see her gears turning. Miriam was almost sold on the idea.

"It might work," she said.

Io felt like they were conspiring to rob a bank instead of trying to find a way to be together.

"Of course it will." He skimmed his palm over her hip, unable to stop himself from touching her.

Miriam drew him in like a field of wildflowers drew in bees. Intoxicated by everything about her, Io drifted and swayed against her as his hand explored lower then slid back up and under her shirt. He sucked in his breath when his fingers touched skin.

Miriam did likewise, her fiery gaze meeting his in wonder.

But unlike before, this time she didn't stop him.

"You're not pushing me away," he said, slowly easing his hand higher.

"No, I'm not." She gently dropped back to the mattress, biting her plump bottom lip as she stared at him and held her breath.

"Are you nervous?" He stared longingly at her lip. Her teeth stretched the skin in a way that made him want to take her lip between his teeth and suck it into his mouth.

She nodded. "A little."

"Why?" The curve of his thumb and index finger found the lower swell of her left breast, and she breathed in sharply.

"Because you excite me so much."

Io couldn't contain his delight and smiled. "Is that a bad thing?"

She grinned shyly. "No, I guess not."

"Then why does my exciting you make you nervous?" His palm cupped the underside of her ample breast and pushed, making the mound of flesh bunch and press against the T-shirt she was wearing. *His* T-shirt.

She squirmed and shifted, letting the fabric loosen so he could more easily feel her.

"Because I've never felt this way before."

"Mmm." Io liked hearing he was the first male to please her. The idea of guiding her through all the pleasures of her body when no other male had explored her path made his chest swell.

"You excite me, too," he said. "And what you did earlier, coming like you did…that excited me."

"It did?" Her back rounded as his palm eased up and over her nipple and his fingers squeezed.

She moaned.

"Yes." Io leaned down and slowly rubbed the side of his nose against her cheek and inhaled long and deep.

She was heavily aroused. Just as she had been earlier.

Her legs parted and he slid one of his between them, his thigh rubbing against hers.

"What are you doing?" she said breathlessly, her voice soft

and drowsy with lust.

"Showing you how good being excited can feel." He dipped his nose against the tender place behind her ear and inhaled her scent again, making her shiver.

"I can't...you can't...we can't do—"

"Shh, baby. I only want to touch you. Just touching. Like we did before, only more skin." He released her breast and smoothed his palm over her flat stomach. She was firm, yet soft. Strong, yet feminine.

Io couldn't deny that he wanted so much more than to touch her, but until she was ready for him, he would take his physical affection only so far. He hoped she wouldn't make him wait too long, because if his calling phase struck him as quickly as the link had fired up between them, he would soon need her in the most extreme sense of the word. And once the calling claimed him, he wouldn't be able to restrain himself from taking her body as often as his hormonal heat required him to.

She relaxed against his caress and moaned. "I like more skin. I like how you're touching me." The tips of her delicate, long fingers tickled a sensuous path up his arm.

He liked it, too. No, he loved it.

If she were any other woman, he would have had her on her back and her legs open already, his body plowing hers like fertile ground. But this was Miriam. Perfect, pristine, absolutely exquisite Miriam. The thought of taking such a female in so careless a way seemed criminal. And if she was, in fact, his mate, she deserved better than that. When he consummated his relationship with Miriam—and by God, he *would* consummate it—he would do so with the utmost care. He would worship her and treat her body like the precious treasure she was.

But for now, this was enough. Touching her skin and feeling her body shiver against his palm was plenty.

"You tremble for me." His lips brushed against her neck as he eased his hand higher once more. Her stomach fluttered.

She responded by nodding and closing her eyes.

When Io's hand covered her breast again, she tensed and

groaned, breathing heavily.

"No male has ever touched your breasts." He whispered the words almost reverently. "I'm the first." He wasn't asking. He already knew the answer, but proclaiming his unique status out loud made the moment more powerful and meaningful.

She nodded, rolling slightly toward him and arching her back.

He looked at her face. Her eyes were closed, her lips parted as she panted. Miriam was unraveling in ecstasy before his very eyes.

He scooted closer and gently pressed his thigh against the apex of her legs. Her eyes blinked open briefly, but as soon as he squeezed the healthy mound of her breast at the same time he rocked his thigh against her core, she closed them again and gasped, her head dropping back to expose the graceful curve of her neck.

The knowledge that no male had ever touched her in this way had Io's cock harder than a marble column. She was his. All his. Untouched and pure. So perfect.

Miriam's erect nipple teased his palm, and from the looks of the peaked fabric over her other breast, she had marvelous nipples that rose like small towers at the crest of her heavy breasts. Io had to see them. He couldn't stand feeling one beneath his palm and seeing how the other teased his T-shirt without letting his sense of sight partake in his exploration of her.

"I want to see you, Miriam. God, but I want to see what your body looks like under my clothes." His voice was raw with lust, but he would keep his promise. He would not take her virtue. He would touch her, taste her, gaze upon her perfect beauty, but he would not violate her.

Miriam opened her eyes again, her gaze filled with curiosity, as well as the hint of something more...the thrill of rebellion, perhaps? She was breaking all the rules now, and it seemed the further she let him go, the further she wanted to take him.

She hesitated then slowly reached for the hem of the shirt

and gradually pulled it up. Io held his breath, his gaze falling to her breasts, waiting for her to reveal them. Her skin was as pristine as he had imagined, unmarked and smooth, lightly tan and exquisite.

Higher the shirt rose until finally she bared herself to him.

"God, you're beautiful," he said, his voice rushing on a breath.

Her rounded, full breasts swayed as she lifted the shirt over her head then self-consciously brought it down to cover her chest, her skin flushing. Apparently, not only had she never been touched, but no male had ever gazed upon her naked flesh, either.

Io grinned. "I've already seen you. No need to hide now." He gently tugged on the T-shirt.

"I've never..." She took a deep breath, the hint of a thrill crossing her face.

"...done anything like this?"

She nodded.

"Miriam, I promise. I won't do anything you don't want. Do you want me to stop?"

God, he hoped not.

"No," she said quickly, shaking her head.

After a moment's hesitation, during which she kept her blue eyes locked to his, she slowly let go of the T-shirt and let him pull it away, exposing her magnificent breasts again.

Her nipples were large and dark pink, and just as he had expected, they stood a good half-inch at attention, as if reaching for him. And who was he to deny them?

He rolled one between his thumb and forefinger, leaning down and kissing the other so softly his lips barely met her skin. She hissed through her teeth, sucking in a blast of air, then moaned as she sank back and exhaled. Her gaze filled with hunger, her eyes watching him with eager anticipation, and he leaned down again and quickly flicked his tongue over her hardened nub. Miriam gasped and squirmed, grinding her hips against his thigh.

The amount of power he had over her was such a turn-on,

but the fact she trusted him not to abuse that power excited him even more.

She took a shuddering breath through parted lips, her gaze locked on his as her chest rose seductively.

"Tell me, Miriam," he said, drawing closer, "how do I make you feel?" His lips brushed over her other nipple, but he kept his gaze connected with hers.

She blinked dreamily and licked her lips, taking another strained breath.

Io swirled his tongue around her hard nipple before sucking it into his mouth. He would make her delirious with need, push her to her limits, make her want him so badly she would never want to leave.

"God, yes." One of her hands clamped onto the back of his head and her fingers fisted into his hair as her chest rose to meet his mouth.

Io loved the way her body responded to him, and he loved that he was the one getting the opportunity to show her the delights a man could give a woman.

"Tell me how I make you feel," he said again, allowing his hand to travel back down her stomach to tease the loose waistband of the sweats she wore.

Miriam's body quaked again. Damn, she was sexy. No female had ever responded to him like this. So raw and primal. Her actions held no ulterior motives, and even under her obvious desire, her innocence was ever-present.

"Decadent. Desirable. Free." Her voice was a mere whisper and she breathed out a sigh between each word.

"And beautiful." Io added.

His hand slipped inside the sweats and her grip on the back of his head tightened as she reached down and grabbed his forearm with her other hand.

An instinctual response?

"Do you want me to stop?" he said. His lips teased her nipple.

A choked groan caught in her throat and she writhed against him, but she didn't pull away or tug on his arm.

"Tell me, Miriam." He took her nipple in his mouth again, flicking it with his tongue.

She shivered and squirmed then released his arm. "No, don't stop."

"Mmm." Io's hand sank deeper.

Io's SUBDUED MOAN SOUNDED ALMOST SERENE, but Miriam knew better. Io was a male. A powerful male. And yet he handled her with tenderness. The dichotomy tingled her spine, and her blood heated further. Who would have thought she would take to such a male? Strong, virile, a member of the working class yet more like a prince with every gentle caress he lavished on her, whether with his hands or his tongue.

Was he always this way with the women he took to his bed? Or just her? Io didn't seem like the kind of male who was used to holding back or putting the pace of the action into someone else's control.

On one hand, she wanted to abuse the power he had given her. This was her chance to have all that a male could give her. All she needed to do was say the word and it was bye-bye virtue. She would finally know the feel of a male. Not just his touch, but how he felt inside her, body-to-body, locked in a primitive dance as old as time.

On the other hand, she didn't want to ruin the beauty of what Io was doing to her. For the first time, she felt like the princess she was, because Io seemed to be worshipping her. To take away what seemed to be a pivotal moment for him, as well as her, by rushing into full-blown sex would be wrong. Talk about a law that shouldn't be broken. This was one of those times.

His fingers glided over her nether lips, and she stirred uncontrollably through the shot of heat that pulsed like rays of sunlight from her center. Her toes tingled, her fingers curled, and her legs opened as he gently rubbed her up and down. Soft and slow, he seduced her body as well as her mind, his teeth nibbling the puckered flesh of her breast.

This was good, so good, so beautiful.

"More," she said, the word more of an exhale than a spoken syllable.

Io complied and lifted himself over her body to take her other nipple between his lips as his index and ring fingers parted her so his middle finger could massage her swollen clitoris.

"You're so wet," he said before opening his mouth and drawing in her entire areola, sucking and licking her into a frenzy.

His middle finger slid through her slick offering and dipped inside. Not far, but far enough that he pushed against the barrier of her hymen with the tip of his finger.

"Oh fuck," he said, his deep voice growling through the words. "You're pure."

The crude obscenity pleased her more than offended, and the satisfaction and reverence in his voice made her insides melt like candle wax against a flame.

"I knew you were, but..." He placed his forehead against her sternum, his finger still inside her but unmoving. His breath rushed out over her chest and against her stomach.

He seemed to be paying homage to her, honoring and admiring her chastity, and she combed her fingers through the hair on the back of his head before flattening her palm against his scalp. Holding, just holding...and breathing.

He lifted his head and looked at her. "I knew you were pure," he repeated, "but feeling it for myself—feeling the proof with my own hand—does something to me. I..." Io hesitated as if choosing his words wisely. "Miriam, you have a hold on me I've never known. I've never wanted anyone the way I want you."

The reverence shining in his eyes and the timbre of his voice, so solid and sure, nearly undid her. Io captivated her. He knew the penalty for what he was doing, but he did it, anyway. Not even the knowledge that her father could kill him for his actions kept him from her.

Some would call him reckless, but she disagreed. Io wasn't reckless. He was fearless. And that was just the quality she needed in a male. To hell with what her father wanted for her. She knew what she wanted, as well as what she needed. And none of the suitors her father would match her with had half the spine and mental prowess Io had. None were strong enough to handle her, let alone meet her halfway.

But with Io, she was putty in his hands. Hot putty ready to be molded and cultivated into a work of art. Io didn't just meet her halfway and handle her with an expert hand, he urged more from her than even she knew she was capable of. The orgasm he had given her earlier, for example, had shattered her. And as her body had slowly glued itself back together after its glorious rapture, she was like a stretched rubber band, unable to return to the exact shape she had been before.

Io was a male she would die and kill for, and who she instinctively knew would die and kill for her.

And that connected them somehow. Miriam couldn't explain it, but something magnetic and larger-than-life was happening between them.

"Io...?" She pushed her fingers through his thick, dark brown hair.

His finger was still inside her, applying pressure that felt heavenly, making her want more.

Io's body shifted against her and she felt his hard length rub against her thigh. His breath rushed over her breast as he rocked his hips against her again, then once more.

He was pure masculinity. All hard male and domineering strength, coiled and powerful.

Suddenly, she needed to feel him, his skin, his fire.

"Take off your shirt," she said, pushing up the hem.

She hated that he had to take his hand away from exploring her, but the payoff was in watching him reach around, grab the back of the shirt at the neck, then pull it off in one husky yank to display his olive skin and chiseled body.

And then his hand was back inside her sweats. His fingers massaged her, his body rose up, and he repositioned himself between her legs, poised partially on his knees so his fingers could continue their fiery caresses against her slick heat.

"Don't stop," she said, tracing her fingers over the swells

of his chest. He had a deep, pronounced dip between his pecs, and she imagined licking him there. Maybe someday she would, but right now, she was enjoying the simple act of admiring his body while he played his fingers over her sex.

The pad of his thumb circled her clit, pressing and stimulating her. She knew she was going to come again. She could feel it working its way to the surface.

"Yes, like that. Just like that, Io."

He was hers. She already knew it. Somehow, she just knew.

CHAPTER 18

IO HAD NEVER TREATED A WOMAN WITH SUCH CARE. He had never given so selflessly of himself. Until now, he hadn't wanted to. For the first time, a woman's pleasure was more important than his own. In fact, her pleasure drove him toward his own. Simply watching her body undulate and shake, listening to her deepening moans and uttered words of encouragement, and feeling her hips rotate against his hand as he stroked her clit with his thumb, was enough to push him to the threshold of his body's sexual limits.

Her arms around him tightened, pulling him down as her legs quivered. The moment his chest pressed against hers, she convulsed and cried out as she came.

He pressed his palm fully against her, feeling her muscles clench and spasm.

"Oh my God, Miriam," he said. His cock ached to spend itself.

"Io…"

That nearly did him in. Hearing her moan his name as she continued coming was better than a blow job, and his cock wept on the inside of his sweatpants as he groaned long, low, and deep.

"Did you…?" she said, flinching through another tiny spasm, catching her breath and moaning. Once she stilled, she tried again. "Did you come?" The tips of her fingers danced down his back then up to his shoulders.

"No." He feared pressing himself against her. If he did, he was sure to climax, and he didn't want this to be about his pleasure. Right now, everything was about Miriam. "But damn, I want to."

"Do it." She pushed him to his back, excitement glinting in her eyes as she licked her lips, straddled him, and slapped her hands down on his chest.

She rose and swiveled her hips against him, moaning as she quivered through an aftershock of her own. Then a devilish smile broke across her face as she churned her hips again. The shock of her unexpected assault blew Io's mind. Sweet, docile Miriam had been replaced with wanton, sex goddess Miriam, and Io couldn't have been happier.

"Fuck." He gritted his teeth and gripped her hips, lifting his own off the bed to strengthen the physical connection between them.

"Can I make you come like this?" Miriam thrust forward, her heavy breasts bobbing as he dry-fucked her.

He growled then purred in response, locking his gaze to hers. "You could make me come with a look, baby. You have no idea what you're doing to me."

She rode him forward and back, massaging his hardened length with her body, and she laughed—a deep, throaty, sexy sound that curled his toes. She looked and sounded like a female who was only just beginning to realize her sexual prowess. She was both bashful and daring, as if she wanted to push further to see just how far she could go. Everything about Miriam was designed to give him pleasure. Her body, her mind, the way she moved, her voice...even her sultry laugh turned him on.

"I want you to come," she said. "I want to know what you look like when you do." Her hips swiveled against him. Yes, most definitely she was discovering herself, and she was doing it in his arms. God love her. "I want to know what you feel like." Her eyes sparkled, and she bit her lip.

Holy shit! She was driving him wild. Through clenched teeth, and with his fingers sinking more harshly into the firm flesh of her thighs, he said, "You keep doing that, and you'll get your wish." He thrust against her. If she wanted to play, he would play.

A self-satisfied smile spread across her face and she leaned down so her incredible nipples brushed over his chest as she rotated her hips around on him again. "I hope so."

"Something tells me you know more about pleasing a male than you've let on." Io slid his hands around to her ass and squeezed, pulling her against him as he pushed his hips up. "Or are you just a natural vixen?" He grinned against her mouth.

"If I am to be prepared for my future mate," she said, taking a dramatically proper air, "I need to know such things, don't you think?" Through her long lashes, she gazed at him, nibbling her bottom lip once more. Clearly, she was teasing him.

Io narrowed his eyes and growled. He didn't like the idea of anyone else with her but him. *He* was her future mate, but something told him he wasn't exactly what daddy had had in mind for a son-in-law.

Too bad. She was his, and it was time he made that perfectly clear.

Io flipped her to her back. She yelped as he rolled on top of her, held down her arms, and pinned her hips to the bed with his before shoving her long legs open with his knees. "Then I'm thankful you've prepared to please *me*."

A momentary flash of fear skirted through her eyes, and then she licked her lips, her gaze turning hot as she moaned and pressed her hips upward, rubbing herself against him.

"You like being manhandled, don't you?" What a thrill for her to react to him that way.

She nodded once, her lips curling into a shallow, mischievous smile.

"The king's daughter likes it rough?" Io let go of her arms and gripped her thighs to yank her closer.

Her breasts bobbed enticingly and her arms slapped down to the pillow on either side of her head as she stared up at him.

"You do, don't you?"

She panted for him, nodding again. "It seems I do."

Io purred low in his chest, beyond ready to show her what he looked like as he came. She had wanted to see, and now he would show her.

"Give me your hand."

She swung one arm toward him and he grabbed her wrist with one hand as he shoved his sweats down with the other. Her gaze dropped as her eyes opened wide. She sucked in her breath as he smacked her palm around his shaft and closed his fist over hers.

With maddening, harsh strokes, he forced her hand up and down on his cock, and Miriam watched in fascination, her lips parted and her nipples puckering as her breasts bounced with the force and speed of his stroking.

He wanted so badly to be inside her, to be staking his claim on her now. To let everyone know who she belonged to. She was his mate and no one else's. To hell with her father. To hell with the law. Miriam belonged to him and he would have her or die.

He glanced down to see that Miriam had dipped her free hand beneath the waistband of her sweats—his sweats. How sexy. She was masturbating, wearing his clothes, putting her heavenly scent on them, moaning with each breath, her eyes glazed with hunger to come again.

"That's it, baby. Come with me." He bent over her, supporting himself on his free arm, his spine tingling and his torso tightening along with his scrotum.

"Io...oh God...Io...." Miriam's chest rose and fell heavily, and her head thrashed side-to-side as if trying to break free the mounting pleasure restrained within her. The flesh of her breasts jiggled as she neared another glorious release.

Just watching her lose herself yet again was enough to send him over.

"I'm about to come, baby. Fuck. Yes. Oh fuck!"

Just as his abdomen clenched and his cock pulsed in their combined grasp, Miriam grunted and cried out, her body arching violently beneath him as she exploded with another powerful release.

"God, yes...fuck, but you're beautiful!" Io gasped and ruptured, shooting his release over her breasts and stomach, his entire body gripping and releasing so that he actually swayed forward and back through each orgasmic wave.

He hadn't intended for this to happen tonight. Io had planned on being good.

Really, he had been ready to remain chaste and proper. But then she had gone into withdrawal, and when she fell into the trademark shame that all addicts carried, his heart had gone out to her. He had wanted only to comfort her, soothe her, make her see that what she was going through was okay and normal, but her beauty when she had looked over her shoulder with eyes glistening with tears had captivated him. What had been meant only to be a gentle peck had, in an instant, morphed into a passionate declaration. From there, things had spiraled out of control, taking on a life of their own.

He had thought about her for two weeks. What he would do or say if he saw her again. How he would sweep her away and make her his. But he hadn't imagined just how powerful the pull she had over him was until she was actually here. What had been only fantasies suddenly became more real than any reality he had ever experienced. He hadn't been able to stop himself, especially after hearing he affected her the same way she did him, and now she lay beneath him, his release streaked across her abdomen, smelling of him, wearing his clothes, and breathing against his neck, looking like an angel.

The reality was better than the dream.

She looked up at him through the strands of tangled hair strewn across her face. They were both breathing heavily, and Io collapsed down on top of her as her arms wrapped around his back. He didn't even care that his semen still lay like an offering over the altar of her torso.

He couldn't speak. No words came to him. He was in the presence of his mate, the one chosen by Fate just for him. If someone would have told him a month ago his mate was waiting just around the corner and that she was the king's daughter, no less, he would have laughed in their face. He had been a ladies man, unbound by commitment and happy to live that way. But now, he was a lady's man—singular. Io belonged to just one lady, and he couldn't imagine going back to his old ways now that he had met and sampled a small taste of Miriam. She had already captured his soul and his heart, and no other female would ever be good enough to replace her. Io was now a kept male, utterly enraptured and owned by the female who sighed beneath him and shifted her embrace to hold him just a little more tightly.

"I don't want to leave," she said quietly against his shoulder.

"Then don't." Io burrowed his face into the side of her neck and whispered softly. If he spoke any louder, he feared he would destroy the moment. "Don't leave. Stay with me, Miriam. I don't think I can survive without you."

She turned her face into his and their lips met in a tender caress that deepened as she pulled him closer.

He couldn't wait to tell Arion the good news.

Oh wait...that's right. He and Ari weren't talking to each other.

Suddenly, he missed his best friend more than ever. The most wonderful thing that had ever happened to him, and he had no one to share it with. Now he knew how Ari had felt.

CHAPTER 19

T͟ʀɪꜱᴛᴀɴ ᴡᴀꜱ ɪɴ ᴛʜᴇ ꜱʜᴏᴡᴇʀ when Josie knocked on the door and poked her head inside.

"Yeah?" Tristan shook the water out of his hair.

"You've got an urgent phone call," Josie said.

"Who is it?"

"Gregos."

Gregos? What did he want? Tristan frowned. Gregos was Arion's father, but surely this didn't have anything to do with Ari or the fact that Ari had quit the team two weeks ago after Sev's incident with Gina. Maybe this had to do with the king. Gregos was one of King Bain's liaisons, but he rarely called Tristan at home to share official news. Shit, he hoped this wasn't royal business.

Ever since the king's daughter had been brought to the compound after overdosing on cobalt, AKM had been in a mini-uproar of gossip and excitement. Especially where Io was concerned. Io had touched Miriam, for God's sake. No one was allowed to touch the king's daughter, but Io had sat on her bed and brushed her hair. Io had fucking touched her and had spent time with her. And it had been clear Miriam had been taken by his charms. God, he hoped those two hadn't found a way to meet outside AKM or that the king hadn't found out what had happened. Tristan had done his best to keep the incident under wraps, but the rumors about Io and the princess had started almost immediately.

"Tell him I'll be right there," Tristan said.

"Okay." Josie closed the door.

Tristan didn't need any royal interference right now. He

was still trying to recover from losing Arion when he had already needed to add more members to his team to begin with. But AKM *was* King Bain's law enforcement agency. It wasn't called All the King's Men for nothing. So if Bain wanted to interfere, there was nothing Tristan could do to stop him.

King Bain had instituted the agency to enforce the truce between the vampires and their distant cousin race, the drecks. Drecks had always resented being inferior to the vampires. The fact that vampire blood, venom, and genes always superseded that of drecks gave the illusion that vampires were stronger, and in many ways they were. But drecks had ways of closing the gap between the two races so they appeared more equal.

Nowadays, AKM not only enforced the truce and maintained the peace between the races, they also battled mutants—mixed-blood vampires whose powers overtook them and changed them into rogues—and even got involved in human affairs.

With cobalt abuse severely on the rise, AKM was short-staffed and needed more enforcers, which meant the last thing Tristan needed was to deal with royal red tape.

He shut off the water and wrapped his towel around his waist then hurried out of the bathroom to the phone.

"Gregos? Hi. Sorry, I was in the shower."

"Sorry to interrupt you, but we have a situation."

"What kind of situation?" *Here we go.*

"The king's daughter has gone missing."

Tristan's gaze immediately flew to the windows. The blinds and drapes were still closed, so he knew it was daytime. Not good that the king's full-blooded vampire daughter was out in the world when the sun was out. "Shit."

"Yeah. Well, we tracked her."

The hair on the back of Tristan's neck prickled. He had a bad feeling about this. "Where is she?" *I don't want to know. I don't want to know.*

Gregos took a deep breath and cleared his throat. "The king's security staff traced the GPS in her phone to an address in the burbs. A check on the address showed it was a home registered to Iobates Liatos."

"Fuck." Tristan took a deep breath and blew it out, running his hand over his water-beaded face.

"That's right, Tristan. Io."

Shit, Tristan had been afraid of this.

"Yeah, I know. He's on my team." Tristan's voice snapped with anger.

"Is there something going on we need to know about, Tristan?"

The mere implication that he knew something and kept it a secret pissed Tristan off. As if he wasn't already angry enough hearing that one of his team members had the royal daughter in his home right now, doing God knew what to her. Because, he had to face facts, Io *was* the team's biggest playboy. He had fucked more women than a mortal porn star.

"What are you saying, Gregos? That I knew about this?" Tristan didn't care that he was yelling into the phone, at a liaison to the king, no less.

"Did you?"

"Fuck no! Look, I'm just as surprised and pissed off about this as you are."

Josie hustled into the room, rubbing her palm over her baby bump, her eyes filled with questions at why he was so angry. He shook his head and waved his hand then held up his index finger. *One minute,* he mouthed.

"Okay, Tristan. Fine. But I have to warn you. The king is livid. He knows Io's reputation."

Tristan had a feeling livid didn't even begin to describe just how angry the king was.

"What happens now?" Tristan paced in frustration, worried. He slicked his hand over his wet, blond hair.

"It all depends what we find when we get there."

In other words, if Io had fucked the princess, he was going to lose his head. Both of them.

"Fuck."

"No kidding. And I thought I had it bad with Arion."

Not that Tristan talked to Gregos much, but in two weeks and three other conversations, this was the first time Gregos had mentioned his broken relationship with his son. Gregos hadn't been pleased to find out Arion was gay and was quitting his job as an enforcer, and he had disowned him. Now it sounded like Gregos might actually be rethinking his actions.

"How bad could this get, Gregos?" Tristan said.

"Bad. You know how the king is about his daughter. He will kill Io if he finds he has been improper with Miriam."

"Isn't that a bit extreme, Gregos?" Tristan had to try to reason and negotiate a better outcome. It was his duty as Io's commander. "We don't live in the Middle Ages, anymore. Things are different today. The world is more lenient and humane."

"I'm not sure the king will be swayed, Tristan."

"Come on, Gregos. Work with me here. I can't lose another member of my team. I can punish him. I can file a reprimand, but—"

"Tristan, it's not my call."

"Goddamn it, Gregos! The king needs to get out more. He's quarantined himself in his fucking home for over a century. Things have changed. You don't just kill people because they touched someone!"

The line was silent and Tristan suddenly realized what he had done. He looked up to see Josie staring wide-eyed at him, her fingers over her gaping mouth. Criticizing the king was strictly taboo. And you never spoke profanely when talking about the king. It was an unwritten rule.

Gregos cleared his throat uncomfortably. "I will present your plea to the king, but don't hold your breath, Tristan."

"Please, forgive me. I didn't mean to speak so candidly. I'm...I just—"

"I know," Gregos said. "I understand."

Did he?

"It's just hard hearing I could lose him." Despite Io's misgivings when it came to females, he was the best hacker at AKM, and he was one of the best in the field, too. Io was a cocky cuss, but he got the job done.

"It's hard for all of us right now, Tristan."

"Understood." Tristan huffed and looked down, feeling defeated.

"The king has sent his personal security to retrieve his daughter and arrest Io. I'll let you know what they find."

"Thanks."

Tristan disconnected and hung his head.

"What's going on?" Josie said, touching his arm.

He hadn't even heard her walk toward him. "Io's in deep shit. The king's daughter is at his house right now."

"What?" Josie's eyebrows popped upward in surprise.

"Yeah. Exactly." Tristan grabbed the phone again and dialed. He needed to find out what happened on Io's shift last night before he did anything else.

"Yeah?" Sev's voice broke on the other end of the line. Tristan had obviously awakened him.

"Sev, it's Tristan."

Muffled noises came from Sev's end. He was probably getting out of bed. "Hold on a sec," he said quietly. He probably didn't want to wake up Ari. The two were still newly mated, so Tristan was glad he hadn't interrupted something more intimate between them than sleep. After several seconds passed, Sev spoke more normally. "Okay, what's up?"

"What went on last night?"

"What do you mean?"

"I mean, how the hell did the king's daughter end up at Io's house?"

Sev didn't say anything. Either he was confused or guilty. Tristan would bet on the latter, or maybe both.

"Look, Sev, I know you were on patrol with him last night. Miriam went missing, and the king's security team traced her to Io's."

"Her phone. Damn it." Sev heaved a loud sigh. "Look, Tristan. I wanted to say something, but she was in bad shape and Io took her to his place. He said he knew how to take care of her, and I believed him."

"What? Another OD?"

"Yeah. She was unconscious when we got to her."

Looked like King Bain had bigger problems he needed to worry about than whether or not Io had dipped his wick and stolen Miriam's chastity. Miriam was turning into an outright junkie, and yet the king was more concerned with where she slept than getting her off the shit.

To be honest, she was probably in the best place she could be right now. Io had knocked the blue shit a year ago, after a long battle with his addiction. There was no doubt in Tristan's mind that Miriam was in capable hands to get her through her overdose and maybe even save her life. Just as long as Io's capable hands didn't wander over her body. Tristan wouldn't take that bet, though. Not with the way Io had looked at her when she had been brought in after her first overdose, and vice versa. Miriam had been as attracted to Io as he had been to her.

Tristan felt that the worst was yet to come with this sitch. Lucky him, being Io's commander and all.

"How did you two find out she needed help?" Tristan said. "I don't recall seeing it dispatched on the report." The night had been fairly quiet, as a matter of fact.

"Io got a direct call."

"Oh?" Now, that was interesting. "From whom?"

"Miriam's friend, Persephone. The girl who was engaged to Ari for all of an hour." A bitter edge colored Sev's words. Apparently he was still sore over recent events, even though he and Arion had ended up together.

"Yeah. I remember."

"She called AKM and asked for him directly. Dispatch treated it like a personal call and texted Io."

Tristan would need to modify the protocol for personal calls. This could have saved him some time if he had known about it sooner. "Okay, so Io got the call, and Persephone told him…?"

"She was in hysterics, but the gist was that Miriam had overdosed and Persephone thought she was dying. We found them, Io took Miriam to his place, and when I got there, he had treated her and she was sleeping."

"Anything else?"

"Nope."

"He wasn't inappropriate with her?"

"No. Like I said, she was sleeping. But that was hours ago."

In other words, anything could have happened since then. And knowing Io, it probably had.

"Okay, well, shit's going to hit the fan. Apparently, King Bain has day walkers on his security team because Gregos just told me the king has sent security to retrieve her and arrest Io."

"Fuck."

"Yeah, fuck."

Neither said anything for a second, and Tristan wondered if Severin was putting two and two together. Severin was one of two day walkers on his team, Trace being the other, but Tristan didn't want to give him an outright order to go pull Io's ass out of the fryer, so he sure hoped the guy would take a hint.

"What do you want me to do?" Sev finally said a few seconds later.

Tristan grinned slyly. "I don't know what you're talking about."

"Yeah, sure you don't."

"You'd better hurry, Sev. You don't want to be late."

"Maybe I'd better call Trace."

Tristan nodded. Now Sev was thinking. "No. Just go. I'll call Trace."

Sev huffed. "Man, you're gonna be in trouble."

Right now, Tristan didn't care. He wouldn't lose another member of his team. And this wouldn't be the first time he'd gone against the king. He glanced at Josie with a fond smile. "Don't you worry about that. Now, hurry up, Sev. Get there and save our boy. I just hope we're not too late."

"Roger that."

Io had Miriam tucked securely against his body. They were fast asleep when the commotion upstairs startled him to the land of the waking.

"What the fuck?"

It sounded like a whole platoon was storming through his house. He jumped out of bed and went for his gun. What time was it, for Christ's sake? Sleep kept the clock out of focus for a second, but then the time registered. It wasn't nightfall, yet, so whoever had invited themselves into his home was one of three things: human, dreck, or day walker. He really hoped for human, but he doubted he could be so lucky.

The door to the basement blasted open and a rush of footsteps descended.

Miriam cried out and yanked the sheets up to cover her nudity as four day walkers wearing the king's insignia burst into the room, assault rifles drawn.

"Get down!" One of the males pointed his gun at Io. "NOW!"

Io dropped to his knees as the other three went for Miriam.

"Don't you touch her!" The deep, possessive echo in his voice startled even him, and he realized he was breathing hard, suddenly wide-awake, with his hands curled into fists and pressed against the floor as if ready to push off and attack.

The four military-style fuckers who had invaded his home all looked at him in surprise. They had obviously caught the mated male tone of his voice just as he had.

The one guarding him stepped forward and backhanded him. "We'll deal with you soon enough, asshole. You dare defile the king's daughter?"

"I defiled no one." Io's words spat out like cobra's venom. His body even felt coiled and ready to strike.

"We'll see about that," the soldier said. The barrel of his gun remained trained on Io's forehead.

Miriam fought off the other three as they went after her again. Rage pushed up within Io. That was his female. She was his to touch, and his alone. The old saying, *Touch a vampire's mate and you touch the mated vampire himself, so best touch lightly or not at all*, came to mind. His mating bond to

Miriam fired full force. He would die for her. He would kill for her. And right now, both options looked like keen possibilities.

When one of the other males grabbed Miriam's arm and yanked her forcibly from the bed so that the sheet fell away and her naked breasts were revealed, Io knew he wouldn't be able to hold himself back from attacking. These males had no right to look upon his female's nudity. That was his right, and his alone. Her bare breasts belonged only to his gaze. They were his to touch, his to suckle. Simply by viewing her flesh, these men were violating his natural rights as Miriam's mate. And they had to pay for their injustice. As her mate, he had to make them pay.

"I said, don't. Touch. Her."

A mated male vampire was a dangerous creature. Only one entity was more dangerous, and that was a mutant: a mixed-blood vampire who had been biologically and genetically consumed by its power. You didn't mess with the mate of a male vampire unless you didn't mind dying.

The other four men in the room seemed to sense this, too, but they were too late. They had already fucked with what belonged to him.

With a spitting hiss that formed into a shriek, Io leaped and tackled the male in front of him, plowing his fist into the guy's nose with such force it knocked him out. One punch. Whoomp! And the fucker was out cold.

The other three scattered and tried to train Io in their sights, but he was fast. He pounced on one of them and slammed him against the wall before rolling back and tossing him over his head. He crouched and hissed as he jumped to shield Miriam, his fangs bared.

Shit went from bad to worse as the fourth male regained consciousness and groaned as he dabbed his fingers against his shattered nose and the blood that had splattered his face. Now it was four against one. Not good odds, but almost fair being that Io was in full-on, mated male rampage.

As long as they didn't try to come after Miriam again, things would be fine. They just had to leave Miriam alone and not try anything heroic.

He got the sense the four were communicating mind-to-mind. Not good. They were plotting. He put his arm up over Miriam and pushed her back so she was more fully behind him. No way would he let them take her. Over his dead...

Two disappeared then suddenly reappeared in front of him. ...body.

They each gripped his arms before he could evade them. His muscles bunched and flexed as he pulled and tried to escape, but they dragged him into the center of the room and shoved him down to his knees while he hissed and growled in warning. It was clear that if they let him go, he would kill the first one of them he could get his hands on.

"Hold him still. Joseph, get her." The one with the broken nose stepped in front of Io.

"She's mine!" Io's voice sounded like a demon's, as if he were possessed. And, in a way, he was. He was captive to his need to protect his mate, to defend her, to honor her and keep her safe.

But he was failing.

"She belongs only to the king. Your foul hands aren't worthy to touch her excrement, dog."

Miriam shot forward and slapped the guard. "How dare you speak of me in such a way, Donovan!"

Io looked around at her and saw that she held his T-shirt to her breasts with her other arm. Her eyes blazed with fire, her chin high and proud.

Donovan's face spun away from her strike, and he averted his gaze as he turned back toward her, holding his head in shame. "Forgive me, Daughter of Bain."

"My name is Miriam."

"Daughter of Bain, you know I am not allowed to address you so casually."

Miriam's plaintive gaze captured Io's in such a way that he realized she longed for what he had given her, even if it had only been for a few hours. He had treated her like she was normal. He had called her Miriam, and even Miri. For just a short time, she had known what it felt like to be average, an everyday citizen, not the daughter of the king. Io got the sense that was what she wanted. More than anything else, she wanted to be treated like she was anything but the king's daughter.

It was becoming clearer what kind of existence Miriam lived inside the king's home and what the allure was to cobalt. For Io, using cobalt had been about risk and living—experiencing the bad just to see if he could overcome it. For Miriam, using was about rebelling against the system and escaping from the oppression she lived under every day.

"This male has defiled you, Daughter of Bain."

"He has not." Fear flashed in Miriam's eyes as she looked back at Donovan. "My virtue remains intact."

"Maybe so, but the scent of his seed covers your body."

"Donovan. No. I forbid you."

"He must die, Daughter of Bain." Donovan took out his sidearm.

"I forbid it!" Miriam tried to slap the gun away, but Joseph pulled her back.

Io's blood boiled. How dare that filthy male handle his mate so roughly.

Donovan cocked the gun. "The king demands it, and his orders are the law."

"NO!" Miriam cried out as Donovan stepped forward and pressed the barrel of the gun between Io's eyes.

Suddenly, the four males froze, becoming like statues.

"Well, well, well. Hello, girls." Trace's deep voice drew Io's gaze around to the stairs. His right arm was stretched out in front of him and the fingers on his hand were splayed. "I knew finding the front door open hadn't been a good sign," he said over his shoulder to Severin, who was coming down the stairs behind him.

"Don't touch her!" Io growled at Trace, still in the throes of mated obsession.

"Cool out, lover boy. I'm not here to pull a sneaky peek at your date." Trace moved his fingers and the guards' grips loosened on Io's arms. He pulled free and immediately rushed to Miriam and pulled her out of Joseph's hold before turning to watch Sev follow Trace into the room.

"What the hell are you thinking?" Sev said, shaking his head.

Io's hold on Miriam tightened. "What are you two doing here?" he said, avoiding Sev's question.

"Saving your ass. Apparently." Sev's gaze fell on the bed then flicked to him and Miriam in silent accusation.

Trace slid a matchstick between his lips and ass-parked against the wall, his arms crossed, his mind still holding the four guards in animated suspension. "You mind telling us what the fuck is going on here? I mean, if I'm going to die, I'd like to know why."

"We're not going to die," Sev said.

Trace rolled his eyes in Sev's direction. "Newsflash, Einstein. These are the king's guards." Trace gestured with a back-and-forth wave of his finger. The four men actually teetered side-to-side. "And that is the king's daughter." Trace pointed at Miriam. "We are now accomplices to the shit that was going on here."

Sev strolled around the four males and sighed in frustration before shaking his head.

"Did Tristan know about this when he called and told me to meet you here?" Trace chewed on the matchstick.

Io glanced back and forth between Trace and Sev. "How did Tristan get involved?"

Sev picked up Miriam's purse and pulled out her phone. "GPS tracker."

Io exchanged glances with Miriam.

"Shit. I didn't think about that," she said.

"Don't worry. It'll be okay." Io held her close, and she kept the T-shirt pressed against her chest. He didn't like how precariously the fabric hung, almost revealing one of her nipples. He ushered her to the bathroom. "Go ahead and get dressed."

She stepped inside and within seconds rejoined them, covered up.

Sev shook his head. "What the hell went on here, Io? What were you thinking? You two slept together?"

"That's none of your concern."

"Like hell it's not," Trace said, chewing the matchstick. "You better not have fucked her, or Tristan will have your ass."

Miriam got in Trace's face and glared at him, repeatedly jabbing her index finger against his chest. His brow furrowed and his mouth screwed up in a half-grin as he looked down at her finger. "We did not *fuck*," she said. If words could cut, Trace would have been bleeding.

Trace raised his gaze to hers and sniffed abruptly. "Then why do you smell like cum?" He cocked his head at her, one brow arched, his arms still crossed and his body still calmly leaning back against the wall.

Miriam gasped. "How dare you."

Io rushed head-on toward Trace. "Fuck you! You don't talk to her like that."

"Bite me, Romeo." Trace scoffed and waved him away, causing the guards to rock back and forth again.

Io pulled Miriam away from him, glaring at Trace. "Up yours. This is my—" He snapped his mouth closed. He had been about to say she was his mate, but thought better of it. "This is the princess. You treat her like one." He pointed at Trace then backed away, taking Miriam with him.

"Holy shit," Sev said.

Io glanced at him. Sev's eyes were filled with suspicion. "What?"

"You didn't. Please tell me you didn't mate her."

Damn it. Sev was a smart SOB. Io spun on him, finger pointed at his chest. "I did not violate her. And you can keep your holier-than-thou bullshit to yourself, too, asshole." Maybe if he diverted their attention from mating to sex, he could get them to drop the subject.

Sev knocked Io's hand aside and barreled down on him until the two stood chest-to-chest. "I'm not talking about fucking, asshole. I'm talking about mating. As in, tell me you are not her mate. Tell me you did not take her as a mate, Io." If Sev had been a dragon, he would have been breathing fire.

So much for diversion. Oh well, it had been worth a shot.

Io took several deep breaths, holding Sev's gaze. But what

could he say? Sev had hit the bulls-eye. Io was a mated male now. His biology had fired up and formed a connection to Miriam the instant he had arrived home with her. He finally looked away and turned toward Miriam. She stood motionless a few feet away, her eyes wide and her mouth open as if she wanted to speak but couldn't find the words.

"Yes. She's my mate."

"Jesus." Trace pushed off the wall and paced toward the four guards.

"Shit." Sev took a step back.

"Io?" Miriam tilted her head, confusion painting her face. "What are you saying?"

He walked toward her and took her hands. Time to fess up. "Somehow over the past twelve hours, my soul chose you, Miri. My mind and body mated to yours."

Fear crossed her features. "Oh my God."

"I'm sorry." Wait a minute. Why the hell was he apologizing? He shouldn't be apologizing for mating her. "I mean, I'm not sorry, but I know this isn't what you need right now."

"No, no. It's not that. I mean, well…" She fidgeted. "My father won't approve."

"Do you?" That was all that mattered, in Io's opinion. Everything else was subordinate. He didn't care what King Bain thought. After all, he hadn't mated the king. He had mated his daughter.

Without hesitation, she nodded. "I do." Her hand tightened around his.

"Great." Trace leaned against one of the guards. "Now what do we do."

Sev took out his phone and punched in a number.

"Who are you calling?" Io didn't like this.

"Yeah, Tristan? We've got a problem." Sev spoke into his phone.

Why was Tristan so involved? What the hell was going on?

Sev continued. "No, nothing like that…hold on…Tristan, calm down…Tristan! He mated her, goddamn it!"

The dead air on the other end of the line was so loud Io could hear it. Then Tristan's voice broke through the silence loud and clear. "WHAT?!"

Sev actually flinched and held the phone away from his ear for a second, then pulled it back in. "No, not like that. As in, he's her mate. Io's her mate, Tris."

The string of expletives that shot out of the phone left nothing to the imagination. Everyone in the room instantly knew how up a pole Tristan was over that little newsflash. "PUT THAT ASSHOLE ON THE PHONE NOW!"

Sev held the phone out to him. "He wants to talk to you."

"Yeah, I get that." Io took the phone. "Hey, boss."

"Don't fucking *hey boss* me, you fucking son-of-a-bitch. What the fuck got inside that fucking head of yours? Fuck!"

Io had never heard Tristan use the f-word so many times in one breath. Another first for Io's list of accomplishments, right up there with, *Yeah, I took a mate. Can you believe it?*

"Get off my back!"

"FUCK YOU! I will *not* get off your back, Io! This was a major fuck-up on your part."

"Taking a mate is a fuck-up?! You're joking, right?"

"No, I'm not joking, asshole. She should never have been in your house to begin with."

"And if she hadn't, she'd be dead now, so which would you have preferred? Me dying because I didn't save her life, or me dying because I did and ended up finding out she's my mate. Because either way this stacks up, I'm dead, right? I might as well die doing something *noble*."

Miriam stepped up beside him and wrapped her hands around his tattooed forearm, concern in her touch.

He shifted, pulling her closer.

Tristan huffed and paused, then said in a more controlled voice, "No one says you're going to die over this, Io."

"Well, the four royal guards in my basement say otherwise."

"What?"

"Yeah, I was about to be executed when Wonder Stud and his sidekick, Eighties Hair Band, showed up." Io looked up to see the long-haired Sev glare at him and mouth, *Really? Eighties hair band?* as he flipped him off.

Io shot the bird back at him then flipped one to Trace while he was at it—just for good measure since he was in such a giving mood. Meanwhile, Miriam tucked herself against his side.

"Okay, okay." Tristan took a deep breath. "Tell Trace to clean up their heads and send them out of there. Then I want all three of you here in thirty, especially you. You got me."

"What about Miriam?"

"Send her home. The sun's setting, so it's safe for her to go outside."

Io wrapped his free arm around Miriam's waist as if protecting her. "Tris. No. She needs my care. She'll go into withdrawal and she'll need—"

"That's not your concern right now," Tristan said.

"Like hell it's not!" Io glared as if Tristan were sitting in front of him. "She's my mate. I won't have her—"

"Goddamn it, Io! You send her ass home NOW!"

"What about the calling?" Io didn't want to be away from his mate when the calling started and gripped him in sexual heaven. To be away from Miriam when the calling began would be more like hell. His body would drive him into agony without her. An agony that would rival cobalt withdrawal. Maybe even put it to shame.

"We'll figure this shit out, Io, but right now, she needs to go home. Trace can implant new memories in the guards' heads about what they found, we can get this mess cleaned up, and then we'll figure out how to get you and your mate together. Now, you keep your shit together and don't do anything stupid. I know how you are, Io, so you check your fly-by-the-seat attitude and get your ass in here now!"

Checkmate. Io was out of moves. For now, anyway.

"Fine." He disconnected and handed the phone back to Sev.

"What did he say?" Sev said.

Io looked at Trace. "He wants you to give these guys new memories about what they found when they got here. Something innocent, I'm guessing."

Trace made a face like he didn't approve, but he would play nice. "Okay. I'm on it."

Io looked at Miriam. "You have to go home."

"No." She shook her head and snuggled closer.

"You have to, baby." He caressed her cheek.

"I don't want to." She tightened her hold on him as if it would allow her to stay with him.

"I don't want you to, either, but we need to sort this out. We'll be together. I promise."

She shook her head again. "Io...? I'm worried. What if...?"

She would go into withdrawal again soon. They both knew it.

"Take a shower so my scent isn't on you, okay? I'll get your clothes out of the dryer and make you another cup of elixir. You'll need to drink it before you go home. And I'll fill a water bottle for you. Hopefully, it will get you through long enough so you don't go into withdrawal before I can see you again."

"What if I do?"

"Fight it. You'll have to fight it, Miriam. But I'll be with you soon. I promise, okay?"

She looked terrified, as if she felt she wouldn't be able to fight her addiction without him by her side.

"Miriam, you're strong. You can do this."

She took a deep breath and nodded.

"Now, go on. Get in the shower. I'll bring you your clothes."

She disappeared into the bathroom and Io turned back around. Trace was puppeteering the four guards up the stairs.

Sev was staring at him.

"What?" Io said.

Sev placed his hands on his hips and looked at the floor then back up at him. "Man, I never thought I'd see this day."

"What do you mean?"

"Fuck me, but you're mated."

Io glanced at himself in the mirror. The playboy was off the market. He didn't look any different, but clearly he was a Lothario no more. "You know, I always thought Ari and I would take mates at the same time if I ever took one." He grinned and looked back up at Sev. "I just never knew it would happen like this."

Sev walked over and clapped a hand on Io's shoulder. "He'd be proud."

"You think so?"

"Hell yeah. I wish Ari could see you now. I mean, you're a damn bonehead, but I guess you can't help who you mate, right?"

Io nodded. If only Ari *could* see him now, but he had messed up their friendship so badly that he couldn't even share this monumental moment with him.

"Damn, Io. You sure know how to pick 'em." Sev chuckled.

"Go big, or go home." It was a motto Io lived by.

Sev's chuckle turned into an outright laugh as he threw his head back and all that long, blond hair fell off his shoulders. "No shit!"

CHAPTER 20

MIRIAM SHOWERED, dressed in her newly cleaned clothes, choked down a mug of the noxious but miraculous elixir-water, and joined Io and his friends upstairs.

Things were complicated now. What were they going to do?

"Hey." Io smiled at her, looking relieved to see her.

She knew how he felt. "Hey." Being near him instantly set her at ease.

His friends hovered nearby, the guards gone. Whatever Trace had done to them was finished, and it looked like they had been sent on their way. Events were now set in motion, and nothing could be undone. How were she and Io going to be together? This was her home now and leaving was as wrong as snow in summer. Was this how it felt to attach to a mate?

Io handed her a one-liter bottle of water. "Here. Take this home with you." He nodded toward the bottle as he brushed his palm gently down her arm.

"Thank you." She took the bottle and stuffed it into her oversized designer bag that functioned as a purse.

Trace turned his gaze toward the door right before it opened. Another male walked in. He had long, black hair that hung past his shoulders and black, groomed stubble lining his jaw and upper lip. His dark, shrewd eyes surveyed the room. "Girls," he said with a nod.

"Micah?" Io frowned at the newcomer as he casually slid his arm around her waist.

Micah clasped hands with Trace. "Brother."

"Glad you could join us, pretty boy," Trace said.

"Why are you here?" Io's fingers curled around the curve of her hip.

Micah seemed to make Io nervous, and Miriam glanced out of the corner of her eyes at him. He was already so protective of her. Her mate. Wow! She had a mate, just like that. Everything had happened so fast she still couldn't grasp the idea. How was she supposed to act? Feel? Behave?

"I'm the chauffeur." Micah popped a piece of gum in his mouth and eyed her. "And it'll come to you." He smiled at her. A kind, knowing smile.

Io looked back and forth between her and Micah, his grip tightening around her waist. "Get out of her head, Micah. And what do you mean, you're the chauffeur?"

"Wait, wait, wait a minute." She held up her hand, shaking her head. "What are you two talking about?"

Trace smirked and crossed his arms, leaning back against the wall as Sev sighed and paced.

"I'll let you tell her while I get a drink." Micah walked past them into the kitchen.

Io absently stroked her arm. "Micah tends to see everyone's thoughts." He turned and glared over his shoulder at Micah. "Which he will *not* do with you. Understood, pretty boy?"

Micah filled a glass with water and came back into the front hallway, drinking, eyeing them both. But he didn't nod, and he didn't agree with Io. Just stared, his gaze full of power and knowledge, piercing them both as if dissecting them.

Miriam shivered. Was Micah burrowing into her thoughts right now?

Trace chuckled and looked at his feet with a shake of his head.

"I said, is that understood?" Io's face was stone hard, his eyes not wavering.

Micah sighed and set the glass down on the table next to him. "You know I can't, Io. But I promise to be nice." With a flourish, Micah dismissed Io and looked at her with a lopsided grin. "Your highness, I'm here to return you to your car and escort you home."

Who was this guy? And what was with the *highness*

bullshit? She would put her foot down on that shit right now.

"Okay, hot shot." She shifted her weight to the side and waggled her finger in front of him. "I don't know who you are or what planet you're from, but one, get out of my head, and two, you can stop with the royal titles." Miriam was going to lay the law with Io's friends right off the bat. She got enough of the ass kissing at home. She didn't need it here, and she certainly didn't need a mind sweep.

The smile that broke over Micah's face could have stopped traffic, and he glanced toward Trace. "Looks like we have a real she-devil here," he said. He held out his hand. "I'm Micah, Miriam. Pleasure's all mine if you've got balls that big."

Io growled softly, and Micah's gaze slid toward him, but he didn't take away his hand.

She arched an eyebrow, wary, but shook his hand. "Good, because I hate the fucking hoity-toity royal crap." Her gaze swept the others. "That goes for all of you. Any of you call me anything resembling your highness and I'll twist your balls so hard you'll curse the day you were born. Is that clear? My name's Miriam. Not Princess, not Your Highness, not Daughter of Bain. Miriam. Got it?"

Micah and the others laughed, nodding as they exchanged approving glances.

"You've got your hands full with this one, Io." Micah chucked his shoulder.

"I know." Io pulled her close and nuzzled her cheek. "And I love it."

She turned into him.

"Does that go for me, too?" he said.

"What?"

"I can't call you Princess?"

Heat filled her cheeks. "Okay, maybe just you."

He pulled her closer, shielding her. "I don't want you to go," he said quietly.

Micah clapped Trace and Sev on the shoulders. "Boys, outside."

Sev began to protest. "We need to get going. Tristan—"

"Tristan can keep his panties twisted up his ass crack a

few minutes longer," Micah said, finishing Sev's sentence. "You're a mated male, Sev. You know how it feels. Let them have a minute to say goodbye, for God's sake."

Trace was already outside, and Sev reluctantly followed Micah, glancing over his shoulder at them. *Hurry up,* he mouthed.

Micah smacked his head. "Leave them alone."

"Hey!" Sev whipped his gaze around, scowling as he brought his hand up to the back of his head, smoothing his hair back into place.

The front door closed and Miriam heard them arguing outside, but turned back to Io. "When can I see you again?" Her pulse quickened as his eyes met hers.

"I don't know. Soon, I hope." His hold on her tightened and he pulled her closer. Their noses touched.

"God, Io." She inhaled his scent. If only she could stay. Dread gnawed her insides, emptiness threatening to take hold. She should be excited about embarking on this new path with him, her mate. All her life, this was what she had wanted, but instead of locking herself away with Io to revel as humans would during a honeymoon, she had to leave him. All because of her father. He ruined everything.

If only they had made love, at least she could take that with her. Would she ever feel him in that way? So much could still go wrong. Her father could still rip Io away from her if he found out what had happened between them.

"How is this going to work?" she said, her voice quiet.

"I don't know, but it has to." He kissed her ear, then lower, and still lower, leaving a trail of kisses down the side of her neck.

Leaning her neck to the side ever-so-slightly, she purred.

"That is so damn sexy," he said, bringing his face around and dipping his forehead against hers as she swiveled her head back toward him.

"What?"

"That you purr when you're aroused. Like a male does." Io's hands skimmed down the small of her back and over the upper swell of her ass.

"Like a male does?" She arched one eyebrow and let her lips brush over his.

He nodded. "I've never met a female who purrs like you do. I like it. A lot."

She raked his broad chest with her fingers. "I like *you*."

He grinned against her mouth. "I certainly hope so."

"Oh, I definitely do."

"We'll be together, Miriam. I promise. They can't keep a mated pair apart."

Her gaze dropped. "*They* aren't my father. He has a way of seeing things differently." Why had she been born into such a rigid family? Why did she have to be the princess? Why couldn't she have a normal father and a normal home life? One where she wasn't bound to inane rules and laws about who touched her, kissed her, swept her off her feet. Because then being with Io wouldn't involve what amounted to an act of treason. She wouldn't have to scheme behind closed doors just to be with him, and she would be free to mate him as nature dictated.

"Surely, he won't keep a mated male from his mate."

She wrapped her arms around him, hanging on for as long as she could. "I don't know, Io. I don't know what he'll do."

"I need to be with you." His arms tightened around her and he held her close, as if his life depended on it. And as a mated male, it probably did.

"I need to be with you, too." What were they going to do? How could they make this work without setting off her father or becoming fugitives?

They stood in the hallway, holding each other but not speaking. There were no words to convey how they felt, but the message got through loud and clear. They would find a way to be together. Neither of them would tolerate the separation for long.

Finally, Miriam pulled away. She not only had to battle her father and the separation from Io, but also her addiction. How would she survive? Sure, Io had given her a bottle of the water and elixir, but that would last her only a day or two.

He leaned forward and kissed her. Unlike last night, she was now used to the feel of him, and she kissed him back, her lips molding perfectly with his.

She wasn't sure how long they stayed like that, savoring every taste, each caress, stretching time in a desperate attempt to remain rooted in place forever.

But forever ended too soon when a knock came at the door. "Ladies? You ready?"

Io groaned as his mouth stilled on hers. She opened her eyes and met his gaze, frozen in the moment, memorizing every line and contour of his face.

"Time to go," she whispered. Her heart cried, but she would not shed tears. If she did, it would blur his face, and she didn't want to remember him that way.

"Uh, yeah," he called to his companions, clearing his throat. He looked at her. "We will be together, Miri."

She smiled even if her heart wasn't in it. "I like that you call me that. Nobody calls me that."

"Why not?"

"It's too informal." No one was allowed to be so casual with her. "But I like it with you."

"Well, then I'll make sure to call you that more often." He took her hand and led her to the door.

"Feel free to do a lot with me more often." Heat burned her cheeks, her gaze flitting back and forth over his face before lowering, her heart racing. Why did she suddenly feel so bashful?

He stopped and touched her chin, lifting her face so he could look at her. "I'll remember you said that." He gave her a lusty look.

Her heart fluttered, and she bit her lip. Io made her body sing with just a single look, his eyes so mesmerizing. "I expect you to teach me many new things, Io."

"I plan on it." He kissed her. A chaste kiss, sweet, but full of promise.

When he opened the door, three pairs of eyes turned toward them.

Micah looked at her. "You ready, Miriam?"

"No, but I guess I have to be." She squeezed Io's hand as he gave her a reassuring glance.

"Micah, you take care of my female," Io said, not looking away from her.

His female. Hearing him call her that made her stomach fill with warmth and spin in her belly like a tornado.

Micah rested his hand on Io's shoulder. "Nothing will happen to her on my watch. Trust me." Micah looked over his shoulder. "Trace, why don't you come with? Give Io more peace of mind."

Trace stepped to her side like a bodyguard then looked at Io, his pale eyes shadowed with confidence. "Mike and I will take care of her."

Sev shook his head. "No, Trace. Tristan will want you with us at the compound. He'll want a debrief."

"Tell Dad I'll be there as soon as Mike and I know Miriam's safe." Trace exchanged glances with Micah, who smirked before heading off to the Suburban. "I'm sure he would want the king's daughter to be of the utmost importance, right?"

"Fine, whatever. Io, let's go," Sev said, waving toward the other Suburban. He sounded irritated, but resigned.

Io locked up the house and joined Sev. "I'll see you soon, Miri."

She nodded, hoping like hell he was right. "Soon." She needed to emphasize the point, as if it wasn't clear enough that she was going to be miserable without him.

Sadness engulfed her heart as she watched Io climb into the other Suburban while Trace ushered her to the passenger side of the one Micah was in. Io had shown her something no other male had ever shown her. His body had given her a pleasure unlike any she could imagine. God, his hands, his lips, the way he looked when he came. He was a magnificent, virile male.

"Okay, I so didn't need to see that," Micah said, putting the Suburban in reverse.

"Huh?" Miriam glanced at him, brow furrowed.

"Io coming." Micah made a sour face.

Trace chuckled, leaning back and glancing out the window.

Oh, that's right. Micah could see her thoughts. "Do you mind?" Miriam tucked her hair behind her ear and gave him a stern glare.

"Sorry. Habit."

"Well, break it around me." She squirmed. He had seen what had been meant only for her. How rude, if not embarrassing.

"You sound like my mate." Micah pulled out onto the street and hit the gas. "And don't be embarrassed. I don't think much of it, and I can't stop it, anyway. I'm not trying to be rude."

"You'll get used to it, Miriam," Trace said, his voice flat and unaffected.

She didn't think she would ever get used to someone invading her thoughts, but there wasn't much she could do about it, from the way it sounded. Might as well change the subject.

"You're mated?" she said to Micah. He seemed too full-on military hard-ass to be mated, but then, he *did* have a soft edge to him. After all, he had been the one to kick the others out so she and Io could have a private moment together. She doubted an unmated male would understand such a need.

"Yep, I'm mated," Micah smiled privately, as if he was remembering some secret moment between him and whoever the lucky lady was.

Trace leaned forward between the seats. "Micah was a real asshole before Sam came along. Amazing what the right female can do for a male."

Miriam sensed a measure of sadness in Trace's voice, but he grinned as his pale eyes met hers. Whatever he was thinking would stay hidden behind his congenial façade.

Micah made a left turn. "I think what Trace is trying to say is that you, little Miss Fireball, have made Io a changed male."

"How so?"

The corner of Micah's mouth turned up. "I've known Io a long-ass time, and I have never—and I mean *never*—seen him behave so admirably with any other female. He looks at you with hearts in his eyes. I've never seen him like this."

Miriam smiled, her heart swelling. "I'm in love with him." The words came out before she could stop them.

"Duh." Micah huffed and hit her with those intense eyes of his, flashing a knowing grin.

She grinned back then glanced down at her lap before looking out the window. The day had been incredible. She had experienced things she had only dreamed about, and just remembering how Io's finger had felt inside her and the way his body had shuddered against hers—

Micah raised one hand off the steering wheel. "Okay, okay, okay. Enough of that. Shit, woman!"

Miriam whipped her head around. Micah was frowning, his jaw clenched. He dashed a sideways glance toward her as he hissed out a heavy, impatient sigh between his teeth.

"Jesus, Miriam! Think of something else, would you? You're going to get me killed if your father finds out I've seen you naked."

She crossed her arms and leaned to the side, glaring at him. "If you'd stay out of my head, you wouldn't have to worry about my father." Really, though, she couldn't bring herself to be mad at the guy. She was too lovesick.

"Give it up," Trace said, rolling his gaze toward hers. "Micah dipping into your mind is like breathing or blinking his eyes. It just happens. He can't stop it."

"Yeah, but some people are excellent blockers." Micah shot Trace a glance.

"Hey, I don't want you roaming through my merry brains. Those are my secrets, brother."

"What-the-fuck-ever," Micah laughed low and deep. "You just don't want me to see those little pink tutus you wear every Friday night when you play with your Barbie dolls."

"Fuck you, Micah."

Micah roared with laughter, slapping his hand on the steering wheel.

Trace looked at her and pointed to Micah. "Can you believe this guy? Pink tutus. He knows I only wear the blue ones he gave to me when he outgrew them." Trace smirked as Micah threw him an eat-shit glance.

"Damn, Trace! Don't be telling the female all my secrets." Micah mock-tsked.

Miriam broke into laughter then Trace joined her. She had never felt so at-ease. She didn't just want to be in Io's world, she belonged in it. His friends and coworkers were her kind of people, and these two were a riot together.

"You're not bad yourself, Miri," Micah said, grinning.

"Stop it!" Miriam slapped his arm.

All three erupted into laughter again, and Miriam didn't even realize she wasn't thinking about her next hit of cobalt… or her father.

Io's world was good for her. No, it was perfect.

CHAPTER 21

Io ALREADY FELT LOST WITHOUT MIRIAM, and they had only just parted.

"How's it feel?" Sev said.

"What? Being mated?"

Sev nodded.

Io thought for a second as a gentle smile curved his lips. "Fucking awesome, but a bit scary."

"Why scary?" Sev glanced at him then looked back at the road.

"Because I don't want to lose her." No, that wasn't it. "Because I *can't* lose her. If her father denies my claim to her..." Io shuddered. He couldn't even think about the king denying his right to Miriam without having a physical reaction. "And the calling, Sev. Damn, he can't deny me if I'm her mate, right?"

"I don't know, Io. I can't believe he would do something like that. It's against the law to deny a male's mated claim to a female, but..." Sev took a heavy, worried breath. "This is Miriam we're talking about."

Io's foot tapped restlessly. He fisted and unclenched his hands over and over. He was a nervous wreck without her. How could he survive if he wasn't allowed to see her?

"Shit, Sev! Is this what it was like for you and Ari?" Io blurted out the question, frustration and aggravation raising his voice.

Sev nodded. "I was fucked up for real, man. You saw. You were there. I got my chest blown open because I didn't give a fuck and got careless. All because I thought I couldn't have him. And now?" Sev shook his head. "If anything happened to Ari, I'd die. I know I would."

"Shit." Io was beginning to see just how undeniable the mating call was. Even if Arion had been strictly hetero, he would never have been able to refuse the mating call to Sev. To do so would have meant insanity or death if Ari was connected to Sev the way he was to Miriam.

In only a short time, Io already felt that way about Miriam. Despite how quickly it had happened, the mating bond had formed a powerful tether to her before he had even realized it. If he had thought his cobalt addiction had been bad, he could already tell his withdrawal from losing Miriam would be devastating if the king took her away. His chest already ached. His nerves were raw, and he was about as fidgety as a crackhead who had just downed three shots of espresso. Miriam wasn't just an addiction, she was an obsession.

He glanced at Sev, seeing his relationship to Arion differently now. Sev and Ari had only been following biology when they mated each other. They hadn't had a choice. It wasn't like Arion and Sev had chosen to be gay. Choice had nothing to do with it. Io could see that now. You loved who you loved. You mated who your biology chose for you.

"Why are you looking at me like that?" Sev watched him out of the corner of his eye.

"Sorry, I was just...." Io sighed. "Shit, I've been an ass. I've been horrible to you and Ari. Fuck, man, but I'm sorry."

Sev stiffened and his lips formed a tight seal as if he didn't know what to say.

Io took another deep breath and looked out the window. For so long, he had been the resident gay-basher at AKM. Nobody had been more vocal about putting down homosexuals than he had. Sure, he still had some deep-seated discomfort, because...well, for one, he couldn't just change overnight, and for another, the idea of a man pumping another man's ass made him feel weird, but that was *his* hang-up. Other people didn't have to live their lives according to his version of what he liked.

And Sev had made a good point last night. Io had no problem with two women together, so really, what was the big difference if two men were together?

So much had changed in the last twenty-four hours. He had already been second-guessing himself about how he had treated Ari, but now that he was mated, he was seeing things regarding Arion in an even broader light.

"Do you think Ari will forgive me?" Io spoke softly, cheeks burning. He looked in Sev's direction but couldn't meet his eyes. He had treated both of them so badly. After all Ari had done for him, Io hadn't been able to see past his own prejudice and show support during a time when Ari needed him.

Sev cleared his throat. "I think so."

"I mean, I'm still working shit out." Io shifted uneasily. "It's still weird to think of you and Ari, you know, fucking, but—"

Sev cut him off. "Why? Do you think about everyone like that? I mean, do you routinely think about Micah fucking Sam? Or Tristan fucking Josie? Or Trace fucking whoever he fucks?"

Io stiffened, swallowing nothing but cotton. His mouth was so damn dry. "No."

"Then why would Ari and I be any different? You can hang out with us, come over and watch the game with us, and I promise we won't drop down and fuck in front of you, Io."

Io bowed his head and closed his eyes, rubbing his palm back and forth across his forehead. He was so messed up. "I guess I still have a ways to go before I'm cured of my problem, huh?" He was such an ass.

"Well, admitting you have a problem is a start."

He had heard that before. In rehab. The first step toward recovery was admitting you had a problem. If you couldn't, then you were just wasting everyone's time. With cobalt, Io had known he had a problem by about a week in to his addiction. Still, it had taken him months to admit it, even when Arion had put up with his sorry ass day in and day out to keep him from killing himself.

"Do you?" Sev said.

"What?"

"Do you have a problem?"

Io met Sev's gaze as they stopped at a red light. Did he? Where Sev and Ari were concerned, did he still have issues that needed to be addressed before he could truly say he was a recovered bigot and no longer walked around with a prejudiced shroud over his eyes? He nodded slowly, the same shame he had endured during his cobalt rehab overtaking him. "Yeah. Yeah, I do."

Sev fought back a grin, but Io could still see something close to pride flicker across his face.

"What?" he said.

"Just you." Sev turned back to front. "I wish it were Arion here with you instead of me. He really needs to hear what you just told me."

Io shrugged and rolled his eyes, feeling about as pathetic as a shaved cat. "Well, if King Bain doesn't kill me for mating his daughter, maybe I will."

"My God. I never thought I'd see this day." Sev hit the gas as the light turned green. "I know I'm still the new guy on the team, but I had you pegged as the resident playboy right from the start. A Grade *A*, chauvinistic ass. I didn't think I would ever really like you." Sev chuckled and glanced at him. "But now? Look at you. I can't believe you're the same guy. Miriam's been good for you, my man. Real good. I sure as hell hope this shit works out, because I'd hate to see you if it doesn't."

"Me, too." Io looked out the window and took an uneasy breath, his sweaty palms pressing together as he fidgeted. "Me, too."

He wondered if Miriam had made it home, yet. And whether or not she would ever be allowed out of the house again.

CHAPTER 22

MIRIAM WAVED TO MICAH AND TRACE, who had followed her home after dropping her off at her car, then she turned into the driveway. The security gate opened automatically, registering the tracking chip in her car. It closed behind her as she drove up to the house.

Trace had filled her in on the story he had implanted in the guards' heads, so if she stuck with the script, she and Io should be okay. Everything depended on her keeping herself together, though. She reached her hand into her bag and palmed the bottle Io had given her, swallowing nervously. Hopefully, this would all work out.

She pulled her car into the garage and entered the house through the kitchen, a massive room where upwards of six chefs and countless assistants worked when her parents held parties for the liaisons, consultants, or other distinguished guests.

"Miriam!" Her father's voice boomed from his office as she approached, and a moment later he barreled out the door into the hall.

He stood nearly seven feet tall, an imposing presence that intimidated others as much as his title did. But he had stopped intimidating her a long time ago. She was still a babe by vampire standards, but old enough to have grown a spine.

"Father." She stopped in front of him with her chin high, shoulders squared.

"Where have you been?"

She raised her eyebrows in mock-surprise and innocence. "Didn't your lackeys inform you when they returned?"

"They returned without you in custody, and I had ordered them not to return without you."

In custody. How nice. "Oh, so I'm a criminal? Am I to be a prisoner, too? Perhaps I should be fitted for my cuffs and shackles now. Would that work for you? I assume you've already added bolts and chains to my room's décor." She was pushing her luck, but who cared? Just being around her father made her skin prickle.

Couldn't he just give her some damn space and ease up with the Gestapo brigade that followed her around as if she were an enemy spy?

Her father growled and Miriam could swear he wanted to slap her for her insolence. But that was one thing he never did. For all his barbaric ways, he never hit her.

"So, are you saying Donovan failed to relay where I've been?" Only she could be so insubordinate with her father. Not even her brother dreamed to talk back the way she did.

"I want to hear it from you. And I wish to know why they failed to retrieve you as I ordered."

She heard a door close quietly down the hall. Probably her mother or one of the many servants hoping to avoid being struck by shrapnel if she and her father made like a P-51 Mustang and a Japanese Zero in a dog fight during World War II. "I was with one of the members of AKM."

Her father's entire face frowned, not just his eyes.

"I had overdosed—"

Her father pulled back and looked away as he always did when her cobalt use entered the conversation, as if avoiding her addiction would be enough to safely tuck the blemish on his family away and out of the public eye. She had only started using in the last two months, but after her infamous overdose two weeks ago, word had spread quickly throughout the vampire community despite her father's attempts to quell the wildfire gossip. His liaisons and consultants weren't even allowed to bring it up in conversation. It was as if he thought that if no one talked about it to him, it wouldn't be true and would just go away.

"Yes, Father, I use cobalt!" She stepped forward, not to be

ignored. "I shoot it up, I snort it, whatever it takes to give me my next high! I'm an addict, Father! And one way or another, you will have to deal with that!"

"ENOUGH!" Her father snarled and hissed as his fangs punched out in anger. "My daughter is not an addict!"

He couldn't even address her in the second person. He spoke as if she were one of his consultants and his daughter was elsewhere while he discussed her.

"Yes, I am! I'm an addict! ME!" She slapped her hand against her chest, leaning forward." Quit ignoring me! Quit ignoring my addiction! It's real! You can't pretend or ignore it away!"

He refused to meet her eyes, and she scoffed at him. If he felt so strongly that she was a disappointment as a daughter, he was just as disappointing as a father. To him, she was nothing more than another person to lord over. Curling her lip, she shoved past him.

"Did he touch you?" Her father said.

He—Io.

She stopped but didn't turn around. "Yes."

The air bristled with aggression.

"How?" he said, his voice a low growl.

"Well, it was either he touched me or Donovan would have brought me back here in a body bag. Or an urn if the sun came up before he found me. Which would you have preferred?"

He didn't answer.

"Maybe you should think about thanking Io instead of killing him," she said before striding away, her arms itching. Shit. Not home fifteen minutes and she already needed a hit. She had gone hours without suffering withdrawal at Io's home, but in her own, she was jonesing right after walking through the door. The potion Io had given her wouldn't last an hour at this rate.

CHAPTER 23

UNABLE TO CONTAIN HIS ANTICIPATION, Bishop slipped from his bed and wrapped his robe around him, tying it at the waist. He didn't even bother with slippers and ended up slinking barefoot through the quiet hallways and rooms, into the kitchen, and farther back to the metal door that led down to his underground lab. Quietly, he descended the stairs.

Milky splashes of light illuminated the shadows as he made his way past the tables and counters of equipment. Monitors hummed, and beeping noises occasionally sounded as the subjects remained monitored during the overnight. One technician stayed up to observe them, but remained in a detached room.

Bishop passed cell after cell of vampires. Some slept. Some rocked restlessly, and it looked like one had died. But he was interested in only one. His prize. Maddox.

When he had flown out over a week ago to meet the two vampires who he had been communicating with for over a year, he hadn't expected to find such a valuable commodity. Bishop had gone into the meeting simply looking for another resource to add to his growing cache of suppliers and allies. The two vampires, Jacob and Haslet, reported having a powerful, ruthless assassin under their control, and when Bishop had inquired how they had managed that, they led him to the basement. Maddox had been lying in an induced coma on a makeshift medical bed that was much too short to hold him. Maddox's feet had hung off the end.

"Who is he?" Bishop had asked.

"The assassin's father." Haslet had replied.

Apparently, Jacob and Haslet held Maddox's safety over the assassin, threatening to kill him if the assassin refused to do as they instructed. The assassin—neither of them would tell Bishop his name—had lost a brother and his mother centuries ago. All he had left was his father, and from the sound of it, the assassin would do anything to ensure his father didn't come to harm.

"And what of this assassin? Will he work for me?" Bishop had been eager to employ the services of such a weapon.

"If we tell him to, he'll do anything we ask," Jacob told him.

"Tell me about him."

"The assassin?"

"Yes."

"What's there to say? He's a mixed-blood with extraordinary talents."

Bishop had perked up at the mention of a mongrel. And that was when the seeds of an idea had begun to form. He had searched for a vampire like Maddox for a long time. He'd known upon seeing him that he wanted him for his own, but learning that his son was a mixed-blood caused his interest to spike beyond mere wanting. Whatever it took, Bishop would obtain Maddox.

"Sell him to me." Bishop nodded toward Maddox as he made the demand.

"What?" Jacob exchanged glances with Haslet, who held up his hand as if to calm him.

"How much will you pay?" Haslet seemed more ready to deal than Jacob.

"Whatever it costs."

The two exchanged glances again, dollar signs lighting up in their eyes.

"Ten million dollars." Haslet suggested.

A mere drop in the bucket of Bishop's hefty cash reserves, and well worth spending for such a fine specimen.

"Done."

Both Jacob and Haslet gasped, but in a pleased way.

"On one condition." Bishop held up his finger at them. "His son, the assassin, is not to find out." If they were using

Maddox to keep him under control, and Bishop ended up wanting to employ the assassin's services down the road, keeping him in the dark about his father's transfer to Bishop was necessary.

"Agreed, but how do we pull that off?" Jacob asked.

"Not my concern. Just make sure he doesn't."

The two vampires nodded, resolved to the deal they had struck with him. "Done."

The three had shaken on it, Maddox had been turned over to him, and he had left with the promise that the assassin would be in his back pocket any time he needed to order a hit. It had been a win-win-win meeting.

As he stopped in front of Maddox's cell, he licked his lips, unable to tear his gaze away from his treasured acquisition. He reached into the pocket of his robe for his case of Sobranies, but in his excitement to get to the lab, he had forgotten to grab them off his bedside table.

"Damn." He tsked at himself and pulled his hand back out of his pocket. If only he could savor the moment with a cigarette.

Maddox remained in the corner of his cell, head down. His long, dark brown hair hung over his face and past his bent knees, which supported his thickly muscled arms. The vampire was apparently sleeping.

As Maddox's custody had been transferred to Bishop, Jacob had explained that Maddox had lain in a sort of self-induced stupor or hibernation for decades and had only recently re-animated as if brought out of the spell he had been under. Bishop had asked what had sent the vampire into such a state, and Jacob had told him that, apparently, when Maddox had lost his mate and other son, he hadn't been able to cope, as most male vampires can't. But his human mate had been a witch or some voodoo sorceress and had sheltered Maddox in protective magic even after her death. In fact, it was as if her death itself had activated the magical mechanism within Maddox to make him fall into sleep so he didn't harm himself or die as a result of losing her. Had she hoped to prevent the mental breakdown that claimed the lives of nearly a third of the males who lost their mates and left the other two-thirds in a state of mental decrepitude marked with violence and self-loathing?

Clever human.

The truth was, Jacob and Haslet had been relieved to be rid of Maddox now that he had awakened. It was why Haslet had been so eager to deal. They weren't sure what he would do or how he would behave now that the spell on him had finally worn off, and they hadn't been eager to find out. That was why they had kept him in an induced coma, because whether or not he would melt down in a rage of destruction once he assimilated the reality that his mate was still dead had kept everyone on pins and needles. Maddox could just as easily react violently as he could with submission.

But Bishop would have none of leaving Maddox in an induced coma. If the big vampire was awake, Bishop would make sure he stayed that way if he could. All the better to see the vampire's mettle and what exactly he was capable of. Bishop wouldn't be able to surmise what to expect once the experiments started if he couldn't study Maddox's behavior and mental state.

With a tap of his fingernail on the glass, Bishop switched on the microphone with his other hand.

"Wake up, my friend." He wiped a touch of saliva from his lip, all wide eyes and greedy eagerness.

The only sign that Maddox had awakened was a slight twitch of his left hand.

"Are you hungry, Maddox?" Bishop tilted his head, studying the impressive musculature of his acquisition, his palm smoothing over the front of his robe.

Slowly, Maddox lifted his head. Strands of hair still hung over his face, but one pale eye peeked through. But what an eye it was. Unlike earlier when Apostle had straggled along for a tour and Maddox had been dull and lifeless, Maddox's gaze now burned with inner animation even as his body remained still as stone. What looked like pure hatred seared Bishop from the single, pale iris he could see through all that thick hair. Maddox's brow was set in a hard line and scrunched over the bridge of his nose. He looked like a pissed off lion crouched in the bushes.

But instead of leaping swiftly, Maddox slowly leaned forward, his movements a deliberate study of deadly grace. Drawing back his shoulders and arching his neck, Maddox pushed out his chin as his lips pulled back from his teeth in a snarl. Long fangs distended from both his upper and lower jaws as a long, deadly hiss issued Bishop a warning.

What a lovely sight. Only the most ancient of the Slavic vampires had lower fangs. Having both upper and lower fangs was a trait only the most barbarous vampires of prehistory possessed. Still, how rude of his guest to hiss at him like that.

"I see we will have to teach you some manners." Taming the wild ones always made him smile.

Not that a lot of wild vampires came through his lab, but he had seen one or two. Bishop had methods to ensure they broke eventually, though. Breaking Maddox and reconstructing him would be a crowning achievement.

The caged vampire shifted and planted one massive hand on the floor and pushed himself up. The beast moved like a gorilla, graceful and measured, despite his incredible size. Bishop was surprised. He thought one such as Maddox, who had just awakened from a centuries-old sleep and had limbs as long as the Jolly Green Giant's, would be as clumsy as an ox. Not so. Maddox moved with fluid grace. Living art.

Once on his feet, Maddox's stature was even more impressive.

"My, you are a tall one." Bishop licked his lips, his gaze traveling up and down Maddox's naked body.

What he had planned for Maddox would change everything, but he mustn't be too eager. Bishop needed to make sure nothing could go wrong before he pulled the trigger on his next series of experiments.

In only two steps, Maddox was standing at the front of the cage, glaring down at him from the other side of the reinforced Plexiglas. As he breathed against the glass, clouds of condensation formed.

Bishop had to turn his head up at a sharp angle to look into Maddox's eyes.

"Very tall." Bishop's body shivered with anticipation, and he grinned.

Maddox had to be over seven feet tall. The tallest vampire Bishop had ever seen.

"Dreck...where my son?" Maddox spoke in broken, heavily accented English.

Bishop had as yet never heard Maddox speak, but his voice did not disappoint. In fact, his voice was so deep and guttural, it created its own echo.

Narrowing his eyes, Bishop grinned at the way Maddox looked at him with pure hatred. Unfortunately for Maddox, he wasn't in control here. Bishop was. Bishop held the knowledge that Maddox had missed since falling into slumber decades ago, and only Bishop held the power to grant Maddox comfort or pain, release or captivation.

"Your son is dead." It would make breaking Maddox easier if he thought he had no one left.

"No." Maddox's frown deepened and his breathing grew labored as he clenched his fists then slammed them against the glass.

"Oh yes. You are all that remains of your family, Maddox." Bishop took a step backward, one arm crossed over his torso and the elbow of the other resting on it. He nonchalantly inspected the fingernails of his raised hand. "Consider me your family now, dear boy."

"NO!" Maddox pounded his fists against the Plexiglas, but it didn't give.

The look on the vampire's face was priceless. His gaze danced over the Plexiglas as if he couldn't believe it hadn't broken. Maddox had never seen Plexiglas before. It hadn't been invented the last time he had roamed as a free vampire. And this Plexiglas was reinforced.

With a roar, Maddox bared his fangs and struck the Plexiglas again, and again, pounding and punching with all his strength until his knuckles cracked and bled.

Streaks of blood covered the inside of the glass by the

time Maddox fell to his ass on the floor, sweat covering him and his chest pumping hard for air.

"Impressive." Bishop's mouth ticked into a manic grin.

Maddox looked up at him, his pale eyes seething. "I kill you...dreck."

"Oh, I very much doubt that, Maddox." Bishop knelt down and studied his new pet. "I have plans for you, Maddox. You and I will become very close in the next few weeks. Very close."

Bishop pressed a button on the panel next to the cell. A hissing noise followed as vapor entered the cell from a vent in the ceiling.

"Fuck y—" Maddox fell backward into unconsciousness before he could finish.

With his heart beating hard with exhilaration, Bishop sat down outside Maddox's cell and watched him sleep, his blue hand pressed against the glass. The vampire was turning out to be a better acquisition than he had first thought. This would be good. Very good.

"Impressive indeed," he whispered.

CHAPTER 24

"**Damn, Io, you've got it bad, don't you?**" Tristan said.

Io glanced up at Tristan. "Huh?"

Tristan shook his head and gave him a look. "You're going to be as bad as Micah, aren't you?"

"What are you talking about?"

"Haven't you heard a word I said?" Tristan frowned.

Had Tristan been talking? Io couldn't remember. "I guess not. Sorry."

"Okay, let me start over. Pay attention this time."

Io nodded. He would try, but he was a spider's nest of agitation. Being away from Miriam after mating her not even twenty-four hours ago was like getting married without a honeymoon.

Newly mated males needed to be with their mates immediately after mating, especially once the calling started. Otherwise, they went stir crazy. And the way Io was feeling, his calling could start any minute.

Tristan snapped his fingers. "Earth to Io."

"Oh, yeah, sorry."

"Do I have your attention now?"

He nodded.

"Good. Maybe I'd better give you the condensed version since your attention span is a bit short-circuited right now. What I was saying was that we need to find a way to soften your mating to Miriam in a way that might go over better with the king. This has all been too abrupt and could backfire."

"What did you have in mind?" Io rubbed his knuckles up

and down his sternum, trying to ease the ache in his chest.

"I want to use your cobalt addiction. Spin it like this: 'Io has first-hand knowledge of cobalt addiction. We can treat her and keep it all hush-hush. Move her into Io's home for a few weeks so he can see her through recovery and withdrawal.' That kind of thing. We could ease into your mating her more slowly, once he's gotten used to you and sees you're not a threat and mean no harm. And I'm sure he would appreciate the matter of privacy and keeping this out of the public eye. If she is admitted here at AKM, it would be common knowledge. What do you think?"

It was brilliant, as far as Io was concerned, because hadn't he had a similar idea while cradling Miriam in his arms earlier?

"What about my work schedule?"

"I'll remove you from rotation for as long as it takes." Tristan punctuated his statement by lightly thumping his fist on his desk. "I'd be taking you out of rotation, anyway, due to your calling, so it's neither here nor there."

"We could play it that she'll need care twenty-four-seven. And we can say that she'll need strict maintenance care after her withdrawal has subsided." Io was feeling more and more confident about their plan.

"Yes, and that she would need after-care every other day."

"By then, I would hope we could tell him we're mated," Io said.

Tristan held up his hands. "I know. But we can hold that ace in our pocket if we need to if he doesn't seem ready to hear it. It's just a thought. It'd be a bitch if you're still in your calling at that time, but hopefully you'll be far enough into it or past it so it's no longer an issue when that time comes."

So far neither of them had mentioned the obvious. Io took a deep breath and held it for a minute.

"Tris"—he emptied his lungs, holding Tristan's gaze—"you know what this means, right? As far as the law goes regarding Miriam."

"About touching her?"

Io nodded. "Yes. Obviously, I have and I will."

Tristan looked as nervous as Io felt. "Yeah. Yeah, I've considered that." Tristan looked down at the pen he was fiddling with on his desk. "Damn, Io, but you're a pain in my ass." Tristan's words lacked the punch they'd had on the phone earlier.

"Sorry."

Tristan snorted and leaned back, spreading his hands on the desk. "Don't be sorry. She's your mate."

Io regarded him a moment, then said, "If she gets pregnant, we won't have long to hide what's happened."

"I know." Tristan settled more deeply into his chair, not meeting Io's gaze.

Io's brow furrowed. Something was on Tristan's mind. "Why are you doing this, Tristan? You could get in a lot of trouble."

Tristan stood and walked across the small office, paused, then turned and paced back. When he sat back down, his gaze fell on a picture of Josie on his desk. He blew out a heavy breath and dropped his head, jaw set, his brow knitted.

"My reasons are my own, Io, but you have a natural right to be with her. You have a valid claim. You and Miriam should be together." Tristan shifted in his chair, his gaze still on his desk, his fingers loosely interlaced.

Io looked from Josie's picture to Tristan, then back to the picture. There was something Tristan wasn't saying. Tristan had never mated Josie, not the way he had mated Miriam, but that hadn't stopped him from breaking the king's law to change her into his *davala*. Was that what was troubling him? That he had broken the law with Josie and was now helping Io break the law, too? Io didn't think so. He got the sense there was more to whatever was going on with Tristan than that.

The fact that Josie was even pregnant when he had never experienced a calling with her was a miracle. Whatever was going on, Tristan didn't look happy. Was he feeling the heartache of knowing that he and Josie would never be true mates, or did something else burden him? Whatever it was, Tristan didn't seem interested in talking about it.

When Tristan didn't say anything further, Io said, "Okay, when?"

Tristan snapped out of whatever reverie his mind had traipsed into and cleared his throat. "I'll place a call to Gregos as soon we're done here and lay the foundation. I won't tell him you're already mated. Oh, and the others have strict orders not to speak of it, and I want you out of here ASAP so no one else picks up on it. At any rate, I'll talk to Gregos and hopefully he can persuade the king to put Miriam in your care. I really don't see any way he could say no. He wants to keep this private. The black spot on his family is an embarrassment. You getting her off *blue* could make you look like a savior to him and he'll be more receptive to your mating." Tristan paused and held his hands palms up. "It's as solid a plan as we're going to get."

"I like it. Let's do it."

"Okay, get out of here." Tristan turned toward his phone. "I'll call you at home as soon as I hear back. Try to relax. This will work out. It's a good plan."

It *was* a good plan. It was an *awesome* plan. It would work. It had to.

CHAPTER 25

MALEK TOSSED HIS WEAPONS INTO HIS LOCKER.

Great, now Io was mated. First Micah, then Sev and Ari, and now Io. La-dee-fucking-da for them.

At least the team had been given the night off while shit got sorted out with the cluster fuck Io's mating had created. He could go to the Black Garter, buy a private dance or two, then go home and take care of the nagging ache in his balls.

"You going to the Garter, Malek?" Micah said, his voice quiet even though they were the only two in the locker room.

"Get out of my head, Micah."

"Actually, I'm making it a point to stay out of your head right now, and you of all people know how hard that is for me to do." Micah paused, tossing a pair of gloves in his locker. "You've just got that look."

"Yeah? What look is that?"

"The same one you've had since Gina left. Only worse"

Malek momentarily froze at the mention of Gina's name. "That's none of your business."

Micah huffed. "You've changed, Mal."

He shoved his feet into his casual shoes after tossing his combat boots into his locker. "So have you, Mike. What of it?"

"Yeah, but you've changed for the worse."

"Fuck you."

"See, you're starting to sound like old me." Micah brushed his fingers through his hair.

"Yeah, well old you knows the real score, doesn't he?" Malek tossed him an over-the-shoulder look that made it clear that he was referring to an even older Micah than

Micah had been talking about.

The two of them went way back, all the way to the time when King Bain's father, Bain the First, ruled the vampire race. In fact, Micah had trained the current King Bain in combat.

Back then, Micah had been Malek's best friend. They had done everything together, and everyone had mistaken them for brothers. They looked enough alike to pass as brothers, too, except Malek was shorter than Micah. They both had black hair that fell over their shoulders, groomed facial stubble, same build. Micah's eyes and mouth were more angular, though. Malek had softer angles to his face.

But the similarities didn't stop there. They had similar pasts, too. They had both lost mates in the Middle Ages. Micah had fallen further into the depths of living hell than Malek had, but only because Malek had hidden it better. Now, everything was unraveling. Micah had found a new mate and was returning to the hero he had been so long ago, but Malek's despair had opened like an old, unhealed wound to seep sewage throughout his system.

And Gina was the cause. Damn her to hell.

Malek stood up and shut his locker. "Mind your own business, Micah."

"Not gonna happen, and you know it. It's time you faced facts, old friend."

Malek spun around and shoved Micah against the line of lockers. "I've had enough of your shit. You have no idea what this is about." He knew it was a lie. Micah knew everything and always would. It was what made Micah...well, Micah.

Micah arched an eyebrow and hit him with a level glare. "You're the one who let her leave, dickhead."

He jerked back and glared at Micah, but he couldn't find the words to offer a smart enough retort.

Micah pushed forward and got in Malek's face. "If you wanted her so badly, why did you let her leave, dumbass? Oh wait, because you still haven't dealt with Carmen's death. That's right."

"You fucking bastard." Malek didn't care if he was half a

foot shorter than Micah. He was still strong and held black belts in every martial arts discipline. He could hold his own. He shoved Micah back hard. "I knew you'd been in my head."

When was Micah not in someone's head? But he usually didn't talk about the shit he found there.

He took a swing at Micah, who blocked him with one hand and sent his other fist into Malek's gut with such ease it looked like the guy hadn't even tried. But that was Micah. It was stupid to have gone up against him like that, because he had the hand-to-hand down like a pro. If Malek was a black belt, Micah was a double black belt.

Malek bent over Micah's arm, his diaphragm paying his lungs a visit as he coughed and gasped for air.

"Have I got your attention?" Micah grabbed him by the collar of his shirt and lifted him up before pushing him back against the lockers.

Malek could only cough and sputter as he tried to catch his breath.

"Good," Micah said. "Now, maybe you'll listen to me. Wake up, Malek. You need to get over this shit now. Your reason for living is out there, asshole. Go. Find. Her."

Malek shook his head, anger and resentment building and filling him with blackness. "Fuck you." He coughed. "I don't want that bitch." Maybe if just kept saying that, it would become true.

Micah sneered and dropped him like he was cold leftovers not fit to feed to his dog. "You can't lie to me, Malek." He jabbed his finger against Malek's temple, making it clear he could see everything—including the truth—inside Malek's melon.

He smacked Micah's hand away.

With a huff, Micah pressed forward and got all up in Malek's grill. "Deny it all you want, but you know I know the truth."

"Yeah, well this time you're wrong." Malek would prove it. Carmen's memory was too pristine to soil with Gina or any other female.

"Uh-huh. Sure I am." Navy blue eyes bore deep into

Malek's. "If I could find my way back, so can you, old friend."

The sincerity of Micah's words dug into Malek's soul, but it only made him angrier. No one had a right to make reference to Carmen. Not even Micah.

Malek pushed him away. "Leave me alone, *old friend.*"

Micah shook his head, obviously disappointed. "Have it your way." He turned for the door. "Tell the girls at the Garter Sam says hi." With that, Micah opened the door and walked out.

Malek sat back down on the bench. Fuck Micah. Who did he think he was, sticking his nose where it didn't belong?

Suddenly, he didn't feel like going to the Garter, anymore. He wanted something else. The woman he had taken home last night. She had been nice.

He left the locker room and hit the underground parking garage where he got in his SUV and pulled out.

In less than ten minutes, he was trolling the streets around Four Alarm, sniffing the air for the woman's scent. Was Jess working? Would she be available? Would she want to go with him again after he tossed his cookies after fucking her last night? Surely, she would. No one else would pay her what he would.

Five minutes later, he spied her leaning down on the passenger side of a car up ahead. She was talking to the driver and reaching for the handle when Malek pulled up and parked on the other side of the car, blocking traffic.

"Jess!"

She popped up and looked at him over the top of the car, and he nodded his head for her to come with him.

"Hey, buddy, she's mine." The driver of the car shot an angry, resentful look his way.

"Wrong, *buddy,*" Malek said, glaring at him. "She's coming with me." He flashed a stack of cash at Jess.

She hustled to the front of the guy's car and Malek pulled up so she could jump in.

"Hi," she said as he quickly pulled away from the curb. "I didn't think I'd see you again."

"Turns out I had a change of heart."

She smiled. "You want to call me Gina again?"

Malek grinned at her. "How about I just call you Jess tonight?"

She took the money he held out and shook her head. "Baby, you can call me anything you want."

Good then. It was settled.

He headed toward his house.

CHAPTER 26

MIRIAM PACED IN HER ROOM. So much had happened in the past twenty-four hours. Being cooped up here drove her nuts.

A light knock came at her door and Persephone poked her head in.

"Seph, hey. What are you doing here?" What a surprise. Under the circumstances, she assumed she wouldn't even be allowed guests.

Seph stepped inside and quietly closed the door. "I came with my dad. He's with the other liaisons and consultants, meeting with your father." Seph's curious grin spread over her face. "So?"

Miriam sat down on her bed with its sheer, lacy canopy. Like Io's, the bed had been custom made, but unlike Io's, it was shaped like a giant oval, not a square. But the dainty canopy was where the princess persona stopped. Miriam had thought it provided an interesting contrast to the black, faux leather comforter and red, silk pillows she had decorated the bed with.

Looking around the room, all the décor contrasted with the furniture. An antique bureau was draped with a black lace runner that hung down both sides. And gargoyle bookends guarded her volumes of classic literature on her handcrafted, cherry wood desk. Two walls were painted a drastic midnight blue, and the other two were a more soothing shade of cream. Lavishly framed portraits of dragons, sorcerers, and other mystical creatures adorned the walls alongside scenic vistas...and even a couple of gorgeous Japanese murals.

Everything in the room was of the finest quality and taste, but the décor made it clear that the decorator was in the middle of an identity crisis.

"So...what?" She said. Her cheeks blazed and she fought back a grin. Clearly, Seph wanted to know what had happened with Io, but she wasn't sure how much she should tell.

Seph flounced into the Elizabethan chair beside the bed. "How did it go with Io? That's what."

"Oh, him." Miriam waved her hand and shrugged.

"Yes. *Him*. You know, the one you were all gaga over." Seph huffed. "Stop playing, Miri. I know he curls your toes."

Miriam issued Seph a sideways glance as she sat down on the edge of the bed and smiled wide then fell back. "Oh God, Seph. He's . . ." she couldn't think of the right words to describe just what Io was and what he did to her.

Seph got up and joined her on the bed, laying down next to her, propped on her elbow. "Yes?"

Miriam turned her head and laughed at the look on Seph's face.

Seph slapped her arm. "Stop it! Now tell me!"

"Hey, okay!" She rubbed where Seph had slapped her. "I'll tell you."

They sat up again and Miri pulled the canopy around the bed, a habit that had formed in her youth when she wanted to disappear from her life. When the canopy was pulled, she fell into her own private world where nothing bad could touch her. Not even her domineering father.

She crawled into the center of the bed with Seph and they sat facing each other, legs crossed.

"Okay, spill," Seph said, her face full of anticipation.

What to tell and what not to tell? Miriam pondered all that had happened between her and Io. The good, the bad, and the ugly.

"Things started out bad. I was messed up when I got there, as you know." Miriam rolled her eyes and picked at a piece of lint on her comforter.

"Yeah, but I can tell something happened." Persephone wiggled closer.

"Oh? How can you tell?" Miriam arched one eyebrow.

Seph squirmed and lifted her shoulders as she leaned forward. "You have this I'm-so-in-love glow about you. Did he kiss you?"

Miriam rolled her eyes again and looked away, trying not to smile. But before she could stop herself, her face lit up. She had to be glowing.

"He did, didn't he? Oh my God." Seph's mouth dropped open and she gasped.

"Maybe a little." Miriam laughed. Seph looked so funny, all gaping astonishment.

Persephone shook her head, smiling. "I knew it!" Sadness filled her eyes for only a moment, but Miriam saw it.

"What's wrong?" Miriam scooted closer and took Seph's hands.

"It's nothing." Seph glanced away as if ashamed to be Debbie Downer.

"No. What is it? Something's wrong. Tell me." Miriam leaned to the side to catch Seph's gaze.

With a sigh, Seph tried to smile, but her gentle, blue-grey eyes remained sad. "Don't get me wrong. I'm happy for you, Miriam. But...."

"But you're thinking about Arion, aren't you?"

Seph nodded. "Yes. But not so much Arion. Sure, I liked him, but I had been more excited at the prospect of being mated, even if Arion never formed a biological link to me." She sighed again. "For a few hours, I had been so happy." A faraway look shone in her eyes.

"Your mate will come, Persephone. And when he does, you'll never give Arion—or any male, for that matter—another thought. You'll be so thankful the mating to Arion fell apart. Your true mate's touch will send you to the moon." Miriam squeezed Seph's hands and her face lit with the knowledge of how Io made her feel. She knew from experience what finding a true mate felt like, and nothing compared. "You'll be the most precious thing to him, and he'll honor you in a way no other male will be capable of."

Seph cocked her head to the side, watching Miriam closely,

her blond brows knitting together. "Miriam?"

Miriam looked at her. "What?"

"Did Io mate you?"

For a moment, Miriam said nothing, but she felt the color drain from her face. It wasn't that she didn't want Seph to know what had happened, but she hadn't meant to blurt it out so soon.

"Oh my God! He did, didn't he?" Seph's face lit up.

There was no use hiding the truth. "Yes." She sounded like she was admitting to doing something she had been told expressly not to do, but in a way that said she would do it again if given the chance. "He did."

Seph gave her a stern but playful look. "When were you going to tell me?"

"I'm telling you now." Miriam shrugged innocently.

"Uh-huh. Okay, so you have to tell me everything. You do know that, right? Because if he mated you, then I know he broke all kinds of your father's rules and touched you."

Miriam smirked and rolled her eyes. "You would bring that up, wouldn't you?"

"Sorry, but it's true."

Miriam wondered just how much she should tell Seph. They were best friends, but in a way, she wanted to keep Io all to herself a little longer. At least the juicy parts.

"Come on, Miri. It's obvious something happened between you two." Seph paused. "I have to live vicariously through you, Miri. What's it like to be a mated female?"

Io had called her Miri. The thought made her grin. Outside her father, only Io and Seph did that. Only they were so casual with her.

Taking a deep breath, Miriam said, "God, Seph, he's so wonderful. He's perfect." She spoke wistfully. "He treats me like I'm a normal person, not the *king's daughter*." She made air quotes with her fingers as she said it. "And he's such an incredible kisser."

Seph pretended to swoon, her eyes going dreamy and misty all at once. "I knew he would be."

Miriam nodded, blushing. "He showed me things, too."

Seph bit her bottom lip conspiratorially, as if she realized that no one else knew what Miriam was about to tell her. "Really? Like what?" Then she gasped and looked at her with shock. "You didn't…? He didn't…. You're not de—?"

"No, no!" Miriam waved her hands in front of her. "We didn't have sex. He didn't deflower me or anything like that. But…"—she looked down—"we touched. A lot."

They scooted closer to each other as if they were about to share state secrets.

"He touched me…you know…down there."

Persephone was a virgin, too. All the liaisons' unmated daughters were. It was strictly forbidden for any of them to have relations before being mated or wed. Which technically meant that Miriam could have sex now, because she was mated, wasn't she?

"What was it like?" Seph said.

Miriam traced her finger over her comforter. "It was incredible. I've never felt anything like it."

Seph sighed wistfully, and Miriam could almost hear her thoughts. She had been close to being wed, but what Seph really wanted was a mate. She wanted to feel that magical connection that Miriam now had with Io. With Arion, she had been willing to sacrifice the greater dream for the smaller one, but now that Miriam had told her about Io, it was clear Seph desperately wanted the same.

"I'm sorry, Seph." Miriam wished she could do or say something that would make Seph feel better. "Your male will come along someday. I know it. And it will be worth it."

"I don't know. I'll probably end up being what humans call an Old Maid."

Miriam placed her hand over Seph's. "No way, Seph. You're too pretty." She smoothed her other hand over Seph's long, blond hair. "No, you're beautiful. Look at you."

"Yeah, well, you're not a male." Seph flashed her a cockeyed smirk.

"Whatever."

The two sat silently for a minute then Miriam said quietly, "We're going to try to convince my father to put me in Io's care."

Seph's eyes grew wide and her jaw dropped. "What?"

Miriam nodded, biting her lip. "You can't tell anyone about this, Seph. You have to promise me."

Seph crossed her finger over her chest. "I promise. We've been friends forever. You know I won't say a word to anyone."

Miriam knew she wouldn't, and she nodded. "Okay, so... we're going to use the approach that Io can treat my addiction. He was an addict, you know."

Seph gasped. "No. Really? He was?"

"Yes." Miriam nodded. "Last year, he was strung out worse than I am."

"And he quit?"

"Yep."

"How?"

"His friend helped him." She refrained from bringing up Arion's name. She didn't want to upset Seph.

Seph pursed her lips. "And the plan is for him to help you?"

"That's the plan. Io is supposed to be working out the details with his boss. Hopefully I'll hear something soon, because I won't make it long without his help." She lifted the bottle of water that had been sitting beside her.

"What's that?"

Miriam took off the cap and sipped, scrunching up her nose. "It's a tonic that curbs the symptoms of withdrawal." She remembered her powerful reaction to the detox from the day before. She didn't want to go through that again.

Seph pinched her thumb and forefinger over her nose and swayed backward. "Phew! It stinks."

"Yeah, I know. But it works." She put the cap back on the bottle and set it aside.

"When are you supposed to hear from him?"

"I don't know, but this plan *has* to work."

Not only did Miriam want to be with Io again, but he knew how to care for her. She had already drunk half the tonic he had sent home with her, and the rest wouldn't last another twelve hours.

"He knows how to rehab and help me through the withdrawal. I'm afraid if I can't get back to him soon..." Her voice trailed off as she looked away and began chewing on her thumbnail.

Seph looked down uncomfortably when Miriam glanced toward her again.

"You know, I think it's time for us both to get off that shit," Seph said, her lips turning up into a reluctant smile. "I was going to tell you when I got here, but then we started talking about Io, and, well…." She shrugged and looked down.

"What?" Miriam said. "What's going on?"

Seph frowned and took Miriam's hands. "You scared me last night. Damn it, Miri, but I thought you were going to die."

Miriam felt bad for putting Seph through last night's hell. "I'm sorry. I didn't mean to scare you. I promise I'm going to try to quit. If I'm allowed to go back to Io, I'm sure I can make it happen."

"I know." Seph took a deep breath and exhaled slowly. "I know you can." She smiled. "And so am I. I told my dad last night that I want to be admitted into AKM's treatment program."

"Really?"

Seph nodded. "Seeing you like that, and knowing that could be me . . .?" She shook her head. "We have to quit, Miri. Both of us."

"Yes, we do. And I'm proud of you." Miriam was truly happy for her friend, but sad for herself. "At least your father listens to you." She looked down at her hands, frustrated that everyone else seemed to have a father willing to listen to them while her dad was Hitler.

Her father wanted to pretend everything was perfect bliss in the royal home. He refused to notice how destructive Miriam had become, and instead of treating her like a daughter, he treated her like a convict.

Miriam had started using cobalt to get her father's attention. She readily admitted it, especially after Io's little provocation last night. And not just get his attention. Miriam wanted him to actually care. She wanted her father to *see* her, *hear* her…to show he still *loved* her and that she wasn't just another minion to order around and rule.

Talk about a backfire. Taking that first hit of cobalt had been a major fail. The second hit had been even more stupid. By the third, Miriam had been totally addicted. Cobalt was nasty shit. Getting off it would be a major ordeal.

"I know you've got problems with your father, Miri." Seph took her hands. "But at least you've got a mate, right?"

Good old Seph, always trying to look at the bright side and cheer her up.

Miriam nodded. "As long as my dad doesn't kill Io when he finds out what's happened." Miriam didn't deny how messed up this situation could still become.

"He won't. He can't. Surely, he'll recognize the significance of a mated male's claim."

Miriam rolled her eyes. "This is my dad we're talking about, Seph."

"True, but..." Seph paused. "Everything will work out. I know it."

Miriam wished she had Seph's confidence, because at the moment, she felt like everything was about to fall apart.

CHAPTER 27

A COUPLE OF HOURS BEFORE DAWN, Io paced the hall, his phone in his hand. Why hadn't anyone called him, yet?

The door opened and Micah walked in with Trace.

"What the hell?" he said, spinning around to glare at them. "That door was locked."

Trace tapped his temple and grinned.

"Oh, I see. Another one of your fancy abilities, I presume?" Io shook his head. The more he learned about Trace, the more he realized he knew very little about how powerful the guy was.

"Yep, Trace is full of tricks," Micah said, walking toward him. "I need a favor."

Did Micah even acknowledge that he had broken into his house? "How 'bout you go back out and knock like a normal person?"

"No time for that." Micah grabbed his arm and led him toward the back of the house.

What was so urgent that they couldn't even knock? "You're kidding, right?"

"Nope." Micah directed Io into his den and pushed him into his chair behind his oversized desk full of laptops, keyboards, and monitors. "I've got a job for you. Something you can do while you're waiting for little Miss Firecracker to return."

Io frowned, but Micah had a good point. He needed something to keep himself busy, and from the looks of things, it would involve working on his computers, and if anything had hope of taking his mind off the agony of being separated from his mate, it was his computers.

"Okay. So what's up?" he said.

Trace sauntered in and sat down on the couch. Micah joined him.

"Gina Carano," Micah said.

"Who?" The name sounded familiar, but Io couldn't remember from where.

"The female who tried to perform open heart surgery on Sev with a bullet a couple of weeks ago."

"Oh, yeah. Her. What about her?"

Micah leaned back and rested his arm over the back of the couch. "I want you to find her."

"Say again?"

"Find her. Contact her. Get her ass back here."

This was an unusual request. "Would you mind telling me why the sudden urgency?"

"Malek needs her."

Either Io was completely out of touch, or Micah was delusional. He looked back and forth between Trace and Micah and saw no hint of psychosis.

"I'm not delusional," Micah said.

"Get out of my head."

"Yeah, that'll happen." Trace said doubtfully.

"Can you find her?" Micah was all business.

Io was the best at digging up intel and hacking systems. "Sure, I can find her. If she wants to be found."

"Make sure she wants to."

Io still didn't understand the urgency. "Why is this so important? What's she got to do with Malek?"

"I think she's his mate."

Okay, hold the phone while a bombshell drops in my office.

"Come again?"

"You heard me."

So this explained why Malek had been walking around like a member of the pissed off walking dead for the past couple of weeks. AKM seemed to be in a mating boom, and ol' Malek looked to be next on the list. What was up with that?

"How will Sev react to this?" After all, Sev was the one Gina tried to kill.

"Who cares? If she's Malek's mate, we need to get her back here. He's not doing so hot."

"Jesus." Io fired up his system. "You heard she had a fling with Sev's father, Lakota, right?"

"Yep." Micah took out his phone as it beeped, read the screen, then punched in a number.

"Lakota won't be happy to see her back here after what she did to his son."

"He'll get over it." Micah turned his attention to his phone. "Hey, babe." He had obviously called Sam. "No, I'm at Io's house…uh-huh…do you need me?" He paused. "Oh?" His eyebrow arched with interest then he chuckled darkly. "You are, huh?" Micah shifted on the couch. "So, you *do* need me."

Awkward.

Trace looked out the window, and Io typed in his password.

Micah chuckled again. "I'll be right there." He hung up and looked at Io. "I've got to run. My mate requires my attention." He grinned and glanced at Trace. "You coming?"

Trace stood and followed Micah to the doorway. Then Micah stopped and turned back toward Io. "Text me when you find her, but get her back here. I don't care what it takes. Tell her Sev changed his mind and decided to press charges if you have to."

Io smirked. "I'll leave that part to you. How's that?"

"Fine. Whatever. Just find her."

As the two left the den, Io realized that Micah would make a good team leader. What an odd thought. Before Sam, he had been the loosest cannon in the history of loose cannons. He had been an asshole loner who nobody liked, but in the months since meeting Sam, he had changed. Micah was turning into someone who commanded respect and displayed sound judgment and concern for his peers. All qualities necessary for a leader, and even though he was constantly in the minds of those around him, he rarely, if ever, used what he found in their thoughts against them, and he never used others' thoughts for his own personal gain. He kept his mouth shut and didn't reveal secrets when it would be so easy for him to do just that. Io had never thought he would like Micah, but for the first time he felt like he and Micah might actually be able to get along…maybe even be friends.

"Wouldn't work!" Micah called from the front hallway.

"Huh?" Io frowned.

"You and me being friends," Micah called back to him. "It wouldn't work, you homophobic bastard. I've fucked guys."

Io heard the hint of humor in Micah's voice. "Yeah, well I seem to be finding a guy's sexuality and what he does with his own dick more and more unimportant these days, Micah. But then again, I've got the feeling you already knew that."

A dark chuckle came from the foyer. "Yep. I've caught that, but I'll still ride your ass about it."

Io had to laugh. "Fuck off, shithead. Go home and make your woman happy."

Micah and Trace both chuckled. "I plan on it," Micah said.

The front door opened and closed, and Io heard the lock engage as he began his search. This would help keep his mind off Miriam. At least for a little while. Because he sure wasn't going to be able to sleep until he had her back here, and pacing endlessly was just going to wear out his carpet.

Now, where could he dig up info on Gina? Pulling up AKM's record of her arrest would be a start. He would find something there to go on, then connect the dots and follow her trail. If Gina really was Malek's mate, Io could understand the importance of getting her back. The way he was suffering, he could only imagine what Malek was going through.

CHAPTER 28

MALEK PUSHED JESS'S HEAD DOWN against the mattress with one hand while he shackled her slender wrists at the small of her back with the other. She was bent over on her knees, his thighs holding her legs open as he fucked her hard from behind.

Anger roiled just beneath his skin, and sweat poured from his body as his muscles strained against his aggression. Damn Micah to hell for making light of his feelings for Carmen. He would show Micah how wrong he was about Gina. Malek didn't need Gina or anyone else.

He punctuated the thought with a violent thrust, grunting harshly as his body slapped hard between Jess's legs, her ass rippling from the impact.

Jess cried out and whimpered. He was hurting her.

Good. As he saw Gina under him instead of Jess, he growled with satisfaction at giving her pain.

"I don't need you, fucking whore." Malek pounded hard inside her again, tightening his grip on her wrists and driving her head further against the mattress. "Do you hear me? There's no room for you here." Again he slammed into her.

Gina yelped again, sounding distressed.

Her cries pleased Malek. He wanted to hurt her, to make her see he had no room in his life for her. Spiraling down further into hell, Malek lashed her body with his, trapping her beneath him, showing her who was boss and that he would never see her as anything more than a fuck to milk his cock when he felt the urge to abuse her. He would never take her as his mate. Never! Fuck biology and fuck his instinctual needs. Malek would never bow down to either and take Gina as his mate. Not at the cost of tainting Carmen's memory.

"You're nothing, Gina. Nothing but a whore." His voice hissed with venomous rage.

He pulled back and flipped her over, manhandling her, bruising her flesh as her wide eyes met his. Fear shone through. She was terrified of him.

Once more, his brutal fucking lashed her, his knees shoving her legs apart before she could close them, his hands pressing down her arms so she couldn't fight him.

"Stop...Ow! Malek, stop!"

Her pleas only fueled him to take her harder, sweat dripping off the tip of his nose, his long hair damp and hanging over his face.

Gina! God, but she was beautiful. NO! He refused to see her as anything more than a vessel. She would never measure up to Carmen's memory. Carmen, sweet Carmen. How he had loved her. Loved and lost, but never would he soil her memory by taking another.

Malek's mind spun out of control, his lust rising, his body answering the call to let loose his desire. But no matter how hard he tried to keep Carmen's face in his mind, it was Gina's that kept pushing forward.

"NO!" He shouted, relentlessly abusing her body to drive back her image as he drove only to give her pain while finding his pleasure.

"Ow! Malek! Stop. Ow! You're hurting me!"

Closing his eyes, Malek struggled to see his perfect, beautiful Carmen, fighting to hold onto her, clashing with Gina's mental image, trying to resist her clawing hands. She reached for him, scratched him, tried to latch on.

When Malek opened his eyes again, he saw that his hands were squeezing Gina's throat. Her arms flailed, her hands slapping him as she gagged and choked.

With a jolt, Malek pulled back.

The woman was no longer Gina, but Jess. God, what had he done?

Jess heaved for air and coughed, gasping as Malek fell

backward. Wide-eyed and terrified of his actions, he could only stare. He had thought the woman with him was Gina. He had tried to kill her and hadn't even realized it.

"Oh my God. Jess. Oh fuck." He tried to reach for her, but she slapped his hand away.

"Stay away from me, you freak! I never said I was in to asphyxiation." She coughed again, sitting up and fixing Malek with a horrified glare. "You almost killed me!"

"I'm sorry…God, I'm sorry." Malek scampered off the bed, paced away in a confused daze, then turned and rushed back, wanting to help her and make this right.

Jess flinched and nearly fell off the bed to get away from him. "Don't touch me!" She got her footing and grabbed her clothes. "I thought you were different. I thought…" She shook her head. "To think I felt sorry for you last night."

"Jess, please. I didn't mean to hurt you."

Malek needed to get his shit together. He didn't know what was happening to him, but he needed to figure it out fast before he hurt somebody. He glanced at Jess. Well, he already *had* hurt somebody, which meant that if he wanted to make sure it didn't happen again, he needed to wrap his head around what was going on.

"Fuck you. You got that. Fuck you. You can keep your goddamn money for all I care. I'm out of here, asshole."

Malek couldn't blame her. After nearly getting choked to death, he would split like his ass was on fire, too. But he couldn't let her leave without paying her. Not after what he had done.

"No…Jess…"

But she was already flying at Mach speed up the stairs.

Malek grabbed his stash of bills and darted after her, but she was already out the door. Not even caring that he was as naked as a jaybird, he ran after her, catching her wrist.

Screaming, she spun around and slapped him. "Let go of me." She continued trying to beat him, crying out as tears streamed her face.

"Just hold on. Let me at least call you a cab. Jess! Stop fighting me."

"I don't want you calling me a cab. I don't want anything from you. Just get away from me and never come looking for me again!" Her palm connected with his face one last time, the slap ringing out like the crack of a whip.

Malek pulled back, letting go of her, stumbling and falling to his ass on his lawn as the realization that he had fucked up beyond all recourse finally sank in. Jess took off, and all he could do was watch her go.

Numb, Malek sat in the grass, staring into space until the cold, early morning air caused him to shiver. Pushing himself off the ground, he gathered his bearings as best he could and went back inside.

He was falling apart. He hadn't meant to hurt Jess, but his conflicting emotions had spun him into delirium, and before he had known what he was doing, he had almost strangled her to death, thinking she was Gina.

If Gina had just stayed in the back of his mind so he could enjoy his precious Carmen, none of this would have happened. But that bitch had bullied her way into his thoughts, forcing him away from the one who mattered most, stealing him away from his first and only mate. Damn Gina to hell for causing this nightmare. This was all her fault.

God help Gina if Malek ever saw her again, because sure as shit, if he got his hands around *her* throat, he wouldn't let go until she stopped breathing.

CHAPTER 29

KING BAIN DISMISSED THE MEETING an hour before dawn, but Gregos stayed behind.

"What's on your mind, Gregos?"

His liaison bowed respectfully and stepped forward. "A matter I feel needs your attention."

"Speak."

Gregos cleared his throat. "Tristan from AKM called me tonight. He offered a solution to the...um...problem that plagues you."

"What problem is that?" His eyes narrowed. He had a feeling this had to do with his daughter. Couldn't this matter just go away on its own?

"Sire, forgive my candor, but Tristan offers a discreet solution to Miriam's...well, to her extracurricular medicinal usage."

Clever phrasing. With the care Gregos used to choose his words, perhaps Bain would listen to his proposal. Obviously Gregos understood how he felt about the matter of Miriam's escapades and defiant behavior.

"Go on." He sat back in the massive, leather chair at the head of the oval table. With a controlled wave of his hand, he gestured toward the chair beside him as he turned to face Gregos.

Gregos bowed again and sat. "Sire, Tristan and I know how delicate this situation is, and I truly feel that Tristan's solution is wise. A member of his team used to have a similar ailment as your daughter, but he was able to overcome it. I understand this person often assists in counseling sessions conducted at AKM on the issue. He is an expert in treatment and I am assured that if you put your daughter in his care, he would treat the situation with the utmost privacy and diplomacy."

King Bain considered the proposal for a moment. "Who is this male?"

Gregos cleared his throat and blinked several times. "Io, Sire. The male who tended to Miriam last night. And saved her life, I might add."

The hair stood up on the back of Bain's neck. Miriam had spent the night and day with Io—in his home, no less. And despite the fact that Io had, indeed, saved Miriam's life as Gregos said, he still didn't like the idea of his daughter being anywhere near him. The male had a reputation as a chauvinistic womanizer. A real Casanova. The fact that he had been a former cobalt addict didn't score him any Brownie points.

However, Donovan and his security team had come back claiming innocence of what they had found in Io's home. They all said the same thing: that Miriam had slept in the bed, perfectly chaste, while Io dozed in a nearby chair so he could monitor her condition.

Bain sighed. Perhaps Gregos's solution was worth a try. He needed to keep Miriam's...*problem*...out of the public eye, but he also needed to make it go away. He couldn't very well put her into a public treatment program, because then everyone would find out about the blemish on his family. Bain wanted to keep his family's affairs private, which was becoming harder to do with Miriam's antics growing worse and more unpredictable each day. Putting Miriam under Io's care would make keeping their dirty secret private much easier.

"How would this work?" he asked, eyeing Gregos.

"Your daughter would stay with Io. Tristan will put him on leave so he can monitor Miriam. Io would oversee her recovery from her...ailment, and then treat her through, um, withdrawal. Then we could work out an aftercare arrangement."

"And how long do you think this will take?" He didn't like

the idea of Miriam living with Io, but Io certainly couldn't come to his home. No one but his liaisons and consultants were allowed inside the royal home.

"Given the state of your daughter's ailment, as well as normal treatment times, I would say we're looking forward to at least three to four weeks for the initial treatment. Then her aftercare would begin and, depending on how well she re-assimilates, that could last a few months or up to a year. But she would return here after the initial treatment and only see Io for follow-up or as needed."

"As needed?"

Gregos nodded. "Yes, if she...relapses, for example. He is a qualified counselor and program sponsor at AKM."

"I see." Bain considered what Gregos had told him, and despite his reservations about Io personally, he had to admit the male did sound qualified to handle Miriam's care and recovery. "The treatment is rather long, don't you think?"

"Yes, Sire. But it's highly successful. All the data support the program is working very well."

King Bain took a moment to think it over.

"What is your opinion, Gregos?"

Gregos tipped his head respectfully. "I believe this is your best choice, Sire. Io comes with high commendations, despite his misgivings in other matters, and Tristan speaks well of him. The best part is that this solution does keep the affair private."

Throughout the conversation, Bain felt himself swaying in the same direction Gregos recommended. Sure, Io was a hedonist and a lecher, but he sounded qualified to handle Miriam's problem. Damn, but Bain just wanted this aggravation to go away. Whatever it took, he wanted Miriam well again.

King Bain sat forward, the decision made. "Arrange it. But, I want a key to the residence, and he will be subject to inspection any time I see fit. He is not to touch her except to treat her, and he is to speak to her only in a manner fit for the princess. Make this clear. If he defies my rules, he will be punished. This is not a vacation for my daughter. She is to be treated, taken seriously, and will return home after she is no longer ill."

Gregos stood and bowed. "Yes, Sire."

"Put together the proper paperwork. I want her treatment to start as soon as possible. Tonight. Make it happen, Gregos."

"Yes, it will be done." Gregos hurried out of the room. He had a lot to do during daylight hours.

Rising from his chair, Bain strode from the large conference room and headed for the stairs that led to the wing of the home where Miriam's room was.

When he reached her door, he knocked. "Miriam?"

"What?" Her obstinate tone bit back at him. When had she grown to hate him so much? All they did was fight now. She had been much more enjoyable when she was younger. If only she were still that way, young and impressionable, gazing upon him as if he were her hero.

He opened the door and found her lying on her bed, the canopy drawn around her. He glanced around the room, frowning. The mish-mash of styles and colors hurt his eyes.

A half-full bottle of water caught his eye on her dresser.

"What's this?" He picked up the bottle.

She huffed. "Io gave me that. It's medicine for my *cobalt addiction*. It helps with withdrawal." She spoke as if trying to hurt him.

He winced at the mention of addiction. She was not an addict. She was merely sick. That's all. But he didn't want to fight with her. Not now when she would be leaving him to get better. He set the bottle back down.

"You are leaving for treatment tonight," he said with unceremonious fanfare.

She sat up and pushed the canopy aside to look at him. She appeared confused. "What?"

"For your ailment. You will return to Io's home, the one who treated you yesterday." He frowned as what looked like excitement crossed her face.

The brief flash of emotion made him uncomfortable. She was attracted to Io, which was unsettling, but he wanted her well. He would have to lay down the law and make it clear to her what this was about. Her foray was not a vacation or a jaunt to be taken lightly.

"This is not to be fun and games, Miriam. You are to follow his orders strictly, and when you return home, I expect no more of this stupidity from you. This problem goes away now. Do you understand?"

She nodded. "Yes."

His eyes narrowed suspiciously. She was suddenly much too accommodating and less argumentative. "You are not to behave inappropriately with him, either. He is not to touch you, and you are forbidden from touching him." He wanted her clear on this point. "Is that understood?"

She nodded and rolled her eyes. "Fine. As always, your orders are understood, Father."

He huffed in frustration. He had been ready for an argument from her, not this blithe acceptance. "Get packed and rest. You depart at nightfall." He shut her door and headed back to the stairs leading to the main hall. Something didn't feel right. Perhaps it was just his discomfort over this whole nasty situation. He just wanted the cobalt out of his house and out of his family. So much so that he was willing to risk putting Miriam in the home of a reputed playboy with hopes that fear of what would happen to Io if he broke propriety with his daughter would keep the male from doing anything regrettable.

CHAPTER 30

MIRIAM LEAPED OUT OF BED and rushed to her closet for her luggage. What should she take? Hell, she wanted to pack up her whole life and leave and never return. This wasn't her home anymore, anyway. Her home was with Io. Wherever he was, that's where she needed to be from now on.

She was going back to her mate. She was going to see Io in a little over twelve hours.

She grabbed her phone and dialed his number.

He picked up almost immediately. "Miriam? Are you okay?"

"Yes, yes, I'm fine." She was whispering, but she didn't know why. It wasn't like her room was monitored, which actually surprised her.

"I miss you," he said. "I miss you so much."

"Well, you'll be seeing me soon."

His voice rose with hope. "What do you mean?"

"My father has agreed to whatever plan you and your boss came up with. I'm supposed to be packing right now. I'll be at your place tonight."

"Tonight?" He sounded relieved. "I need to see you. I'm going crazy without you."

"Me, too."

"I can't stop thinking about you. I can't sleep."

"I can't, either." Her body heated in all the right places hearing him speak of how much he missed and needed her. She had never hoped to hear a man say such things to her for fear she never would, but now she had found the one she was meant to be with forever. And he spoke with such desire for her. It made her feel purely feminine and utterly wanton.

"I want to kiss you, Miriam. I need to feel you."

Her knees went weak and she had to sit down to keep from collapsing to the floor. "I keep replaying our day together in my mind."

"So do I. I'm supposed to be working on a case, but I keep drifting off as I remember how you looked and felt against me. You're so beautiful."

"Stop that. You're making me . . ."

"What?" he said. "What am I making you?"

She heard the smile in his voice and bit her lip. "You're making me warm."

"Warm is a good thing." He paused and she got the sense he was leaning back as she heard a rustling noise. "Tell me where I make you warm, Miriam."

She lay back on her bed just as the clock struck 6:00 a.m. "You make me warm everywhere."

"Between your legs? Are you warm there?"

She grinned. Definitely. She was definitely warm between her legs. "Yes."

"Mmm."

"What are you doing?" she said.

He paused then said, "I'm touching myself."

"You are?"

"Uh-huh." He moaned quietly.

"You're hard?"

"Yes." His voice cracked on the single syllable. "Very hard."

Butterflies fluttered in the pit of her stomach and she felt moisture slick her core. "My voice did that to you?" The thought that just her voice and the thought of her could excite him filled her with a sense of power.

"Your voice does all kinds of things to me, Miri."

She ran her palm down her stomach and over the apex of her legs as she parted her thighs. "Yours does things to me, too."

"Mmm, are you touching yourself?"

She nodded. "Yes. Is that okay?"

"Oh God, yes baby." He groaned long and low.

So, yeah, her touching herself was okay. She performed a one-handed unsnap and unzip of her jeans and took a deep breath before sliding her hand inside her satin panties. She had very little hair down there, and what hair she did have was short and downy soft.

"Are you wet?" he said. He purred into the phone. He was heavily aroused.

"Yes." She purred back as her middle finger dipped between her lips and found her hardened clit. Was she really doing this? Inside the royal home, no less? But it was too good to stop.

"Stroke yourself for me, baby. Imagine it's my hand and my fingers on you. Imagine it's my tongue licking you."

His tongue? The mental image of his head between her legs alone was enough to make her shudder as she sucked in her breath and exhaled on a moan.

"You like that, don't you?" he said.

"Yes." The word sounded more like a breath than a word.

"Then I'll have to show you how good my tongue can make you feel once I have you here. Would you like that?"

Oh God, she was going to come. "Yes." She trembled and her breath shuddered out from her parted lips.

"You're going to come, aren't you? Thinking of my tongue teasing your clit and licking you is going to make you come. Mmm, Miri. I can't wait to taste you. I can't wait until you come against my tongue and wrap those long legs around my head and hold me against you while your pussy quivers against my mouth."

"Oh God, oh God!" Her fingers swirled over her hard nub as it swelled and suddenly everything exploded. She whimpered and moaned through her orgasm, whispering his name on a breathy exhale.

"That's my girl. Umph. Yeah. Just...fuck...just like that. Fuck!" He growled and cried out, clearly reaching his own climax as he listened to her breathe and gasp through the tail end of hers.

Nothing was said for a minute. The only sounds involved

catching their breath alongside the occasional purr as their bodies slowly came back down from their orgasms.

"Is it nightfall, yet?" Io said, his voice wistful.

She glanced at the clock. If only she could speed up time. "No, but I wish it were."

"I think I might lose my mind before I see you."

"I can help you find it again."

He chuckled. "I'm sure you could." He blew out a heavy breath. "How is the elixir holding up?"

"Okay. I'm nursing it. I've got about a quarter of the bottle left."

"That should last until you get here. You might get a little fidgety, but you can hold out, baby."

She loved when he called her baby. It was informal and unlike anything else anyone called her.

"Knowing I'll be seeing you is enough to make me know I'll be okay, Io."

He paused. "I want to keep you on the phone all day."

"I know, but I have to pack."

"And I have to work."

She finally pulled her hand out of her panties. "But I'll see you soon."

"Yes, and I can't wait."

"Go on now," she said. "Go work."

"Bye, baby."

"Bye, Io."

"Bye."

She laughed. "Hang up."

"I can't."

"You have to."

He groaned in frustration. "You hang up."

"I can't." She laughed again.

"See, it's not easy, is it?"

They laughed at each other.

"On the count of three?" she said.

"Okay."

"One, two…" She paused.

"Two-and-a-half…"

He cracked her up. "Three." She waited.

Nothing.

"Are you still there?" she said.

"Yes."

She broke into laughter again, and he joined her.

"Just hang up," she said.

He growled. "I don't want to."

"Be strong."

"Fine. On three."

"One, two…three." She hit the *end call* button before she could stop herself.

Instantly, she wished she hadn't, but they would have only kept on, and she really needed to pack.

She got up and took a sip of the elixir mixture—yuck, but it was getting easier to tolerate the taste—then opened the top drawer of her dresser and grabbed a neatly folded stack of matching lingerie to put in her suitcase. She had a feeling that would come in handy.

"MIRIAM?" IO SAT SILENTLY AND LISTENED. "Miri?"

Damn, she had hung up. She was stronger than he was. He set down his phone and looked at the mess he had made on his stomach then grabbed a tissue from the box beside him and wiped himself off.

With a sigh, he tossed the tissue in the trash and zipped up his pants. He was making excellent progress on his search for Gina. Finding where she had gone had been easier than he thought, but Gina would have to wait a bit longer. He needed a shower and one more round with his hand before he could focus on the last leg of his search.

And he had a feeling Tristan would be calling him any minute with the good news. He would have to act surprised. No sense in letting the cat out of the bag that he already knew Miriam would be with him tonight.

CHAPTER 31

APOSTLE WAS BACK IN CHICAGO, having arrived only a few hours ago.

This sucks.

He hated being back here. It was cold, and that just made him itch even more from the residual scorpion venom. And the last thing he wanted was for whoever had wiped out his entire team and his twin in such spectacular fashion to find out he was still alive.

He was sure that special little welcoming committee would love to get their hands on him.

His new human form was still much too puny, only because his dreck body was still so emaciated. But he couldn't build a house without a foundation, which meant he needed to pack in some calories.

He parked in front of his favorite Italian joint, RoSal's. The place had a mafia family vibe, with white tablecloth service. And as far as Apostle was concerned, the food couldn't be beat.

After being seated and ordering an appetizer of their Famous Fried Ravioli, stuffed mushrooms, and a plate of Tortellini Alfredo, he sat back and looked around at the other patrons. All humans. Of course, the sun hadn't set, yet. Once it did, the vampires would come out to play.

Apostle checked his watch. His friends were late. He needed to learn what had happened while he had been locked away in his brother's home.

"You look good for a dead guy." Apostle looked up to see Jarek take the seat across from him a few minutes later.

Chezmu, who simply went by Chez, took one of the other

seats. Both were drecks.

"What can I say?" Apostle shrugged. "I wear death well."

Chez and Jarek chuckled before Jarek tapped his index finger on the cloth-covered table then leaned back. "Seriously, man. What happened? I heard the scene was pretty gruesome at your place."

Apostle sipped his wine. "They got the wrong guy."

When the two only gave him inquisitive looks, he added, "Whoever was after me killed my brother. They got Deacon, not me."

"Whoa!" Chez's eyebrows popped as he exchanged glances with Jarek. "I bet Bishop was pissed."

"Gee, thanks." Apostle shook his head.

Apostle couldn't get any respect, not even from those he considered friends. Well, maybe not friends, but at least close associates.

"That's not what I meant. It's just that—"

"Forget about it." Apostle wasn't into their sentimental bullshit. "Everyone knows Bishop favored Deacon over me, but I'm not here to talk about Deacon."

Jarek and Chez nodded warily, as if they knew Apostle had already been through hell and back and could blow a fuse any second.

"Tell me what you've heard about who did it." Apostle leaned back as the server brought his appetizers.

Jarek waited until the server left then leaned in so he could keep his voice down. "Word is there's a bad-ass mixed-blood working at AKM. Seems the guy can mass compel or some shit, and he has some wicked abilities. My bet is he did it, but if he did, he's not talking about it. Officially, the murders remain unsolved."

"And unofficially?"

Jarek's eyebrows lifted. "Unofficially, the dreck community is running scared. At least the element of the dreck community we run with. Whoever pulled off that hit gave everyone something to think about, know what I mean?"

Apostle stuffed a ravioli in his mouth and fought back a moan. He was so hungry, and the food here was good enough to give a guy an orgasm.

"I can imagine." Apostle swallowed and shoveled in more ravioli. "How do you know all this about the mongrel at AKM anyway?" Apostle mumbled through two full cheeks of food, not caring about table manners when his stomach was a pit full of empty.

Jarek and Chez exchanged glances. "We have a guy on the inside."

"Really?" This piqued Apostle's interest. "How did you manage that?"

Chez half-shrugged smugly. "The usual. Threats. Coercion. We told him if he doesn't give us information we'll kill his human mother and then systematically kill everyone in his extended family."

"So he's a mongrel, too?" Apostle popped a stuffed mushroom in his mouth.

Chez nodded. "Yep."

"That's ballsy going after someone inside AKM like that. Especially a mix." Apostle wasn't sure he would pull such a stunt. Too many things could go wrong. But Jarek and Chez had balls. He respected that.

"We keep him well monitored. And his talents aren't the kind that could cause much damage."

"Oh? What? Is he one of those mystics?"

Chez grinned. "Something like that."

Apostle took a bite of garlic bread. "So, how do you keep him monitored?"

"We have our ways." Jarek grinned.

"Fine, keep your secrets," Apostle said. "For now. But eventually, I want to know everything you've got going on."

Both nodded in agreement. "Absolutely," Chez said.

He was their boss, and they knew that if he didn't like what they told him, they would have to deal with Bishop. And no one wanted to deal with Bishop. Something Apostle now understood first-hand.

"What else is happening? How's business?" Apostle polished off the ravioli and pushed the plate aside.

Chez and Jarek were his central regional dealers in

Chicago. Product didn't touch the streets here without running through their distribution facility first.

"Product is moving well, and sales have increased despite— or maybe because of—some recent high profile activity."

"What do you mean?"

Chez chuckled and leaned closer. "Rumor is that King Bain's daughter is a junkie and that she overdosed a couple of weeks ago. And being that all her previous dealers' calls come to us now, we can confirm that, yes, she uses."

Apostle's eyebrows shot up. He could use this to his advantage, and Bishop would probably shit himself with delight to know that he had *His Royal Highness's* daughter as a customer. "The king's daughter, huh? I bet that's gone over well with the king."

"I'm sure," Jarek said, then added, "Photos of her have been circulating on the Internet."

This just got better and better. King Bain had taken tremendous pains to keep his family, and especially his daughter, out of the public eye. No one was allowed to take pictures of anyone in the royal family. Looked like things were getting interesting in Chicago.

"How did those get out?" Apostle sat back as his plates were cleared.

Jarek waved his hand dismissively and sat back. "They were taken at some party. Went viral in both the vampire and dreck communities in less than twenty-four hours before the king's techies and legal eagles could take them down. Now they just keep popping up everywhere."

"Sloppy." Apostle rested his arm on the table, picked up his wine glass, and swirled the red liquid around and around.

One of Apostle's assignments upon returning to Chicago was to find strong vampires for more experiments. Who could be a better candidate than a member of the king's family, whose bloodlines were pure back to the beginning of the race?

Bishop had brought him up to speed on some of what he was working on in his laboratory, and one experiment in its final stage involved combining vampire genes with dreck genes to create their own form of mongrel: a new species, if you will. One who was strong enough to rid the world of vampires forever so the drecks could take over and control the human race. Bishop already had a prototype, or so he claimed. If he could get his hands on the king's daughter, and swipe some of her blood, those pure genes could be quite useful to Bishop as he started production.

However, taking a member of the royal family was dangerous. If the king found out who took her and why, it would mean all-out war. But if he could find a way to make it look like an isolated incident, he might be able to pull it off. All they needed was her blood, which he could obtain easily enough without carting her back to Bishop's lab.

"Who's her dealer?" Apostle said, glancing at Chez.

"Her last two dealers got busted. We had their phone calls transferred to my mobile, so she's been talking to me. And because she's...well...*who* she is, Jarek and I were thinking about dealing directly with her rather than finding her a new dealer."

"Don't." Apostle didn't want to lose his regional managers, and with the way the plan was forming in his mind, whoever her next dealer ended up being would probably take a heavy fall.

Chez and Jarek exchanged glances then looked at him curiously. "We could have Grotek and Chane handle her," Jarek said.

"Are they disposable?" Apostle set his wine glass down and leaned on his elbows, interlacing his fingers and pressing them thoughtfully to his mouth as he looked between Chez and Jarek.

The implied message came across loud and clear, and realization dawned on their faces. Chez took a deep breath and shifted uncomfortably. Jarek cleared his throat and looked over his shoulder as if wanting to make sure no one was around to overhear their discussion.

The restaurant was alive and loud, and Apostle had chosen this table because no one was seated near it. Their conversation was secure.

Jarek's eyes narrowed as he turned back. "Sure, they're disposable. What's on your mind?"

Apostle leaned closer. "One of the things Bishop wanted me to do while I was here was find him strong subjects for his experiments. Either actual subjects or blood samples. I don't think we can get away with kidnapping the king's daughter, but we can sure get some of her blood."

"Whoa." Chez sat back, letting the single syllable stretch with a healthy dose of shock.

"Damn, Apostle, you've got balls," Jarek leaned back and chuckled respectfully. "Barely back from the dead and already planning a heist of suicidal proportions."

"What? You don't think it can work?"

Apostle's tortellini arrived and they stopped talking until the server left the table.

"Oh, I think it can work, but it's damn risky," Chez said. "But if the king finds out, you're dead."

"That's what Grotek and Chane are for. Insurance." Apostle speared two pieces of tortellini with his fork and shoved them in his mouth.

"Yeah, I kinda figured that." Chez snagged a slice of complimentary garlic bread and tore it in half.

The plan was good, at least at this point. There was still a lot to work out, though. Perhaps he should call Bishop and let him know what was going on here. After what he had just suffered for the past two months, he didn't dare piss Bishop off.

Apostle set his fork down and dabbed his cloth napkin to the corner of his mouth before pushing back from the table.

"Excuse me a minute. I'm going to call Bishop and let him know what's up."

Leaving Jarek and Chez behind, he stepped outside, took out his mobile, and dialed his brother.

"Yes?" Bishop's voice sounded distracted, as if he was admiring his scorpions or leaning back in his chair smoking one of those God-awful cigarettes of his.

"I just heard something I think might interest you," Apostle said.

"Oh? What?"

"King Bain's daughter uses."

There was a long pause, and Apostle imagined a slow smile spreading over Bishop's face.

"Yes, I can see how that would interest me," Bishop said, the humor evident in his voice. "Very good, Apostle. Very good. I assume you're thinking I would like her blood, yes?"

"That's my thought. You said you wanted strong samples, and very few vampires are as pure as King Bain and his children." Apostle turned away from a cold wind that whipped between the buildings, nearly knocking him over.

"What do you propose, Apostle? How do we get her blood without igniting a war and showing our hand?"

"We simply have to wait for her to make contact for her next buy. For now, she contacts Chez when she's out of product. Next time she calls, I'm going to have them send a couple of fall guys to the meet in case things go south. My thought is that we knock her out, take her blood, and make it look like an isolated case of a drug deal gone bad. Since she's going viral and has now become a celebrity in both the vampire community and ours, it won't be too hard to sell the notion that a couple of enterprising drug dealers thought to ransom her or some shit, as long as we make it look like a random incident." If even a clue got out that this was part of a bigger venture, doing anything to the princess could nullify the truce between their races.

"Good." Bishop sounded like he was pacing. "That could work, Apostle, but I don't want there to be any chance of her seeing your face. I don't want her to be able to identify you afterward. I'll send a courier to your hotel to assist and bring back the sample. And don't kill him when he arrives. He's a vampire."

The line went dead, and Apostle frowned as he held his phone in front of him and stared at it like it was the one who had hung up on him.

"Yeah, okay. Bye. And you're welcome, asshole." Apostle scowled and tucked his phone back in his pocket and headed inside.

"What'd he say?" Chez asked.

Apostle sat back down and picked up his fork. "We're on." He took a bite of tortellini then pointed his fork back and forth between them. "When will you see her again?"

"Who? Miriam?" Jarek said.

"Yes. When does she normally make her buys?"

Jarek placed his hands on the table and brushed them over the surface of the tablecloth. "We've only been selling to her for a couple of weeks. Just since her last dealers got busted. She burns through product pretty fast, though, so I expect to hear from her soon."

"Then we need to work this out ASAP. You two meet me back at my hotel later so we can build a plan."

"Sure. If you'll buy us dinner to go." Chez grinned at him.

"Fuck you. Buy your own goddamn food." Apostle shoveled in more tortellini just to prove a point.

Chez and Jarek both chuckled at him as Chez waved to get the waiter's attention and motioned for menus.

"Damn good to have you back, Apostle," Jarek said.

Yeah, yeah. Whatever. Apostle waved them off, ready to finish his meal and get to the hotel. His skin itched and he just wanted to get back to his room and shift into his dreck form, which helped ease the discomfort. But at least things were beginning to look up in other areas. And once he had Princess Miriam's blood, shit would get even better.

CHAPTER 32

KING BAIN SAT IN THE LIMOUSINE with his daughter. She had looked shocked when he joined her.

"You never go out in public," she had said.

"Today is an exception," he'd replied.

He wouldn't see Miriam for at least three weeks, based on what Gregos had told him about her treatment, and while he and Miriam didn't get along the way they used to, she was his daughter. The thought of not seeing her for so long hurt his heart. He wasn't accustomed to feeling this way.

"You're okay with this arrangement?" he said, keeping his gaze straight ahead. Showing tenderness and emotion was a sign of weakness, and he knew if he looked at his daughter right now, his eyes would tear up. He was already fighting the lump in his throat.

"Yes." Her voice was cold, as it always was with him now. She kept her face turned away from him, her gaze on the passing scenery.

He didn't know how to reach his daughter, anymore. She was still so young, but yet...not. He could remember like it was yesterday how she used to sit on his lap while he conducted business. Her soft hair would fall over his arms as she watched him draw up decrees, and he would bounce her on his knee while dictating orders to his liaisons. After everyone had left, she would turn on his lap and hug him with her tiny arms and pat her small hands on his face.

"Let's play Barbie," she would say in her high-pitched little girl voice.

"No, Daddy has work to do, Miri. Another time."

But another time had never come, and after a while, Miriam had stopped asking him to play, and then she had stopped joining him while he worked, and then they had stopped talking to each other altogether. Now they only argued and traded glares.

His little girl was lost to him. He had lost her a long time ago and had missed her entire life.

The rest of the drive to AKM was silent. Neither spoke, and the atmosphere in the car felt about as warm and inviting as an oil spill. He just didn't know what to say to her. What could he say that wouldn't spark a retaliatory retort or a bite of sarcasm? Or worse?

Miriam was just so damned rebellious now. Obstinate to a fault. When had she become so angry and disobedient? Bain remembered when Miriam had trailed after him, all smiles and giggles, full of admiration and always so eager to please him. Now she was anything but.

When they pulled into the back lot of the AKM building, he cleared his throat. "Well, take care of yourself. And behave."

She glanced over her shoulder, already pushing the door open as if she couldn't get away from him fast enough. "Whatever," she said, practically leaping from the car.

One-word sentences were about all he got from her these days, unless she was arguing with him.

She slammed the door, and suddenly he was alone, the air clearing of the tension and unspoken words. Even so, Bain felt worse. Miriam possessed such a strong vitality that even though she hadn't said more than a word the entire trip over, she had filled the closed-in space with life. Now the car just felt dead. Without Miriam, his life was meaningless and empty. Bain lowered his gaze as his face dropped. His long, black hair hid his features.

And that was a good thing, because for the first time since he could remember, the mighty king cried.

MIRIAM WAS ONE STEP CLOSER TO SEEING IO. One step closer to

being back in his arms.

She was ushered immediately into a Suburban while her luggage was pulled from the trunk of the limousine.

"You ready?" Micah said from behind the wheel.

She smiled. Despite his bad habit of stripping her thoughts, she liked Micah. "Yes. Have you talked to him? How is he?"

Trace and Severin walked out the back door of AKM and approached the SUV.

"He's dying to see you. I know that much," Micah said. His gaze swept toward the limousine. He frowned as if he'd heard an unusual noise and was trying to figure out what it was.

"What?" She followed his gaze.

"Oh, nothing." He looked back at her with a tight smile.

"Hey, ladies," Trace said as he pulled himself into the seat behind Micah's. His deep voice was luscious. Miriam imagined he had plenty of lady friends who simply wanted him to talk to them.

Micah chuckled and she shot him a warning glance, knowing he had just seen what she was thinking. He held up his hands innocently and looked out the window, making it clear he had no intention of revealing her thoughts to the others.

Severin settled in behind her. "Hi, Miriam," he said.

"Hey, guys." Miriam smiled at Trace and Sev before facing forward again. She was fidgety. Was she slipping into withdrawal or just anxious about getting back to Io?

After unloading her bags from the limo, the chauffeur went around to the back of the SUV and, with Malek's help, packed her suitcases in to the rear compartment. Malek shut the hatch as the chauffeur approached Micah's window. "Do you have the key?"

Micah handed over a key attached to a bright yellow tag. "As agreed."

"Thank you. I'll make sure the king gets this."

Micah turned toward her. "Part of the agreement. Your father insisted on having a key to Io's house. I think he'll have someone conduct surprise inspections to ensure the arrangements in the house are *proper.*" He gave her a hard look to make sure she understood what that meant.

"I see," she said.

Micah turned and looked in the back. "Jesus, woman. Did you bring enough shit?" He looked back at her with a snarky grin on his face, one brow arched.

"Leave me alone," she said. "I'll be staying with Io for a while."

"You're telling me," Trace said.

She turned to see him slip a matchstick between his lips. He had a big-ass grin on his face. She met his gaze and smiled. He was right. If everything went well, she would be staying with Io a good, long time. As in, forever. So, yeah, she had packed a lot of extras.

She looked at the limousine as the chauffeur got in and shut the door. Why had her father come with her today? She hadn't expected that.

Micah glanced at her knowingly. His gaze was soft and compassionate, but he wasn't talking. Whatever he knew, he wasn't going to let her in on it. But she could tell he knew something. Was he feeling sorry for her? Had he picked up on her father's animosity toward her and the situation?

Micah sighed then put the SUV in gear and followed the limousine out of the parking lot. The limousine turned left. The Suburban turned right.

And just like that, Miriam felt the oppressive ties between her and her father sever. Free at last.

Thank God.

CHAPTER 33

Io NEARLY LEAPED OUT OF HIS SKIN when he heard the Suburban pull into the driveway. He shot to the door and opened it just as Miriam was getting out of the passenger side.

Micah, Trace, and Sev piled out and went to the back as he rushed out to greet her.

He was about to hug her when Micah turned and shouted, "NO!"

Miriam and Io both stopped and looked at him.

"You two need to be careful. Someone could be watching." Micah spoke quietly. "You need to act like a concerned caregiver," he said to Io. "And you," he looked at Miriam, "need to act like a patient with an attitude problem."

Micah was right. Io couldn't lose sight that this was the king's daughter and at any moment, one of the king's many employees could be watching.

"Welcome back," he said to Miriam, trying to keep his voice unaffected as he gestured toward his open front door.

"Whatever." She walked past him, brushing her arm against his. "I can't believe my dad is making me do this."

His blood boiled and his cock instantly hardened from the small caress, as well as her scent. Damn, he needed the boys to hurry and get her things inside and leave, because he didn't know how long he could hold himself off going into full I-need-you-now mode on Miriam. He had felt the signs of the calling scratching at his insides for the past several hours and knew shit could go critical any minute.

He hurried around to the back of the SUV and grabbed the last bag as if his ass were on fire.

"Calm down, stallion," Micah said. "We'll be gone soon enough. Keep your pecker in your pants."

Trace chuckled and led them to the house.

Sev pulled up beside him. "By the way, Ari says hello."

Io glanced over at him, eyes wide. "He does?" Why did he sound so surprised?

Sev rolled his eyes. "Don't get too excited. He's still pretty sore."

"Well, tell him…" Io paused. "No, never mind. Just tell him I said hi, okay?" Io didn't want Sev doing what he should do himself. "And save me a seat at the bar one night when all this is behind us. Can you do that for me?" He wanted to mend fences and make things right. He had to try.

Sev nodded and fought back a grin. "I can do that."

Miriam waited inside for them and grabbed one of the bags out of Trace's hand. The others set down the rest of her luggage, said goodbye, and turned to head out.

Micah paused in front of Io. "Did you get what I asked for?"

Io nodded. "Yep. Sent her a message a couple of hours ago. No response, yet."

Micah glanced back at Miriam then to him. "Well, after you two say a proper hello to each other, make sure you keep me informed on your progress."

Io grinned and looked at Miriam as she blushed and glanced down at the floor. A proper hello could take a while. He turned back toward Micah. "I'll do that."

"Okay," Micah gave Io's cheek a light, affectionate smack and chuckled. "Now get to your female." He waved to Miriam. "Bye, Miri. Be good." He paused and grinned. "Fuck that. Be naughty as hell." He walked out and shut the door, making sure it was locked first.

As soon as the door closed, he and Miriam flung themselves toward one another, meeting halfway in a rush of fire. Her arms wrapped around his shoulders, and his wound around her waist, gripping her tightly. In a blaze of heat, their mouths fused together, their tongues dancing in an erotic tasting that filled Io with relief, as well as lust.

She felt perfect against him. Her body fit his like it had

been made expressly for him. And, hadn't it? She was his mate. They had been destined to be together from the inception of time.

He brought his hand around and cupped it over one of her ample breasts, squeezing as his other arm tightened around the small of her back. She moaned and let her head fall back, displaying the elegant column of her neck.

"I need you," he said before nipping the tender flesh she had so readily revealed to him.

With every passing second, it became more and more clear that his calling would fully claim him within days if not sooner. He could feel its power building inside him, preparing his body to take hers in a fever of endless hunger that would leave them both spent and delirious for one another.

WHAT **M**IRIAM FELT FOR **I**O WENT FAR BEYOND NEED.

She leaned into him as he released her neck and pulled her up. With her forehead touching his, she closed her eyes and purred softly. Io's arms tightened around her, and the most erotic moan vibrated through his throat. The sound encouraged her while chipping away any last remnants of logical thought and self-control.

"Take me to bed tonight?" Her whispered words lilted like a question as her lips brushed against his.

She had never lain with a male, but the thought of going one more day without feeling Io inside her was intolerable. Miriam was ready to grow up and put her innocence behind her. She had made her choice, and it would be Io or no one.

A low purr resonated from deep within his chest. His entire body seemed to bend and mold more snugly against every curve of hers as his fingers curled over the mound of her breast.

"Are you sure?" He bent and licked her neck once more.

She nodded and trembled, nervous, yet certain that she was making the right decision.

"Yes." She swallowed impulsively, shuddering as tiny crackles flamed her nerves. "I want you to."

The pit of her stomach clenched with an ache that felt both agonizing and delicious, and somehow she knew that having Io inside her would soothe the tightening knot in her belly.

Until she met Io, she had merely been an empty vase sitting on a shelf, unfilled, with no purpose. But now Io was like water, filling her and flowing around her curves, giving her purpose, preparing her for a beautiful bouquet so she could become the glorious centerpiece she had always wanted to be.

Not that she was vain. That wasn't it at all. But she had been pushed into the shadows by her father and held back from her full potential for so long that she had forgotten what it felt like to mean something to someone. She had forgotten how it felt to be wanted and acknowledged, and she had never felt beautiful. Not really. Not until Io had wrapped her up in his gaze and dared to tread on a minefield to be with her.

Io wanted her. She was important to him, and he showed her as much in the way he looked at her with pure adoration, in the way he touched her with reverence, and in the way he spoke to her with complete devotion. And all those things made her feel truly beautiful and important for the first time in her life.

As Io murmured loving words against her neck and caressed her back as if she were made of delicate crystal, Miriam's emotions got the best of her and tears broke in her eyes.

Someone wanted her. Io hadn't let royal titles and stupid laws scare him away. He treated her like she was simply a random female he had met in passing. The irony was that she had never felt more like a princess than she did when she was with him, and his lack of formality with her was the reason why. No one else had ever made her feel so exquisite and special, and it was by treating her like she was a commoner that Io had achieved what no one else had.

"Miri?" Io pulled back, sniffing the air as if he had scented her emotional upheaval. When he saw her tears he frowned. "Are you okay?"

She nodded and sniffled, swiping her fingers over her cheeks to brush away her fallen tears. "Yes. Never better."

The crooked, confused grin he gave her endeared him to her.

"Then why are you crying?" He lifted his hand to her face and brushed away the lingering moisture with the pad of his thumb.

"Because you've made me feel things I've never felt," she said. "I've never felt more like a princess than I do right now, and it's all because of you."

She brushed the backs of her fingers down his cheek.

He grinned. "And I've never felt more like a prince."

"My prince?" She smiled and leaned in to meet his lips with hers.

"Mm-hm." Io's mouth played softly over hers. "I'm a better male since I met you."

They were good for one another. A perfect match. Impeccably paired. Both becoming better versions of themselves because of the other.

"Let me feel how much better I make you, Io." Miriam trailed her hand down his chest and torso, tilting her face against his and brushing their cheeks together as her hand slid seductively over the bulge in his pants.

"Mmm, just as long as I can make you feel more that you've never felt before." He reached around and tenderly gripped her bottom.

"Oh, I think you've got that covered, baby." She nipped his cheek, then flicked the tip of her tongue over his skin.

Without another word, he grabbed under the curves of her ass with both hands, hefting her up easily. She wrapped her legs around his waist and his gaze met hers.

"You're mine." His deep voice announced his claim.

He walked her to the stairs that led to his basement bedroom, and she hugged his shoulders as she buried her face against the side of his neck.

"I'm yours." Her voice was a reverent whisper.

Down they went, drawing nearer to her deflowering with each step.

If she was a goddess, Io was her god. He even felt like one—magnificent and larger than life, all sculpted muscle and power.

Funny how things worked out. If her father had actually behaved like a father, she never would have started using cobalt to get away from the miserable reality of her existence, which meant she never would have overdosed and met Io. But all the pieces had lined up perfectly, and she had finally found someone worthy to call her mate. Through the pain and hell of addiction, Miriam had found her prince.

A small night-light plugged in a few feet away from the bed provided the only illumination in the large room, casting gentle shadows over the furniture.

When they reached the middle of the room, Io stopped. She unfolded her legs from around his waist and he set her down then stepped back.

She swallowed heavily. His gaze drifted down her body then back up to her face. Before, his scrutiny would have made her self-conscious, but not anymore. She wanted him to look at her, because the way his eyes glazed and he rubbed his lips together—slowly, thoughtfully...*hungrily*—lit butterflies in her stomach. Sexy, lusty, wanton butterflies.

"This is your first time." His words carried portent, a promise hidden just under the surface that tonight would forever change them. As he breathed, his gaze dropped to his fingertips as they outlined the curve of her breast, caressing her like a feather. "It should be special." His fingers skimmed down her stomach, his hands disappearing under her shirt after a moment's hesitation. He inched the fabric up to reveal her skin.

She lifted her arms, moving just as slowly, and he tugged her shirt over her head before tossing it aside. It landed on the floor with a soft *thwump*, and his palms slid up and over her lace-covered breasts. His fingers played with the scalloped edges of her bra as she reached around and unfastened it. The material loosened, and his hands glided underneath and over her skin. She tossed the bra aside so it joined her shirt on the floor.

Io seemed fascinated with her breasts, his gaze following his hands as he massaged, squeezed, and caressed them.

"Are you okay?" she said.

Without lifting his gaze, he nodded. "Yes. I've just never seen more perfect breasts, and to think they're mine...they—you—all of you...you belong to me, and I belong to you. I just never thought..." He trailed off.

"You never thought what, Io?" She placed one of her hands over one of his.

He smiled, and this time his eyes lifted to meet hers. "I never thought I would take a mate."

"And...? How do you feel about that now that you have?" She smoothed her hand down his arm.

"I can't imagine ever going back to the way I was. You're perfect, Miri. Perfect for me, and perfect in every way."

She felt the same way. Everything about Io screamed *I'm your mate.* He was bold and outspoken. He took risks and went after what he wanted. He refused to be intimidated by money, titles, or even her royal blood.

"Claim me," she said, whispering.

His gaze blazed hot, and his full lips parted seductively. "Precious Miriam, make no mistake, your body will be fully and well-claimed by morning."

The tone of his voice heated her blood, and her breath quickened as he knelt in front of her and took off her shoes. She stepped out of them. Then he reached for the fastenings on her jeans.

She had worn such casual clothes as a general *fuck off* to her father. He hated seeing her in jeans. But somehow she doubted her father would be happy about her taking them off, especially since Io was doing the honors.

Io's fingers made short work of the button and zipper and peeled the denim down her long legs. He bathed her with a sigh that sounded like a half-moan as he leaned forward to kiss the teardrop of her left thigh, just above the knee.

She was fully naked except for the lacy panty that matched the discarded bra, but even that had to go as Io hooked his fingers inside the delicate elastic at the sides of her hips and slowly pulled down.

Now she was fully naked.

Io leaned forward and buried his nose against the nearly hairless flesh of her femininity as he wrapped his arms around her hips. She gasped as his tongue forced between her lips and licked her just once, lingering against her hard nub for an eternity as he inhaled and exhaled over and over. Hot air rushed over her, then her skin cooled as he sucked her aroma back in, then he blew out once more, and then in. Repeat.

"So perfect," he said, then growled against her.

He dragged his mouth up her stomach, rising with deliberate ease to stand in front of her. Her fingers pushed into his thick, dark hair. He was so damn sexy. He gazed at her breasts again, sighing, admiring, making her tremble as he bent down. When his mouth closed over one rosy, tight nipple, Miriam dropped her head back so that the ends of her hair swayed over the rounded top of her buttocks.

"Io." She breathed out his name.

"Mmm." One hand spanned the small of her back while the other molded to the round softness of her breast and squeezed to pucker her nipple more deeply inside his mouth. His wicked tongue flicked the hardened flesh as he sucked the expanse of her nipple between his lips. His teeth nipped just once then he sucked again before pulling away to release her breast with a gentle, yet erotic, pop.

"God, I love your breasts!" He rose to his full height and brushed his lips over hers, urging her toward the bed.

When the backs of her thighs met the edge of the mattress, she climbed backward onto her knees, her lips separating from Io's as he pulled away. Poised on her knees, she froze. Io was a god, more virile than Zeus. His muscles stretched and bunched as he untucked his shirt and drew it up and over his head. *Best show in town.* She reached to help him.

"No," he said, grabbing her hand. If looks could start a fire, she'd have been a blaze. "Just lie down."

"You don't want my help?" She grinned as he shook his head in a way that let her know tonight was all about her, and that he wanted her to watch. "Fine, I'll wait." She sprawled back, propping herself on her elbows, swaying her bent legs back and forth. Funny how last night she had been nervous, but now all she wanted was to feel him. Amazing the difference twenty-four hours could make.

Io tossed his shirt to the floor, razing her with his gaze, then went to work on his belt. "You'll get plenty of opportunity to help. Don't worry." He pulled his belt free and unfastened his jeans.

Biting her lip, Miriam hardly moved, hardly breathed, and could only stare as he pushed down his jeans and stepped out of them.

He didn't have on underwear, and his erection jutted out in front of him, full and heavy and large. Suddenly, her nerves made a marked reappearance. How was he going to get that large rod of flesh inside her? Would it hurt? She had heard that first times hurt for a female. Now she understood why. Sure, she had seen him yesterday. She had even wrapped her hand around him. But for some reason, she hadn't thought—really, truly thought—about *that* going in *there* until just now.

Miriam didn't want it to hurt with Io. She wanted it to be perfect.

"Sshh," he said. He had rightly sensed her worry. "Just relax. Roll over."

Huh? "Roll over?"

"Trust me, baby."

She did as he said and rolled onto her stomach then felt the bed shift as he crawled up over her. The inside of his legs rubbed against the outside of hers and she shivered when she felt the head of his erection brush over her ass. What was he doing? Was he going to take her from behind?

Then his weight settled over her as he straddled her hips and sat on her bottom.

"Am I too heavy?" he said.

She shook her head. "No." She practically held her breath in anticipation.

His hand combed aside her hair, then his fingertips skimmed the length of her back from the arch down low up to her shoulders then down again. Over and over, he lightly caressed her back, then her shoulders and down her arms.

"Mmm, that feels good." She relaxed into the mattress as he increased the pressure of his touch. When had a massage ever felt so good? And been so unexpected? She wouldn't have taken Io as a foreplay-savvy kind of guy. Several minutes passed before he shifted his concentration to the lower portion of her back, and he scooted down.

She stiffened as his erection slid down her ass. But he didn't try to open her. He didn't push her legs apart. Instead, he slowly drew his palms down over her ass then kneaded her cheeks before caressing further down to the backs of her thighs. As he pushed his hands back up her legs, his thumbs pressed against her inner thighs and made contact with her labia as his fingers reached her buttocks. Repeatedly, he rubbed up and down her thighs, always pressing his thumbs against her tender flesh at the end of every ascent, getting her hotter with each passing second.

Miriam practically gushed between her legs when he urged her to roll to her back a few minutes later. Her body was alive, and every nerve ending sizzled, her breath coming in heady, rapid pulses. She could hardly think, only feel, a bouquet of lusty impulses she only barely contained. Faint light and shadows played over them both, but she was sure if he turned on a lamp, her entire body would be flushed crimson with arousal.

As if to punctuate her point, a soft purr lit in her chest, and she saw Io's erection twitch at the sound.

He bent over her body, doing to her front what he had done to her back, moving from her breasts to her stomach and still lower. He pointedly avoided the heart of her, but teased ruthlessly with his fingertips as she parted her legs for him. His strong hands kneaded her hips, her thighs, the insides her legs, and his fingertips grazed lightly down the junctures where her legs and torso met. Damn, Io had her lit up brighter than a spotlight, and just as fiery hot.

When he urged her legs to part, she didn't resist. She wasn't even nervous. She was so hot for him nothing else mattered than getting him inside her. Now.

He lowered himself between her legs and drew the tip of his tongue up her inner thigh.

Jesus! Was he trying to kill her?

He switched to the other leg, then back again, crawling ever higher. Was she even breathing? Everything centered around his tongue and the inch-by-inch upward journey it was making toward her quivering heat. His lips brushed farther up, his tongue followed, his fingers teased, and her body tensed with what was sure to be an even more powerful orgasm than the one he'd given her yesterday.

His mouth passed over her slit and just the feel of his breath on her clit nearly sent her into orgasm. *Christ!* A full body shudder quaked her, and she choked back a stifled groan. And still he refused to put his mouth directly on her core. His lips kissed from side-to-side, almost as if he was worshipping her. Each kiss drew closer…so close, ever closer, until finally….

He closed his mouth over her swollen nub and licked just once, long and with a drawn-out exhale that sounded more like a sigh of relief.

Head thrown back, eyes slammed shut, her fingers dug into the bed as she sucked in her breath. She was going to come. There was no stopping it.

Io's hands pressed against her inner thighs, holding her open, and his thumbs pulled her labia apart as he licked her again once more.

She nearly blacked out from the force of her orgasm. Her entire body lifted off the bed as she blew apart, crying out.

In an instant, he was above her, the head of his erection opening her as he pressed in. She felt a pinch, then tightness, and then his body was flush with hers. She was still in the throes of orgasm, coming against all his steely hardness. If anything, his hard presence served only to intensify her orgasm and she locked her arms around him and cried out again, quaking violently.

"That's my girl," he said, grinding his pelvic bone against her clit. "That's my baby."

Then he bit her, just sank his fangs right into her shoulder and rocked against her body as the venomous euphoria took her, making her come again as her body relaxed as if she were floating on a sea of clouds. The pleasure of climaxing during venom euphoria was unreal, and Miriam could only choke out an abrupt gasp from the force of the sudden rapture.

IO HAD WORKED HER INTO WELCOMING HIS BODY in the way he had learned ages ago. He hadn't thought he would ever have need of the technique, but now he was grateful to have learned it. A female's first time could be uncomfortable or pleasurable, depending on the care given her by the male claiming her flower. And Io had made sure Miriam's first time was as pleasurable as he could make it.

Paving the way by exciting her, then taking her while she climaxed, was much better than taking her when she hadn't been properly prepared. Dosing her with euphoria was the final step in persuading her body to relax enough to accept his size. And the way Miriam shuddered and cried out again told him she was good and relaxed. Only a fully relaxed female could climax again so quickly after already having two powerful releases.

He sucked hard on her neck as his body tightened, taking in her blood as it flowed over his tongue like spirits. Her feminine sheath contracted around him through another, less powerful release and he couldn't hold back any longer. Giving her long, hard strokes, he felt his already-tight scrotum strain higher.

He growled. It was time to take what was his...to claim her as a properly mated male.

Pushing himself up on his arms, he released her neck and slammed his hips into her as his seed poured into her body.

"I'm coming, baby."

Her glossy, blue eyes sparkled in the scant light as her gaze met his. Her body was spent, and soon his would be, too. At least for a little while. And then he would do it all over again. The day without her had infused him with a need to take her as many times as his body would allow before giving out. He needed to mark her, put his scent all over her, implant her with his body's offerings until he had nothing left but his mangled, sated body. He had never felt anything like this before—this overwhelming need to take the same woman over and over until his body was dry and completely wasted and unmoving. The urge felt almost instinctual. Was this part of the mating bond? Surely, his calling hadn't gone into full effect already. It was too soon.

Io lifted himself off Miriam and rolled to his back, taking her with him. As she collapsed on top of him, he pulled her close, caressing her back. Her long, black hair fell over his chest and shoulders in waves of silk. She purred and rubbed her cheek over his chest, slithering against him as she settled in.

He kissed the top of her head. "You okay, baby? Did I hurt you?" Rarely in the past had he been concerned about a female's comfort, but Miriam's was all he seemed able to think about now.

She turned her face into his skin and kissed the generous swell of his pec. "No, you didn't hurt me." *Kiss.* "I'm surprised. I thought it would be painful."

"It *can* be." He caressed her face with the backs of his fingers. "But I took extra care with you. I didn't want to hurt you."

"My thoughtful male. You honor me."

"No, Miri. It's you who honor me." He cupped his palm against her face, cradling it. "You've entrusted me with the most valuable gift you can give, and I promise always to cherish your virtue and hold it next to my heart as if my life depends on it."

Io had never been one for romantic proclamations, but with Miriam he was Shakespeare. Her Romeo. Waxing poetic spilled from him as if he'd been writing poetry all his life.

"I love you, Miriam. You are my lifemate, my lover, my friend. You are my life now." He spoke the words in their ancient tongue. "I will honor you always above all others."

Her eyes lit with recognition of the ancient vow between mates. Obviously, Miriam had been versed in the old traditions and knew what his words meant. They were the equivalent of human marriage vows, only stronger.

She replied in the ancient tongue, as well. "I love you, too, Io. You are my lifemate, my lover, and my friend. Your life is my life, and mine is yours. I will honor you forever."

He pulled her close, kissed her, and then she snuggled against him. They were mates, and now it was official. They didn't need a ceremony, or anyone to witness their promise to one another. What he and Miriam had just done was akin to running off to Vegas to get married. They had eloped and spoken the vows that would forever link them. Vampires took the ancient vows very seriously. No marriage certificate was required. No rings needed to be exchanged. Say the words, and that was all. And he had just said them, and so had she.

He was bound to her forever, and she to him. He was off the market. Who would have thought monogamy would appeal to him so deeply?

Only one thing could have made him happier: being able to share the news with his best friend.

CHAPTER 34

AFTER HAVING THE CHAUFFEUR DRIVE HIM around the streets of Chicago so he could get his emotions in check and think, King Bain returned home and met Donovan at the door.

"Here." Bain handed over the key to Io's house.

Donovan took the key and removed the bright yellow tag before attaching it to a gold keychain. "When would you like me to go?"

King Bain considered his question a moment. "Tonight."

"Sire?"

Miriam's easy acceptance of the situation, in combination with the odd way his guards had returned from Io's house two days ago had made Bain more and more uneasy on the drive home. She had been too eager to go. Something wasn't right.

"Yes, Don, tonight. They won't be expecting an inspection so soon. If something is going on, I want to know about it now." He narrowed his eyes on his head guard. "Are you sure you found nothing when you were at his house before?"

"Yes, Sire. I found her chaste. The gentleman was asleep in a chair."

"And your broken nose? How did that happen again?"

Donovan reached up and touched his nose, which still showed a hint of black and blue. The doctor on staff had had to re-break it and reset it when Donovan had arrived home. "I startled the master of the house with our intrusion. He apparently thought we were there to hurt your daughter."

"Io didn't see the royal insignia on your clothing?" King Bain was feeling worse and worse about the situation. He should have listened to his gut before sending Miriam back to Io's house, but he'd been in too much of a hurry to see her illness treated. Now, his carelessness might prove costly.

"As I said, we startled him."

King Bain had a feeling he would have to call in Cordray. She was a day walker whose power, among other things, allowed her to sift through the minds of others and find where memories had been altered. Then she could release the original memories. Her gifts came in handy during legal proceedings, but he kept her close for other reasons, as well.

"Donovan, gather the team you took to Io's house and meet me in the conference room in half-an-hour." He wiped his palms over his face. He wanted to get some sleep, but this couldn't wait.

"Yes, Sire." Donovan bowed his head and followed him into the house.

The two parted as Donovan headed off in the direction of the security office, and King Bain marched upstairs to the master suite that took up the entire top floor of the mansion.

His queen was settled on a chaise lounge, reading. She looked up. "How did it go?"

"Too easily for my comfort, Cara." He whipped off his wool scarf and shrugged out of his leather jacket before hanging them in the closet.

"What do you mean?" Cara set down her book.

"I mean she was much too agreeable. She didn't argue or fight like she always does. I think more is going on here than we've been led to believe. I'm calling in Cordray."

Cara drew back, her hand shooting to her throat as she inhaled sharply. She didn't like Cordray. Cara said Cord made her uncomfortable, which was understandable. She made a lot of people uncomfortable, and not just because of her powers. It was Cord's appearance and demeanor that usually put people off. But she was thorough and skilled at what she did. There was no one better in her field. Bain's fondness for her went beyond business, but no one, not even Cara, knew the real relationship between Bain and Cordray, which was a secret they both protected.

"Is that necessary?" Cara fingered the ruby pendant that sat between her collarbones.

"Yes." King Bain turned and left, not wanting to deal with Cara's criticism of his half-sister, who happened to be his most trusted consultant. He took the spiral staircase two-at-a-time as he descended. Something was going on with his daughter, he just didn't know what. But he could guess, and none of his guesses eased his mind.

When he reached the main floor, he took out his cell and punched in Cordray's speed dial.

"Yes?" The female's husky voice answered after only one ring.

"I need you here. I need a sweep."

"Who?"

"Donovan and his team."

"I'll be there in fifteen."

The line went dead. But that was how conversations went with Cord. Short, crisp, and to the point. Admittedly, he afforded her a long leash in exchange for her expertise, as well as for who she was. Only she could get away with being so cold and cavalier toward him. So far, no one had questioned him about how she got away with talking to him the way she did, but if anyone ever did, that person would learn how the term, "None of your business," could actually break bones. He only barely tolerated Cara's vague remarks where Cordray was concerned.

Cord was a merciless firecracker. Well, she was more like full-on TNT than a firecracker, but then maybe that was simply a side effect of her inability to feel physically. She could touch, but not feel. Pain that would cripple a warrior was but an inconsequential pinprick to Cordray.

Bain had once met with her after she had retrieved a bounty. Gunshots had been fired during the skirmish, but, as always, Cord had taken the man down. During their conversation, Bain had noticed what appeared to be a stain on her black shirt, just above her elbow. After the stain grew larger, he had asked her about it, and she had pulled up her sleeve. She had been shot.

"Oh, I didn't know," she had said, poking her finger into the wound and digging around until she pulled out a slug.

Afterward, she had lowered her sleeve and continued her discussion with him as if she hadn't just performed outpatient surgery on herself with a finger.

What would it be like not to feel? Not to suffer pain, whether physical or emotional. One thing was certain, Bain wouldn't be feeling so helpless and keyed up right now over what might or might not be happening to his daughter. And that would be a blessing.

The idea that he could have been duped pissed him off. Had this whole thing been a trick for her to get back to Io's house? And if so, how deep did the lie run? Tristan? Gregos? His gut told him that whatever was going on between Miriam and Io had required the assistance of others. And it had started that first night. Something had been done to his guards' memories. Somehow Io had been able to alter their minds. The filthy heathen! How had Bain missed this? Why hadn't he thought of this before? And how could Miriam have done this to him?

Twelve minutes later, the intercom beeped in the room.

"Yes?"

"Cordray Buveau, Sire."

"Send her down."

King Bain stepped into the hall and saw Cord walk through the large double doors at the entrance. She wore black, black, and more black. A long leather trench that looked more like plastic flared at her ankles as her measured, purposeful strides ate up the floor. Black, skintight leggings hugged long, slender legs, and a loose, black shirt covered her ample breasts under her coat.

Her choice of footwear surprised him, though. Knee-high combat boots with thick soles and silver hooks for the laces made her look like a gothic mercenary. She usually wore stylish shoes from top designers, but the one thing Bain knew about Cordray's fashion tastes was that she had a shoe addiction. No doubt she had an entire wing of the mansion he'd given her devoted to her collection of shoes. The boots were no doubt another addition to her growing horde.

"Hell, Bain. I could hear your thoughts from outside," she said from halfway down the hall. She flipped her hair off her shoulder.

She had a new hairstyle, too. Surprise, surprise. When did Cordray not do something bizarre to her head of long, black hair that hung down past her ass? Today, it looked like she had a mix of twists and braids that tracked over her scalp before falling in thick, heavy, serpentine tails over her shoulders and down her back. And she had dyed sections a bright shade of aquamarine. The color accented her brilliant, blue eyes perfectly.

A strap of leather with a hook on it served as a choker around her neck, and wide leather cuffs adorned each wrist. A variety of silver and gemstone rings decorated each finger with skulls, snakes, dragons, scorpions, spiders, and Celtic designs, and a silver hoop pierced one nostril. The colorful, feathered wings of a dragon tattoo that wrapped around her torso could be seen on the exposed skin of her chest and shoulders.

In short, Cordray was a walking conversation piece, scary-looking and unbending, with the chutzpah to back up the image if anyone pushed her.

She stopped in front of him, her intense blue eyes flashing. "What's got you so pissed off?" Her eyes narrowed, brow knitted. She was more concerned for him than she needed to be. As usual.

"Do I really need to answer that?"

She shrugged one shoulder, smirking. "We'll talk later."

He nodded once. "Thank you for coming. As always." He tried to maintain an air of entitlement with her, but sometimes he didn't want to have to work that hard.

"Of course." She glanced over his shoulder. "Where are they?"

As if on cue, Donovan, Joseph, and the other members of Don's team entered through the main doors.

Their steps slowed when they saw the six-one Cordray standing next to him. As with Cara, his guards weren't huge fans of her either.

"I'll wait inside," Cord said flatly, one brow arched as she cast the four guards a disdainful glance. She knew how she was perceived. She accepted it, but Bain could plainly see the guards' reactions got on her nerves.

She walked around him and into the conference room.

Donovan and each member of his team bowed their heads as they passed the king and followed her. He took a deep breath and went inside, closing the door behind him. Now he would find out the truth.

CHAPTER 35

MIRIAM AWOKE WITH HER HEAD ON IO'S CHEST. The two of them had dozed off after he had claimed her. She still couldn't believe how pleasurable her deflowering had been. She had thought it would be uncomfortable, but Io had expertly tended to her. He had known just what to do, and other than a minor pinch and a little bleeding, her first time had been memorable for all the right reasons.

She smiled against his chest. She loved him, and he loved her. They had spoken the vows to each other. Her father would be furious, but she didn't care.

Suddenly, she shivered and a tingle zipped through her body. Instantly, her skin began to itch.

"Are you okay?" Io immediately awoke and sat up beside her, rubbing his palm over his face. "Withdrawal?"

She nodded and shivered again. "Yes. How did you...?" Her brow furrowed, a perplexed grin splashing across her mouth between shivers.

"It's a mated male thing. I connected my mind with yours as we dozed off."

"Oh." This mated business just got more and more interesting.

Io hopped out of bed and put on a pair of sweats. "I'll go make you a cup of elixir."

She shivered again, and her teeth chattered. "Okay."

He hurried up the stairs, and she got up and went to the restroom. A sudden wave of nausea swept through her.

Whoa! Bending over the sink, she quickly turned on the faucet, splashed water on her face and throat, and tried taking deep breaths to calm the queasy feeling that broke her out in a cold sweat.

She must have been in the bathroom longer than she thought, because Io suddenly appeared with a mug of elixir. Oddly enough, just the putrid scent of it calmed her stomach, and she guzzled it down as if her body craved it.

"You okay, baby?" Io sounded concerned, and he rubbed his hand over her back and pulled her to him as he took the cup with his free hand and set it on the counter.

"Yes. I think so." She placed her hand on her stomach and took another deep breath and blew it out. "I just got a bit queasy."

He held her for a minute, soothing her skin with his palms and combing his fingers through her hair. "That's normal during detox. It'll get better." Io kissed her forehead. "You should have seen me. I was a mess. In way worse shape than you are."

She nodded, feeling her body calm, then turned her face into his neck and kissed him.

He felt good. Hard, strong, like her protector. Big. Solid and sexy as hell. Her withdrawal pushed into the back of her mind and now all she wanted was to be back in his arms, his body marking hers again, making her feel decadent and sensual once more.

"Come on, let's get you back to bed." Io took her hand.

His marvelous green-brown eyes twinkled with lust, and she noticed the tent in his sweats. He needed the same thing she did.

She turned off the bathroom light and followed him back to the bedroom. Her body hummed with arousal, as if answering the call of his, and she wanted to spend the next several hours wrapped around his body.

As if reading her mind, he let go of her hand and took off his sweats before lifting the covers and climbing underneath. He rolled to his back and held the covers up for her to join him.

As soon as she slid in beside him, he dropped the blankets over them and engulfed her, pulling her on top of him.

"I can't get over how hard I am for you." He smoothed his hands over the cheeks of her ass. "How badly I want you." His hands squeezed and pulled her as he shifted his hips down, making his cock slide down the center of her, parting her.

She gasped.

"Mmm." He pushed her back down and rocked his hips forward, creating a friction between them that was beyond amazing.

Her breasts mashed against his chest and she planted her mouth over his as she lifted her hips and reached down for his erection. He worked with her, their bodies shifting and moving gently until the head of his cock breached her. As she bore down and took him all the way, they both sighed then moaned.

"Baby, you're tight." Io wrapped his arms around her, holding her snugly against him, gently rocking. "And wet."

Now that he had already taken her, this time was easier. She closed her eyes and focused on how he felt. Big. He felt big, and all that hard size stretched her, but in a way that felt so right.

"Baby, fuck me. Take what's yours," Io tensed beneath her, his lips pressing against her throat on a moan.

"How? I don't know how." Being on top was intimidating, and self-consciousness halted her body. What if she moved wrong? Would she look stupid? Would Io be underwhelmed with her novice ability?

"Ride me. The way you did the other night, but with me inside you this time." His voice cracked. "I'll help you."

He pushed her up so her body wasn't flush against his. "Sit up on me. That's it. Sit up where I can see you."

She did as she was told and his hands instantly thrust up and over her breasts, teasing her nipples into tight peaks. "My God, but you're beautiful. So damn beautiful."

Her heart somersaulted, and another layer of her soul melted for him. He didn't seem to care that she had never done this before, or that she fumbled to figure things out.

"Now, move your hips against me," he said.

She worked forward and back tentatively. Was she doing it right? Should she go slow? Fast? Where should she put her hands? She nibbled her lip. This was harder than being on the bottom. On the bottom, he took control and she just went along, but now she played the dominant role. She wasn't very good at it.

She was about to stop and beg him to be on top again when he released her breasts and grabbed her hips. "Like this." He pushed and pulled, working her the way he wanted her to move. "That's it. Hard like that. Just ride me, forward and back." He pursed his lips, groaned, and gasped as he continued to help her get a rhythm. "Damn, Miri."

Once she got the hang of it, he released her hips and clutched her breasts again, squeezing, teasing, working her nipples into hard nubs.

She ground her hips forward and back and around in tight circles, swiveling and rocking. Mmm, this was nice… getting nicer.

"See, like that," he said. "Yeah, God yes, that's it. Like that."

The position lent to a nice massaging of her clit against his pubic bone, but if she angled her hips just a little forward… yes, just like that—Yes, the contact between pubic bone and clit intensified.

"God, baby, that's sexy."

She tossed her head forward, and her long hair cascaded over her face so that the ends brushed his chest and stomach. With her hands pressed against his chest, she looked down and lifted up then lowered back down, watching his ridged shaft disappear inside her. The sight made her moan.

"That's it. Watch what you're doing. Watch me disappear inside you."

The visual was enough to make her catch her breath and curl her toes, especially when he moaned his own approval as their bodies met. Over and over, she pulled up then lowered herself back down, his cock burying deep.

"This is nice," she said, finally bringing her gaze back to his.

"I can think of another word for it." Io pulled her flush

with his body again, and her breasts mashed against his chest as he began to drive into her hard and fast from below. She exclaimed with each pounding thrust, her lower body bouncing up and down in time with his jackhammer action as he held her upper body securely in place.

"Harder, Io!" She wanted him to be rough. She had already had soft and romantic. She wanted to know the other side of sex.

And he gave it to her. With a heavy growl, he pushed her off him and jumped around behind her. In a heartbeat, she was on her knees, and he yanked her back, positioning the head of his erection between her swollen labia. Growling, he surged into her.

Oh my God! He hit her differently inside. Better.

"Yes! More...*more!*" Damn, she didn't know sex could get better, but this new position. Wow! Yes! Better didn't describe it. Her whole body reacted to the way his cock rode up and down against her inner walls, the friction sparking heat to flood her everywhere and her breath to come in prolonged, heavy pants. And was that her voice? Moaning and begging him not to stop? She was lost to him, wanton and in need.

One of his arms wrapped around her waist, pushing and pulling her with each harsh, insistent thrust. His other hand brushed her hair off one shoulder then swung around to grip her breast almost painfully. But pain was good. So good. It intensified the pleasure. Io grunted with each forward plunge, hoarse, sucking down oxygen with a rasping inhale every time he pulled back.

The sounds he made were hot and sexy, and every choked groan sent her further toward yet another orgasm.

When his hand shot down between her legs and his fingers began urgently rubbing her clit with tight circles, she saw stars.

"I'm gonna come again, baby. Come with me. I'm close. Baby, you're so fucking sexy." Io licked her shoulder. Once, twice. Then....

"YES!" She cried out and threw her head back against his shoulder as his fangs pierced her skin and his venom coursed into her body.

Within seconds, she splintered into euphoric orgasm, her body convulsing uncontrollably as he struggled to hold her up against the first wave of his climax.

Io's jaw tightened, his fangs sinking deeper, and she imagined his eyes were slammed closed as he growled low in his throat—almost a long, sustained groan really. And then warmth flooded her between her legs, inside her and down her inner thighs as he continued to pump hard and fast, riding out his orgasm.

Finally he pushed her forward and collapsed over her back before releasing her shoulder with a heavy gasp.

"I love you." He tucked his arms around her and held her tightly. "I can't believe I love you this much already."

It was the mated male coming out of him. Miriam smiled to herself as she locked her fingers around his and tucked their joined hands against the side of her breast. She had found her mate, and it had been her cobalt addiction that had led them to one another. Life sure worked in mysterious ways.

CHAPTER 36

BEHIND CLOSED EYES, Cordray worked through the heads of Donovan and the other guards. Someone *had* tampered with their memories, just as Bain suspected.

One-by-one, she unwound the false memories and reopened the real ones, seeing a dark-skinned vampire with a bald head and pale eyes as the one who had performed the mind job on them.

He was a powerful vampire. Dangerous, too, but only to his enemies. Through the minds of Bain's guards, Cordray sensed that he meant well. Unfortunately, he had screwed up. Bain would never allow his actions to go unpunished.

And, based on what she saw get unlocked in these four guards' memories, the vampire known as Io would be lucky to live beyond the next twenty-four hours.

This was one fucked-up covert op these other vampires had going on. One she feared wouldn't end well.

Not that she necessarily enjoyed or wanted to rat anyone out, but she had a job to do. She would do it. It was that simple. Io and that dark-skinned vampire—Trace, his name was—had to be accountable for their actions. If they couldn't do the time, they shouldn't have committed the crime. And not only was playing house with the king's daughter considered a criminal activity, so was tampering with the minds of anyone in the king's employ.

She opened her eyes and looked at Bain as the guards remained compelled and tranquil.

"They were altered." She sat back and twirled the wide, silver band on her left thumb.

Bain cursed and stood, paced, then turned back toward her. "Tell me what you saw."

"The one known as Io has taken liberties with Miriam."

If a volcanic eruption had a face, Bain would have been it. "In what way?"

Cordray leaned back and steepled her fingers in front of her. How to put this? She was usually blunt, but this was Bain's daughter they were talking about—Cordray's half-niece—and she tried to filter her words when they talked about Miriam. Now was an excellent time to filter. "They shared a bed. It's unclear whether they had sex, but she smelled like semen. She was also topless, as was Io, so he looked upon her flesh." A cardinal sin, according to Bain. Io had broken about ten different laws where Miriam was concerned, and that was only what she had seen in the minds of the guards. No telling how many laws he had broken that they weren't aware of.

Honestly though, she thought Bain was too protective, his laws archaic where her half-niece was concerned. But she usually tried to keep from lecturing him on how to be a father. He was too stubborn to listen anyway. "There was a... *closeness* about them." She paused, narrowing her eyes and preparing for the outburst her next revelation would cause. "He might be her mate."

Bain's face turned beet red, clearly nonplussed and livid, but he didn't speak. The concept of a volcano filling with lava before blowing out the crater came to mind.

"Who else was involved? Who altered my guards?"

Cordray placed her foot in the chair and loosely wrapped her arms around her leg as she sat back. "I see two other vampires. Traceon and Severin. Trace is the one who altered the guards." She pointed around the room at them. "And a phone call was made to Tristan. From what I gathered, Tristan gave the order to erase their memories."

"Tristan?" Bain looked down and placed his hands on his hips. "Why?" The last he asked as if to himself.

"I don't know. Do you need anything else?" She stood and grabbed her coat from the back of the chair. Her work was finished as far as she was concerned, and she had a guest waiting for her at home. She really wanted to get back.

"No, that's all." Bain spoke between clenched teeth, but she knew he wasn't angry with her.

She nodded and released the guards from her mind's hold. The tension that bristled among them as their original memories resurfaced smelled like fizz in a soda, bubbling under her nose.

Bain stopped her as she proceeded toward the exit. "Cordray, when the time comes, I will need you to testify."

She had figured as much. "Fine. Let me know when."

Bain tilted his head in deference. "I'll be in touch."

Bain still looked like he was on the verge of tearing his home down with his bare hands, but that wasn't her problem. She left the room, left the house, and dematerialized back to the front yard of her tree-obscured mansion on the outskirts of the city. She hardly used the mansion, but tonight she'd needed companionship.

The sky was black as pitch in the deep of night, and it was perfectly quiet as she approached the porch.

Cordray stepped inside, removed her coat and gloves, and then started up the grand staircase in the dark as she began peeling off her shirt.

The human female she had picked up earlier was still in her bed when Cordray entered her bedroom, but the woman was asleep. Cordray had needed to feed earlier, and this human had caught her eye. Perhaps next time she would select a male, but tonight, she had been drawn to this woman. Blondes did something for her.

Cordray sat down on the edge of the bed and took off her boots and leggings, leaving her in nothing but her tattooed skin and piercings, then climbed on top of the human.

"Mmm, hi." The pale-haired beauty rolled to her back under her. "You're back."

"Yes." Cordray bent down and kissed the human as she pulled the sheets down to reveal her breasts. Cord smiled at the way her black hair looked against the woman's blond tresses. Sexy. A duality...the light and dark together. She had a way with symbolism.

Gentle hands skimmed around her back and pulled her down. "I'm glad."

Cordray climbed under the sheets with her. "Me, too."

The interlude was about feeding, but there was no reason why she couldn't give another pleasure while she took sustenance. Being that she could no longer feel, giving pleasure to another was as close as she came to experiencing it herself.

CHAPTER 37

KING BAIN'S GUARDS WERE FULL OF PISSED-OFF and ready-to-kill.

"That motherfucker jacked with our memories!"

"I'll kill him. I swear to God I'll kill him."

"I knew something wasn't right about all this. I just knew it."

Damn it, they needed to shut up. It wasn't like they had daughters who had defied them, had been touched by unworthy hands, and who now had a...my God...a mate, if what Cordray said was true.

How could this have happened? His daughter was supposed to take an approved mate, someone worthy of her royal blood, someone Bain endorsed and had hand-selected, not...*Io!* He was so far down on the unapproved list he didn't even rank.

Bain didn't know where to start. Which problem did he tackle first? His gaze swept the room, from the bitching guards, to the floor, to the window, back to the floor, and then to the ceiling as if he was going to find the answers floating in the air. He was numb. He couldn't focus. The anger and confusion roiling through his mind were so strong it nearly blinded him. He had been lied to. Not just by those who worked for him, but by his own daughter. Had her illness only been a ruse? Was she really ill or not? She had to be. How else do you fake an overdose? Unless her only intention was to craft a way to see Io. How far back did this scheme go? And who else was implicated besides Tristan and Traceon?

But the worst of it was that Miriam was back in Io's home,

maybe even in his arms…or his bed.

The thought stopped him in his tracks. *His bed?*

"Shut up!" He swung his attention around to his still quibbling guards.

Donovan and the others instantly quieted and bowed their heads in apology.

"Get over to his house and get my daughter." His voice was dangerously lethal, low and seething. He was barely keeping the lid on his aggression.

"Yes, Sire. And what of the male? Io? Shall we kill him?"

The idea was tempting, but this was one execution he wanted to handle himself. "No. Bring him to me. I will see to him personally."

"Yes, Sire." Donovan nodded briskly then led the others out.

King Bain paced. His long, black hair hung down the sides of his face and over his chest to his waist, swaying as he turned and looked out the window. He felt defeated. Had Gregos known the truth? He doubted it, but certainly Tristan had known. How could he not? He had given the order to alter his guards' memories. They all had to be punished. They would all suffer for their lack of fealty and disregard for the law, especially Io and Trace, who had committed the worst offenses of all involved. Trace had altered his guards' minds. Even though Tristan had given the order, Trace should have refused, because ultimately, everyone answered to the king's law. And Io had…well, Io had done what Io was good at doing. He had soiled his daughter. That philandering manwhore had dared lay his vile hands on her. Everyone knew the laws surrounding his family, and especially Miriam. Io would pay for his crimes.

He took out his phone and punched in Gregos's number.

Gregos answered swiftly, as he always did. "Sire?"

"Contact Stryker. Tell him to arrest Traceon. Then bring me Tristan. Now."

Gregos hesitated long enough for King Bain to realize the liaison didn't know what to think about Bain's commands then said, "Of course. Right away."

Bain disconnected, set his phone on the table, then linked

his hands behind his back as he walked toward the window and looked out into the darkness. All he could do now was wait. And seethe. Seething was good. It gave him time to fantasize about exactly how he would kill Io once he got his hands on him.

CHAPTER 38

Io's FINGERS PLAYED OVER THE CURVES of Miriam's body. They had made love for what felt like hours, deep into the night. He had taken her every way imaginable, and still, he wanted more. If this was how it was for a mated male even without the calling in full force, he was all for it. Sex had never been more satisfying.

Her hand was wrapped around the back of his neck, her lips working against his in rhythmic caresses as her latest orgasm continued to simmer her flesh and milk another of his releases from his cock.

How many times had he come inside her? He hadn't known he could even come so much in one night, but as soon as one orgasm ended, another began to build as her body called to his to continue mating. He couldn't explain it. Maybe his calling had started and he just didn't realize it, because he did feel an undeniable pull toward her. It was like she was a lioness in heat, and he was the lion chosen to serve her. Except that wasn't how it worked with vampires. With vampires, it was the male who determined fertility. It was the male who went into heat, as it were, during his calling. And so far, it didn't feel as though his calling had officially begun. But then again, when had Io ever taken a mate? He had no first-hand experience to go on. Calling phases were a learn-as-you-go affair, not something set in stone that could be taught.

Calling or not, Miriam seemed just as willing to continue their lovemaking as he was, her body begging for more as she kept right up with him.

As if on cue, she purred. Damn, he hoped he never got

used to that. It was sexy as hell.

"Still aroused, are you?" he said, pulling away.

She nodded. "Yes." Her hands brushed up and over his chest, and her fingers squeezed his pecs.

"Me, too."

She smiled, and he kissed her gently.

"Unfortunately, it's time for another dose of elixir," he said.

She sighed. "Don't go."

"I'll be right back." He grinned. "I wouldn't want to shirk my duties as your rehabilitation and recovery counselor now would I?"

"Ha." She rolled her eyes at him.

He pulled out of her and fought to get out of bed. Damn, but he hated leaving the cocoon of her body. He just wanted to stay inside her for the next several hours. Shit, he even wanted to fall asleep with his cock inside her. She was the perfect sheath for him.

He filled the cup she had been using with water, squeezed in a drop of elixir, then returned to bed. "Here."

She drank it readily then handed the empty cup back as she smacked her lips and made a face at the aftertaste. At least she seemed to be getting more used to the pungent flavor.

"How long will the withdrawal last?" she said.

"It depends. The longer you use, the longer the withdrawal."

"I only used for a couple of months."

Io brushed her hair off her face and away from her eyes. "Then you'll probably have it bad for a few days. After that, it will be a little easier for a couple of weeks."

"I don't feel like it's bad." She traced a graceful finger down his throat to his chest, where it danced back and forth, up and down, around in circles, tickling his skin.

Her coy flirting made him lick his lips and grin. "Ah, but that's because I'm excellent at distracting you." He plucked her finger from his sternum and brought it to his mouth, licked it, took it between his lips, tasted her skin, and caressed it with his tongue.

Miriam's lips parted, and she stared at what he was doing with his mouth as if she had never seen anything so captivating.

After releasing her finger, he kissed her palm and settled in beside her, propped on his elbow. Her skin was smooth and warm, her body firm, made for his hand and his alone.

She lay down facing him. "How about you? How long did your withdrawal last?" Her eyes closed as he caressed her face and brushed back her hair.

He could smell his countless offerings wafting out of her. He liked that she smelled of him.

"I was in bad shape. It took me a couple of months to get through." He skimmed his palm down her abdomen to the curve of her hip. "Mmm, but I didn't have such a beautiful distraction to help me, though." He scooted closer and kissed her. "But I was overdosing practically every night and had used for over six months, too."

"How did you get through that?" She draped her leg over his, her fingers stroking lightly on his chest.

"Arion stayed with me. He helped me through."

"He was the one engaged to Persephone for about a heartbeat. What did he do for you? Was he a former addict, too?"

Io shook his head. "No. He never used. But he took care of me while I did." He looked down. Damn, he missed Ari. "Ari was the best friend a guy could have. He practically lived with me for six months, taking care of me, helping me get off the shit. It had to have been hell for him, but he never complained. He just held me while I puked, cleaned me up, poured that shit down my throat—even when I physically fought him, I might add." He glanced at Miriam and grinned. "He was...well, he was my best friend. What can I say? That's what friends do for one another."

"Was?" Miriam frowned at him. "What happened?"

Io shook his head and averted his gaze. Talking about Arion hurt.

Miriam's hand caressed his arm, but she didn't say anything, as if she knew he needed to reveal his thoughts at his own pace. He loved her even more for that.

"Arion and I had a falling out the night I met you." Had it really been almost three weeks ago?

"A falling out over what?"

Io took a deep breath and blew it out. "It's silly, really."

"I won't laugh."

Their eyes met and he saw his mate's love, pure and comforting, shining back at him. He felt completely safe, as if he could confess his most shameful behavior to her and she would absolve him and make him clean again.

"Arion's gay," he said, and before he could stop himself, the whole story poured out about Arion and Severin, as well as everything that had happened the night she was brought in to AKM during her first overdose.

She sat quietly and listened to every word.

"I treated him horribly, Miri. My best friend, who had been with me through everything, and I abandoned him. All because I was an ignorant ass. He's happy with Sev. They were made for each other like I was made for you, but I said awful things to him. I treated him badly. I'm such a terrible friend." He looked away, not wanting her to see the emotion welling in his eyes.

She reached up and turned his face back to hers. "You miss him." It wasn't a question.

"Yes, I do. I really miss him."

"Then apologize to him."

"I want to, but I'm afraid it's too late. I'm afraid I've done too much damage for it to ever be the same."

"You won't know unless you try, Io. But I don't think it's too late. I bet he misses you just as much."

"Sev says he does."

She perked up. "Well, see."

"Yeah, but—"

"Io, I'm sure it will be awkward at first. Maybe he'll be upset with you and won't be as friendly as he once was for a while, but I'll bet he comes around. You two were friends for so long. People can't just throw that kind of closeness away so easily."

Io wrapped his arms around her and pulled her against him. "I love you." How did you fall in love with someone you just met? Io had never thought it would be possible, but without question, it had happened to him.

She hugged him back. "I love you, too."

A loud crash exploded upstairs. It sounded like the front door had been busted right off its hinges, followed by a rush of footsteps.

"Oh my God!" Miriam jumped away and scurried for her clothes as he bolted out of the bed and did the same.

It didn't take an Einstein to know who had just barged into his home. But damn, they could have rung the doorbell.

"I didn't know they would do an inspection so soon," he said, yanking on a shirt after pulling on his boxer shorts.

"I didn't either!" Fear filled her eyes.

There would be no way for them to hide what had been going on between them. His scent was all over her and hers on him. He rushed to her after pulling on his sweats and helped her yank on her shirt then clutched her protectively in his arms. She gripped him tightly then kissed him.

"I'm sorry," she said.

There was no time to respond as the door to the basement splintered and the same guards from the other day barreled down the stairs. Miriam's hold tightened, and he tried to push her behind him, but she had none of that. She seemed intent on facing the guards by his side.

Donovan, whose face still showed signs of a broken nose, was a picture of menace as he stalked forward and backhanded Io.

"No!" Miriam yelled at him, but Donovan ignored her and hit Io again.

Seemed ol' Donovan had some pent-up anger left over from the last time they'd met.

"You ingrate," Donovan said, his lip curling. The bruised, brownish-yellow flesh around both eyes held the shadows of the damage Io had inflicted on him.

Io snarled. This was still his home, and Miriam was his mate. The instinct to protect both was greater than logical thought, which dictated he not fight back for fear of making the situation worse.

Miriam slapped Donovan. "Io is my mate and you will not

speak to him like that." She stood tall, head up and shoulders back. "You will address him in a manner fit for a prince."

This was clearly her arena, not his, and Io barely managed to remain silent as she unfurled her royal entitlements in an effort to protect them both.

"He has defiled the Daughter of Bain, and he has lied to the king," Donovan said.

"He has not defiled me." Miriam spoke with confidence and social grace. Io imagined she would make a fine politician. "He is my mate. As such, he is entitled to claim me, as it is written in law."

"That doesn't matter, Daughter of Bain. The law as it pertains to you supersedes all other laws, so Io must be arrested." Donovan reached for him.

"No." Miriam latched on to Io and pulled him back.

"Unhand him," Donovan commanded. "King's orders. He is to stand trial."

"No!" Miriam tried to protest and struck out at Donovan, but his men were already pulling Io out of her arms.

The physical distance stretching between them as the guards pulled him away was intolerable. An ache sprouted in his chest, and he reached for her. When the guards resisted and jerked on his arm, he whipped his head around and hissed at them, his fangs punching out.

Shit was about to get critical if they didn't let him go.

"Donovan! Let him go! I command you." Miriam glared at the head guard.

"No."

She slapped him, and tears sprung in her eyes. They were losing, and she knew it. They had gambled and lost. Score one for the king. Behind him, he heard the telltale sound of handcuffs. No fucking way was he being cuffed. Hell to the no!

Snarling, he began to resist until a pinprick in the side of the neck drew his attention. He snapped his head around and saw one of the guards pull away a syringe. The fucker sneered as if he'd just stolen the bride from the groom.

"Nighty-night," the guy said with a little finger wave.

Miriam sobbed nearby. "NO!"

But it was too late. Everything went hazy, then black.

Checkmate. Io out.

CHAPTER 39

STRYKER HUNG UP THE PHONE AND PUSHED AWAY from his desk, grumbling to himself. He had to arrest one of his own? Over someone taking a damn mate? Good thing he was mateless, girlfriendless, and wanted nothing to do with either. Love and romance and all that sexual shit were too much trouble. Messy. Not worth the effort. Let other males deal with that shit. He would keep his life simple. His hand was enough for him. He didn't need a female to give him his jollies, and he had carefully structured his life to keep exposure to the fairer sex at a minimum so he didn't risk tripping his inner I'll-fuck-your-world-all-up-and-take-a-mate mechanism.

Look at what had happened to Micah after losing Katarina. And Malek after losing Carmen all those centuries ago. Hell, even Severin and Arion had nearly died over mating one another. And now Io was playing the hi-I'm-your-mate game with the king's daughter?

Taking a mate. Nothing but trouble. Trouble Stryker didn't want, didn't need, and would avoid at all costs. He liked his orderly, plain-Joe life, thank you very much.

After stopping by dispatch to order a call to Devon and Bauer to meet him out front in five, he marched crisply down the hall to Tristan's office, full-on military hard-ass, his boots thunking heavily on the tile. Tristan was just hanging up his phone, his face pale. He looked up and met Stryker's gaze.

"You're aware?" Stryker asked.

Tristan nodded. "I just got off the phone with Gregos."

Man, this shit sucked elephant balls. He hated arresting Tristan. But orders were orders.

"You need to come with me, Tristan. I'm sorry."

Tristan stood up and grabbed his jacket. "Don't be. I knew what I was doing."

"Where's your boy?" It would save them a lot of time if Tristan could tell him where Trace was so they didn't have to look all over God's green earth for him.

"He stays at Micah's most of the time."

"You think he's there now?"

"Probably."

"Let's go." Stryker turned and began the long trek up the hall to the front.

Tristan fell in behind him. The waves of emotional pain pouring off him felt like sludge oozing out of the walls.

"We'll get this over with as fast as possible, Tris," he said, pushing open the door to the front. Comforting wasn't his thing, but he did feel for Tristan. This had to be tough, especially since he already worried over his pregnant mate.

Bauer and Devon were already waiting, a wall of big, tough, and muscular. Hopefully Trace would come quietly. He didn't want any confrontations, and he knew how bad-ass Trace was.

"Devon, you drive." Stryker got in the back seat of the Suburban on the driver's side as Tristan climbed in next to him. Bauer took the front.

Within minutes, they were at The Sentinel, where Micah lived. Stryker had heard Micah was moving back to his home in the burbs, but that he would be keeping the apartment, as well. With any luck, Micah was at the apartment tonight so they could get this shit done and over without a lot of wasted time to fill with awkward, uncomfortable silence.

"Official business," Stryker told the security guard who looked up and frowned at what must have looked like a football team's offensive line on the other side of his desk. Stryker liked to operate by the book and flashed his credentials and a very convincing badge. If the guard didn't let him up, he would have to compel him, but he hoped he wouldn't have to.

Thankfully, the guard got his drift and decided not to play

hero. He waved them past. "Go on up."

A couple of minutes later, they all stood outside Micah's door on the eighteenth floor. Stryker rang the bell once then knocked.

After what felt like too long, Micah opened the door, a scowl on his face. Apparently, he had been poking through their thoughts from the other side of the door and didn't like what he saw.

Micah was considered a young ancient, and he was extremely powerful, possessing an unusual ability to see inside the minds of everyone around him without even trying. Stryker didn't know where the unusual ability came from, because as far as he knew, Micah didn't have any mixed-bloods in his family tree. If he did, no one knew about it. Not even Micah.

Still, Micah was a natural-born leader. That much was evident by how he had changed since meeting Samantha. His gift of sight could make him a contender for the head of all AKM facilities, a role the king had left unfilled for decades since removing the last division head. In fact, if Micah's first mate hadn't been killed, sending him into a tailspin that had nearly destroyed him, he likely would have risen to the rank of AKM commander hundreds of years ago and would already be entrenched as the division head by now. Micah was highly intelligent, cunning, and now that he had Sam, he was unusually compassionate, which was a side of Micah Stryker had never seen before.

"What's this shit about?" Micah said.

And he was just as blunt and raw as ever.

MICAH GLARED AT THE ENTOURAGE OUTSIDE HIS DOOR. They had come to arrest Trace because he had followed Tristan's orders. How fucked up was that?

Tristan stepped forward. "Micah, just let us in. Don't cause any more trouble than there already is."

Trace appeared in the hall behind him. "What's going on?"

Micah held his arm up toward Trace, not wanting him to come any closer. If Stryker, Devon, or Bauer made a move, shit would go down and create a bigger disaster than they already had. "Nothing, Trace. Just hang, okay?" He turned his attention back to Tristan. "He was following *your* orders."

"I know," Tristan said.

To Stryker's credit, he hung back, letting him work things out with Tristan. Bauer and Devon stood on either side of Stryker, hands on their side arms, ready to go bodyguard at a second's notice.

Sam came around the corner, stopping behind Trace, worry on her face. "Micah, what's going on?"

"They're here to arrest Trace."

"Why?" She grabbed Trace's arm and stepped closer to him. Micah could see concern raging in her mind and wished there was something he could do or say to calm her.

"Because he followed Tristan's orders." Micah threw an accusatory glance at Tristan.

"What?" Sam looked confused.

"Never mind," Micah said. Then he looked between Tristan and Stryker. "If you arrest Trace, you have to arrest me, too. I knew about what was going on between Io and Miriam, and I helped."

"But you didn't actually break the law, Micah," Stryker said. "Trace did when he altered the king's guards' memories."

"At my order," Tristan said, tossing a challenging look at Micah as if to point out that he was, in fact, owning up to his part in what had happened. "So, I'm under arrest, too, in a manner of speaking."

"A manner of speaking?" Micah scoffed and stepped in front of Trace, blocking anyone from getting by. "I don't see you shackled, Tristan."

"No, but I'll be reprimanded."

"Yeah, and Trace will be arrested and put into containment. I can see what's going down." Micah tapped his temple.

"I know you can." Tristan sighed. "But believe me, this isn't easy for me, either."

"Fuck you." Micah glowered in disgust and looked down,

jacking his hands up on his hips.

Micah had pulled Tristan's ass out of the fire and saved his life more times than he could count back when Micah had been in charge of the King's Army. Tristan had joined his and Malek's company soon after Micah had become old enough to go into battle. In truth, it was Micah who should be in charge of the team now, not Tristan, but things had gotten fucked up after Katarina's death, and Micah had found himself lucky to even be allowed to continue on in AKM for all the hell he had put the others through. Still, after saving Tristan so many times, couldn't the guy return the favor and pull Trace's ass out of the sling just this once?

"Fuck!" Micah pounded the side of his fist against the wall. There was nothing anyone could do. He couldn't fix this without causing even more trouble for everybody.

"I'm sorry, Micah, but we have to take him in." Stryker looked over Micah's shoulder and addressed Traceon. "Trace, I need you to come with us."

Trace looked from Micah to Stryker, then back to Micah.

"I'm going with you," Micah told him, holding his gaze in a solemn, silent oath. "If they take you, they take me."

Trace looked at Sam, who immediately protested as she reached for Micah with one hand while keeping hold of Trace with the other.

"I'm sorry, Sam," Trace said. "It's my fault."

"No, Trace. You put a lid on that shit right now. This is not your fault. You were only following orders, and as far as my going with you? It's my choice. I won't let you go without me. You got that?" He wrapped his arms around Sam and kissed her forehead. "We'll be fine, babe. I'll take good care of him."

Stryker stepped forward to bind Trace. Sam winced and looked away.

"I've got him." Micah took over and swiped the binders from Stryker without asking, and then turned toward Trace, whose hard, pale eyes lifted without emotion to his.

As soon as their gazes met, an unspoken submission passed from Trace to him, making Micah's inner Dom stand up and take notice.

Ever since the night he and Sam had seen Trace at the BDSM party, and Micah had been invited by Trace's Domme, Mistress Diamond, to join her in working Trace over, Micah had exercised a measure of his Dom prowess over Trace. Simple shit, such as making Trace sit on the floor next to him like a dog or cuffing his hands behind his back and forcing him to watch Micah make love to Sam or even to watch him lightly work Sam over in his dungeon. But Trace had yet to give himself completely to Micah, and Micah hadn't pushed, despite wanting to take Diamond's place as Trace's full-time—and only—master. Micah could only do so much with Sam, but Trace was a treasure trove of Dom-worthy submissive that Micah wanted to sink his teeth—or rather his whip—into.

But with one look, right now, this very moment, Trace told Micah he wanted the exact same thing. So, why hadn't Trace taken that step with him? Why hadn't he asked Micah to give him exactly what he wanted? If only he could see inside Trace's thoughts the way he could everyone else's, finding answers wouldn't be so damn hard.

His brow furrowed as he eyed Trace and stepped forward, the binders held out in front of him. "Trace?" His tone was clear. They *would* discuss this as soon as they had the chance.

A flicker of understanding echoed through Trace's eyes, but he refused to look away. *Bad little submissive.* "Micah." He slowly raised his arms in front of him, his hands in loose fists, palms up. He looked almost eager. "Cuff me, Micah." Trace nudged his joined arms forward. "Bind my wrists."

Micah heard the excited thoughts racing through Sam's mind. He had talked to her at length about wanting to Dom Trace, and she had made it clear that the idea turned her on, even though she felt like a freak for admitting such a thing. As she watched Micah lift the binders to Trace's outstretched wrists, she instinctively knew what was happening between them, and her thoughts tittered excitedly, even if the circumstances were less than agreeable.

Micah glanced from Sam back down to Trace's wrists and wrapped the plastic binder strip around them, then pulled the end through as the plastic zipped over itself, the loop tightening. When he finished, Trace kept his hands extended and pushed them into the air.

"What?" Micah said.

"Too loose." Trace pushed his hands toward him again.

Micah's eyes narrowed. So Trace wanted to get things started right now, did he? He grabbed the end of the pull strip then licked his lips before yanking the cuff tighter. "You dare question me, slave?" He spoke quietly, leaning toward Trace, who dropped his gaze to the floor almost shamefully.

Sam's mind ran rampant with cautious excitement, but the minds of Stryker, Tristan, and the others shifted uncomfortably. They could tell something else was going on between Micah and Trace, but weren't sure what. Micah was picking up a lot of *What the fuck?* from them.

He tightened the binding further, causing Trace to grunt and wince then let out a sigh that sounded more like relief than suffering as he lowered his wrists. "No." He paused. "Master."

Ah, so there it was—what Micah had wanted to hear.

Stryker cleared his throat as if he were interrupting two lovers saying goodbye. "Okay, let's go." He kept his gaze down but urged them toward the door.

Micah and Trace exchanged glances one last time then Micah turned and kissed Sam.

"We'll be back soon, babe."

Her eyes sparkled knowingly. Micah had a new toy to play with, which meant she did, too. And no matter what happened with Trace's arrest, they both knew that this was what they had been waiting for.

CHAPTER 40

Apostle had just finished reviewing his plan with Chez and Jarek when a knock came on his hotel room door. With just a thought, he morphed back from his blue-skinned dreck form to the human form Bishop had assigned to him. The itching began instantly and he tugged the T-shirt he'd changed into away from his body as he pushed away from the round table where he, Chez, and Jarek had been going over details.

"This is probably Bishop's lackey," he said.

Chez and Jarek looked on with interest as he approached the door, apparently curious what kind of vampire Bishop would have in his employ.

When Apostle opened the door, an unremarkable vampire holding a plastic case bowed his head at him.

"I'm Jessup. Bishop sent me." Jessup didn't wait for an invitation into the room, walking in straight away.

Something was off with Jessup. He seemed too docile, too calm, as if he had been trained not to disobey.

Probably one of Bishop's experimental subjects. Apostle wondered if Jessup had been subjected to the scorpion torture test, too. He could see how a weaker-minded vampire could be tamed or brainwashed with such torture.

"What've you got there?" Apostle shut the door and shifted back to blue, nodding at the case Jessup still held.

"It's a collection kit. I was told we were retrieving blood from a vampire?"

"Yes, we will be. We're waiting for her to contact us. When she does, you'll go to room nine-oh-nine and join our associates to wait for her. I assume Bishop provided you with something to knock her out."

"Yes."

"Can I have it?"

Jessup set the case on the bed, popped open the latches, and pushed back the top. The inside was lined with foam, and several empty vials were situated in pre-shaped spaces, along with two syringes and a tiny bottle of blue liquid. Jessup pulled the liquid and one syringe out.

"Jarek." Apostle took the items and looked over his shoulder.

Jarek stood up. "Yes."

"Take this to Grotek and Chane." He handed over the bottle and syringe. "When Miriam makes contact, I want them to make sure she gets a dose of this instead of cobalt. After they confirm she's unconscious, we'll go in and get her blood.

Jessup looked between them as Jarek made for the door and left the room. "I also have orders to remove us from Grotek's and Chane's thoughts so they can't rat us out if they're caught."

"Good. I had hoped you'd say that." Apostle grinned.

He had every intention of making sure Grotek and Chane got caught. If he framed them, it would tie up the incident with the king's daughter in a nice, neat bow. The king and his enforcers would think they had the perpetrators and there would be no reason to look further for those responsible. It was a perfect plan. Apostle would get her blood, he and Jessup would never be implicated, Grotek and Chane would take the fall, and Bishop would get what he wanted: pure, powerful, vampire blood to create whatever Frankensteins he was working on in his lab.

"Now what?" Jessup looked around the room.

"We wait." Apostle arched an eyebrow at the small vampire.

"Is she on her way?"

"No. We're waiting to hear from her."

"How long?"

"As long as it takes." What was with the twenty questions? "If that means we wait a week, we wait a week."

"What if she never shows?"

Apostle deferred to Jarek, who shrugged. "I can't see why she wouldn't."

"But if she doesn't...?" Jessup looked between Apostle and Jarek.

Apostle sighed. "Then we'll come up with another plan. Satisfied?" Stupid, curious little vampire.

Jessup's forehead creased, but he nodded tightly. "Yes."

This just didn't add up. A vampire working with Drecks? Sure, it had happened, but it was rare, and Jessup didn't seem the type.

"Tell me, Jessup, why are you working with us?"

Jessup cocked his head quizzically and made a face. He appeared confused, as if Apostle's question confounded him. "What do you mean?"

"I mean...well, you're a vampire, Jessup. We're drecks. Don't you think it's unusual for a vampire to be working with drecks?"

Jessup frowned and looked down at his arms, his head tilting from side to side as if he was working through a problem. Then he glanced back up, his eyes clear and his face calm. "I'm sorry. What did you ask me?"

Apostle exchanged glances with Chez, whose eyebrows popped up as if to say he wasn't going near this one.

"Never mind, Jessup." Jessup had obviously undergone some type of intense programming, but Apostle wouldn't pursue the matter further. The less he knew about Bishop's experiments, the better. "Why don't you have a seat and rest up while we wait." He gestured toward the bed.

With a nod, Jessup shut the case and lay down as if just the mere suggestion that he rest made him tired. Creepy.

Apostle rubbed his palm over his arm uncomfortably, staring at Jessup, trying not to shudder at the memory of Bishop's scorpions stinging him over and over. Yes, he was fine not knowing the details of Bishop's experiments. Totally fine.

CHAPTER 41

MIRIAM STAYED GLUED TO IO'S SIDE as the guards dragged him up the steps and inside her home. Well, her father's home. She didn't consider this place *her* home anymore. Her father stood like an impressive but pissed off statue in the center of the grand foyer, his arms linked behind his back and his booted feet planted two feet apart on the tile. His brilliant blue eyes—so like hers—radiated a fury she had never seen in him.

Even so, she refused to wilt in cowardice. "Father—"

"To your room. Now." He didn't yell or move, but the deep timbre and dark echo of his voice indicated he was not to be tested.

Too bad for him, because Miriam intended to do just that. She took a deep breath, knowing she was in for a confrontation, the likes of which resembled Mount Saint Helens erupting. "No."

For the first time since they had entered, her father moved, his eyes flicking to hers a split-second before his head snapped toward her. "Now." The word drew out of him like a lion's snarl right before it attacked, long and deadly.

She stiffened her resolve and clasped her hands around Io's arm, stepping closer to him. "No." She matched her father's tone, leveling her gaze on him in a challenge.

"MIRIAM! NOW!" Her father's voice boomed as if through a loud speaker, echoing and vibrating the floor and walls.

Once the echo diminished and the air stilled, she simply squeezed closer to Io and repeated, "No."

So, they were at an impasse. Donovan and the other guards

stood behind her and Io, and her father stood in front. She had no escape any way she looked at it. She might be able to outrun the guards, but not her father, and she would go nowhere without Io.

Her father's jaw clenched and relaxed like he was chewing on something, but she knew that just meant he was pissed off. And goody for that. Because she didn't care. In fact....

"Io is my mate, Father. You have to honor him as my mate. It's the law." Her chin jutted out proudly.

Her father's face turned crimson. "It is also the law that you are not to be touched, daughter."

"Bullshit! Where is it written in those law creeds you pass that I am to remain untouched? Where?" She let go of Io and stormed her father like a bull. "Or that I am to be referred to as *Daughter of Bain* as if I don't have a name? Huh? Tell me. Tell me!"

Her father puffed up so that he looked six inches taller. "That is the law of this house." Again, his voice rang out and echoed. By now, it was likely that all the servants knew what was taking place and had taken cover.

"I am your daughter!" Her voice cracked as she screamed at him. "I am not one of your subjects! I am your goddamn daughter! You treat me like I'm no more than a peasant. I don't need a ruler, I need a fucking father! Why can't you just be my father?"

The two snarled and breathed heavily at each other, both standing firmly in their conviction but bracing for a fight.

"Take her to her room!" Her father gestured for the guards to come forward.

Before she could resist, the guards' hands closed around her arms. Io growled dangerously low in his throat. She swung her head around, trying to break free and get back to him. Io looked like a predator, his head tilted forward, eyes narrowed on the men pulling her away. Fangs flashed as he hissed, then his top lip curled up in a snarl. He pulled against Donovan and Joseph, his muscles bunching and his neck straining.

"She's mine." Io's voice was pure menace.

"She is no one's. Least of all yours." Her father snapped his fingers and the guards pulled her away as she kicked and screamed for her mate.

"Io!" She tried to wrench free, but it was useless. Every time she pulled from one fisted hand, another clamped down on her. She was surrounded. "Io!" Her chest ached, her heart shattering.

"No!" Io's deep voice echoed with mated aggression.

She turned, yanked, fought with all her strength, pulling against the guards. "Let me go! I need him. I *need* him!"

His feral eyes locked onto hers as he doubled his efforts to break free. "Let me go. She's mine. She belongs to me! Miriam!"

Miriam tried in vain to pull loose from the guards, but they dragged her up the stairs.

Within seconds, she was yanked out of sight of her mate. She screamed as pain knifed her chest. Half a heartbeat later, Io's answering howl ripped her soul. If she was hurting this much, she could only imagine the pain he was feeling.

CHAPTER 42

KING BAIN CLOSED HIS EYES as his daughter's and Io's cries pierced his ears. When he heard Miriam's screams become muffled behind the closed door of her room, he opened his eyes again and looked at the crumpled male in front of him. Io had fallen to his knees, his head reared back and his cries and growls sustained by what seemed to be an endless supply of air.

"Silence him," he said.

Donovan pulled another syringe from his pocket, bit down on the cap to pull it off, and then jabbed the needle into Io's neck.

Within seconds, Io slumped forward, quieted and unconscious.

"Lock him up," Bain said to Donovan. "In the basement."

Few prisoners were held in-residence, but he had special plans for Io. Bain wouldn't risk his escaping by transporting him to the off-site dungeon. And keeping him here hardly mattered, since he wouldn't survive the next twenty-four hours.

They dragged Io away, leaving Bain to consider what to do about Miriam. She had lied to him. She had defied him and knowingly broken the rules. And she thought Io was her mate, but he couldn't possibly be. Io wasn't good enough for her. Bain had envisioned so much more for Miriam than Io could provide, and in time she would see that.

Bain turned and headed up the stairs and down the hall to her room. Guards were posted outside her door and stepped aside to allow him in.

Miriam was sitting at her vanity, her face in her hands, shoulders hiccupping as she sobbed.

He frowned, pain blooming in his chest. When was the last time he had seen her cry? Seeing her upset...affected him. "It's for the best, you know."

MIRIAM JUMPED AND SPUN AROUND to see her father standing in her doorway. She spat at him. How dare he try to tell her what was best for her.

"For who? You? The people?" She sniffled and wiped her face with her palm. "It's certainly not the best for me, or have you even noticed?" She sure as hell hoped her father hadn't come in to give her a you'll-get-over-this-and-see-I'm-right-someday pep talk, because she really wasn't in the mood. As in, not even remotely close.

"You don't know what's right and best for you, Miri."

"Don't be so casual with me," she said, her words snapping like whips. "I'm to be called *Daughter of Bain*, or haven't you heard? I have no name. I am merely a poster child for propriety. My life isn't my own, and my father is a bastard. Hell, I don't even have a father anymore."

Her father flinched, her words leaving their mark.

"That's right." She continued, marching across the room to grab a tissue so she could wipe her nose. "I haven't had a father since I was a little girl, and even then, he wasn't much of one. Work always came first. I always took second seat...to the point I eventually became invisible and he could no longer hear my voice." She turned and glared at him, catching her momentum. "And how dare you tell me I don't know what's right. Io is my mate, Father. He mated to me. His soul chose mine, and mine chose his. And now you're going to punish him because of that." She waved her hand as if to dismiss him then turned away toward the heavily draped window.

"Miriam, he is not right for you. Io is not of your standard. He—"

"How dare you insult my mate!" She whirled on her father like a cyclone, her words flying fast and hard, punctuated by jabs of her finger. "And how dare you dispute the mating call you so adamantly uphold in your own court. I've seen you hand down orders and verdicts against suitors trying to stake a claim to a mated female. You have always upheld the rights of a mated male. Even in a case where a female was already wed, you have supported the dissolution of the marriage to allow a mated male the right to the claim nature granted him."

"That's different."

"How? Why? Because I'm your daughter?" She scoffed. "Really? You can't be serious. Do you realize how hypocritical you sound?"

"Miriam, you are special. You deserve more than Io can give."

She laughed, mocking him. "I wish you could hear yourself, Father." She shook her head and barked out a staccato laugh. "I deserve what every member of our race deserves: the right to be with my mate. If I had not been intended for Io, nature would not have seen fit to bond his soul to mine. So excuse me and go fuck yourself." She took a step back and crossed her arms, glaring at him.

Her father shook his head and turned for the door. He looked defeated but resolute.

She wouldn't let him leave that easily. "If you deny him, you break your own laws, Father. And if you hurt him, I will hate you forever."

Her father stopped, hesitated, then turned his head slightly to the side without looking back at her. "You already hate me."

With that, he walked out of the room.

Miriam could only watch him leave, stunned silent by the revelation that he might be right.

CHAPTER 43

IO AWOKE IN THE DARK CELL to his own voice shouting uncontrollably in a single, long wail that only broke long enough for him to breathe before continuing.

Excruciating pain pounded through his body, making his muscles feel like raw meat under a tenderizing mallet. *Pound-pound-pound*. With each beat of his heart, the sharp ache pulsed, driving him mad with agony.

And he had a hard-on as solid as steel.

Fuck! He *had* entered his calling with Miriam.

Snapping his mouth closed, he sat up and looked through the shadows for her. He needed her. Now! They needed to mate!

But she wasn't here. Miriam wasn't with him.

Shooting up off the dank mattress that felt like hardened, lumpy oatmeal, he attacked the iron bars, trying with all his might to pull them apart, but they wouldn't budge.

"MIRIAM!' He cried out for his mate, needing her in a way only a mated male understood.

When she didn't answer, he renewed his efforts to break out of his cell, flailing and throwing himself against the bars as he pulled and pushed.

Io needed release, and he needed it now. He felt like he would die if he didn't get it.

Pushing back from the cell door, he thrust himself into the darkened, back corner and shoved down the sweatpants he was still wearing and latched on to his cock with his fist. Pumping furiously, he cried out as he came almost instantly, not caring if he spilled on the wall, the floor, or wherever.

Still hard and in need, he continued fisting himself until he came again. The orgasms held no pleasure, only a harsh ache that ebbed as he shuddered through the last of the agonizing release.

His body eased up enough for him to collapse back to the mattress, but within minutes, the pain returned. Once more, Io lunged for the door, manic in his need to be with his mate.

"MIRIAM!" He cried out as a jolt of pain doubled him over.

"Do something!" Miriam stopped pacing and shouted at the guard at her bedroom door, tears streaking her cheeks. Her thumb rubbed up and down against her sternum, between breasts that throbbed with a kind of pain she had never felt. Why were her breasts so tender? Why did her chest ache so badly?

The sun had risen and set since she and Io had been dragged back to her home. Without Io's tonic, her arms itched and her head pounded, and she was getting worse. Listening to her mate in the dungeon below the house wasn't helping to ease the growing symptoms of withdrawal that threatened to overcome her, either.

"Can't you hear him?!" Miriam rushed toward the guard and slapped him. "He's in his calling, you asshole! He needs me! Let me go to him. Please!"

The guard's eyes wavered, probably because he understood as well as Miriam did just what was happening to Io right now. The calling without a mate was the equivalent of being kicked in the nuts with a sledgehammer dropped from a ten-story building, and like any sane male, just the thought was enough to make even the guard mentally cross his legs and wince.

"My orders are to ensure you stay in your room, Daughter of Bain."

Miriam screeched in frustration, throwing her hands in the air before pounding her fists against the guard's chest.

"Let me go! He needs me! You bastard, he needs me!" And

she needed him.

Withdrawal was reclaiming her, and she didn't have Io's tonic. Any progress they'd made to get her off cobalt was about to go out the window, because if she didn't get either tonic or cobalt soon, she would be in as bad a shape as Io, and it wouldn't be pretty for anyone who got in her way, if her outburst at Io's house the other day was any indication.

Another heart-ripping cry shot up from the basement, and Miriam threw herself against the guard, sobbing.

"Can't you give him something? Something to ease the pain or knock him out again so that he doesn't have to feel what he's feeling?" Miriam clung to the guard's shoulders, her head bowed in surrender. "Please. If you won't let me go to him, tell my father to give him something so he won't feel the pain anymore."

The guard shifted against her hold, and Miriam looked up. The guard's expression was cautious and dark. He almost looked guilty.

"What?" Miriam's blood ran cold. Something was wrong.

The guard remained silent, pursing his lips stubbornly.

"TELL ME!" She shoved him back against the door, her mounting withdrawal making her strong as she screamed at him.

He gasped and stared at her in shock, then said, "He who defiled you is to be put to death by moonfall, Daughter of Bain. He will be out of his misery soon enough."

By moonfall. By morning.

Miriam stumbled backward, her mental faculties short-circuiting. "No." The word licked from her on a staccato beat, and she fixed the guard in her gaze. "No. I don't believe you."

"It is to be so, Daughter of Bain."

Her room seemed to draw in on her as if she were flying backward into a tunnel as the walls caved and collapsed. Io was her mate. He was her life. They had sworn themselves to each other in the ancient words of commitment and devotion. She couldn't lose him. Not now. Not when she had just found him.

Io had been the only one to understand her. He had made

her feel alive again and had given her hope. Could her father really be so cruel as to take the one thing — the *only* thing — that mattered away from her?

She turned and staggered away from the guard, scratching her arms violently. The news that Io would be executed within hours got along with her growing withdrawal about as well as T-Rex would get along with New York. She was sinking fast, her mind fritzing out and blinking back on as if she were a lightning rod in a storm. Io. Cobalt. Io. Cobalt. Each took turns being more important than the other in her mind as she fell further into withdrawal. Five minutes passed, then ten, her staggering turning to agitated pacing, her thoughts turning to withdrawal-fueled need and obsession, as well as revenge.

She had to make her father pay. Her father and everyone else who had stolen away her happiness. What had they taken from her again? Oh yes. Io. That's right. Io...Io... where was he again? Her brain was misfiring. She couldn't remember. Where was she? She looked around her bedroom. The place looked familiar, but she couldn't quite recognize it. Oh yes, this was her room. Where was Io? He should be here. She darted her head around toward the guard, scratching— endlessly scratching her arms.

Through the withdrawal-induced haze, Miriam was swiftly losing her mind. And behind the withdrawal, another feeling—a much stronger one that she couldn't identify—tormented her, pulling and rattling her thoughts to...what? What was the important thing she couldn't remember? Rage boiled inside her...and a need that was almost sexual. Reality became a blur. Something important was happening, but all she could see was cobalt, cobalt, more cobalt. And retribution. Her body trembled for both, inner voices screaming at her to run, just run, and find her next hit and then to punish her father for hurting her.

Cobalt. She needed to find more cobalt. Now. And make her father pay. Cobalt and revenge. Revenge for...? Why did she need to make her father pay? She couldn't remember, but it was important. He had stolen something precious from her, and she needed to hurt him as payback. She knew she had to get away and punish him.

In a panicked frenzy, Miriam spun around and around, making herself dizzy as she looked for an escape. Out. She needed out.

She grabbed her purse, her entire body twitching as the incessant itching intensified. Turning toward her bedroom door, she stopped and frowned.

"What are y...you doing h...here?" she said to the guard.

The guard looked at her as if she were a stranger. "I've been assigned to watch you," he said slowly, as if he was confused by Miriam's behavior.

"Watch me?" Miriam spat at him. "My father's lackey." She curled her lip in disgust. "Get out of my way."

The guard stiffened as if readying himself to fight.

"Move. Now." Miriam took a single, stalking step toward him, her eyes narrowing.

"I'm under king's orders—"

Before he could utter another word, Miriam rushed him, shrieking, rage and need making her powerful. She shoved him back against the door, which he hit so hard the thick wood cracked and splintered. With an animalistic snarl, she grabbed the collar of his shit-brown, military-style T-shirt and pulled as she fell backward and rolled, tossing him behind her. When she flipped herself up to her knees and spun, her wild hair fanned and flew around her face. Not giving the guard a chance to pull his weapon or defend himself, Miriam landed on him, clamping her legs around his torso on either side of his chest as she thrust the butt of her right hand against his nose, shattering it.

The guard cried out then grunted into silence as she tightened her legs against his torso, rocked, lifted him, and then slammed him into the floor again.

He tried to push her off, but she grabbed one of his wrists and twisted. As a pure-breed vampire, she was strong, but riding a violent wave of cobalt detox-induced withdrawal— and whatever else this sensation was that raged through her body—made her even stronger, and the guard's wrist snapped like a dry twig.

As he screamed in pain, she clamped her hand over his mouth, the blood from his broken nose coating her skin, and bent down so that her disarrayed hair hung in his face. "The k...king is a fool," she said, her body shuddering violently. "You tell him I'll m...make him pay. I'll make y...you all p...pay. You'll all be sorry for w...what you've d...done."

The door busted open behind her, the sound of splintering wood ripping the air, and Miriam spun around and hopped up in a crouch, hissing.

More like a savage animal, she was lost in withdrawal's grip—withdrawal and something else—something primal and savagely protective. Seeing her exit suddenly closed off, she hissed again, snatched her purse from the floor, and leaped for the window. She punched her fists through the glass and crashed through, somersaulting to the ground below.

As soon as she touched down, she took off running. She heard footsteps behind her, but the farther she ran, the farther behind the footsteps grew. No one but her father could run faster than she could.

A guard materialized in front of her, but she ran him over.

The woods. She needed to escape into the woods. She could lose them there then dematerialize to the city once she could focus.

Hustling into the shadows, she led her pursuers farther into the blackness. Quieter and quieter their footsteps became until she couldn't even hear them anymore. But they were still following. She knew they were tracking her scent like the dogs they were. Her father's dogs.

Miriam ducked around the trunk of a large maple tree then shimmied down the slope of a hill sideways until she hit the bottom. Following the shallow ravine, she let her body calm and her mind focus so she could dematerialize to the city.

Footsteps tromped over the leaves, growing closer, but they were too late. They would track her this far, but then the trail would go cold.

Miriam closed her eyes and turned to mist and then was gone.

Free. At last. She never wanted to set foot inside that house again.

Never.

But she'd left something behind. Something important. If only she could remember what it was.

CHAPTER 44

Micah looked around the small room where he and Trace were being held. He knew from the thoughts of those who had put them in the cell that this place wasn't the king's residence—it was too small and official looking for that anyway. The king conducted business here. Mostly trials and legal proceedings.

Even though he couldn't tap into the king's thoughts, Micah could feel his presence, just as he had when Miriam was taken to AKM to be returned to Io. Micah had been surprised to sense the king in the back of the limousine, knowing that King Bain never went out in public. It showed just how much he cared for his daughter, even if his way of showing it was unorthodox and a bit...well, tyrannical.

Back in the Middle Ages, Micah had trained King Bain, who had only been a young prince then. He had been a serious student, and Micah's training had likely saved his life on more than one occasion over the centuries.

But now wasn't the time to be thinking about the good ol' days. He and Trace needed to talk about what had happened back at the apartment.

Trace sat in silence next to him, his eyes closed and his head resting back against the brick wall.

He, Sam, and Trace had developed an unusual, intimate bond in the past couple of months. One where they found pleasure in exhibitionism, voyeurism, and a touch of BDSM, but Micah wanted more from Trace. As in, more submission, more calling him "Master." More desire to be tied up and dominated in a way only Micah could provide.

Glancing at his friend, frustration welled inside him over how Trace had reacted back at the apartment. For two months, he had wanted nothing more than to become Trace's Master, but Trace hadn't taken that step with him. Until today. Now Micah wondered exactly where they stood. Clearly, Trace wanted to be Micah's submissive, but why now? Why had he waited?

"What's on your mind, Micah?" Trace kept his face forward, eyes closed.

Micah stared at him, not sure if he was mad, excited, or confused.

Trace's eyelids cracked open and his pale eyes slid to Micah's, all cool calm and impassive. For several seconds, they only stared at each other.

"Why haven't you approached me before today about being your Dom?"

Trace broke eye contact, sighed, and leaned his head back against the wall again. "I don't know what you're talking about." He closed his eyes almost wearily. Or maybe he was just preparing himself for Micah's response.

"Fuck that shit. Don't give me that line of crap." He tapped Trace's temple with the tip of his index finger.

Trace blinked his eyes open at the contact, but otherwise didn't move as his gaze lifted to Micah's and he frowned. "You saw my thoughts?"

"I didn't have to." Micah pointed to his own eyes. "You showed me everything I needed to know in the way you looked at me and called me 'Master.'" Micah squinted at Trace, trying to figure the guy out. "So, what's going on? Why haven't you allowed me to be your Master until now? Your *only* Master?"

What he had seen in Trace's eyes at the apartment had made his inner Dom jump up and wave its little, leather-clad hands with excitement. *Lemme at him! Lemme at him!*

Trace shook his head and looked away. "You've got Sam. I'm not going to get in the way of that, Micah."

Ever since he had introduced Sam to his playroom at his home in the suburbs, she had come to enjoy bondage games and let him unleash a little of his mastery on her, but he would never go total Dom on Sam. She wouldn't be able to take that. But Trace? He was a different story. From what Micah had seen at the BDSM party, Trace liked it rough and harsh. In fact, the harder the better.

"What the hell does that mean?" Micah's inner Dom was already checking its supply of isopropyl alcohol and oiling the whip. Damn, when was the last time Micah had engaged in fire play? Playing mind games with Trace was one thing, but the thought of getting more physical and giving Trace the pain he so desperately needed to keep his powers at bay was enough to make him pant. Shit, he needed to stop thinking like this or he'd start drooling.

"What are you thinking about there, Micah?"

The two exchanged glances, and Micah swore Trace could see inside his thoughts. An eager glint lit in those pale depths—a hunger for what Micah was capable of sparking to life. So, why did Trace hold himself back when Micah clearly wanted to give him what he needed?

"You answer me first." Micah kept his eyes on Trace, watching for his nuances, not that he had many.

"What? Why I didn't tell you how badly I needed it? Or how I've wanted the pain you can give since I met you?" Trace dropped his gaze and rubbed his palms on his thighs.

"All of it." Micah frowned at Trace's uncharacteristically nervous behavior.

Trace shrugged. "I knew how you were."

In other words, Trace was afraid Micah would have told him to go fuck himself and exactly how he could place his hand on his own cock to do so. Until recently, he hadn't been the nicest or most approachable guy on the block.

"Things are different now, Trace. You know that." Micah leaned forward and eyed Trace. "I'm not that person anymore. Thanks in large part to you for watching over my sorry ass. And you should know by now, after all that's happened between you, Sam, and me that I would never turn you away."

"Whatever." Trace waved him off.

"Fuck that. You tell me what's going on? Why, Trace? Why don't you want me to Dom you?" Why was Trace being so evasive?

"You know why."

What the fuck? Where was Trace going with this shit? "If you're worried about Sam, I've already told you. She's fine with it."

"Yeah, well maybe I'm not." Trace's gaze snapped to Micah's, fire lighting in his eyes.

"Why not?"

Trace scowled and looked down before meeting Micah's gaze again. "Because I'm fucked up, Micah! The shit I need to keep my power in check is fucked up, kinked-out-the-ass shit. What I need is—"

"Is me," Micah said, cutting him off. "You need *me*."

The two stared at each other, the weight of this new element of their friendship sinking in. But there was more. Micah could see it in the pained expression that fell over Trace's face and in the way he averted his gaze.

"What? What else is there, Trace?" Micah grabbed Trace's shoulder and forced him to look at him. "Because I know it's not all about your fucked-up needs, because you know by now I've seen it all. Hell, I've *done* it all." In that respect, Micah knew this wasn't about the kinky way Trace needed to be worked. There was something else going on here.

Trace shook his head. "Nothing."

"Fuck you. I can tell there's something else, so what is it?"

But Trace only looked away, scowling, setting his jaw and sealing his lips.

"Damn you, Trace!"

Trace spun around, guilt shrouding his features under his anger. "Because I'm attracted to her, god damn it! Fuck!" He slammed his head back against the wall, refusing to look at Micah. "Fuck."

Micah's brow knit together as confusion and shock fused and threw him into a spin. "Sam?"

"Yeah. Sam. Now do you get it? Do you understand now why I can't...?" He trailed off.

"No, I don't understand." Simply being attracted to Sam didn't explain why Trace didn't want Micah becoming his Master. "Maybe you need to explain it to me, Trace." He sat back and crossed his arms, glaring at him.

"I'm attracted to her." Trace lifted his hands and looked at him as if to ask what more was there? When Micah only stared back, Trace shook his head and sighed. "She's your mate. What if I can't stop myself? What if I touch her the wrong way? What if…?" He sighed, trailing off.

"So what if you do?" Trace and Sam had touched before during the playtime the three of them shared. Mostly, it was Sam touching him, but—and this was the freaky-odd part since Sam was his mate, and mated males usually didn't take kindly to another male fondling what belonged to them—Micah liked it. Seeing Trace and Sam together turned him on, even as innocent as their contact was. What would happen if Trace reciprocated and got more physical with Sam? Would Micah get even more turned on, or would it throw off the balance and send him into a mated male rage? He actually wanted to know the answer to that question. It would be worth the risk if the reward was deeper intimacy with Sam, as well as a more hardcore relationship with Trace.

But Trace wasn't seeing it that way. "You'd kill me, Micah. I'm not going to fuck up our friendship like that. No fucking way. Not after what it took for me to get in with you."

"You don't know that it would fuck things up. And you know it turns me on to see the two of you together." Micah wasn't sure what he was feeling. This had come out of nowhere and would take some time to fully sink in.

"What about her?" Trace looked at him. "Does she like it?" Was that hope in his voice?

Micah narrowed his eyes on Trace. "Yes, actually, she does."

"I don't want her to think I'm a freak."

"Funny, but she's worried you'll think *she's* a freak."

Trace frowned. "Why?"

"Because she gets so turned on by what the three of us do together."

"She does?"

"You should know by now that she does." Micah felt like he was talking to a kid who had a crush on a girl he hoped liked him back. He wasn't completely sure how he felt about that, being that the girl was Sam. Only time and experimentation would answer that question. Micah shifted and sat back against the wall.

Trace got quiet, and the two didn't say anything for a couple of minutes.

"Sam's not the only one in this arrangement I'm attracted to," Trace said quietly.

So the truth finally comes out.

Micah glanced over at him. "Oh yeah?" He had been with a male before. Back in the days after Kat's death he had been a depraved bastard, taking opportunity where he could find it. If that meant fucking a male, then that's what he did. And then last year he had partially mated Jackson. That relationship had ended badly, but Micah and Jackson had been a couple for a long time. He didn't see Trace the same way he had seen Jackson, but the idea that Traceon was attracted to him didn't upset him. In fact, it was something he could use if he was, in fact, going to be Trace's Master. "Nothing wrong with that, Trace."

"You're okay with that?" Trace looked surprised.

Micah shrugged. He wasn't sure how he felt about Trace's attraction toward Sam, but he was more than okay with Trace being attracted to him. "Why shouldn't I be?"

"What if I got carried away with you? What if—"

Micah held up his hand. "Enough with the what ifs, Trace?" His brow furrowed. "Are you worried about frisking me in a scene? Is that it?"

Trace eyed him and shrugged.

"And you really think I'd let you?" Micah smirked. "I can assure you, Trace, when I'm running a scene, the sub does only what I want him or her to do. Nothing more. If you tried anything with me and I didn't allow it, I would make damn sure you paid."

Trace's eyes narrowed and his lips pursed ever so slightly,

obviously getting a nice visual of exactly what he meant by making him pay.

For several seconds, they sat in silence, coming to terms with how things were changing between them. A lot had been revealed, and Micah had yet to assimilate all of it, but he knew without a doubt that he wanted to be Trace's Master. He was done sharing him with Mistress Diamond.

"So, I'm your Master now, Trace." Not a question. Decision made. Right now, this moment, Trace became his. Trace needed to accept that.

"As long as you know what you're getting into with me." Trace's words came out tough, but Micah knew he was about to bust from the anticipation that Micah would be his one and only Master from now on. It didn't take reading Trace's mind to know that he had wanted this all along.

"Oh, it's knowing what I'm getting into with you that is precisely why I *want* the job, Trace." He would have to work through his emotions over how Sam fit into all this, but he had wanted to fill this role with Trace for two months. He wasn't going to back down because of something that could end up being a non-issue.

"Fine." Trace looked down at his hands, which had curled into fists as if on their own. Clearly, he was working hard to keep his enthusiasm contained.

Good thing, too. Micah wasn't down with Trace going all mushy and sentimental.

"From now on, when you need service, no matter the time of day or night, you see me." Micah leaned back and gazed up at the ceiling as if the discussion was over. "I'll take care of letting Diamond know."

Trace nodded, his head still bowed in subservience. The power transfer was complete. One Master, one servant. Just like that, the dynamic came to fruition. At last.

Micah leaned back. "When we get out of here—"

The door opened, cutting Micah off, and Tristan walked in.

"You should be in containment, too," Micah said without missing a beat.

"I know, I know, Micah. Just drop it." Tristan held up his

hand to quiet him.

"Yeah, well"—Micah looked back toward Trace—"this is fucked up."

"I said to drop it."

Little shit. He and Tristan would have to discuss this matter privately after the dust settled on the proceedings. A fist-to-fist, bloody kind of conversation. He didn't give a shit what kind of problems Tristan had at home.

Two guards stepped in behind Tristan.

"What's this?" Trace looked from the guards to Tristan.

Tristan sat down and combed his hand through his blond hair. "It's time to face the king, but I want to give you an update first. Io's been arrested by the king's guards. He's to be executed within the hour."

"What?" Micah shot forward, jumping to his feet. "Why? For taking a goddamn mate?"

Tristan jumped up with him, lifting his hands to hold Micah back. "Who just so happens to be the king's daughter."

"As if he can control something like that," Micah shot back.

"Hey, I'm just telling you what's going down." Tristan paced away, looking frustrated. "I don't like it, either, Micah. This is more fucked up than a Hollywood whore, but there's nothing I can do."

"Like hell!"

Tristan spun back and nailed Micah with a hand to the throat. "We've got our own problems to worry about!"

Trace jumped up, his eyes flaring wide and his right hand twitching.

Ah hell, Tristan had done it now. If he wasn't more careful, Trace would be walking into court to be tried for murder in addition to his other charges. And that would wreck Micah's week even more than it already was. He was really looking forward to that conversation with Tristan and would hate to see Trace kill the guy before he could have some fun.

"Get the fuck off me." He sounded like the business end of a gun about to go off. "Before I give Trace the go-ahead to rearrange your organs."

Tristan pulled back with an apologetic jerk of his head, his mouth set in a hard line and a frown creasing his brow. "I'm sorry. I'm just…fuck, but I feel so goddamn helpless."

"Well, at least you're not locked in a cell." Micah straightened his shirt. He didn't care how bad Tristan felt. It wasn't fair that he was free and Trace was locked up.

"Fuck you, Micah. Just fuck you, all right. I fucking wish I was locked up, because then I wouldn't have to be out there"— he flung his arm toward the door—"listening to everything being said and knowing I can't do a goddamn thing to stop it."

Nothing was said for a moment.

Tristan spoke first. "Just so you know, I'll be on house arrest for a month for my part in this, and Severin is being suspended without pay for a week. I don't know who'll be in charge while I'm gone, probably Stryker."

Micah didn't care. Right now, he wasn't feeling anything but irritation for Tristan, who jacked his fists up on his hips and huffed, looking down.

"Fine. Let's go," Micah said, gesturing toward Trace to join him. "After you," he said to Tristan, eyeing the guards before looking back at Trace.

An unspoken promise passed between them. Micah wouldn't abandon Trace. Not now. Not ever. They would work through the rest after this ordeal was over.

Trace nodded subtly then turned to follow Tristan out of the room. Micah grabbed his arm.

Trace stopped and looked over his shoulder.

He wrapped his free arm around Trace's head, pulling his face down against his shoulder. "I've got you, buddy. You hear me? I've got *you* this time. Just as you've had my back so many times, now I've got yours."

Trace hesitated for a heartbeat then wrapped one arm around Micah and held on like his life depended on it. "I hear you." He spoke quietly into Micah's shoulder.

Neither of them moved for a couple of seconds, and then the threat to their man cards urged them to separate and clear their throats.

Micah gestured toward the door. "Let's get this over with."

Trace took a deep breath and led Micah out of the room,

where they joined Tristan and another set of guards in the hall.

Time to face the music.

CHAPTER 45

As soon as Miriam reappeared downtown in the shadows of an alley she used when she traveled by mist, she shoved her hand into her purse and dug until she found her phone. With fingers that trembled so violently she could barely open her contact list, it took her six attempts and several bursts of colorful language to dial her dealer.

She wasn't supposed to be doing this. Somehow, calling her dealer was supposed to be wrong, but how could something that felt so right on the surface be wrong? The vague notion that someone important to her didn't want her using cobalt anymore raced just outside her mind's periphery. Like the sounds of birds singing or cars driving on a far-off freeway, the idea buzzed in the background like white noise, easy to disregard with the roar of addiction and withdrawal screaming in her ear and slapping her face. More like full-on, fist-to-the-nose action.

She swore under her breath as she walked briskly out of the alley with the phone to her ear and her other arm wrapped around her torso as if she were cold. Keeping her head down and her feet moving, her teeth chattered as she listened to the electric buzz of ringing on the other end.

"Yes?" A male answered.

Miriam thanked the gods of extracurricular drug use at the sound of his voice.

"It's C...Candy." She gave her fake name.

There was a short pause and then the dreck on the other end said, "Hi, Candy. But we both know your name isn't Candy, don't we?"

"But..." How did they know she was lying? Well, duh. After recent events, her real identity shouldn't have been a secret to anyone anymore.

"Don't worry," the male's voice said, "I just want to make this easier for you. With a high profile like yours, we want to keep you safe. You want to be safe, don't you, Candy?"

How nice to find someone who understood. All she wanted was to be safe. Her father didn't understand that, but this nice male on the phone—Mr. Candyman—she almost laughed at the name—he understood. He would give her what she needed. "Yes. Okay, y...yes."

"You need product, Candy?"

"Y...yes." She darted in and out of pedestrian traffic as she hurried along the sidewalk.

There was a pause, followed by a rustling noise. "I've got someone at the Hotel Burnham on Washington. It's safe. I promise. No one will see you there, Candy. Are you close to the Burnham?"

Miriam looked around as she approached an intersection. She was less than five miles from the Burnham. Running part of the way and dematerializing from shadow to shadow, she could get there fairly quickly. "Yes. I c...can be there in less than a half-hour."

"Okay, we'll let him know you're on your way. Be careful, Candy." He gave her the room number then hung up. As she turned for the Burnham and started running, she realized what she had to do. The idea had been simmering in the back of her mind like a promise she couldn't remember making, but now the thought surged forward. She had nothing to live for anymore. Her father had taken something from her tonight. Something important. So important it was her only reason to stay alive. But through her shit-infested mind, whatever that was hung just out of reach, right where her father wanted it to remain.

Well, fuck him. Fuck her goddamn father. She would teach him. She would show him how done she was with his bullshit rules and his oppressive control.

With every step, her resolve strengthened and she grew

closer to her fate. Soon, her suffering would be over. Just one more fix. That's all she needed.

CHAPTER 46

CHEZ TURNED TOWARD APOSTLE, who was lounging on a fancy but comfortable gold couch with a diamond pattern woven into the fabric.

"She's on her way."

"Good." Apostle snapped his fingers at Jessup. "Get ready." He turned back to Chez. "Nice touch with all that 'safety, be careful' shit."

Chez grinned. "No problem."

Jessup wiped his hands on his napkin and abandoned the plate of room service he had been eating to go to the bathroom and clean up. Apostle reached over and plucked an artichoke from the plate and popped it in his mouth.

"And you're sure it's her?" Apostle licked his fingers and grabbed another bite of food off the plate.

"Yes. She uses the name Candy. When I called her on it, she didn't correct me. It's Princess Miriam."

Apostle wiped his fingers on Jessup's napkin and stood up, pulling out his phone. He dialed Bishop's number.

"Do you have it?" Bishop asked, not bothering with hello.

"Not yet. But she's on her way."

"Excellent. Don't fuck this up, Apostle."

Nice vote of confidence, asshole.

"I won't. We've got a good plan."

"Mmm, the same kind of plan that got Deacon killed?"

Apostle bit his tongue. Would he ever live down his twin's death? "Don't worry, Bishop. This will work."

"It had better. I have plans for that royal blood, and I don't want to be disappointed."

"Jessup will return with her blood as soon as it's finished." Apostle stared at his reflection in the window.

His long blue-black hair hung to his waist and his face looked a bit less gaunt than it had. At least he was beginning to put on weight.

"I shall await Jessup's return then." Bishop disconnected and Apostle shoved his phone in his pocket.

If this plan of theirs didn't work, he didn't want to think about what Bishop would do to him.

CHAPTER 47

KING BAIN PACED IN HIS TOMBLIKE OFFICE during a short recess in the proceedings. He had already sentenced Tristan and Severin, and now Trace was being brought in with Micah.

Micah. That powerful bastard had trained Bain back in the Old World. Talented with a bow and arrow, and even better with a knife, Micah should have been in charge of Bain's entire fighting force by now. If not for what had happened to Katarina, he would have been. Such a shame. Bain shook his head at the memory of what had happened a long time ago.

He had been thinking a lot about the past, his mind drifting to family and his own upbringing. He had been a stubborn child, rebellious and headstrong. Miriam was definitely following in his footsteps, making him see just how much grief he had given his own parents.

Even so, things had been different then. Sure, they had lived in constant fear of wars and fighting with the drecks, and even humans had turned on them, making the vampire community hide away and live in secret. It was his duty to protect Miriam from becoming a victim in this new world where vampires not only had to protect themselves from drecks, but also from humans. Couldn't she see that he only wanted to protect her?

And what father didn't want the best for his daughter?

"You're overthinking it," Cordray said, slipping quietly into his office.

He spun around. He had been so wrapped up in his own thoughts, he hadn't even heard her come down the hall. "Cordray?"

She wore metallic, print denim pants that looked like a second skin, as well as a black leather bustier that laced up the front and shoved her breasts into healthy mounds. Studded cuffs wrapped around her wrists, and she had to be wearing twenty different chains, rings, and piercings. But it was the tattoos of rainbow-colored birds and exotic flowers across both shoulders and down both arms, as well as what he could see of the dragon tattoo wrapped around her torso, that stole the show.

She crossed the masterpieces known as her arms and leaned against the wall. "You're overthinking it," she said again.

Only Cordray could get away with poking around in his thoughts without permission. "Overthinking what?"

She arched an eyebrow and gave him a knowing look, her mouth quirking into a crooked grin. They both knew exactly what she was talking about. He could hide nothing from her—never had been able to, either. "Don't give me that, Bain," she said. "You know what I'm talking about, and you need to quit comparing how our father raised you to how you're raising Miriam."

Cordray knew him better than anyone. Better even than Cara. The two shared a secret no one else knew. Bain's father had never mated to Bain's mother. It was nearly miraculous he had been conceived at all. Unfortunately for the queen, over one hundred years later, the first King Bain found his true mate in a human who served in his castle, and within the year, Cordray was born.

The situation had been difficult for all involved, and new laws had been passed pertaining to the changing of human mates so that Bain the First could rightfully turn his mate from human to immortal and spend the rest of his life with her. But everyone who knew the true relationship between Bain and Cordray had died a long time ago. Cordray was all Bain had left of his family, and they kept their relationship a sacred secret for fear of stirring up dissidence in the community. There was nothing like a scandal to weaken solidarity, which was something Bain couldn't afford.

"I want what's best for her," Bain said.

Cordray cocked her head in that no-nonsense way of hers and sighed. "What's best for her is for her to live her own life, idiot." She pushed away from the wall and turned before looking over her shoulder at him. "She's not a normal female, you know. She has too much of you in her." She began to walk away. "Micah and Trace are ready for you." Her three-inch, platform heels clicked across the hardwood floor, and then she left the room.

His heart was heavy with personal burden. Miriam's words had cut him deeply earlier, and now Cordray's weighed just as heavily.

Were they both right? Was he being overly cautious and too controlling where Miriam was concerned? He only wanted what was best for her, and she deserved a worthy male with strong bloodlines. In his opinion, that wasn't Io. But Io had mated her. Just like his father had mated the unlikely human servant, Io had formed a link to his daughter.

Still, Io had lied to him, in a manner of speaking. So had Miriam, and so had Io's commander and teammates. What kind of king would he be if he allowed such insubordination to go without punishment? If word got out he had bent on what had been perceived as common law for decades, if not centuries, as it pertained to the royal family, would that open him up to scrutiny? Would those he ruled see that as weakness and try to exploit it?

Bain had ruled since his father had been killed in battle over seven centuries ago. Fear had kept the race compliant and orderly ever since. He couldn't afford to show weakness. He couldn't let his people think he was going soft. His rules and his laws had to be followed, and if they weren't, it was his responsibility to make those who broke them suffer.

But Miriam had a point. His law also supported the rights of a mated male to claim the female he had mated, regardless of all else. He had broken up countless marriages to ensure the mating call was answered between a male and his female. With vampires, the male's mating claim was sacrosanct.

He sighed and picked up the picture he had kept on his desk ever since it had been taken when Miriam was only six years old. The photo was black and white, and she was sitting on his lap. She had been in a fit of laughter when the picture had been taken, her face turned up to his, her little arms reaching for him.

When was the last time Miriam had reached for him?

He set the picture back down and turned away. She and Io had put him in a tough predicament. His decision today would either push his daughter away forever or open him up to ridicule from his people. Either was a no-win scenario.

Bain smoothed his hands over the red, satin stole that draped over the heavy, black cassock he wore, then he fingered the ancient, bronze medallion passed down from his father. It was heavy and round, and its surface was embellished with ancient glyphs and two ornate, crossed swords over a full moon. He wore the medallion during legal proceedings or other official business.

What would his father do if he were in his place? If only he weren't the king, hard decisions like this would fall on someone else's shoulders.

When he re-entered the main chamber, everyone was seated and ready to proceed. His gaze met Micah's for all of a second, but long enough to see concern simmering like burning soup within the depths of his eyes. Clearly he and Trace were as close as he had been led to believe, which meant Micah wasn't going to like what was about to go down. Not one bit.

CHAPTER 48

DONOVAN BARKED ORDERS INTO HIS RADIO as he ran back to the king's residence. Miriam's trail had gone cold in the ravine two miles into the woods.

"Track her, damn it! She's got to have her phone on her!"

Shit. Donovan didn't have time for this. The king needed to know immediately what had happened. He hit the king's cell phone again, but it went straight to voicemail. Of course he wouldn't have it on while in trial, but this was one time he wished the king had made an exception.

He would have to hoof it to the Justice Center. Donovan only hoped they could retrieve Miriam before she did anything stupid.

TRACE GLANCED AT MICAH, who bobbed his head at him as if to remind him to keep his chin up. The rest of the team sat in a tightknit group around him.

He was surprisingly relieved that Micah had forced the Dom issue, but he couldn't get a bead on what Micah thought about what he'd said about Sam. It wasn't that he wanted to fuck Sam. Or Micah. But he couldn't deny how much he enjoyed their physical beauty. What if a time came when he pushed for more from either or both of them? It wasn't out of the question. Being unmated, he could easily bend to his attraction and take things too far. He could already feel himself being pulled toward Sam, and he couldn't jeopardize his friendship with Micah like that. Not without letting him know up front what was going on…that he *did* find her—and him—attractive.

Shit. If only he knew what was going on inside Micah's head the way Micah seemed to know what was going on inside everyone else's. But Trace wasn't one to poke around in someone's mind without permission or good reason to, whereas Micah simply couldn't help it. And from what he could tell, when Micah was traipsing through people's thoughts, they couldn't feel it like they could with others.

Case in point, Trace glanced toward the female sitting in the row of chairs against the wall. Her catlike eyes, perfectly outlined in dark eye shadow and liner, turned toward him and narrowed with familiarity as one corner of her red- and black-stained lips curved upward. He had never seen her before, but she clearly knew him.

She immediately attempted to invade his mind again. This was the third time in five minutes. What felt like worms probing at his grey matter squirmed inside his skull. He clamped down on his thoughts and glared at her. She arched an eyebrow and shrugged as if to say he couldn't blame her for trying, but instead of backing off, she dug harder. The worms turned to snakes that slid into the crevices of his brain and squeezed.

What was her story and who the hell was she? She looked like his kind of woman. Tattoos and piercings, lots of black leather and skintight clothes. Whoever she was, she was a tough little bitch. He bet she could rough him up good. But she would have to learn that his thoughts were off-limits. *Slam!* He shoved her out like a rude host. She ricocheted back in her chair, her lips curling into a mischievous grin as one brow arched. Oh, she liked that, did she?

"Trace."

He snapped his attention to the front.

King Bain was looking at him as if he had been waiting longer than a moment. "Would you care to join us, Trace? After all, this is your trial."

He exchanged glances with Micah, who was frowning at him. Looked like he had been so preoccupied with the odd female to the side that he had missed his name being called.

"Uh...yes. I'm sorry Your Honor, or Excellency, or...King." What the hell did you call the king when he was acting as judge and jury, as well as the king? He had never been in this situation before.

The king sighed. "Your Honor is acceptable, Trace. Now, please step forward."

Micah patted him once on the shoulder for encouragement, then he walked to the front.

King Bain looked to the side. "Cordray?"

Trace looked over and saw the inked up female stand and join him. She took the place in front of the bench, just to King Bain's left, looking at him. What did she have to do with him?

"Cordray, is this the one who manipulated the memories of my guards?"

"Yes." Her voice was low and sultry, and her eyes penetrated his.

"Please relay as evidence what memories he changed, how he changed them, and the new memories he implanted." King Bain looked down at his notes.

So *she* was the reason the king had found out what had happened and that he was involved. Cordray's stock plummeted. Attraction turned to disgust, curiosity to disdain. The rounds he had fantasized about going with her in the playroom turned to rounds in a boxing ring.

"The guards entered Io's home and found him with Miriam in a compromising situation. They were both only partially clothed, and the scent of his semen was on her. Clearly, the two had been engaged in sexual relations. Traceon hid those memories from the guards and implanted new memories that showed them walking in to find Io sleeping in a chair where he was startled and attacked them in self-defense."

Trace scowled at Cordray. How did she know what he had done? Trace met her eyes again and they glared at each other, those vividly blue eyes of hers piercing him. And just like that, any last remnant of his attraction to her vaporized. She was a threat. A major threat. And threats were meant to be neutralized.

King Bain fidgeted uncomfortably, obviously affected by Cordray's recount of what had gone on between Io and his daughter.

After clearing his throat, Bain went on to ask her other questions regarding the details of the memories he had changed in the minds of the guards. Every question Cordray answered as if she owned his soul. He had always lived in fear, but what he felt now, with Cordray cutting him apart and laying him bare, went beyond fear. His breathing quickened, and his palms began to sweat.

When the king dismissed her, she exchanged one last glance with Trace then turned and walked back to her seat. He watched her go, scowling after her as she worked her stilettos and skintight clothing like a stripper. All she needed was a pole.

"Traceon," the king said, pulling his attention back to the bench. "Do you deny these accusations?"

Trace shook his head, frowning, rubbing his palms up and down the front of his thighs. "No."

"You admit that you willingly altered the memories of the members of the king's guard?"

"Yes." He flicked a furtive glance toward Cordray. She had exposed him. Stripped him. Vulnerability sat with him about as well as having his dick chopped off, and he wrestled between fear and anger. He wanted to make her pay in the most brutal way, but he was terrified of her at the same time. Why? His reaction didn't make sense.

King Bain paused and flipped a page of his notes. "Traceon, to tamper with any person in my employ is a serious crime and can result in death. Do you understand?"

Micah made a noise of protest behind him and King Bain's gaze shot up to issue a warning for those in attendance not to speak.

"Calm down, Micah," Arion whispered.

King Bain looked back at Traceon. "Do you understand, Traceon?"

He nodded, a quick, jerky motion. "Yes." He swallowed,

but all that went down was dry air.

"Traceon, I will spare your life, but for your willful, criminal actions, I decree you are to be held in the king's prison for one month, without visitation, and are to be suspended indefinitely without pay from your position as an enforcer at AKM."

A commotion erupted behind him and Trace turned to see Micah jump out of his chair as the others tried to restrain him.

"He was following orders!" Micah's voice echoed through the room. "Damn it, Tristan!" Micah turned on their commander. "You told him to. *You* gave the order!"

"Restrain him!" King Bain ordered his guards forward to take Micah, who continued to struggle against Arion and Malek, who fought to hold him back.

Micah's eyes met his.

"He was just following orders, damn it! Fuck!" Micah pulled out of Malek's and Arion's holds and sprang forward. "Tristan gets a vacation at home for a month," Micah said, "but Trace is imprisoned and released from AKM indefinitely? That's bullshit!"

"That's quite enough, Micah," Bain said, rising. "Guards."

The guards grabbed Micah, but he resisted, struggling against them. One of them punched him and Micah's head whipped back. Trace's power rose up. As if it needed much coaxing. As anxious as Cordray made him, it was a wonder he hadn't already gone mutant.

"Don't you touch him!" Trace growled low and deep, full of menace. "He's my charge!" Nobody touched Micah like that. Nobody hurt Micah or they answered to him, damn it. There weren't many Trace would lay his life down for, but Micah was one of them.

The guards ignored him and chaos erupted as Arion and Sev tried to pull Micah back while the guards swung again. Another fist connected with Micah's jaw, and that was all it took.

Trace lunged into the fray and splayed his hand at the guards. Their bodies froze except for their eyes, which turned toward Trace in fear. He grabbed Micah with his other arm and pulled him back, hissing like a viper. He wanted to crush their skulls. He wanted to feel their brains burst in his fist for hurting Micah. Micah was his to protect, and fuck all to anyone who tried to harm him. He had already lost one brother. He wouldn't lose another, even if Micah wasn't his brother by blood.

"It's okay, buddy," Micah said, his voice gentle, his hands grabbing on to Trace's forearm. He sounded like he was trying to tame a lion into a kitten.

More guards closed in and Trace splayed his fingers even farther, pulling them all into his realm of compulsion, halting them in their tracks. His gaze shot to Cordray, and for a moment, he wanted to pull her into his death hold, too, even though she made no move to interfere.

"Trace," Tristan stepped forward, fear in his eyes.

"No," Trace said. He didn't care what happened to him, as long as nothing happened to Micah. "No one touches him but me. No one!" His voice resonated with menace, and he knew from experience his eyes had changed from pale green to vivid yellow. He could feel it. Only when he was this emotionally charged did his eyes change color like that.

They hadn't changed color in a long time. Not since—No. He wouldn't go there. He would keep the memories of his youth locked, especially with Peek-a-boo Bitch over there, staring at him, most likely trying to worm her way into his head again.

He was scared and angry all at once. He felt like a threatened, feral cat backed into a corner, pissed off that it couldn't break free, back hunched, claws protracted, ears back, and fur standing straight on end. The thought of being confined for a month away from his new master scared the shit out of him. What if he lost control of his power? What if the scales tipped too far and he slipped into mutant? That was his greatest fear, and never before had he been tested to find his limits. Could he even go a month without the abuse he required to stay in control?

And how dare the guards treat Micah that way. He growled

at the one who had hit Micah, crouching to the floor and pulling Micah down with him, blanketing him protectively even as Micah tried to resist.

His voice dropped to a deadly whisper, body bent, fangs bared. "No one touches Micah."

Cordray had risen from her chair on the other side of the room and watched him with interest but didn't make a move to interfere. Smart bitch. Because he would ice her just for her damning testimony if she took one step forward. Of everyone in the room, she was the most threatening. He was certain of that even if the idea didn't make sense.

Everyone hovered precariously. It seemed no one knew what to do and could only wait until he calmed down before trying to approach him.

Micah patted his arm and said quietly, "It's okay, Trace. I'm okay."

Trace looked down to find Micah's navy blues turned up to his. "I'm scared," he said. How foreign the word sounded coming from him. Nothing scared him, but being threatened with prison, and faced with a tattooed succubus wearing designer pumps, fear crept in.

"I know you are."

Trace could see in Micah's eyes that he knew exactly what Trace was scared of, too.

He swallowed nervously. "What if I don't make it?"

"You'll make it. You'll find a way. And I'll take care of you when you're out. You have my word. I'll be here the moment you're free."

"Fuck...don't you be late." Trace had a feeling he would be ripped and primed with need by the time his sentence was up, if he made it that long.

"I know, brother. And I won't be late. I promise. I've got your back, remember?"

"I've got yours."

"I know you do." Micah gave him a playful smack, making it harder than it needed to be. "But how about you take the day off and leave the back watch to me." He smacked his cheek again.

Trace had a feeling Micah had hit him harder than necessary on purpose, because the sting of pain *did* calm him.

"Come on. Let me up, buddy," Micah said. "You can let me go. I'm okay. They won't hurt me."

Trace slowly rose, keeping his free arm around the front of Micah's waist protectively as his other continued to hold the guards at bay.

Micah turned to the king. "My apologies for my outburst." He bowed his head in apology. "This is my fault. Trace is..." He paused and looked over his shoulder at Trace. "Well, he's very protective of me."

The king acknowledged him with a head dip of his own then looked at Trace. "That's some power you have there, Traceon."

Trace slowly maneuvered himself and Micah back to the podium, keeping his arm outstretched and his eyes on the guards. He wouldn't release them until he knew Micah was safe from harm.

"Don't worry, Traceon," King Bain said, as if reading his thoughts. "Guards, you are not to touch Micah or any other member of Tristan's team for the duration of this trial, with the understanding that there will be no more outbursts." The king looked at Trace, then Micah, then Tristan and the others. "Understood?"

Everyone nodded.

"Would you release my guards now, Traceon?" King Bain said.

Trace frowned shamefully and nodded, then lowered his hand and let go of Micah at the same time. The guards fell out of compulsion and stepped away from him.

"Micah, you may return to your seat," King Bain said.

"If it's all the same to you, I'll remain with Trace."

King Bain sighed. "Very well."

He probably realized that allowing Micah to stay was a good way to ensure Trace didn't go bionic hand again.

King Bain cleared his throat and looked back down at his papers then continued now that the excitement was over. "As I was saying, Traceon, you are to be confined for one month and suspended indefinitely from your job as enforcer at AKM. You will also perform community service at the shelter two nights, or days in your case, since you're a day walker, per week. You will be evaluated in three months, and if your performance and behavior have been satisfactory, your reinstatement at AKM will be considered."

Trace bowed his head. He didn't know how he would get by for the next month in confinement, but even after his release, it would be no walk in the park. He took a measure of satisfaction from his work. Being an enforcer made him feel like he was somebody and not just a random face in the crowd. His powers could be put to use for good as an enforcer. What would happen over the next few months until his evaluation? Would he go crazy from the inactivity?

He looked at Micah.

"Don't worry, brother. I'll take care of you. We'll get through this. Trust me."

Micah's reassurance helped, but it only went so far. There was only so much Micah could do for him. Already, he could feel his mind slipping into the past and to the blood brother he had lost with his father after his mother's death. Where was Brak now? Had he survived? Sometimes Trace thought he could feel his twin, but most of the time he felt nothing. He didn't want to be alone and idle, where his thoughts could open up to the past, but he didn't have a choice.

"Guards, shackle him." King Bain signaled the guards forward.

They approached him warily, clearly not wanting to set him off.

"Here, let me." Micah stepped forward and grabbed the chained cuffs from the guards. "I think I need to do it, anyway. Don't I, buddy?"

Trace glanced from the guards to the metal cuffs and heavy steel chains as they passed from hand to hand. Then, he slowly lifted his gaze to Micah's. This was his master. Micah was the one who would set it all right for him.

But before Micah could shackle him, another guard burst through the door and rushed inside.

"My lord!"

Everyone jumped and turned toward the commotion as more guards poured into the room.

Donovan ran forward with a sense of urgency.

King Bain rose. "What's going on here? Why have you—?"

"Miriam's gone!" Donovan gasped for air as if he'd run the one hundred meter dash in record time. "She's gone!"

CHAPTER 49

TRACE WAS SUDDENLY FORGOTTEN. Miriam's disappearance took center stage.

Everyone in the room shot to action, surging away from their chairs, but no one moved faster than King Bain, who leaped over the bench and rushed forward.

"What?"

"She escaped, my lord. She's gone."

"Where is she? Were you able to track her?"

"Yes, but I fear for her safety." Donovan gasped for air.

"Why?" King Bain's face had lost all color.

"She was not"—Donovan stopped and visibly trembled. From fear?—"She was not herself when she left."

"What do you mean?" King Bain was beside himself as he gripped Donovan's shoulders.

Donovan grimaced as if he didn't want to speak openly in front of such a large crowd.

"Tell me!" Bain shook him.

Donovan tensed. "She was in withdrawal." He shook his head. "Violent and despondent."

The room practically exploded with tension.

King Bain recoiled, fear and raw emotion overtaking him.

"I don't like this." Cordray appeared at the king's side and turned on Donovan. "Did Miriam know of Bain's intentions to execute Io?"

"I don't know, but it's possible."

Cordray's brow creased, and Donovan went still, his eyes suddenly vacant. "Shit," Cordray said.

"What?" The king grabbed her wrist as the guard reanimated.

"She's in a female calling." Cordray cursed again.

"Is that even possible?" Micah asked, dismayed.

The king could only shake his head in denial.

"It's rare, but Miriam isn't a typical female. In a lot of ways, she's like…" Cordray turned toward the king. "She's like her father. She inherited your essence, Bain. And from what I'm seeing, she's not just in withdrawal. She's attached herself to Io the way a male attaches to a mate, just not quite as strong, but strong enough to send her into a mental breakdown and cause the physical symptoms."

"How…?" King Bain looked sick, his face pale.

Cordray grabbed his arm. "I know what I'm seeing, Bain." She shook him. "Wake up! You have to fix this."

Trace frowned at her. Who was this bitch who got away with what stronger men would be squashed for doing?

"And how do you propose I do that?" The king glared at her.

Good for him. Now maybe he would put that bitch in her place.

Cordray huffed as if talking to a six-year-old. "Send Io for her."

The king recoiled, obviously not liking that idea.

"Listen to me," Cordray said, "if you send anyone else, it could set her off. If she thinks Io is dead, she could do something stupid, such as kill herself. But if you send Io, she'll see for herself he's still alive. And he's her mate." She knocked her knuckles on the side of Bain's head, and several gasps erupted around the room. "Hello! Think about that, Bain. He's her mate. He'll home in on her like she's a beacon with the hormonal overload he's on."

Bain didn't look like he was buying it.

"Io is your only hope, Bain." Cordray grabbed his arm.

By now, everyone had assembled in a disorganized mass nearby, ready and awaiting the king's order.

King Bain erupted with anger. "Go after her! Bring her home!"

Cordray turned back to the king. "Damn it, Bain! You must send Io. If you send your guards, you will only provoke her. She won't come home until she knows Io is safe, and the only way she will believe he's safe is if she sees him with her own eyes."

The king's face flushed such a deep shade of red, he looked painted. "No."

"You have to."

The king paced away, but didn't say anything.

"We're wasting time," Cordray said flatly. "The longer you wait to decide, the more likely it will be that you'll find Miriam dead."

Trace glanced around the room at the other shocked faces. None of them knew who Cordray was, but everyone seemed to be just as surprised as he was by her behavior.

"Fine!" King Bain spun around, his face the picture of menace and hostility. "Release him! Send Io after my daughter."

"A wise choice," Cordray said, as Donovan waved to one of the other guards and nodded. The guard immediately darted out of the room, followed by two others. "Only a mutant is more powerful than a mated male without his mate. Io will protect her well." Cordray turned and bobbed her head toward Trace. "And send him, too."

Trace glared at her.

"What?" King Bain took an aggressive step forward, but Cordray remained steadfast.

Micah was already handing the shackles back over to one of the guards.

"As you saw, Trace has a unique and powerful gift." Cordray glanced back toward the center of the room where he had performed his magic act earlier. "If there *is* danger, he will be an asset to Io, who will be thinking of only one thing once he finds Miriam, since he has entered his calling."

Everyone in the room knew what that one thing was, too. Io had already gone far too long without Miriam, and if he was in his calling, he was probably about to rip his skin off to mate with her.

Trace had to admit, as much as he disliked Cordray, she was smart and level-headed, thinking proactively while everyone else was in reaction mode.

King Bain waved his hand. "Fine. Release him. But as soon as this incident is over, you will serve your time," he said, pointing at Trace. "Now go. Find my daughter and bring her home."

"Let's go." Micah clapped him on the shoulder and made for the door as the rest prepared to move out.

He was about to hurry after Micah when a hand clamped down on his arm. As soon as he saw the silver-ringed fingers and tattooed hand, Trace scowled. With a severe yank, he pulled his arm away and jerked around to see Cordray standing next to him.

Her face was frozen in wonder, and she was staring at her hand as if it weren't part of her body. It was as if she had forgotten Trace was even there.

"Do *not* touch me." Trace punctuated the demand by bending down, getting in her pretty face.

Cordray's gaze lifted, and Trace could swear he saw fear in her eyes. Fear or shock. Maybe both. Either way, he really didn't give a shit. She needed to be afraid of him, because *his* earlier fear of *her* was subsiding, leaving only anger.

Fueled by her show of emotion, Trace sneered and loomed closer. "Do I scare you, little girl?"

Cordray's face blanched, and she appeared momentarily flustered.

"No. It's just...you...I..." Cordray, who until now had been so eloquent, was at a loss for words.

"Spit it out, honey. I've got work to do." Trace really did *not* like Cordray or the mind job she had pulled on him. The bitch needed to stay out of his thoughts and out of his way if she knew what was good for her. He had no reservations about icing her permanently after what she had done to him.

As if coming back to her senses, hot anger flared in her eyes as she composed herself. "Make sure you bring back any humans or drecks you find with her. Do you think you can handle that, wonder stud?"

Trace glowered, his right hand going twitchy. "They might not give me a choice, sweetheart. When I'm ass-deep in the drink with fuckers who want to play hero with their stupidity, sometimes shit happens." He pressed forward, looking down his nose at her. "But for someone like you, who spends her time indoors instead of out in the trenches, you probably don't understand that."

"Well, Superman, make sure shit *doesn't* happen. And what makes you think I spend my time indoors, hotshot?"

Trace got the distinct impression that if she could shoot fire from her eyes he would have been scorched by now.

When Trace didn't answer, she glanced askance at Bain who was gesturing with animation as he spoke to his guards. "You know, I may not be the indoorsy type, but others are. And they're a lot more dangerous to your health than I am." She looked back at Trace with a satisfied smirk. "And he's a lot tougher on shitheads with itchy trigger fingers than I am, too. You remember that."

With that, Cordray turned and walked out the door, calling over her shoulder, "Time's ticking, asshole."

Cordray had trumped him. Clever bitch.

He would get his chance to put her in her place or die trying.

As he stormed out of the room and hurried to catch up to Micah, he didn't even realize he had a hard-on.

CORDRAY DUCKED AROUND A CORNER and slammed her back against the wall, gasping as she looked up at the ceiling.

She had felt Trace. She had actually experienced physical sensation when she grabbed his arm. So much so that he had lit her up like a Roman candle on the Fourth of July. When was the last time she had ever felt anyone or even been aroused like this?

Running her palm down one inked up arm, she panted harshly and bent forward.

What did this mean? How had that unbelievably powerful mixed-blood affected her like this? Was it just another attribute of his power, or was it something else?

All she knew was that her body was lit up like New York City on New Year's Eve, a sensation she hadn't felt in so long that she had forgotten just how torturous being aroused without a partner was. Too bad she wanted nothing to do with Trace to further explore whatever this was he had awakened inside her. In fact, she wanted nothing more than to see that smirk on his face get wiped off by Bain's fist.

Fuck Trace. She'd find another outlet, because the last thing she wanted was that pompous dick's hands on her.

CHAPTER 50

MIRIAM ENTERED THE HOTEL, relentlessly scratching her arms, and smiled nervously at the desk clerk as she made her way to the elevator bay. The lobby of the Hotel Burnham had a nostalgic but elegant feel, as if the motif was modern-day 1930s.

Stepping into the elevator, she could barely hold her shivering hand still long enough to tap the button for the ninth floor, but soon the doors closed and the elevator began its climb toward freedom.

Even though her mind was completely lost to reality, one thought grew stronger with each passing second. She was done. Whatever her father had taken from her—which hung just beyond her realm of consciousness, in a place she couldn't find through her haze of withdrawal and the dull ache in her chest—was too important to live without. It frustrated her to feel its importance but not be able to remember what it was, but she knew she couldn't survive without it.

The elevator stopped on the ninth floor, and she stepped out.

After looking up and down the hall, she turned and made her way until she found the right room, took a deep breath, and knocked.

Within seconds, the door opened. A dreck stared back at her and she could see another one inside prepping a syringe.

Good. They could dose her so she wouldn't have to.

"I'm Candy," she said.

The dreck stepped aside. "I'm Grotek. That's Chane. Come in."

One more deep breath, and Miriam entered the room. The door clicked shut behind her. Blue bliss in a syringe awaited.

THE DOOR TO IO'S CELL UNLOCKED with a series of loud clangs, and then the door swung open with a scream of metal on metal.

In a flash, Io was on his feet and rushing out the door. A mass of bodies greeted him, some he recognized, some he didn't, but all of whom were in his way of getting to his mate. He needed her. Io was going crazy without Miriam.

With a shriek, he attacked the first guard in his path, easily dispatching him before moving on to the second. He was mad with fury and lust, clawing at the guards.

"I told you!" A voice shouted from behind him.

"Do something!" another cried.

"TRACE! Get over here! NOW!" Micah's voice cut through the melee.

"Io...stop it, Io! You're free! No one's going to hurt you!" A familiar voice called to him, but he couldn't place it.

"Give it up, Ari. He's lost to the calling," someone else said.

Ari?

Suddenly, Io released the guard and spun around. Ari? He knew Ari. Io's chest rose and fell as he studied the group of vampires surrounding him, but especially the one in front, with the short, dark hair and tawny eyes.

"Ari." Io's voice sounded foreign even to him, as if he was more beast than vampire.

Trace stood with his arm outstretched and his hand fisted as if ready to drop Io if he did anything stupid.

"Io," Ari said, stepping forward. "You need to calm down. There isn't much time."

"Ari!" Io lunged forward, and everybody flinched.

He hugged his best friend—they were still best friends, right?—as if Ari were a parachute and he was in a free fall, which he damn near felt like he was.

"Okay, buddy. I'm here, but we need you now. Miriam

needs you. She's in danger."

That got Io's attention in a heartbeat, and he pulled back, on the alert. His mind was misfiring with a kaleidoscope of emotions. One second he was angry, the next sad, and now he was overwhelmed with urgency.

"Where is she? Where's Miriam?"

"They've tracked her to the Hotel Burnham," Micah said, stepping forward. "She's in withdrawal, and some think"— Micah shot a glance toward an unfamiliar female with long hair and enough ink to fill a rainbow—"Some think she might try to hurt herself."

"Or worse," Trace said.

His mate, his mate, his mate. Miriam was in danger. He needed to save her. Panic pushed him to near hyperventilation as he felt the link that had formed to Miriam fire up.

Miriam! I need to find her! Need to save her!

"Lead the way, Io. I'm with you." Trace latched on to his forearm. "Take us to your mate."

Without another word, Io looked up at Trace then connected their molecular structures to one another.

"Hold on," he said.

And then he pulled Trace with him as he dematerialized from the king's dungeon to the shadows near the hotel.

CHAPTER 51

APOSTLE GLANCED DOWN AT MIRIAM, who lay passed out on the bed. Jessup had already gone *vanishing vampire* and taken the blood samples back with him to Bishop's lab.

"By the way," he said over his shoulder to Grotek and Chane. "Nice work."

The two dealers lay in a stupor on the opposite bed. Jessup had mentally tranqed them not to awaken until Apostle was gone. They would awaken thinking that Miriam had passed out after taking too much cobalt. All memory of Apostle, Jessup, the withdrawal of her blood, and anything to do with any of the above had been stripped from their minds.

His phone rang.

Bishop.

"Yes?"

"Good work," Bishop said.

"Do you have enough of her blood?"

"Plenty. You've done well, brother."

Someone spoke excitedly in the background.

"What?" Bishop said, his voice fainter as if he had turned away from the phone. "Pregnant?! Are you sure? Check again."

The voice in the background said, "I've checked three times."

"God in Heaven," Bishop said.

What was going on? Apostle turned and looked down at Miriam's belly. Were they saying she was pregnant? She didn't look pregnant.

"Apostle!" Bishop barked him back to attention.

"Yes?"

"Change of plans. I want her. I don't care what it takes. I

want that unborn child."

Apostle's mind raced. "How—"

"I'm sending Jessup back. As soon as he arrives, get out of there. He'll give Grotek and Chane new memories so they take the fall. Then he'll bring the princess here."

Shit had just gone in a direction he hadn't expected. "Okay, but—"

A second later, Jessup reappeared in the room.

"Get out of here," the vampire said. "I'll take care of this."

No need to tell Apostle twice. He had a bad feeling about this and didn't want to be anywhere near what was about to go down.

"Bishop, I'm out of here," he said. "I'll call you when I'm clear."

"I'm about to be transfused. If I don't answer, I'll call you right back."

"Fine. Whatever." Apostle disconnected, not wanting to know what Bishop had meant by being transfused.

He looked around quickly then headed for the door, leaving Grotek, Chane, and the princess in what he hoped were Jessup's capable hands as he raced for the elevator bay.

How the hell had the princess gotten pregnant? This shit just didn't add up. The vampire king had made it well known his daughter was not to be touched, and yet, she was with child. Which meant…?

Fuck. Had she been mated?

Apostle was too agitated to wait for an elevator and headed for the stairs. He just wanted to keep moving. Especially if she had a mate. He didn't want to be around if the unlucky male showed up. He knew how mated vampire males could be. All too well, in fact. And this one wouldn't find a happy ending once he discovered what had happened to Miriam.

The question was, who the hell was Miriam's mate?

Io RUSHED OUT OF THE ELEVATOR with Trace right behind. They had already inspected the lower floors, but there had been no sign of Miriam.

On the ninth floor, however, he caught her scent.

"She's here." Io's entire body raged to be with her, and he was only barely keeping himself pulled together so he could find her and sate the violent urgings stringing him out.

"I smell drecks," Trace said from behind him.

"And cobalt. Shit." Io couldn't let Miriam begin using again. She needed to stay clean.

Racing down the hall, he stopped so abruptly that Trace ran into him and nearly sent the two of them careening to the floor.

"Damn, Io!"

"Ssshh." Io pushed Trace back and stared at the door they had just passed then inhaled long and deep.

Trace stood back, letting him scent out his female.

"There!" Io shot forward and kicked the door open. It slammed into the wall and ricocheted back.

What the fuck? A vampire stood over Miriam. She was passed out on one of the beds. Two drecks lay prone on the other, apparently locked into a compulsive state.

The vampire's gaze flew to his and shot wide, and then he reached for Miriam.

"No!" Both he and Trace surged forward and grabbed Miriam's legs just as the vampire dematerialized with her.

And wouldn't you know it? The fucker sucked them into the vapor tunnel with him and Miriam.

Io felt himself squeezed tight as if in a straw, flying at the speed of light, and then everything opened and he came back into his animated state, still holding Miriam, Trace right next to him.

The vampire stared in shock at them.

Io had no idea how he and Trace had managed the vapor caper with the asshole who had tried to take Miriam without asking his permission, but here they were in...holy fuck! Where in God's name were they?

Drecks stood frozen and gaping all around them. They were wearing white lab coats, and a couple who had been in dreck form quickly shifted to their human visage as if they hoped to hide themselves. Io stared wide-eyed, looking around what appeared to be a giant laboratory.

"Trace, are you getting this shit?"

"Holy fuck," was Trace's answer. He sounded as shocked and awed as Io felt.

Holding cells—at least fifty of them—lined the walls of the sterile room. In each one was a vampire in various stages of captivity, abuse, and torture.

To their right, a massive vampire with long, dark hair lay prone on a table. Tubes were attached to his arms and it looked like they were doing some kind of transfusion or something to him, being that the tubes led to a dreck lying on another table a few feet away.

The dreck on the table opened his eyes as if he realized unwelcome guests had arrived. When his gaze met Io's, he let out a shriek and jumped up, yanking the tubes from his arms.

"Get them!" He pointed at Trace and Io.

"Fuck you, Dr. Dread!" Io turned toward Trace. "Ice 'em!"

But Trace's hand had already come up, fingers splayed wide. Every dreck in the room froze, along with the vampire who still had hold of Miriam.

Io pried the dickshit's fingers from around Miriam's upper arms, struggling against the strong hold Trace had on him. Finally, he pulled Miriam free and hugged her to his body. She was breathing, but drugged. But not on cobalt. Thank God.

"Miriam. Can you hear me? Baby, I'm here." He kissed her perfect face while Trace slowly walked away from him.

"Trace?" Io hoisted Miriam up into his arms and cradled her close, ready to fly out of this hellhole. "Can you tell where we are?"

They needed to send an army back here to infiltrate and release all these vampires. He and Trace couldn't do it alone.

"Arizona." Trace picked up a small shipping box and showed it to Io. "I've got the address right here."

Io could tell Trace wanted to go superpower on the drecks whose lives he held, literally, in the palm of his hand.

"Don't, Trace. You know you can't."

"What? Kill these rats?" Trace walked over to the one who had stood up on the table next to the massive vampire who still had tubes sticking out of his arms. "Do you think they deserve to live, Io?"

He spoke to Io, but his gaze remained on the dreck.

"Trace, you'll start another war."

"And what do you think this is, Io?" Trace waved his arm in an arc, sending drecks flying like puppets thrown across the room.

Glass shattered. Papers scattered. Tables were knocked over.

Io's body screamed for him to take Miriam and flee to safety where he could let the calling properly claim him, but he couldn't leave Trace here. Not like this.

"We don't know what this is, Trace. This could be an independent. We need to investigate. You know as enforcers we can't go vigilante." Io prayed Trace wouldn't lose it.

He heard a snap and looked at the vampire next to him. His forearm hung at an odd angle. Another snap, and Io watched his other forearm bend in the middle.

"Oh yeah?" Trace said. "Well, the law doesn't apply to traitors, does it?"

Trace flicked the index finger of his left hand and the vampire's jaw broke.

"Trace. We need to go. We need to get out of here."

Just then Trace looked down at the large, naked vampire on the table, and his face paled.

Io frowned. "What is it? What's wrong?"

It looked like Trace was about to be sick.

Trace bent closer, inspecting the large vampire's face and sniffing him. "Father?"

Io's mouth dropped open and his eyes shot wide as he pulled Miriam closer. Was that behemoth on the lab table Trace's father?

Trace's rage bubbled up with such violence, Io could actually feel it. The dark energy became a living entity, and wind began blowing through the room, growing stronger with each passing second.

"You motherfuckers!" Trace cried out.

The vampire who'd tried to kidnap Miriam exploded in a shower of flesh, blood, and shattered bones as Trace fisted his left hand. After the gore settled, he reached down and yanked the tube's out of his father's arms.

With unbelievable strength, Trace bent and lifted his father over his left shoulder, all while keeping the drecks suspended with his right hand.

Trace turned and shouted back at the drecks, "You're all dead, motherfuckers! All of you! I'll kill every last fucking one of you goddamn animals! Fuck the truce!"

Io had never seen Trace this angry. Wind whipped all around them, and Io knew Trace was causing it. Just how powerful was Traceon? It scared the living shit out of him to think that this was his teammate and he'd never known just how powerful he was. "Trace! Now! We need to go now!"

Trace turned toward him, fixing him with yellow irises. *Yellow irises?* Trace just got freakier and freakier by the second.

"Go back to the hotel and grab those drecks if they haven't left, then get back to AKM and tell the others about this place. We need to get a team here pronto." Io shifted Miriam in his arms, squinting as papers flew past his face. "I'm taking Miriam to my place."

With his yellow eyes, Trace looked like a freak, but he nodded then disappeared with his father.

The wind immediately let up and the drecks re-animated as Io locked himself to Miriam and dematerialized, leaving behind the nightmare he and Trace had landed in.

CHAPTER 52

BISHOP PUSHED HIMSELF UP OFF THE TABLE the hairless vampire had thrown him against. Jessup's flesh was everywhere. All over everything.

But it didn't matter.

"Evacuation Code Red. Pack it up. Now!" The big vampire's venom and blood were shooting through him, sapping his strength, but he could rest later. They needed to get out of here before vampires overran the place.

Anything vital had to go with him. They would have to leave most of the vampires behind, but he would take a few of his more prized subjects.

Losing Maddox was a crushing blow, but he still had Miriam's blood. Royal blood. And he had already drawn enough of Maddox's blood and venom to hopefully complete what he had started today.

As the lab assistants rushed to gather anything critical they could scavenge from the mess the hairless vampire had made, Bishop rubbed his palm over the padded table where Maddox had been laying. He had heard everything. The hairless vampire was named Trace, and Maddox was his father. How very interesting.

"I want that vampire," Bishop said aloud.

"Who, Maddox?" One of his assistants paused and frowned at him.

The corner of Bishop's mouth turned up slyly. "If we can get him back, yes. But the one I want...the one I *really* want? Is Trace." He raised his voice so the entire room could hear him. "If anyone can find a way to bring me Trace, you will be handsomely rewarded." Trace was clearly a mongrel with exceptional powers, and that gave Bishop a mental hard-on. Trace would be a fabulous mixed-blood to test his mutant theories on.

The vital materials of the lab were already one-third packed up, the evacuation plan running like clockwork. He would never return to this facility, but the destruction and evac would be worth it if he could get his hands on Trace. That mongrel would make a fine addition to his collection.

CHAPTER 53

Io APPEARED WITH MIRIAM IN HIS LIVING ROOM.

She groaned and rolled her head from side to side as he laid her on the couch.

"Miriam. Miriam? Wake up, baby. Come on. Wake up for me." He knelt beside her, stroking her hair off her face.

When her eyes fluttered open, he bowed his head and said a silent prayer of thanks.

"Io?" She sounded so damn weak as she frowned and blinked. Did she recognize him?

Lifting his face to hers, he smiled. "I'm here, baby. I'm with you."

"Is this Heaven?" She blinked drowsily.

Whatever those drecks had given her to knock her out had been strong, but he didn't detect any cobalt in her system.

"No, baby. This isn't Heaven." Io skimmed his fingers over her face, his body crying out with need for her. But he wouldn't claim her until she was lucid and able to understand what was happening. "You're in my home. I saved you."

With heavy lids, Miriam forced herself to keep her eyes open so she could look at him. Io could tell she was struggling to focus, but she tried to lift a shaking hand to his cheek.

"How do you feel?" he said, dipping his face into her hand.

She trembled and groaned, closing her eyes and curling in on herself.

Withdrawal. Io jumped up and ran to his kitchen and quickly prepared her a cup of tonic. Once back by her side, he held the cup toward her and lifted her head off the couch. "Drink, baby. You'll feel better."

She wrinkled her nose at the smell but didn't resist, taking a sip, then a drink, and finally a gulp that all but killed the contents of the cup.

The minutes ticked by and her trembling diminished until, finally, she took a deep breath and relaxed. She rolled her head toward him, tears balancing on the rims of her eyes.

"You're alive?" She sounded confused. Her eyes blinked again and again as if she was trying to focus. "Io?"

"Yes, honey. I'm alive. Your dad spared me so I could save you." He stroked her face again.

What sounded like a choked sob croaked in her throat, and Miriam's eyes slammed shut and squeezed out her tears so they streamed her cheeks. Within seconds, painful sobs wracked her body, her shoulders convulsing with each hiccupping attempt to breathe.

"Ssshhh. Miriam, it's okay." Io lifted her into his arms and hugged her close.

Her arms flung around him, and her fingers curled like claws as she gripped the back of his shirt in her fists, latching onto him like a vise and burying her face against his neck.

"Io! I love you. God, I love you. Don't ever leave me. I'm never going home again. Never. They'd have to kill me first to take me away from you."

Tears of his own balanced on the rims of his eyes. All his life he'd never expected mating to feel like this, like his life depended entirely on another. Io had never comprehended what taking a mate was like, but now that he had, he knew with certainty that if anything happened to Miriam, he would die. She was his reason for living now. Miriam was his life.

"What I feel for you I can't put into words, Miriam. It goes so far beyond love that saying I love you is a disservice."

Her hold on him tightened and she nodded against him as if she understood completely but was unable to speak.

Io finally let his tears flow and held her, knowing exactly how she felt.

CHAPTER 54

AFTER DEPOSITING HIS FATHER ON ONE OF THE BEDS, Trace chased after the two drecks who had flown out the door right after he had poofed back into the room. Catching up to them in the stairwell, his hand shot out, and they both froze as he caught them into compulsion.

"Where you goin', boys?"

Their eyes locked to his in fear, then he forced them to turn around.

"Back to the room. Now."

Like a puppet master with a pair of marionettes, Trace marched them up the stairs and back into the hall on the ninth floor, where he walked them toward the room, having a little fun and directing them into the wall a couple of times.

"Oops."

His vision was still extra sharp and crystal clear, so he knew his eyes hadn't changed back yet. Shit, with all this emotional upheaval, he was shocked he wasn't ready to crawl out of his skin. He'd had a hell of a day. First Micah had agreed to be his Master, then Cordray had...well, just Cordray. 'Nuff said on that bitch. Then he'd been sentenced to what felt like Hell, and now he had found his father strapped to a lab table having God only knew what being done to him. What was next? Would his dead brother materialize from thin air? Or maybe he wasn't dead after all. If his allegedly dead father had shown up, then maybe his brother would, too.

Once they reached the room, Trace stepped in front of them, opened the door, then turned as he backed in, waving his fingers in a come-here motion so that the shoes of the two drecks dragged across the floor. After getting them inside, he waved his left hand, making the door slam shut behind them. Well, it didn't really slam. Not with Io's heavy foot action on it earlier, which had torn out a piece of the jamb. But at least it shut. Then he picked up the handset on the room's phone.

"Have a seat," he said to the drecks, dropping them to the floor and holding them there while he dialed out.

Tristan picked up. "This is Tristan."

"It's Trace. Io has Miriam. She's safe. She was drugged, but alive."

"Shit. Overdose?"

"No." Trace looked around the room until his gaze landed on his father. He didn't know where to begin with all he and Io had seen. "I need you to send someone to the Burnham. I have two prisoners here."

"Who are they?"

"Drecks. Two of them. Dealers. But whatever they were doing to Miriam, they weren't shooting her up with cobalt."

"What do you mean?"

Trace frowned, emotion beginning to overcome him as memories of his past began to invade his mind. "Fuck, Tristan. We've got a problem." He swiped his palm over his scalp. "I think they were planning on kidnapping her. There was another vampire here, but he was working with the drecks. He was taking her. Io and I hitched a ride as he vapored into some kind of..." Trace hesitated, his thoughts scrambling over what he had seen. All those vampires held like animals in cells. No. Test subjects. Lab rats. Those vampires back at that lab were rats for God only knew what kinds of experiments. He looked at his father again. What had they been doing to him?

"Trace?" Tristan's voice jolted him back into the room.

"Tristan. I've got an address. You need to send a team immediately. This is important." He rattled off the address. "It's a lab of some kind. There's going to be heavy retrieval. Must be forty or fifty vampires locked down in cells there. They..." Trace looked at his father again. "They had my father."

The line went silent, then Tristan said, "Say again?"

"My father, Tristan. I swear to God, this is my father." He stood over the prone male sprawled and unconscious on the bed. "I got him out. He's here. Send medics, but get a force out to that address in Arizona."

A knock sounded on the door before it opened. Micah entered, leading Severin and that bitch, Cordray, inside. Trace immediately yanked the cover up and over his father. He didn't like the thought of Cordray seeing his naked flesh.

"How many drecks were there, Trace?" Tristan asked.

"A lot. But they're probably already packing up and getting out of Dodge. But some of those vampires were in bad shape and in no condition to travel. We need to rescue them.

"Roger that. I've already texted AKM's Phoenix substation, and I'm asking Stryker if he can put together a team to go out and assist. We'll get 'em out."

Trace felt Cordray worming into his mind and shot her with an acid glare.

"I've gotta go, Tristan. Micah, Sev, and that witch are here."

Micah frowned and glanced between him and Cordray then back at him, mouthing *Witch?*

Cordray flipped him off, but refused to pull herself from his mind, threading her way in.

Trace slammed the phone down and growled right before taking one long, forceful stride to get in Cordray's face, dropping his right hand and allowing the drecks to fall out of compulsion and right into Micah's and Sev's waiting fists.

"Stay out of my thoughts, bitch!" Trace hadn't felt such a powerful reaction to anyone in a long time.

"I don't take orders from you." She met his glare with one of her own, her catlike eyes narrowing.

"Oh, and you've been ordered to probe my head?"

"That's right," she said with a sneer. "Bain wants me to report back what you and Io found."

The sound of Micah and Sev working over the drecks hardly distracted him.

"You can ask, and I'll tell you," he said, still glowering at her.

"My way is much more efficient."

Trace snarled. "Well, you can suck my dick, because I want you OUT." He reinforced the mental block he kept up around his thoughts, slamming the door on her.

She sneered. "That's okay. I already got what I needed." Cordray walked away and stood by the window.

Trace watched her go, shooting eye daggers at her back before turning toward Micah and Severin. Sev cinched a binding strip around one dreck's wrists and shoved him down on the floor. Micah had knocked his opponent out and was sitting on the bed, combing his fingers through his long, black hair, pushing it off his face.

"Who's that?" Micah nodded toward his father.

"His name's Maddox," Cordray said. "He's Trace's daddy."

Trace turned to see Cordray standing beside the other bed. The sarcastic, I-dare-you-to-try-something expression on her face made it clear she took a particular joy in stealing his thunder and outing him.

"Get away from him!" Trace made to lunge for her, but Micah jumped up and pulled him back.

Cordray's smirk widened and she stepped around the bed and got right in Trace's grill. Sev joined Micah and fought to keep him from attacking her, but it was all they could do to prevent him from breaking free and coldcocking the bitch.

Narrowing her eyes, Cordray reached out and pressed the tip of her index finger against his sternum with deadly quietness. "Don't ever tell me to suck your dick again, because next time it happens, I'll do more than just steal your thunder. I'll bite the goddamn thing clean off."

This time around, with Cordray steadfastly standing her ground against him, Trace became fully aware of just how hard his dick was. And as Cordray flicked her long leather trench and sauntered toward the door, it shocked him to realize his power was completely and complacently in check.

He didn't know what that meant, but he had a feeling he wasn't going to like it when he found out.

CHAPTER 55

MIRIAM LEANED BACK AND GAZED at Io's handsome, perfect face, still in shock that he was actually there.

"What happened?"

She had gone to the Burnham, met with the dealers, thought she was being injected with cobalt, but instead had passed out.

"You were drugged." Io's face looked pained.

"Why?"

"I don't know," he said. "But I think they were trying to kidnap you."

He told her about what had happened. "I think they wanted to use you..." Io winced and grunted, clutching his stomach.

Miriam sprang upright. "Are you okay?"

He was panting.

"The calling"—his entire body jerked as if in a spasm—"is hitting me...ungh...hard ...now that you're safe." He doubled over, gripping his abdomen.

Oh God! That's right. Io had entered his calling phase with her. She reached for him.

"What can I...?"

But she couldn't speak another word as a wave of hormonal heat pulsed through her own body like the shockwave from an explosion. Miriam literally fell back against the couch cushions from the power of the pulse of core-moistening arousal.

She moaned as a rush of Io's heat answered her own and pounded through her, and damn if she didn't almost have an orgasm on the spot.

"Forgive me," he said, sweeping up and over her, grabbing the waist of her pants. "I know you've been through hell, but—"

"Do what you have to, Io." She knew what he needed, and if her body was going to react like this, and his was going to put off that kind of heat, she would be helpless to stop him anyway.

"Don't want...to hurt you." Io's fingers curled around the waist of her pants, gripping the fabric so tightly his knuckles turned white as he fought not to lose control.

Miriam needed to take care of her male. Io was in physical anguish, more worried about her than about the demands his body had placed on him. They could talk later about what had happened, but right now, Io couldn't wait another second.

"Baby," she whispered against his ear, pulling him down. "Let yourself go and take what you need."

Something broke inside Io at her words. Miriam felt the change immediately. His hormonal heat flooded her as if he'd been holding it back. With a primal, guttural growl, his hands practically shredded her clothes as he tore them off. And she just as violently and urgently stripped him free of his, reacting to the basic, animalistic urge to mate.

"I'm sorry, I'm sorry, God, I'm sorry." Io picked her up and tossed her on the floor, tears streaking his face.

As badly as he wanted her—to the point he could barely control himself—Miriam could tell that somewhere inside himself it pained him to treat her so roughly after what she had been through. His reaction made her love him all the more, because she knew in that moment that he would never hurt her. He would always strive to take care of her and see to her comfort.

"Ssshhh, baby. I belong to you. Do what you need to." Miriam dug her nails into his shoulders as he shoved her legs apart and sank down on her, thrusting himself inside.

AFTER SO LONG AWAY FROM HER during this critical phase in their relationship, Io came the instant the head of his cock breached her. Just that simple friction was enough to send him careening into the most violent orgasm he'd ever had.

His ass tightened, forcing him deeper into her as he cried out, practically convulsing out of his skin as surge after torrential surge of climactic force blew him apart. It felt like his bones were splintering from the fierce constriction of his muscles, tightening him into a tense, stretched mass of flesh that would snap with just the tiniest flinch.

And before he knew what was happening, he came again, and again, and yet a fourth time. His calling was good and pissed off at having been denied the pleasure of Miriam's inner warmth for so long, letting him know it by spinning him like he was an out-of-control bumper car at the carnival. Io couldn't focus, feeling as though he were spiraling into a black hole in the middle of the universe, lights shimmering and disappearing, his vision going dark but his body remaining lit up brighter than a supernova.

From somewhere, Miriam's cry of pleasure assaulted his senses. Her nails raked down his back. The insides of her thighs shuddered against his hips before her legs wrapped around him.

That was when Io felt it—the telltale waves of heat coming off her. She was reacting the way a mated male did in his calling. He had never heard of a female calling, but sure as hell, she was having one, and her hormonal release pulled him, prolonging his orgasm, intensifying it.

Finally, Io stopped spilling inside her, his body calming until he lowered himself to the side in a spent heap of heavy breathing. His still-hard cock slipped out of her, leaving her saturated and pleasantly wafting of his fragrance. Instinctively, his hand slid to her flat stomach and pressed down as he kissed her breasts and tenderly played an oral trail down her torso.

He had maybe minutes—or perhaps even seconds—before another wave of fertile fire forced him to take her again, and if her body continued to push off wave after wave of her own calling, this would be a long, yet pleasurable, night.

Miriam practically glowed as her legs scissored in a

glorious display of post-orgasmic bliss, her back arching and a moan floating from her throat like a honeyed song as she lifted her body to his mouth. With hunger flooding him to have her yet again, he passed his tongue up and over the mound of one breast, sweeping it over her taut nipple, sending her into another small, quivering orgasm. She was on fire beneath his touch, lost to her heat and his.

Suddenly, he stilled and lifted up on his elbow, pressing his palm more firmly against her abdomen. He stared at her stomach. "Miriam...?"

"Hmm?" She sounded dreamily distracted and skimmed her long fingers up his arm.

Io couldn't believe it. He had already achieved what the calling had urged him to create. Life stirred inside Miriam's belly. New and still too small to see without a microscope, but it was there. Its warmth and unique life signature flowed apart from Miriam's but in tune with it. As the male, it was his job to feel his child's life force. If he had been paying attention, he would have felt the moment Miriam had conceived, but he hadn't realized at the time how far he was into his calling. He had been more concerned with treating her withdrawal.

"You're pregnant, baby." Io turned his face toward Miriam's just as her eyes flashed open.

"What?" Her hand planted down over his. She looked at him as if she feared she hadn't heard him right.

When he held her gaze and nodded, she looked at him in disbelief. A proud grin spread over his mouth.

"Who's the man?" he said playfully, not caring about her father, the punishment he had been sentenced to, or the fucked up laboratory he had pulled her from. All that mattered was that he had succeeded. He had made new life. With Miriam.

The calling dictated only one thing: that he propagate the species by creating a child. He had done just that.

Out of all the members on his team, he was the most unlikely to play the role of loving mate and doting father, but here he was, going from playboy to expecting father in a

matter of days, and Miri was the reason. She was his savior…
his queen.

"I love you, Miri. You've made me so happy. So damn
happy." He bowed his head against her stomach and kissed
the smooth skin that held his future child in her protective
cocoon.

"I'm seriously pregnant?" Miriam's fingers wove into his
hair and held him against her stomach.

"Yes." Io kissed her belly button, his pride and ego swelling.

He had gotten Miriam pregnant when he hadn't even
realized he was in his calling. How about those potent little
soldiers of his? Who's the man indeed? If he wasn't already
preoccupied with giving his girl all she deserved and more,
he'd have hopped up and strutted like a peacock.

Miriam tugged on his hair, and Io rose up her body to
taste her waiting lips.

"We created a new life, Io," she whispered softly. "You and
I created a miracle."

The wonder in her eyes made Io feel even more like a
hero. "It's all because of you." He kissed her. "I was nothing
without you. Now…?" He smiled and kissed her again.
"You've allowed me to be more than I ever thought I could
be. And now you're going to make me a father."

Miriam bit her bottom lip as she smiled, her blue eyes
twinkling. "And here I thought you were a rebel."

"Baby, if you only knew." He nibbled her chin as she tilted
her head back.

"What do you mean?"

He smiled against her throat. "Taking you as a mate has
been my greatest act of rebellion. I defied the king to have
you. I defied everyone to make you mine. Even myself."

Miriam pushed him to his back and straddled his hips,
her long, raven hair spilling over her breasts. "You're such a
bad boy."

"Only because you're such a bad girl."

She grinned. "I am that, aren't I?"

He nodded, playing his palms up her naked thighs.
"Mmm, we're so perfect together."

"Two rebels?"

He lifted her up so she could reach down and position his still-erect cock beneath her.

"Mmm, God yes." He moaned as he slid into her slick channel. "Don't you ever go playing it safe with me, either. I love you this way."

Miriam swung forward and mashed her breasts to his chest. "Ditto."

As the calling rose once more, Miriam rocked hard against him, taking him to new heights.

I'm going to be a father. Io wrapped his arms around the mother of his child and swore he would never let go.

CHAPTER 56

CORDRAY SAT ACROSS FROM THE TWO DRECKS, filtering through their broken memories and unlocking what was real and discarding what was false. These two had been mind-fucked not just once, but twice in the past twenty-four hours, and they had been held in a semi-lucid, almost hypnotic state for part of the time. But through their unlocked memories, she saw the other players in the room and heard all the conversations that had taken place.

Donovan was situated to her right. King Bain sat to her left, tense and fidgeting, because Io had not yet returned with Miriam, and it was daylight out. It was surprising Bain was able to focus at all.

And that prick, Trace, sat with the others who had been re-assembled to finish the trial that had been disrupted earlier.

"Bishop," she said. "He's in charge. Jessup is—was—the vampire who worked for him." She fixed Trace in a knowing stare.

When she had looked inside Trace's mind earlier, she had seen Jessup's gruesome demise, as well as his reaction to finding his father having God knew what being done to him.

She actually felt bad for Trace having to find his father like that. Medics had taken Maddox to the AKM facility before she and the others had returned to King Bain's courthouse, and she sensed that it was killing Trace not to be there when his father woke up.

But she couldn't think about that now. She had work to do. She turned her attention back to the two drecks.

"Their names are Grotek and Chane." She pointed to each

in turn, signaling who was who.

She let their memories wash through her. "And Apostle. John Apostle. He's there, too, and—"

"No. That's impossible!" Micah barked. He shook his head, hands in the air as if pushing her words back at her.

"You're wrong," Trace added, his voice deep and powerful.

"No, I'm not."

She knew why Trace sounded so certain, though. When she had been in Trace's mind earlier, she had caught a glimpse of what he had done to the dreck he thought had been Apostle. If Bain knew Trace was responsible for that massacre from two months ago, Trace's punishment would be a lot harsher than it already was. That little stunt had taken a lot of finagling and political diplomacy for Bain to smooth over with Royce, the dreck liege.

"I heard Apostle was killed, Cordray?" King Bain said.

"The report of his death was a mistake." Cordray looked from Trace to Micah and back again.

It was clear from their expressions that they knew she knew the truth.

"Apostle had a twin," she said, her voice steady as she narrowed her eyes on Micah, whose brow furrowed at her words. She knew what she was about to say would cause an uproar. "His name was Deacon." Realization began to alight in the eyes of those around the table. "Deacon was the one who was killed, not Apostle. And Bishop is Apostle's other brother. Bishop is far deadlier than Apostle, based on what I'm picking up from these two." She nodded toward Grotek and Chane. "Bishop's the one you have to worry about, but Apostle's no picnic, either."

The color drained from Micah's face as he and Trace exchanged glances, and within an instant, Micah had his cell phone in his hand, probably sending a message to Sam to warn her. Cordray knew the connection between Apostle and Sam from the thoughts she had picked up from both Micah and Trace, and Micah had good reason to be concerned. Still, she didn't think Micah had cause to worry in the immediate future.

"I don't think Apostle is after Sam, Micah." Granted, she only had the thoughts of Grotek and Chane to sift through, but deductive reasoning dictated that if Apostle was more concerned with Miriam, he likely didn't know about Sam. If he knew she was still alive, he would likely go after her over anyone else to exact revenge.

Micah shot her an eat-shit glance and continued typing on his phone.

Murmurs broke out around the table, and everyone turned a nervous, concerned eye toward Micah. Apparently, they all knew what Apostle's return to Chicago meant, too. Micah and Sam could be in danger. Apostle would have a serious bone to pick with Micah for what had happened in January.

But as big a splash as the news about Apostle had created, she knew what she had to say next would make an even bigger one.

"There's more," she said, turning back to the two drecks, who remained still as stone as she kept them tranced during her mind sweep. "Miriam…."

"What about her? What's wrong?" King Bain shot forward in his chair.

"She's fine. Better than fine." Cordray paused. "She's pregnant. I would say Io is the father."

As expected, the room exploded into an uproar, voices talking over one another. But when Bain's fist landed on the massive, round table, everyone fell silent.

"I want Io! He'll pay for this!"

Cordray swung her gaze around. "No. Haven't you learned a thing from what's happened here?" Her half-brother could be so dense when he wasn't acting as the king.

Several gasps broke from the others in attendance. She had always been granted an amazing margin of leniency when addressing him. No one else had to know why, and she had no problem keeping her relationship to him a secret, so to hell with everyone else when it came to how she and Bain talked to one another.

Bain stared at her. "What do you mean?"

"What I mean is you almost lost your daughter, Bain. And she has formed an attachment to Io the way a male attaches to a mate. If you kill Io or even try to harm him, it could kill her or cause irreversible damage." She stared at him. "Do you hear me?"

More gasps, but she didn't care. Her main concern was Miriam, and Bain was out of line. He had been for a long time where Miriam was concerned.

"But Io broke the law. He knew the consequences."

Cordray stood her ground. "And so do you. If you kill Io, Miriam could die. If you hurt him or take him away from her, she will hate you forever. You will lose Miriam forever, Bain. Do you understand? I advise you to think long and hard about how you will handle this situation, because your reaction will directly affect Miriam's reaction. And since she has your blood in her veins, she will be just as stubborn and convicted of her choice as you are of yours, only she will have biology on her side through her link to Io. That gives her the advantage."

She knew that if anyone else had spoken so candidly to him, they would already have been removed from his presence, but Bain knew she only had his best interests at heart and that she only spoke the truth. They shared a bond that was stronger than that of even full-blooded siblings. She and Bain were truly bound to one another through not only their father's blood, but also through a mutual devotion to the well-being of the other.

Cordray didn't kiss his ass or blow smoke up it. She said it like it was and didn't mince words. Not with anyone, but especially not with Bain.

All of the above made her one of Bain's most trusted consultants. All the others had their noses so far up his ass it was a wonder they didn't spit his shit. When Bain wanted honesty, he came to her.

Case in point, Bain's gaze wavered on hers then darted across the room. She knew she had gotten through.

"I will consider your advice," Bain said, jutting his chin out as if the decision had been his and no one else's.

"Good." Cordray looked back to Grotek and Chane before Trace caught her eye again.

She turned toward him. "May I help you with something, Traceon?"

He shook his head, his pale eyes narrowing. "You have big balls there, sweetheart."

She had wondered how long it would take before he voiced his thoughts about her. She had been reading them since the trial. He didn't like her and couldn't believe how she talked to Bain. Well, fuck him.

"That's quite enough, Trace." King Bain's voice boomed beside her. "You're already in enough trouble, or would you like me to extend your sentence?"

Trace's gaze nearly cut through her as if he blamed her for the king's reaction.

"No, Sire. My apologies." With a final glare at her, Trace looked away.

But Micah refused to follow suit, his dark eyes shooting daggers at her. Obviously, those two had each other's backs through thick and thin, just as she and Bain had each other's. She also got the feeling without digging through his thoughts that Micah didn't like that she knew the truth of what had happened to get Apostle's twin killed. She held one hell of an ace over them with that tidbit of information. She had no intention of playing it, but they didn't need to know that.

Lucky for her she had a mental barrier stronger than Trace's to keep Micah's little probey-dobey head out of hers. Cordray didn't like anyone poking around in her thoughts. She had too much she wanted to keep hidden.

"Is there anything else, Cordray?" King Bain seemed restless.

She huffed, staring at Trace. He had done well in Miriam's rescue, and he had suffered—was still suffering—from finding his father the way he had. As much as she didn't want to admit it, the guy deserved some slack.

"I think you should consider shortening Trace's sentence," she said, knowing that Trace was already concerned about being locked away. She had caught a glimpse as to why, but it had only been a glimpse. He was one fucked up male, that was for sure.

"Why?" Bain arched a black eyebrow at her, his jaw tensing. She might have had leeway, but in some things he didn't like being challenged.

Trace and Micah both looked suspicious of her intentions.

"He helped save your daughter," she said. "And he helped shut down a laboratory that served as a torture chamber. If our preliminary counts are accurate from our counterparts in Phoenix, he helped rescue over thirty vampires, including his father." She turned toward Bain. "Don't you think that deserves some leniency?"

Bain pursed his lips and rubbed his chin, glancing toward Trace as if measuring him up. "We'll see."

"I don't need your charity, honey," Trace said, practically spitting the words at her.

"It's not charity, tough guy. Just shut up and hope he cuts your sentence." She sneered at him. "I know the thought of being locked up for a month scares the shit out of you, and I know why." She looked from Trace to Micah and back again. "So just say thank you and zip your trap."

The two glared at each other, Trace's eyes tightening as he pulled back slightly in his chair. He looked threatened, like a raccoon spooked by humans, freezing and rearing back on its hind legs. Obviously, Trace wasn't used to letting others know so much, and the fact he couldn't stop her from getting inside his thoughts didn't sit well with him.

"Enough," Bain said, shaking his head at them. "Fine. Traceon, for your contribution toward saving my daughter, as well as for your heroic sacrifice, I will reduce your sentence from one month to fifteen days. Is that acceptable, Cordray?"

She turned toward Bain. "Yes."

"Is there anything else?" he asked.

"Nothing of consequence."

"Good, then with nothing further, the punishments I handed down earlier will commence immediately. Tristan, you are to return home and remain there under house arrest for one month. Severin, you are suspended for one week without pay. And Traceon..." The King stood. "You will serve fifteen days in confinement and be suspended indefinitely without pay, pending review in three months."

Micah stood and shouted, "He's still suspended? What about—?"

King Bain raised his hand, cutting Micah off, and gave the guards a vicious glare to keep them back. Obviously, he remembered what had happened earlier when his guards had manhandled Micah, and he didn't want to provoke Trace into a repeat performance.

"Micah, my decision is final. I will take his assistance into consideration in three months when we consider his reinstatement to AKM, but for now, that is my ruling."

"What about me?" Micah said, jutting out his chin. "I was involved with helping Io and Miriam, too, but you haven't punished me?"

"You weren't involved in giving the order, or party to the mental manipulation of my guards, Micah," King Bain said patiently.

"But I helped deceive you."

What the hell was Micah doing? Did he *want* to be punished?

"Very well, Micah." Bain sounded tired, as if he were suddenly weary and wanted only to rest. "I sentence you to one day suspension, without pay, to be enforced immediately. And then you will take over the team in Tristan's absence." The king gave Micah a long, hard look as both he and Tristan gaped. "And you will become the leader you were always meant to become. Is that understood?"

Cordray slowly stood and looked from Bain to Micah. This was an unexpected turn of events.

Bain ambled slowly around the table and stopped in front of Micah. "I am ready to see you fulfill the role you were meant to fulfill, Micah. The role my father and I had always intended for you to fill before"—Bain pressed his lips together and shook his head once—"Before Katarina's death."

"What role is that?" Micah stared at him suspiciously.

"In time, Micah." The king rested a hand on Micah's shoulder, smiled tightly, then turned and began to walk away. "For now, just know that I have grown weary of waiting. Now that you have Sam, and you seem to be back on track, I have my eye on you. Don't disappoint me, Micah. Now, everyone, leave me."

Cordray watched her brother trudge away as if the weight of the world rested on his shoulders. He had a lot to think about. And when her gaze met Trace's as the guards pulled him away, she realized that she did, too.

CHAPTER 57

BISHOP STOOD WITH HIS HANDS clasped behind his back, staring out the window of his new residence in a wooded, rolling area of northern Indiana. He had carefully selected the location from a dozen choices, choosing it because it was the crossroads between east and west. It was only a day or two's drive to all the major cities surrounding it. New York, Chicago, Pittsburgh, St. Louis, Indianapolis. Even Florida could be reached in less than twenty-four hours if he drove straight through. He would be able to run a more efficient operation here, shipping subjects into his lab and back out to the streets in a fraction of the time he'd been able to from Arizona.

The place was still a mess, and it aggravated him no end that he'd had to move before he'd been ready, but it was what it was, and he could either be a sourpuss about it or look at the bright side. He chose the latter, even if the bright side was as dim as a twenty-five watt light bulb.

He had only been able to bring a handful of his test subjects, so he would have to begin an immediate re-stock. Luckily, this new facility had twice the number of cells as the one in Arizona, and the lab was bigger and better equipped.

Okay, so make that a forty-five watt light bulb.

After taking out one of his brown cigarettes, he closed his lips around the gold filter and flicked up a flame on his etched, gold lighter. With a deep inhale, he turned and waved away the assistant who was arranging the last scorpion aquarium on the shelf in his new den.

The assistant scuttled away, and Bishop lifted the lid of

one aquarium and beckoned his pet onto his hand.

Apostle's voice shot out from the corner of his new office. "It wasn't my fault!"

Time to christen the home.

With a sigh, Bishop walked toward him and knelt down. "I know, dear brother. But Jessup…" Bishop feigned remorse and shrugged one shoulder. "Well, he's dead already, and someone needs to be punished for this failure."

"I didn't fail!" Apostle pulled on the chain that bound him to the reinforced wall, his eyes full of terror. "You're the one who ordered her to be taken. If you had just stuck to *my* plan, none of this would have happened!"

"I know, brother. I know." Bishop lowered his hand and the scorpion scurried onto Apostle's leg, which jerked and twitched.

But Apostle's ankles were shackled to bolts in the floor, so he couldn't get away.

Bishop slowly stood and took a leisurely draw on his Sobranie. "From now on, you will convey to those who work for me what will happen if they fail, Apostle."

"But you're the one who failed!"

Apostle's terrorized screams cut him off and touched Bishop's ears like a symphony. He closed his eyes and tilted his head back to listen.

"I will make a strong leader out of you yet, my brother. Now, sing for me. Sing for me some more."

What do you know? Apostle followed his order to the letter this time.

CHAPTER 58

TRACE HAD BEEN LOCKED UP FOR OVER TWO DAYS. No one had been allowed to see him, and hardly a sound reached him this far back in the king's holding cells. He was completely alone, and with the rampant thoughts running amok through his mind, Trace wasn't sure how much longer he could stand the isolation and sensory deprivation.

His greatest fear had always been that he would humiliate himself by losing hold of his power and going mutant. Now, he feared learning the truth of where his father had been all this time would tip the scale.

The last memory he had of his father had been tainted with pain and blame, and Trace had thought his father had been killed long ago, along with his brother.

Life without his brother had been hard in and of itself. Brak had been Trace's proverbial lightning rod. The one person Trace had been able to count on to keep him grounded. Losing Brak had been devastating, but thinking he had lost his father had left Trace feeling even emptier.

But now his father was back. Maddox was alive. It made him wonder if Brak was still out there somewhere, too. Unlikely, but hope bubbled in his heart nonetheless.

How long had his father been held in that lab? Where had he been? Was he okay? Had he finally accepted what had happened to Trace's mother?

Sitting with bent legs on the small bed in his cell, Trace bowed his head and settled his forehead on his folded arms, which rested on his knees.

He didn't know how long he sat that way before he became

aware he was being watched. Snapping his head up, he saw Cordray standing outside his cell. Her long hair was pulled up in a tight ponytail that draped over her shoulder and down the front of her body.

Trace lowered his feet to the floor and frowned, bristling. "You sure enjoy breaking the king's rules, honey." He wondered how she had been permitted to see him when the king had clearly stated he wasn't allowed to have visitors.

"Don't you worry about me," she said, eyeing him.

Trace snorted. "Don't compliment yourself."

"Fuck you, Trace."

He flipped her off without meeting her gaze. "Will that be all?"

Cordray's face remained placid. "I thought I could help."

Trace scoffed. "I don't need your help, honey."

"I could have told Bain what you did to Deacon, but I didn't."

Trace pushed up off the tiny bed and stalked to the front of his cell. "Don't go doing me any favors. You're the reason I'm in here to begin with."

"No, *you're* the reason you're in here, Traceon." Cordray arched a slender eyebrow at him, her brilliant blue eyes locking onto his.

"Whatever." Trace turned and marched away. "Fuck off, okay. How about you just fuck off and leave me alone?"

Obviously not one to be deterred, Cordray pushed onward. "You had a choice, Traceon. You knew the law and you chose to break it. Actions lead to consequences. If you can't take—"

Trace spun around. "Spare me your philosophical ruminations, bitch. I don't need your bullshit right now."

She shot needles at him from her eyes. "Fuck you. I'm not the one locked behind bars, and I'll do and say whatever I want." She tilted her head to the side. "And I'll go wherever I want, too. If you don't like it, you can suck my ass, because I don't give two shits about you or whether you live or die. You got that?"

"Then why are you here? Afraid I'll die without saying goodbye?"

A flash of emotion crossed her face—one Trace couldn't

identify, but which reminded him of dismay or surprise.

"You'd better get used to me, Traceon," she said, composing herself as quickly as she had faltered, taking a step back and placing her hands behind her as if she was at military at ease.

Wearing a black, sequined tank top with the image of a black widow on the front, along with black cargo pants and studded platform boots with three-inch heels, she looked like more like the military fashion police than a soldier. Especially with all that ink and metal decorating her body.

"Why's that? You moving in to the cell next to mine?" Oh joy, what a ride that would be.

"No, dickhead. Because when you're out of here, I'll be your boss."

A haughty laugh punched out of Trace's throat. "You couldn't boss my dick, bitch."

The corners of Cordray's mouth turned up almost wickedly, her eyes narrowing with self-satisfaction.

Trace stopped laughing. "You're serious?"

"Oh yeah, big guy. Dead serious. You'll be serving your community service at *my* shelter. If you ever want to work at AKM again, you'll do as I tell you." Her eyes dropped to his crotch. "And what was that you were saying about bossing your dick?" Her bright eyes lifted to his, one brow arching. And then she spun on her heel and sashayed away, head held high. Self-righteous little huss.

Trace looked down.

What the fuck? His pecker had sprouted to full attention, making a healthy tent in the scratchy canvas pants he'd been forced to put on before going into lockup. The bulge left nothing to the imagination.

"That's quite a package...*Traceon*," Cordray called back, sniggering quietly.

"Fuck off...*Cordray*." He really hated that bitch. Damn her. But she had him by the short and curlies, and didn't that just suck a donkey's dick?

At least fighting with her gave him an outlet for his power. But if he wasn't careful, he could get addicted to verbally sparring with her, and that was something he really didn't want to see happen.

He'd just as soon knock Cordray out the first opportunity he got. Someone needed to put her in her place, and Trace hoped the task would fall to him. Soon.

CHAPTER 59

Io's RINGING CELL PHONE AWOKE HIM, and he rolled into Miriam's warmth, trying to ignore it.

"That's the third time it's rung in the last fifteen minutes," Miriam said, stroking her fingers across his cheek and kissing his forehead.

"I know, but I don't want to answer it." He had a feeling he knew who it was, or at least what the incessant phone calls were about.

Honestly, he was shocked the king's guards hadn't come busting down his door to retrieve Miriam by now. Having King Bain's men interrupt his time with Miriam was becoming the status quo—a fucked-up déjà vu he lived over and over. He and Miriam hadn't made any efforts to flee or hide, choosing to stay in his home and steal as much time as they had together before being ripped apart, but here they were, four days later, and still no one had come to arrest him and take her back home.

The call went to voicemail and he nuzzled his face against Miriam's neck. She smelled of him. His scent was all over her, and hers was all over him. Not surprising since they had spent the past four days without an inch between them. His calling hadn't cared that a child already grew within Miriam's belly. It had continued to demand he make regular deposits of his fertile offering, a command Io was more than happy to comply with.

"How do you feel?" he said, snuggling closer.

"Good."

He grinned at the sound of the lazy smile in her voice.

"No withdrawal?" He had faithfully been preparing doses of elixir for her every six hours, but the last dose had been over seven hours ago.

"No." She relaxed more fully against him and kissed the top of his head. "You've taken excellent care of me, Io."

His eyes remained closed, and he grinned as they shifted so that he spooned her. "You're getting better already." He opened his eyes and brushed her hair aside to kiss the back of her neck.

"I know. I can feel it."

The phone started ringing again.

"Fuck." Io sighed heavily.

"You should answer it. Get it over with." Miriam dropped her face into the pillow, obviously not liking the disruption to the peaceful existence they had created during the past four days.

Miriam was right, of course. He was only putting off the inevitable.

With another sigh, he rolled back and snagged his phone from the nightstand.

It was Micah. Not exactly who he had expected, but close enough.

"Yeah?"

"Sorry to interrupt you, Io. I know you're busy and all..." Micah cleared his throat. "You've been summoned to appear before King Bain for your sentencing to be carried out."

And there was the hammer falling. Io's heart dropped.

"When?"

"An hour after sundown, which is in about..." Micah paused as if checking the time. "That's about two hours from now."

Miriam turned and laid her head on his chest, wrapping her arms around him.

"We'll be there," Io said.

"We?"

"I'm bringing Miriam with me. She doesn't leave my sight." His free arm encircled her and held her tightly.

"Understood. I'd feel the same way if it were Sam."

Io frowned, realizing something. "Hey, why are you calling me instead of Tristan?"

A long pause, then, "Because I'm in charge now."

"What?" If Io had still been drowsy, he was now wide awake.

"You heard me. Tristan got suspended and King Bain put me in charge in the interim."

"There goes the neighborhood."

"Yeah, fuck you, too."

Io actually smiled. In the past few weeks, he'd come to like Micah. "You'll make a good boss."

"Don't blow smoke up my ass."

"I'm being serious, asshole." Io wished he could live long enough to see how well Micah ran the team, but he knew he was as good as dead when he returned Miriam to her father.

"Yeah, well..." Micah trailed off as if he didn't know how to take the compliment. "Just get in here, you got me?"

"Yeah, I've got you." Io glanced down at the top of Miriam's head. He could already smell her tears. "And don't worry. I won't play hero this time. I'll turn myself in without a fight, okay?"

"Okay, buddy. See you soon."

"See ya."

He hung up and set his phone down.

"Miriam, look at me, baby." He tucked his index finger under her chin and urged her to look up.

Her beautiful eyes glistened with tears.

"I don't want you to go," she said.

"It's okay. I'm okay now. But you have to promise me. You will have our baby and raise it for us. For *both* of us. Don't do anything stupid, okay? Promise me."

She fought not to sob but failed, breaking down.

"Promise me, Miri. I need to know you'll take care of yourself and our baby."

The fantasy that he would be a father was over. They wouldn't be together forever or raise their child together. He was sentenced for execution. The royal decree had already been announced. He couldn't hope that his saving King

Bain's daughter would grant him leniency.

Miriam sobbed, and her tears fell against his chest. "I promise, Io. I promise."

"Come here," he pulled her up and kissed her. "Make love to me again. One last time before we go. I want to feel you one last time, Miri."

Miriam gave him everything she had to give, opening her body and her soul to him. And when she came, he let himself go, too, pouring all the love he had in his heart into his release, hoping it would be enough to sustain her after he was gone.

CHAPTER 60

KING BAIN SAT AT THE RICHLY CARVED DESK in his chambers. The desk had been his father's before his, and his father's before him. The elegant antique had weathered time through exquisite care and love, having been crafted by hands older than he was and restored numerous times.

He ran his large hand over the smooth surface and looked at the picture of his daughter, so small on his lap, with her dark curls hanging around her heart-shaped face.

But Miriam was no longer a babe. She had grown into a mature and strong-willed female, stubborn and independent, decisive and passionate, ready to die for what she believed in. At one time, Bain had thought the traits to be a weakness in her, but now he realized that those same attributes were what made him such an effective and powerful king.

Miriam would make a fine ruler of the race if it ever came to that. *Queen Miriam.* Unlike with her brother, Colin, who didn't have the spine to rule, King Bain felt no trepidation if he suddenly died and had to leave the future of the race in her hands. She was more than capable to take care of anything that needed done.

But for now, Bain was still in charge, and he had hard decisions to make. Decisions that put his family second and risked estranging his daughter from him forever. But that was what it meant to be king.

He rose and headed for the door, weary of all that had happened and all that he still had to face, but Io and Miriam were waiting for him. It was time to get this over with.

Opening the door, he walked the short distance down

the hall and entered the large room where he had met with the others a few days ago, where Cordray had picked apart the minds of the two drecks, who were now locked in his dungeon.

Io and Miriam sat at the far end of the table, holding each other as if they would never let go. Their eyes lifted in unison and looked at him as he approached.

Io made to stand, but Bain lifted his hand.

"No, Io. Stay seated."

Io frowned and settled back into Miriam's arms. It was obvious she had been crying.

"Let's make this quick," Io said. "I don't want Miriam to suffer any longer than she has to."

Bain slammed his fist down on the table, causing the posted guards to jump. One cleared his throat awkwardly, as if embarrassed.

"You insufferable bastard. Do you think I wish for my daughter to suffer, Io? She is my *daughter.* I should know her better than—" King Bain's voice cracked and he quickly turned away.

He refused to break in front of his daughter or her mate. A strong front and solid show of power were critical for a king, who needed to remain personally detached from his work.

He bowed his head and pinched the bridge of his nose between his thumb and forefinger. The truth was Bain couldn't remain personally detached. That was his daughter. His blood. His child. His baby. And while he should know her better than anyone, he didn't. Because he had ceased being a critical part of her life a long time ago.

"Father?" Miriam's perfect voice touched his ears with concern.

Drawing in a lungful of air, Bain held it, fighting his emotions before blowing it out and clearing his throat. His baby wasn't a baby anymore. She was all grown up. Carrying a child of her own. His grandchild and future heir.

"Daddy?" Despite being an adult, Bain heard the little girl she had been over forty years ago speaking to him, her high-pitched voice ringing like silver bells as she patted his cheeks, smiling her precious little-girl smile.

Daddy, play Barbie with me.

Not now, honey. Daddy has work to do.

Damn him for never giving Miriam the time she had deserved. All she had wanted was for him to play with her and give her a little attention, but he had always been too busy being king to be a father.

He didn't want to miss any more of Miriam's life, and he didn't want her child growing up without a father the way he'd condemned Miriam to grow up without one.

Breaking down, he bowed his head into his hands, and for the first time in his life, he cried in front of others. Never since his childhood had he allowed himself the luxury of sorrow where others could see it. Not even when his father died had he broken down until he was safely alone.

"Leave us," he heard Miriam say from behind him.

He assumed she was telling the guards to leave, and within seconds he heard the door open and close as they did.

"Daddy?" Her hand touched the back of his shoulder.

That was all it took for him to completely shatter. Her tender caress undid him, and in an instant, he whipped around and pulled her into his grasp, hugging her harder than he could ever remember.

"I love you, Miri. I love you so much. I'm so sorry. I've never been the father you deserved. But if you'll let me, I'll make it up to you or die trying. I promise." He sobbed through his words, burying his face in her hair.

MIRIAM COULD HARDLY BREATHE. Her father held her so tightly.

It took her a moment to shift gears, but before she could stop herself, she threw her arms around him and let fresh tears flow down her cheeks and against his shirt.

"Daddy..." She hadn't called him daddy since she was a little girl who thought of him as her hero.

"I can't lose you, Miri. You mean too much to me." He kissed her hair and reinforced his hold on her.

"I'm still here, Daddy." Her own embrace tightened. "You just haven't listened."

"I know, sweetheart. God, I know." He spoke against the top of her head, washing her scalp in warmth. "But that stops right now. I promise."

She let herself get lost in her father's outpouring of love, feasting on it, having craved it for so long, and then she pushed away.

He resisted, but she had to make sure he knew she was a package deal now. If he couldn't accept Io as her mate, his breakthrough and show of emotion wouldn't matter, because if he forced her to choose, she would choose Io.

"Father," she said, wiping her tears away and composing herself. She needed him to take her seriously.

Her father frowned, but it was an expression of pain, not anger.

"Father, I love you, but..." She turned and looked at Io, who had stood but remained back by the table, giving her room to work this out with her father. "Io is my mate, Father. If you want to make amends with me—"

But her father was walking away from her, toward Io, wiping his face with his palm as if he didn't hear her.

As he drew near Io, Miriam feared the worst and held her breath as she watched Io take a wary step backward.

"Forgive me." Her father extended his hand toward Io. "I'm Miriam's father. It's..." It was obvious that sucking up his pride was hard for him and that he still needed to work through the ghosts that haunted him over realizing she was no longer his little girl. But he was making an effort. "It's a pleasure to meet you, Io."

Io glanced at her, his eyes wide. Then he stared down at her father's outstretched hand as if it were a poisonous snake before looking up and meeting his eyes.

Miriam could only imagine how confused Io was.

He took her father's hand. "Iobates Liatos, sire. The pleasure's mine." Io said the right words, but it was obvious his guard was still up. This new side of her father would take getting used to...for both of them. Hell, for *all* of them, her father included.

The two most important males in her life shook hands as she blew out the breath she had been holding, and another round of tears began to fall as she covered her nose and mouth with her hands. She had her father back. Somehow she had gotten through.

"You take good care of my daughter, Io. She's one of a kind." Her father gave Io's hand another hardy shake.

"Yes, Sire, she is."

Her father released Io's hand. "Call me...." He cleared his throat, biting back his pride. "Call me Bain, Io. You're family now."

Miriam rushed forward and hugged Io and looked up at her father with a sense of wonder. What had happened to change his mind?

She knew it would take him time to fully adjust to Io, but he seemed ready to commit to making things right with her. After all this time, she felt like she and her father had a chance to make peace and become reacquainted with one another.

"You're not going to punish him?" she asked as her father turned away.

Looking back over his shoulder, her father shook his head. "Don't you think he's been punished enough?"

Miriam opened her mouth, but no words came out.

"What? No sassy comeback this time, my daughter." Her father smiled at her. "Have I finally made you speechless?"

A broad grin spread over her face. "Um, well...sure, you could say that."

With a nod of deferment, her father turned and began walking away, chuckling. "Besides, Io will be punished enough if you birth him a little girl."

Miriam gasped. "You knew?" So that explained the sudden change. Well, maybe part of it.

Without turning around, her father hesitated in the doorway. "I know everything I need to know, Miri." He paused, his long hair falling like a black waterfall down his back. "I love you. Now go on. Take your mate and go home. But I warn you...." He turned and held up his hand, his index finger pointing. "You'll be hearing from my security team. I want to make sure your home is well protected."

"Absolutely," Io said, hugging her close. "Yes sir. I'll take good care of her."

"I know you will, now go on before I change my mind." Her father winked then disappeared through the doorway, leaving them alone. She turned to Io, meeting his gaze.

"Is it over?" he asked.

"Is what over?" She brushed her fingertips over his brow, unsure what to feel now that her father had surprised the hell out of her. Of all she and Io had expected by coming here, his blessing was the last thing they thought they would get.

"All of it. Everything. Am I...? Am I safe? I mean, did he just give us his blessing?"

Miriam nodded. "Yes. I do believe he did."

Poor Io. He looked shell-shocked. "I'm not going to be executed? Put back in the dungeon? Not even cuffed?"

She laughed at him, arching one eyebrow. "Well, I'm sure I can cuff you if that's what you want."

His eyes twinkled as a grin spread across his face. "Mmm, you won't get any complaints from me." Io dipped his forehead to rest against hers.

"Then I'd better get you home."

Home. With Io. Her mate. With her father's blessing.

"Yes, I think you should."

She took Io's hand and led him out. It would take a little while for all that had just happened to sink in, but she had a feeling when it did, she and Io would be off the grid for a few days.

CHAPTER 61

ONCE THE REALITY THAT HE WASN'T GOING TO DIE had finally settled in, Io and Miriam had spent the next few days in each other's arms. His calling was gradually subsiding, so they hadn't spent the entire time making love, but he couldn't imagine not holding her and feeling her arms around him. Even if they were just watching a movie, he needed to feel her and keep his hand on her belly to feel the tiny life growing inside her.

Now that he and the king were on a first name basis and Miriam was becoming settled into his home, he had only one more person he had to make things right with.

Arion.

He already knew that Arion was performing at the Blue Turtle tonight, and he had every intention of going there, gay bar or not, to make amends.

"How do I look?" He brushed his hand over the burnished red cashmere sweater.

"Like a million dollars." Miriam stepped up behind him and wound her arms around his waist.

He smiled at her reflection and stepped aside, looking around with a low whistle while giving her the once-over.

"Baby, you're going to make me a jealous male tonight."

"Why's that?"

"Because every eye in the place will be on you."

She wore a red, silk blouse with a plunging neckline, along with a pair of fashionable, wide-leg black slacks and black platform pumps. Long, ebony waves framed her face.

"I thought you said this was a gay bar." She lifted one eyebrow.

"Well, even gay men can appreciate this kind of beauty." He waved his arm up and down.

"You flatter me."

"It's just the truth."

He took her hand and led her up the stairs and grabbed her bottle of tonic off the kitchen counter.

"We'll leave it in the car in case you need it," he said.

She was doing remarkably well fighting through withdrawal, and he hoped that within a couple of weeks they wouldn't even need the elixir anymore.

A half-hour later, they parked across the street from the Blue Turtle and made their way inside hand-in-hand. As he suspected, every eye in the place turned and took in his Miri, but she seemed oblivious, falling into the circle of his arm as he wrapped it around her waist.

Severin sat at a table against the far wall and waved them over.

"Miriam, I think you know Sev."

"Yes." She smiled and held out her hand.

Sev shook it. "Nice to see you doing so well, Miriam."

"Thank you. It's all Io's fault." She flashed him a coquettish smile.

They chuckled, and Io looked around the room, searching for Ari. "Where is he?" He helped Miriam into one of the chairs.

"Restroom." Sev nodded toward the back. "Don't tell him I said this, but I think he's got a nervous bladder."

"Really? Does he always get nervous before he performs?" Io remained standing, his arm around Miriam's shoulders. She reached up and placed her hand on his.

Sev shook his head. "He's not nervous about performing, Io." Sev gave him a knowing look.

"Oh." Io nodded then looked down. "I see."

Ari was nervous about seeing him. That's what Sev was saying.

Miriam tightened her hand around his, instinctively knowing he needed her support.

Sev turned and looked toward the back. "There he is. Why don't you go talk to him? I'll keep Miriam company."

Io turned and saw Ari break through the crowd and come to a sudden stop when their eyes met.

"Okay, yeah." Io lifted Miriam's hand and kissed it. "I'll be right back. I need to speak to him alone."

"Take your time, baby. I'm fine." Miriam gave him an encouraging smile and waved him away.

Taking a deep breath, he walked toward Ari, who turned and headed toward a hallway in the back. Io followed, feeling as if they were engaging in espionage, arranging a secret meeting or something.

Ari led him to a back door then outside into a back alley.

It was unseasonably warm.

After closing the door behind him, Io turned around. Ari paced away, his hands on his hips, head down. Nothing was said for at least a minute, and Ari wouldn't even look at him.

Io cleared his throat. "Uh, how're you doing, Ari?" He scratched the back of his neck and looked over his shoulder toward the door. He might need a quick escape if Ari's behavior was any indication.

Ari shook his head and spun around. "How do you think I'm doing?"

The two stared at each other, a dripping noise coming from somewhere down the alley. The air was heavy with humidity.

"I, uh...I'm..." Io couldn't seem to get the words to flow. "Hell, Ari, I don't know. That's why I asked."

Clearing the air with Ari was proving to be a lot harder than he thought it would.

"Well, I'll tell you how I am." Ari took an aggressive step forward, pointing a finger at Io. "You reckless bastard." Ari pulled back and cursed as he spun away briefly then turned back toward him again. "What the hell were you thinking? Huh? You always were reckless. Always taking risks a crazy person would be smart enough to avoid. But not you. Noooo. You go off and do shit that could get you killed. Killed, Io!"

Io's face scrunched up as he frowned. He gnawed on the

inside of his lip. Ari was really pissed off. "Look Ari, I didn't come here to fight with you. I—"

"You careless bastard! Do you think I enjoyed this? Do you think I liked knowing I was going to lose my best friend twice?"

"Ari...calm down. Just cool out."

"Don't tell me to cool out, you jackass!" Ari shoved him. "After I pulled your ass out of the gutter more times than I can count, don't you dare tell me to cool out." He shoved Io again. "I have a right to be pissed. The king could have killed you. He was *going* to! Damn you!"

Io jerked backward as Ari shoved him again. "But he didn't! He didn't, okay? You have a right to be pissed, but if you'll just listen to me! Ari! Stop it!" Io swatted Ari's arm away before he could shove him again.

"Asshole!" Ari swung his left arm—his tattooed arm—at Io.

Io reached out with his right hand and caught it. The arms they had tattooed together as a show of their friendship and brotherly closeness now linked them to one another, and they both stilled and stared at the hint of ink that peeked out from the cuff of Io's shirt. It perfectly matched Ari's. For a moment, both quieted, arms linked, their gazes draped over the connection as if the memory of their friendship hung between them.

Io spoke softly. "Damn it, Ari, I know I've fucked shit up between us. Maybe beyond repair. I don't know, but I hope not. But if you'll give me a chance, I want to make things right with you. I don't deserve it, but damn it, brother...I miss you. And God, I'm so sorry. I treated you and Sev...well, I was awful to you both. I wasn't there for you. You needed me and I wasn't there." He dropped his gaze to the ground as shame flooded him. This was so hard, but he had to get it out. All of it. "You were the best friend I've ever had. You were there for me when I needed you. You pulled me through the hardest time in my life, Ari, but when you needed me, I abandoned you. I walked away and left you hanging. I was stupid. I said things...awful things." He cringed. "God, Ari, I'm so sorry."

Ari's tawny eyes lifted, and he glared at Io as he breathed

heavily. From physical exertion, emotion, or both? But he didn't reply.

For at least a minute, they just stared at each other until finally Io took a deep breath and stepped back, toward the door. "Okay, well…I'm sorry." He let go of Ari's wrist and took another step back and straightened his shirt. The darkened alley closed in. Had his apology been all for naught? "That's all I wanted to say." With a tight smile, he turned to leave.

Suddenly, Ari grabbed him, swung him around, and yanked him back into a bear hug the likes of which would have squeezed the life out of King Kong.

"You goddamn selfish bastard," Ari said, thumping a fist on Io's back. "Don't you ever scare me like that again. I thought…you just…you're so fucking reckless…damn you."

Ari didn't mention the real issue. In fact, he seemed to be avoiding Io's previously homophobic stupidity altogether, but that was okay. He knew Ari well enough to know that he was simply deflecting. After all, Ari hadn't gone his whole life pretending to be straight because he was good at addressing conflict. If he wanted to transfer his emotions over their falling out onto his anger over what had gone down with King Bain, Io was fine with that.

He slowly wrapped his arms around Ari and hugged him back. "I'm not going anywhere, brother. And I promise to be more careful from now on."

"You'd better be or I'll kill you myself." Ari let go of him and pushed him away before wiping his hand over his face and clearing the emotion from his throat.

"No you won't. You love me too much." Io grinned, trying to lighten the mood.

"Pompous ass." Ari started for the door.

Io grabbed his arm. "So, we good?" He paused. "I need us to be good with each other again, Ari."

"Why's that?" Ari arched an eyebrow and tongued the inside of his cheek to squelch a smile.

Io took a deep breath, blew it out. "Because I can't think of a better godfather to my unborn child."

Ari's eyes sharpened for a heartbeat, his gaze flickering

as the corner of his mouth ticked upward. Then he licked and pursed his lips and the momentary smile was gone, replaced with hard edges Io got the impression were just for show. "We'll see."

"Is that a yes?"

"No. But it's not a no, either." Ari's face softened, but he looked away before Io could see if he was smiling.

"Okay. That's cool." Io kept his voice even. He knew Ari well enough to know that it would just take time and they would be back to the friends they once were, with one big difference. They were both mated males now.

Ari walked toward the door and stopped without turning around, his head down and his hand on the doorknob. "You staying for the show?"

"I'd planned on it. Do you want me to leave?"

"No...no." Ari shook his head, keeping it bowed. "You should stay. The music's good here."

Io grinned at the back of Ari's head. "That's what I hear, especially when you're playing."

Ari didn't move for several seconds, keeping his head down. His body rose and fell rhythmically as he breathed, and Io sensed the pride and gratitude pulsing off him. His compliment had pleased Ari, whether he wanted to admit it or not.

Finally, Ari stood tall once more and pulled the door open. "Don't blow smoke up my ass." Without another look back, Ari left him in the alley, but Io had heard the smile in Ari's voice even if he hadn't seen it.

Io smiled and leaned back against the brick wall. Yes, everything between he and Ari was going to be just fine. It didn't look like it on the surface, but Io could tell. It was obvious that the separation had been killing Ari just as much as it had been killing him.

When he went back inside and reached the table, he was positively beaming. Ari was already up on stage.

"It went well, I take it?" Sev said.

He nodded and sat down next to Miriam, taking her hand. "Yes."

"You didn't come back inside with him." Sev eyed him curiously. "But Ari stopped by the table before heading up to the stage. Whatever you two talked about certainly put a sparkle in his eye. It's been a while since I've seen him in such a good mood."

Io glanced up at Ari, who was tuning his guitar.

It was still weird thinking about Ari with a male, but he had a greater appreciation for what Ari had gone through and how he and Sev felt for one another now that he had mated Miriam. And after having a brush with death, Io no longer saw homosexuality as that big of an issue. Death had a way of putting things in perspective. Who cared who Ari loved? Just as long as he was happy.

A waitress came by their table and delivered their drinks, and Miriam leaned over and rested her head on his shoulder.

"You okay, baby?" he said.

She nodded. "Perfect."

Io looked up and caught Sev's eye. Sev grinned at him but didn't say anything. But Io knew what he was thinking. No doubt Sev had never seen this day coming, but then again, neither had Io.

But sometimes that's how life worked out. You took chances and let life lead you, and when you came across something good, you grabbed on and fought for it.

"How you feeling?" Miriam said, looking over her shoulder at him.

She was his *something good*. Miriam was that something he had come across that had been worth fighting for. She had a long way to go toward breaking completely free from her father, and she was only just beginning to figure out exactly who she was, but that was the neat thing about being mated to her. He could share that journey with her—participate in her self-discovery and even help her figure herself out.

He grinned. "Like a rebel."

She smiled and leaned back, pressing her lips to his ear. "Don't you go changing, either."

"Oh? Why's that?" His arms slid further around her slender waist.

"Because I've become obsessed with you just the way you are."

Io turned and pressed his lips to hers. "Ditto, baby."

He gazed into her blue eyes, lost in her. He'd been to hell and back, but through the flames he had come out a new male. Where once he had been a reckless playboy, he was now a stable family man, ready to settle down and discard his proverbial little black book.

With a glance back up at his best friend, he had never felt happier. He had experienced the ultimate rebellion—against himself. He had become a better male by thumbing his nose at who he once was and daring to take a new path. One he had always been terrified to tread.

Who would have thought monogamy and humility would be a part of his vocabulary? Few had seen any promise that Io would amount to anything more than a philandering chauvinist and a bigot, but he had shown them. He had proven everyone wrong.

Even himself.

EPILOGUE

"**ARE YOU NERVOUS?**" Io held Miriam's hand as they walked through the halls of AKM toward the conference center.

"A little."

"I'll be right beside you." Io lifted her hand and kissed her knuckles.

"What if my being here is too disruptive?" She leaned into him as they walked.

"I think the better question is whether *my* being here will be too disruptive." The king said, stepping out from a side hallway to join them.

"Father?" Miriam stopped, emotion obviously overcoming her. "What are you doing here? I didn't think—"

"That I would support my own daughter while she battled addiction?" King Bain said, cutting her off.

Miriam fought back her tears, looking from her father to Io. "Did you know about this?" she asked him.

Io grinned. "I was the one who asked him to come."

She wrapped her arms around him and hugged him before turning to her father. He pulled her to him, kissing the top of her head.

"Miri, I want to be here for you. I wasn't before, and I regret that. But now...." The king looked up at Io. "You've got a worthy mate, Miri. He made me see how important it was for me to be here. I'm part of the problem, and that stops right now." He pushed Miri away and fiercely met her gaze. "Right this minute, Miri. No more denying what is so obviously right before my eyes."

Io gave them a moment to talk and wandered toward the

conference room. He could hear the others in the group talking and milling around.

Within a couple of minutes, the king and Miriam joined him.

Io shook the king's hand, noting the bodyguards filtering into the hall. "You have no idea how powerful your being here is." He had already had this conversation with Miriam's father once, but he couldn't stop himself from reaffirming how pivotal the king's decision was to join them.

"I agree, Io," the king said. "I didn't realize how bad the problem was, but if what you say about cobalt is true, and if the drecks are using it to weaken us…." He paused and looked at Miriam. "That alone should cause me to take pause and address the issue. But my reasons for being here tonight?" He took Miriam's hand. "Those are personal. I'm here for my daughter."

"Absolutely, Sire."

King Bain gave him an impatient look. "I told you on the phone. Please call me Bain. You're family now, Io. As much as I fought that before, I can fight it no longer. And for you to address me so formally grates my ears."

Io tried not to smile. He liked this new side to Miriam's father. He could tell Bain had to work at being congenial, but the fact that he did spoke volumes about how important he felt it was to mend the relationship with both him and his daughter, and he seemed willing to do whatever it took to make that happen.

"Of course, Sire. I mean Bain."

"That's better."

Io turned his attention to Miriam. "You're an inspiration, Miri. I think the group will take away a new sense of comfort knowing that even the king's daughter can become an addict. You're more important to these people than you know. So is your father."

Miriam took a deep breath, fortifying herself as she clutched both his hand and her father's. "Okay. I want to help. I want to do something right for a change."

Just as Io did.

He pressed his free palm against her belly and felt the strengthening life force of his child growing inside her. "I love you."

She let go of her father's hand and covered Io's with hers. "I love you, too." She turned to her father. "And I love you. Thank you for being here."

King Bain nodded, remaining stoic. "You're my daughter. I will do anything for you."

Miri smiled and met Io's gaze again. He had searched a lifetime for her, and finally he had found her. She was the most exquisite female to walk the earth, as far as he was concerned.

After a quick, reassuring nuzzle and tender kiss, both of which made Bain fidget and look away, he pulled back and opened the door, and then followed her into the room. Six sets of curious eyes turned and greeted them, followed immediately by six mouths falling open as King Bain entered.

"Hi guys," Io said, still holding Miriam's hand as he grabbed an extra chair from the side and pulled it behind him toward the circle. "I'm sorry I haven't been here in a few weeks. I was busy getting mated." He put his arm around Miriam's waist, presenting her. "Everybody, this is Miriam, my mate." He beamed as he said it, meeting Miriam's eye. "And this is her father, King Bain."

Everyone in the group looked around at each other in awkward silence, unsure of what to do or say.

Bain cleared his throat and stepped forward. "Hello, my name is Bain, and I'm here to support my daughter, who is...." He took a deep breath, and Io could tell he was fighting to keep his composure. "She's...." He looked at Miriam, who stepped toward him and took his hand.

"I'm a cobalt addict," she said.

King Bain nodded and pulled her close, wrapping his arm around her and clearing the emotion from his throat. "Yes, she's a cobalt addict. And I'm the reason why. So I'm here to support her to make sure this never happens again, and to lend my support to each of you." Bain looked around the room. "I'm here to listen…and learn…and be strong for my daughter."

Hope dawned on each face in the group. In the royal family's tragedy, they saw salvation for themselves. They knew now that cobalt addiction didn't just happen to those who weren't privileged. It could happen to anybody, even someone as highly placed as the princess.

King Bain bowed his head, deferring to Miriam as he backed away and took a seat in the background, giving her the floor. His message was clear: This was her time to shine. It was her time to let her voice be heard.

"Hi, my name is Miriam," she said, twisting her fingers nervously. She looked over her shoulder at Io as he sat down, watching her with more love than he'd ever felt. She continued, her voice growing stronger. "My name is Miriam. And, uh…and I'm a cobalt addict."

To the members of the group, who sat enthralled as Miriam spoke, she recounted how she had begun to use cobalt as a means of escape, as well as to draw the attention of her father. She continued until she came to her first overdose, where she turned and looked at Io.

"When I overdosed the first time is when I met Io. When I overdosed the second time is when he saved me." Fond admiration spread a sort of joy over her features as she looked at him, then she turned back to the group. "It's funny really, because if I hadn't become an addict, I never would have met him. Isn't it strange how something so awful and painful can lead to the one thing that can bring salvation?" A few of the group members nodded, and Miriam continued on. "I used to ask myself why. Why did I have to almost die? Why did I have to go through this hell just to find him?" She pointed at Io. "And him." She looked at her father. "But there is no good answer. Sometimes things just are. Sometimes we have to walk through the fire to find water. Sometimes we have to be completely torn down so we can reinvent ourselves into who we're meant to be."

Miriam held the group in her grasp.

"You all went through the fire, just as I did," she said.

"You've survived. Whatever the reason, this happened to you as it did to me, and now you're becoming who you were meant to become because of that. I firmly believe that, because without cobalt, I would only be half a person. Cobalt led me to Io. And Io led me back to my father." She turned and looked at the king.

Io stood and joined her, staying silent as she finished.

"I don't know how or why, but cobalt gave me my mate, and they both gave me back my father, and now I have to put my past behind me so I can move into my future...with him...and with our family." She placed her hand on her belly. "My life is more important than to waste it on cobalt. I know that now. And each of you is more important, too. Each of you has a purpose. Otherwise, you wouldn't be here."

Io couldn't have felt more in love than in that moment. Miriam had connected with the group. He could see it in their eyes. Hope shone on their faces. Hope that they had more to look forward to than the pain they had known through their addiction, and possibly even before.

Io thought back to something Miriam had said earlier, about how he had saved her. As he watched the members of the group come up one-by-one and hug her and shake the king's hand, he realized that even though he might have saved her, she had done the same for him. Miriam had given him purpose again, and she had helped him to complete his transformation from reckless playboy to a responsible adult.

Miriam was his obsession, and he was hers.

Who would have thought Io would ever settle down? But then, he was a rebel like that. Good thing for him that Miriam was, too.

DID YOU ENJOY READING THIS BOOK?

If you did, please help others enjoy it, too:

Recommend it.

Review it at Amazon, iBooks, or Goodreads

If you leave a review, please send me an email at donya@donyalynne.com or message me on Facebook so that I can thank you with a personal e-mail.

ABOUT THE AUTHOR

DONYA LYNNE is the bestselling author of the award winning All the King's Men Series and a member of Romance Writers of America. Making her home in a wooded suburb north of Indianapolis with her husband, Donya has lived in Indiana most of her life and knew at a young age that she was destined to be a writer. She started writing poetry in grade school and won her first short story contest in fourth grade. In junior high, she began writing romantic stories for her friends, and by her sophomore year, she'd been dubbed *Most Likely to Become a Romance Novelist*. In 2012, she made that dream come true by publishing her first two novels and a novella. Her work has earned her two IPPYs (one gold, one silver) and two eLit Awards (one gold, one silver) as well as numerous accolades. When she's not writing, she can be found cheering on the Indianapolis Colts or doing her cats' bidding.

For more information on Donya's books or just to say hello, visit her on Facebook or swing by her website.

www.facebook.com/DonyaLynne

www.donyalynne.com